ENTROPY

LUCY ROY

Entropy

Tessa Avery Book Three

ISBN (hardcover): 978-1-7353385-4-5

ISBN (paperback): 978-1-7353385-8-3

ISBN (ebook): 978-1735338545

Cover art: Denise Worisch

Edited by: Jenifer Knox

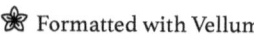 Formatted with Vellum

To my daughters
(I think you'll like this one)

ALSO BY LUCY ROY

Major Greek Gods

PART I

1

MARY

I had a dream once when I was young where I fell down a well. I'd been about twelve, and completely unbeknownst to our guardians, had just spent a large part of the day swimming in an old quarry with Tessa, Leila, and Eric. When we got home, the three of us had gotten the mother of all scoldings. "Underwater currents" and "freezing temperatures" and "the gods only know what else" were a few things listed as the hidden dangers we'd been lectured on, along with the typical, "you're not immortal yet!" that we'd all received a time or three growing up.

That night, I dreamt someone tossed me down a well. I remember waking up thinking it was weird because I'd never actually *seen* one of those old-school wells with the bucket and rope, but there I was dreaming about one, anyway. All I remembered was a heavy push followed by one hit after another against a wet stone wall as I bounced down to the freezing water below that was most *certainly* filled with "the gods know what".

Now, seven years later, I felt an odd sense of deja vu. The damp walls that surrounded me in my cell weren't as physically tight as that well had seemed, but they were just as confining and just as gloomy.

It had been six days since Iapetus had kidnapped me from the arena and dropped me in a dank cell with three missing witches. Six days of being unable to move more than a few feet from the very *real* stone wall, thanks to the godsbane-infused shackles on my wrists. Six days since I'd been ripped from the massacred arena not knowing which of my friends had lived or died. Not knowing whether my captors were lying when they told me one of my oldest friends, along with the rest of the recruits and mentors, were dead at the hands of Tessa's father.

The days that the Pleiades and I spent in our small, damp stone chamber were long and dull, with only a small square of sunlight above our heads to show any passage of time. The sisters had kept track of the passing time with small scratch marks on the stone floor —there had been twelve on the day I arrived.

Once in awhile, the monotony would be broken when Cronus or Iapetus would come in and take one of the witches or dole out some punishment to me.

BANG!

The door flew open, crashing against the stone wall behind it and knocking me from my thoughts. Cronus strode in, filling up the small space with his enormous, vicious presence, followed by three guards. I tried to get a good look at them to figure out what species they were, but they kept their faces averted, so all I saw was dark hair.

"You know where to go," Cronus snapped, jerking his chin toward the three witch-sisters who sat slumped on the floor across from me.

A moment later, Cronus and I were left alone, his dark, intimidating presence causing the size of the cell to shrink in size. Tendrils of fear twisted around me as he stood, unmoving, above me, muscles straining against his shirt.

My trademark sass had evaporated days ago, replaced by a moroseness that scared even me. As Cronus glared at me, I simply stared back, hoping this wouldn't be the day he decided he wanted to drain my powers but knowing I was too weak to try to defend myself if he did.

Everything about him screamed "apex predator." He was the wolf, and I was the goddamn sheep.

As though sensing my fear, a small, cruel smirk twisted his lips. He loomed over me, standing so close that the toes of his heavy black boots were nearly touching my bare feet. One step and he could shatter every bone in my foot.

Folding his arms across his chest, he arched a brow. "What, no snappy remarks today?"

When I didn't respond, he sighed, then crouched in front of me.

My lower lip begin to tremble, and my heart thundered in my chest as his face filled my vision. I focused on the collar of his shirt, refusing to look at the cold, cruel face just above.

"Look at me."

I felt frozen, my eyes refusing to answer my mind's command to obey him.

Look at him look at him look at him.

You know what'll happen if you don't.

My silence was received with a backhand to the face.

I cried out, the sheer force of his blow nearly knocking me to the floor. My chains stopped me from face-planting, digging into my wrists and yanking me to a stop right before I hit the damp stone. Cronus latched on to my hair and gave a vicious twist, causing my neck to strain and the godsbane-infused shackles to dig into my skin.

"Please!" I began to sob, my entire body shaking. Physical pain mingled with nausea that pummeled through my body. "Please, stop!"

His only response was to backhand me again. My vision blurred with tears, and I wondered if this was how it'd felt for Tessa when Menoetius had taken and tortured her. Tessa was strong, even if she didn't know it, but even the strongest person could become weak in the worst of circumstances.

Don't try to compare yourself to her, a voice whispered in my head. *She's a Titaness. A Mimic. She's got infinite strength. All you've got is just a little bit of water.*

I squeezed my eyes shut, shrinking back from Cronus' next blow as I tried to silence the voices in my mind.

Cronus dropped his hand and angled his head to the side. "I

struggle to understand why the Fates saw fit to bless you with the power of my children. The power *I* gave them." Cruel eyes dragged across my filthy training uniform, blood and grime-encrusted hair, and tear-streaked face. "There must've been thousands of other humans they could've instilled with the gods' magic, who would've begged for it, but instead, they gave it to *you*." He gave a lock of my hair another yank, and I hissed at the quick pain. "It's disappointing to see someone with such power reduced to this."

"Did you chain me up just to pull my hair and insult me?" I rasped, struggling to find some sense of myself through the pain. I shot him a smirk. "I guess that's all bullies are good for, huh?"

His expression remained unchanged as he delivered another backhand to my face, this time to the other cheek.

"Your water abilities... they belonged to my son once, you know." He shook his head as the look of disgust he wore deepened. "I wonder what Poseidon would say if he knew the drop of power he'd handed over had been wasted on such a pathetic—"

The heavy iron door opened, ushering in a gust of cool air.

"Cronus, I think she's had enough."

The pain of Cronus' beating transformed into a leaden feeling in my gut at the sound of Josh's voice. I slumped against the wall, my head still ringing from that last hit, and refused to look at him.

At my *friend*.

Former friend. Don't you forget it.

Cronus' lip curled in annoyance as he stood to face Josh. A moment later, he strode through the door, leaving me alone with Josh, who closed the door, and slid down to sit beside me. His knees were bent, forearms propped casually on top as he rested his head against the wall.

Tears stung my eyes as the air shifted, and I was hit with his familiar scent—either his soap or aftershave, or maybe just him, I wasn't sure. All I knew was that it was the familiar smell of family, of someone I'd shared nearly every day with for the past four years. The fact that he still smelled like the guy I'd loved like a brother was a torture all its own.

In the week I'd been here, I'd seen him only twice—the day Iapetus and Cronus dragged me back here after slaughtering the other Ischyra recruits in the arena and again a few days later. I'd been out of it when I arrived here, groggy from both the godsbane that had poisoned me and from the blast of Tessa's power that had taken everyone in the arena down. The second time had been two days before when he'd strolled into the room, looked around, and left, as though he'd come in for something and forgotten what it was.

The pain from Cronus' hits was receding, but it was a struggle not to focus on the boy—or whatever he was—at my side.

"How ya doing, Mare?"

"Fuck off," I muttered, wincing when my jaw protested at the movement.

He nudged me with his elbow. "You know, you shouldn't antagonize him. It takes a lot longer to heal in here than it does out there."

I shifted baleful eyes toward him. "Fuck. Off."

He sniffed out a laugh. "Do you want to know a secret?"

"Probably not," I grumbled, although secretly I was morbidly curious.

"*I* think it was silly of Iapetus to take you," he whispered conspiratorially. "I plan to let you go eventually, don't worry, but I thought it might be fun to make Tessa stew a bit first, get her nice and riled. What do you think?"

Slowly, I slid him a disbelieving look.

"You know, this isn't the girl I remember," he said with a click of his tongue. "Where's your fight, Mare?"

"I must've left it back on Olympus when you freaks poisoned me, beat me, and dragged me away from the people I love."

"Technically it's 'person,' now, right?"

"What?"

"You said 'people I love.'" He shrugged. "Tessa's the only one left."

"Shockingly, I met new people while I was there," I snapped. "Believe it or not, I'm capable of making new friends."

"Mary Miller brought people into her inner circle?" He stuck out his lower lip and nodded. "I don't remember you being so *inclusive* in

Renville. But yes, I suppose we *could* classify Yana and Anette in the 'people you love' category."

I rolled my eyes but tried not to let on how upset I actually was. As each day passed, I was losing more and more hope that I'd ever see the people I cared for again. Tessa was the only person left from my old life now, but the new additions—Yana, Anette, Nate and his stupid brothers, and Tessa's brothers—had surprisingly found a place in my heart, and the thought of not seeing them again hurt like a bitch.

I turned my head to resume my staring contest with the wall across from me, but Josh gripped my jaw and forced me to look at him, eyes narrowed.

My fingers tugged feebly at his arm. "What the—"

"Quiet," he snapped, dropping his human act. His cold brown eyes searched mine, then a satisfied smile curved his lips. "Sorry, Tess. This conversation is for our ears, only. It's good to see you got that mind link down, though. Keep up the good work."

My eyes widened as I took in his meaning, but before I could rally my brain to reach out to her, I felt a hard *flick*, then his eyes shifted their focus back to me.

He smirked. "Sorry about that. Can't have prying eyes looking in all the time, can we?"

I opened my mouth to tell him we most certainly *could*, but my lips refused to form the words.

"Now, let's chat."

2

TESSA

With a frustrated growl, I released Hermes' hands and dropped down on Nate's bed, then braced my hands on my knees as I sucked in heavy mouthfuls of air. Slowly, the magic that I'd used to link my mind to Mary's began to fade, along with any lingering feelings of her presence.

Hermes sat down next to me and slid a comforting arm around my shoulders, pulling me against his chest and resting his chin on my head as the sound of Cronus' hits replayed over and over in my mind.

"It'll be alright, Tessa," he murmured.

"Didn't you see what he did to her?" I cried as I shoved him away.

They were *beating* her. Hurting her. Probably draining her power at this point, too.

"And we're going to get her back," Epimetheus said soothingly, moving to stand in front of me. He leaned down and placed his hands on my shoulders, meeting my gaze. "That's why we're doing this."

"I know it's hard, but we have to keep trying, alright?" Hermes said.

"Gods, I *know* that!" I shoved my brother away and began pacing Nate's bedroom. I ran a hand roughly through my hair as fury and frustration began to mingle with fear for my best friend.

Over the last several days, Hermes had been acting as an anchor for my body while I sent my consciousness to other places on the astral realm, in the dream realm, and along the mental connections on the physical plane that, according to him, connected us all. We'd hoped to home in on Mary and the Pleiades, but we'd quickly discovered that was nearly impossible. Whatever magic was being used to conceal her prison rarely faltered, and when it did, it wasn't for more than a few moments. We'd had brief success with astral projection, but I was only ever able to see the space immediately around Mary and nothing more. Any distinguishing features of her prison remained hidden.

"What did you see?" Epimetheus asked carefully. "How is she doing?"

I wiped at my eyes and tried to compose myself. "She's doing... alright, I think. Scared, pissed off that she's scared, and she misses us." I gave Hermes a watery smile. "Including Nate's stupid brothers."

His blond eyebrows shot up. "She called us stupid? Dionysus will be heartbroken."

Epimetheus snorted. "Her spirits must not be so bad, then."

"I guess." I rubbed my fingers over my eyes, my hands shaking as I tried to forget the sound of Cronus' huge hand against Mary's cheek, the looks of fear on the three Pleiades' faces as they were dragged from the room. It took all I had not to break down in a sobbing mess.

Focus, Tessa.

After a moment, I looked at Hermes. "I thought a mind link would be harder to detect than astral projection."

"It *is* harder to detect if you're not looking for it." Hermes shrugged. "I wouldn't be surprised if Josh had been waiting for you to drop in."

"Pretty convenient he happened to pay her a visit right when you showed up," Epimetheus muttered. "Do you think he can sense intrusions, like that empousa that was in Atlas' mind?"

"That could be it," Hermes said. "Or maybe he was just waiting. He's a witch, after all. My guess is he's got some kind of warning system that will sense any type of magical intrusion. The dungeons here at the palace are set up similarly."

"Yeah, maybe," I said quietly, hoping it was something that simple. Systems could be taken apart. Maybe not easily, but it could be done.

Hermes laid down on the bed and folded his arms under his head. "Alright, let's look at what we know, then. What did you just see?"

I lay down next to him, mimicking his pose. Epimetheus took a seat near the end of the bed and frowned, awaiting my response. "A stone room, the three Pleiades getting dragged off, and Cronus and Josh."

"And what else did you learn?"

I clasped my hands over my stomach, tapping my fingers against the waistband of my jeans as I thought. "Mindlinking works, but only briefly. We got through, so whatever magic is being used to block the room is fallible. And now Mary knows I can get into her head. If nothing else, maybe that'll improve her morale a little bit, hopefully." Which was a good thing, relatively speaking, unless Josh did something witchy and blocked me out permanently.

"Exactly." Hermes propped himself up on his arm and looked down at me with a grin. "Considering how miserable she seemed, I would imagine that knowledge might improve her spirits a good deal."

I chewed my lip uncertainly. I didn't need to bother mentioning how little fight Mary seemed to have in her. It didn't seem as though they'd been draining her powers, but the sheer hopelessness that was plaguing her was like a knife to the gut. The girl I'd just linked to... that wasn't my best friend. That was a mere shadow of the feisty, stubborn, no-nonsense person I'd grown up with. That her experience was so similar to my own had pity surging inside me, which I quickly tamped down. Pity wouldn't help her right now; it would only make things harder for those trying to find her.

Closing my eyes, I reached back, desperately searching for something in her mind that had told me she wasn't entirely lost. It had been there, a small spark, but it was quickly dwindling.

"Mary's no idiot," Epimetheus said softly. "If she knows you were there, she knows you're doing all you can to find them."

Sitting up, Hermes patted my leg, his golden fingers giving my calf a reassuring squeeze. "Try not to worry. You got into her head once. It won't be a problem for you to do it again."

"You've been running yourself ragged," Epimetheus added. "You need to try and save some of your energy if you're going to keep trying to find her."

I shot him a look that told him I'd be doing no such thing, and he just shrugged in response.

"Gods, I just wish we could do a dream walk!" I exclaimed, exasperated.

"That didn't work the first five times we tried, so shelve that one for now," Hermes said. "We need to figure out our next approach. Have you ever used Splitter powers?"

"You mean that hive mind power?" I shuddered. "No. Telepathy is as far as I like to go with mental conversing." I stared up at the skylight, watching as the clouds slowly drifted past the cabin while I ran through my other powers. There were a few I hadn't tried that I could still tap into, although most of those were ones I hadn't had much practice with. "But...now that we know Mary is with the missing Pleiades, it might be worth a shot, as long as I can limit it to their immediate space. If I can get through to even *one* of them..."

"You may want to touch base with the sisters who weren't taken, then," Epimetheus suggested. "They might be better suited to help guide you."

Hermes arched a brow. "You think they haven't already tried to locate them?"

"It's more than likely, but it could be worth trying," Epimetheus replied.

"If they'd had any kind of success, we would've heard about it," I said.

"It's still worth a shot," Hermes said patiently. I could tell he was getting annoyed with my negativity, but these constant failures were wearing on me more each day.

I took a deep breath and nodded. "Yeah," I said quietly. "You're right."

"Will you bring Atlas?" Epimetheus asked.

His question gave me pause. In the short time Atlas had been back on Olympus, he hadn't been down to Demeter's house in the valley, where three of his seven daughters were living temporarily. From conversations we'd had, I knew he wanted to build a relationship with them, something he hadn't been able to do in the past. He was scared, though, something he would never openly admit.

"I don't know," I finally said. I rubbed my fingers across my brow, suddenly feeling overcome with exhaustion. "Probably. My brain hurts."

Hermes put his sandaled feet to the floor and stood, then held out his hand. "Come on, then. Let's head outside."

I gave him a dubious look as I took his hand. "For what?"

"So you can practice your elemental powers."

Epimetheus stood beside him and smiled gently. "You've been so focused on Mentalist abilities the last few days; your head needs a break."

"That's for damn sure." I slipped the hair tie off my wrist and twisted my hair up into a bun. "But don't you guys have places to be?"

Hermes shrugged. "Eventually. Besides, I told Nathaniel I'd keep you company, though."

"It'd be nice if Zeus gave him a damn break for once," I muttered. "He's been dealing with Menoetius all week."

"We're heading into war," he said simply. "This is how it goes, at least from what I've been told, and digging into prisoners' minds... well, that's what Nathaniel is good at."

I swallowed hard, knowing just how much Nate hated that fact.

Epimetheus gave my shoulder a quick squeeze.

'We're all going to do things we might otherwise find unseemly by the time this is all over. Nathaniel isn't one to lose sight of himself, Tessa.'

I patted his hand in thanks. *'I know.'*

As soon as he pulled the door open, the sounds of bickering from the living room reached my ears, nearly causing me to retreat back into the bedroom that had become our near-permanent residence the last few days. Epimetheus caught me by the shoulders and nudged me forward, stopping my attempt to flee from what was becoming an increasingly common annoyance.

"Change of plans," Hermes muttered as we listened to yet another argument between Apollo and Yana.

"It has been three days! You cannot keep me locked up here—"

"You are not locked up, Yana." Apollo's voice rang with irritation. "It's safer for you to remain here."

I couldn't help but smirk at the patience Apollo was struggling to force into his voice. Dealing with Yana the last few days had been... trying. She'd slept for three days after Menoetius had drained her powers and snapped her neck. When she woke up, she was a spitting ball of fury and fought almost every attempt Apollo made to heal the broken connections to her magic. They'd been futile attempts, as we all knew they would be, and I think they upset her more than if he'd done nothing at all.

And while he hadn't said it outright, I was pretty sure it upset Apollo more than anyone that this had become a problem he was unable to fix.

"Up until a week ago, we thought this whole mountain was safe!" Yana shot back. "Now you are saying I cannot even return to my room to get my things—"

"I've already *told* you we are sending someone to retrieve your belongings."

Yana dragged her hands through her short, black hair and let out a string of rapid-fire Romanian.

"Bringing my mother into this is highly improper," Apollo snapped.

"Screw your propriety *and* your mother," Yana growled. "I am going to get my things!"

Apollo's face took on a look of outrage. "How *dare* you speak to me that way!"

"You want to give him a hand?" Epimetheus murmured to me. "Apollo looks a bit out of his depth."

Bracing myself for Yana's ire, I stepped into the living room. "I can take her down to the dorms to get her stuff, Apollo."

He shot me an icy glare, clearly irritated I'd just circumvented his order that she stay put.

I smiled sweetly. "Don't you think I can keep her safe?"

"I can keep myself safe," Yana spat, turning her stormy eyes on me.

"She needs to get out of the house, and you need to stop playing babysitter," I told him, ignoring her.

"As far as everyone in Olympia knows, all of the recruits, save Mary, Andrei, and Anette, were killed in the attack," Apollo said slowly. "Menoetius thinks draining Yana's powers also drained her immortality, meaning she should be dead right now. If he or anyone else finds out she's still alive—"

"Menoetius doesn't care whether or not Yana is alive," I told him. "And even if he did, he's locked in the palace dungeons. She could parade around Olympia naked, and they'd never find out." I walked toward them and linked my arm through hers, then gave him a bright smile. "And we don't need your permission."

His mouth barely had time to twist into a scowl before I'd teleported us away, coming to a stop just inside the dorms that, up until a week ago, had housed all fifty of this generation's Ischyra recruits.

For a few moments, Yana and I stood there, taking it in. Nothing about the stone courtyard—the granite slabs that made up the floor, the stone fountain or the surrounding benches—looked different, but I could feel it. It was just...empty. Even the quiet sound of the fountain's burbling water seemed morose, as though it were sad there was no one there to enjoy its calming presence.

"It is so quiet," Yana said. Her voice was hardly more than a whisper, but it seemed to echo through the empty space.

"Yeah." I angled my head toward the archway that led to the female recruits' hall. "Come on, let's go."

Wordlessly, we made our way through the covered walkway that encircled the courtyard toward the hall. It'd been a month since I'd slept in my old bed, and nearly as long since Mary had moved out of her room with Anette and in with Yana. It felt more like years, though. Eons.

Neither of us looked at the closed doors that used to belong to the other recruits as we passed.

Yana pushed open the dark door with the elegant gold script that still bore both of our names and stepped inside, holding the door long enough for me to follow. She didn't spare Mary's unmade bed a glance as she tugged her large duffel bag from under her bed and began systematically opening drawers and emptying them. As she picked up a book that she'd left on the foot of her bed, she looked at me with lifted brows. "Do you want to get any of Mary's things while we are here? For when we find her?"

I felt a lump form in my throat as I thought of my best friend trapped in whatever dark hole Cronus and Iapetus had shoved her in. The fact that Yana was so certain we'd find her alive and in one piece made me think she hadn't lost as much hope as it had initially seemed.

"Yeah." I cleared my throat and nodded, then turned toward her bed. "Yeah, I'll grab her things."

So, while Yana finished packing up her things, I began to pack up Mary's, all the while making her a silent promise that she'd be the one to unpack them.

When we were finished, I hoisted Mary's suitcase off the ground and turned toward the door, not wanting to take in the room now that it appeared so desolate. We stepped into the hall, and I eyed the closed doors that ran along either side.

"The funeral is in two days," I remarked.

Yana pressed her lips into a thin line. "Each recruit should take something with them. Not just coins. Maybe photos? I think all of us brought at least one or two."

"I think the guardians would appreciate that."

Quietly, Yana and I went room to room, and I used my telekinesis to unlock each door. We'd all brought very few personal objects with us from Earth—books, jewelry, or some other small thing, but Yana was right. The one thing we'd all brought were photos, so we took those.

Once we'd gotten a stack of pictures to take back with us, we packed up the rest of their belongings in their respective suitcases or duffel bags and set them on their beds, just in case their former guardians wanted to take their things back to Earth. I didn't know if they'd all appreciate it or not, but I know if I'd been in their shoes, packing up the belongings of the person I'd raised for eighteen years by myself would be the epitome of painful.

When we reached Anette's room, I hesitated. Since they discovered she'd been connected to Josh through a mind link, Anette hadn't been released from the palace dungeon. No matter how much Nate or I tried to convince Zeus she would be fine, he wouldn't relent.

"Where will she stay once she is let out?" Yana asked, picking up on my thoughts.

"No idea. She's welcome at Nate's, obviously. He's got the room. There are apartments in Olympia, though, so maybe she'd want one of those?" I shook my head as I gazed around the room. "I don't know. I can't imagine any of you will be forced to stay here."

"I will refuse." Her tone left no room for argument. "This place is a tomb. I cannot stay here." She gave a small frown. "If they even allow me to. If I have no powers, what good will I be?"

I gave her shoulder a squeeze. "I wouldn't worry about that just yet. You're still badass, even if you can't electrocute us anymore."

She gave a small huff, then moved to Anette's dresser and opened the top drawer. "I am going to pack up her things. We can bring them back to Nate's for now, but they should not stay here."

We spent the next few minutes scouring Anette's room, piling clothes, books, and other knick knacks into her bag. Once the bag was full, Yana scrunched her face in confusion as she stared at the pile of clothes that was still on her bed.

"How in all the realms did she fit all of this in her bag?"

"Ziploc bags." I smiled, remembering that I'd asked the same thing when I met Anette. "She packed all her clothes in Ziploc bags, sucked the air out so they were flat. Just leave the rest. I'll come back and get everything else later."

We left the girls' hall and went across the courtyard to where the guys' hall entrance was. We repeated the same process in their rooms until finally, only one room was left.

When we reached Eric and Andrei's door, Yana gave me a reassuring pat on the back. "I will wait for you out here."

I smiled gratefully. Hesitantly, I placed my hand on the knob, knowing I would be hit with a thousand memories once I entered his room. Memories that I knew I needed to face alone.

When I entered, I sat down on his unmade bed and closed my eyes, my fingers curling tightly around the rumpled sheets. As I did, the painful scent of citrus mixed with cedar hit my nose, immediately bringing tears to my eyes. I'd always hated the smell of his body wash, but it was so unmistakably *Eric* that the tears I'd been holding back finally began to flow. Drawing his pillow to my face, I inhaled, breathing in my old friend, the guy I'd spent day after day with and who I'd never see again.

Quiet sobs shook my shoulders as my grip on his pillow tightened. There was nothing left of Eric except *things*—sheets and clothes and pictures. All I wanted was my friend back.

No. All I wanted was my old life back.

It angered me to think that, because I knew it wasn't entirely true.

And yet, if I were still the same girl I'd been when I came to Olympus, Mary wouldn't be missing. Eric—and all the recruits— would still be alive. I wouldn't need to clutch his pillow to remind myself of what it was like to get one of his bone-crushing hugs, the kind that spoke volumes about the kind of person he was.

Loving. Carefree. Happy. Loyal.

And now, gone.

Lifting my tear-filled eyes, I stared at the bed across from Eric's, perfectly made, and waves of fury rolled inside me as I thought of who'd once slept there. Andrei had been Eric's roommate and first friend on Olympus, and now he was rotting away in the palace dungeons, awaiting execution.

How in all the realms had it come to this? How had we gone from group dinners, crushes, and training, to murder and betrayal?

I shook my head and wiped the tears from my cheeks. Taking a few deep breaths, I tried to steady myself. There would be a day for dwelling on the things we all could've done differently, but today wasn't it. Grief wasn't a luxury I could afford just yet. Maybe ever, considering how things were going these days.

Standing, I swiped a few photos out of Eric's top drawer—ones of me and him with Mary and another of him and his guardians—and slid them into my back pocket. I hesitated when I saw the photo of us from prom—Eric and I had gone together, along with Mary, our human friend, Kellan... and Josh and Leila.

It had been one of the best nights in high school, one I knew I'd never forget. We'd celebrated that night, one last hurrah before Mary, Eric, and I left for Olympus. We'd danced like fools with the rest of the senior class before taking the party back to Josh's house, set deep in the woods outside Renville. It had been a night that celebrated friendship, our love for each other... the kind of love that would transcend the separation of our mortal and immortal lives.

Until it didn't.

Now when I looked at that photo, all I felt was rage, sharp and hot, mixed with an unrelenting sadness.

I tossed the picture in the trash can by Eric's dresser, then bent down to pull his duffel bag out from under his bed. Quickly, I packed up all his things, then set the duffel on top of his bed for his guardians, Joanne and Evan, to decide what to do with when they arrived.

Wiping the remainder of the tears from my face, I left, not bothering with any of Andrei's things. Maybe it was unfair to his guardians, but I couldn't handle taking the time and care needed to pack up his belongings when he'd wronged us so badly. If anything, I wanted to take them to the Underworld and toss them in the Phlegethon, letting its fire wipe all reminders of him from existence.

Yana was leaning against the wall across from Eric's room when I emerged a few moments later.

"Ready?" she asked.

"As I'll ever be."

3

NATE

Spending my days picking apart the mental shield of a creature like Menoetius was akin to having needles shoved under my fingernails. With each few threads of his magic I ripped free, one would bite back, nipping at my powers like a stinging insect. His powers were as vile as he was, twisting into thorny ropes around my own tendrils of Coercion as I tried to find out whatever it was he was hiding.

"It might help if you got my baby sister in here, you know." Menoetius' chest heaved as he stared up at me and Hades from where he was slumped against the wall of his cell. "She's finally coming into those powers of hers, after all. Tell me, which one of you gave her that last push to embrace what the Fates gave her?"

I gritted my teeth at was probably his tenth attempt to lure me into an argument with Tessa's former lover. If I didn't know how important it was for us to get through his walls, I would've thought my father sending me down here to work with Hades was some sort of punishment. Both of them were as antagonistic as they were vicious, but I only had the luxury of leaving one behind.

"Do you ever get tired of hearing yourself speak?" Hades asked dryly, narrowing his eyes as I pulled apart a few more strands of

Menoetius' shield. We'd been trying—and failing, for the most part —to get information from Menoetius for the last week. As I attempted to disassemble his shields, Hades tried to pull information from his memory.

But everyone had their weaknesses, and we would find his.

"Your shields are impressive," I commented, slowly sliding free another dull, brown thread of magic from his shield. "It's been three days, and I've barely been able to get anything from you. How long did they take you to build?"

"Centuries," he said with a smirk. "I'm curious to see how long it takes you to unravel them, to be honest." He angled his head to the side. "I wonder if you'll be happy with what you see once you do."

"If you want that to happen, why fight me?" Four threads.

"Are you *that* eager to see all the glorious things I did to Tessa, Nathaniel?" He grinned wickedly. "And here I thought Hades was the resident sadist." He gave Hades a considering look. "Or is it masochist? You're spending a great deal of time with your lost lover's new mate. Are you hoping he might share, or do you just enjoy torturing yourself?"

I swallowed back the urge to reach through the bars and throttle him, and Hades let out a quiet growl.

Ignoring them both, I went back to work.

'Did you see that?' Hades asked as an image flashed in the space where I'd just created a small crevice in Menoetius' shield.

'Mountains?'

'We'll share it with Persephone later. She may know the place he's remembering.'

I gave him a quick nod. All we'd gotten the last few days were small flashes—mountains, the sea, and a couple brief glimpses of Tessa's hometown of Renville. So far, though, we'd had no luck figuring out what any of it meant.

"Really, though. How long do you plan to do this on your own before you put your stubbornness aside and bring Tessa in here to assist?" Menoetius asked.

The corner of my mouth curved up. "Why do you think I haven't brought her in?"

He let out a low chuckle. "Well, then, if you're going to insist on sheltering her like my moronic brothers, might I suggest we bring in a bottle of wine to share since we'll be spending so much time together?"

"You don't strike me as the wine and dine type, Menoetius." Two threads.

Snap.

I held back my hiss of pain as his power stabbed at mine, but the wobble of his lips told me he'd caught my reaction. The pain was brief but intense, a shock that traveled through the tendrils of power I'd sent out.

"These shields take on a mind of their own after awhile, don't they? You'd think the witches would've concocted a way to spell these rooms to disable involuntary magic." He looked around his cell and shook his head. "It'd make things much easier."

"They have," Hades told him. "Why do you think we find yours so fascinating?"

Gritting my teeth, I stood up from the stool I'd been sitting on and cracked my neck.

"Leaving so soon?" Menoetius gave me an amused look. "And here I thought you might want to hear about the dreams Tessa had after Hades returned her memories." His expression turned wicked. "They were quite...vivid."

"Sorry to disappoint," I muttered. "I'll be back soon, don't worry."

Not bothering to wait for Hades, I turned and strode down the hall, away from Menoetius' cell. As much as I hated to admit it, I needed a break from his constant attempts to pit me and Hades against one another. Regardless of my trust in Tessa, there was no denying the fact that feelings had awoken in Hades for her that had been dormant for millennia.

He wouldn't stray from Persephone. I knew that as well as anyone. It didn't change the fact that the thought of Tessa dreaming of their time together made me feel a bit ill, even if it was just the result of memories resettling themselves in her mind.

As I traveled down the long hall of stone cells that made up the underground dungeon, I ruminated on how to handle Menoetius' shields. They were the most complex I'd ever seen; far more than the Giants I'd questioned in the Underworld, and they were direct descendants of Gaia and Ouranos themselves. The Giants' shields had been made of brute strength: effective, but easy to break through with the right amount of power, if not a little painful for them.

I had no trouble believing Menoetius when he said his own had taken centuries to create, but I also didn't believe for a second that he'd been the one to create them. They seemed to be made up of sheer intelligence and cunning. The trip wires woven in blended into the rest of his magic seamlessly, making it nearly impossible, so far as I could tell, to differentiate between the two.

As I neared the door that would lead back up to the palace, I paused when I heard a prisoner's voice from the second to last cell.

Andrei had been mostly quiet the last few days, with the exception of a few occasional taunts as Hades or I walked past his cell. After spending the first few days banging on his bars and screaming obscenities, he'd resorted to the occasional snide comment, seemingly accepting his fate and the fact that his masters would not be coming for him.

"Coercer!" Andrei's voice was rough with disuse. "I know you are out there!"

"Ignore him," Hades said, coming to a stop behind me.

"That's the third time in as many days he's tried to get my attention," I muttered as I continued past his cell. Frowning, I ascended the stairs that led back up to the palace. "It's irritating."

"Does our infallible Coercer think he missed something?" Hades mused.

I cocked a brow. "Considering recent events, I really wouldn't throw barbs about missing key pieces of information, Hades. And no, I don't believe I missed anything."

His amused expression immediately slipped into a glower, and he remained silent as we made the trek through the gilded halls of the palace to my father's war room.

A heated argument could be heard through the door, the raised voices of Zeus, Atlas, Prometheus, and Poseidon carrying clearly through the heavy wood. It had been typical the last few days—one would suggest something, Zeus would shoot it down. Rinse, repeat.

"Ah, Nathaniel, Hades!" Zeus smiled when we walked in, ignoring the looks of annoyance on the other gods' faces. "How are things with Menoetius? Any luck?"

I nodded a greeting at the other three gods, then shook my head. "His walls are too complex to break with brute force, so it's taking longer than I'd hoped, but it'll get done."

"If I didn't know better, I might think he was enjoying this," Hades said, shaking his head. "Whoever helped build his shields—"

"Knew exactly what they were doing," I finished.

"Are you planning on asking Tessa for assistance?" Atlas asked.

I cast him a look. "I am. We need the help, and it will be good for her."

"Brother, you're admitting you need assistance?" Zeus appraised Hades, his tone taunting. "That's somewhat unlike you."

Hades gave Zeus a withering look. "Knowing when to put my pride down and accept help is *quite* like me, actually. You'd do well to take a page from my book now and again."

My father's lip curled in annoyance.

"When do you plan to bring Tessa in?" Poseidon asked me wearily, cutting off yet another spat between his brothers.

"Tomorrow after the briefing," I said.

"Is it really necessary to include her in this?" Atlas asked, his face stormy.

"She'll be fine," Prometheus said reassuringly. His expression was reluctant, but he'd come to acknowledge Tessa's abilities for what they were in the last two weeks. "You need to trust her."

"I do," Atlas snapped. "I just don't want her near him. He can smell her fear, feeds off it." He shook his head. "Her being there will be amusing to him."

"She won't be alone," I pointed out, my patience waning. "Hades and I will be with her."

"And fear isn't what's driving her now," Hades said. "Vengeance is. She's well-prepared."

"Is that any better?" Atlas murmured, more to himself. He ran a hand through his hair and sighed.

"The others will be here tomorrow morning for a full briefing, so I'm hoping you'll have more information when you go back in," Zeus said. "Dionysus and Chiron have brought back representatives from several groups, and the Titans who've agreed to help are all on their way. I need you all here first thing."

I braced my hands on the table and looked over the wooden markers that indicated sightings of Cronus' allies. Red circles dotted areas throughout Earth, marking attacks by empousa, which seemed to be the most widespread of Cronus' forces. Blue marked the shapeshifting crocotta, and marked in green were the crop failures and other incidences of poisoning that had been facilitated by the Telchines—including that of the attack on the Ischyra compound in Athens. Several red markers that hadn't been there the day before were scattered across northern Asia.

"Those are new." I pointed at the swath of circles in Siberia. "What's happened in Russia?"

"Empousa attacks," Poseidon said, his expression grim.

"I thought the lamia had them in hand?" I asked, confused.

"They do now." Poseidon shrugged. "There are far fewer lamia than there are empousa, though, and Hecate had sent the bulk of them to other regions where large numbers of empousa have been reported."

"There were only a handful in Siberia," Prometheus said. "They released poison into the water supply in a few small towns there." He took on a pained expression. "Everyone was killed, man, woman, and child."

"How many have they killed?" Hades asked, frowning down at the newest addition to the map.

"A few thousand humans," Prometheus replied, his face pained.

"There doesn't seem to be any rhyme or reason to where they've chosen to attack."

I rubbed the bridge of my nose, then dropped my hand to my side. "We need to take them out," I said flatly, looking at my father. "The Tels. They've got a hand in everything."

"Agreed," Atlas growled.

"Yes, I'd like to come up with a plan to deal with them fully as soon as possible," Poseidon replied.

"Do we have any idea where they're holed up?" I asked. "Where they're getting their supplies? Why they chose the area they did?"

"Eris is doing some reconnaissance tonight, so we should know more when she returns," Zeus replied. He tossed another green marker over Norway. "At last report, however, she thought they were in Scandinavia, possibly somewhere in Iceland. We're hoping she'll be able to pinpoint a location soon."

"That's their only location?" I asked dubiously. "That doesn't seem terribly prudent."

"They're cocky," Hades said. "That doesn't have a tendency to mix well with prudent."

"No, it does not," Zeus said. "Once she has a more precise location, I'll have Artemis send out teams to monitor their activity."

"If they're in one spot, we should just take them all at once," I said.

My father nodded. "That would be ideal. Although an attack like that requires careful planning, so we need to be smart about it."

"Send Tessa in with Eris," Poseidon suggested. "With Tessa absorbing Eris' power, while drawing on the others she's become proficient in—"

"No." Zeus' tone rang with finality. "We don't need our enemy knowing just how valuable a weapon she is just yet."

"I would appreciate it if you stopped referring to my sister as a weapon," Atlas said quietly. "The last time someone did that, she died."

Zeus sent him a level look. "We're all weapons in this war, Atlas. It just so happens she is one that the world has yet to fully understand.

Waiting until the opportune time to release her is of the utmost importance."

A headache began to build at the base of my skull. This was an argument that was becoming cyclical at this point, and I just didn't have it in me to join in.

Without bothering with a goodbye, I turned and left, then teleported myself home the moment I stepped outside.

4

NATHANIEL

Foolishly, when I returned from questioning Menoetius, I'd hoped to find my house quiet—and preferably empty of anyone who wasn't currently living there. As with most things lately, I had no such luck.

When I opened the front door, I found Apollo and Hermes on my couch, each holding a glass of wine—*my* wine—and Tessa and Yana were nowhere to be seen. I paused when I stepped inside, contemplating suggesting they both go enjoy their own supplies of alcohol, but I couldn't muster up enough energy for that much snark. Instead, I dropped down on the couch across from Apollo and leaned my head on the back of the sofa.

"Rough day?" Hermes asked.

"You could say that," I murmured, closing my eyes. "Where are Tessa and Yana?"

"Tessa took Yana to the dorms to get her belongings," Apollo replied tersely.

I arched a brow and lifted my head to look at him. "I'm surprised you let them go."

Hermes snorted, then topped off his glass from the bottle of wine that was sitting on the coffee table. "He didn't. They went."

Giving in, I took a glass off the cabinet behind the sofa and poured some for myself. "Yana should have her things here if she's going to be staying. She's been wearing Tessa's clothes the last two days."

"I offered to send someone for her, but she wouldn't have it," Apollo groused.

Hermes' lips wobbled. "Then she insulted his mother."

I gave Apollo a surprised look. "She insulted Leto, and she's still breathing?"

His lip curled in a sneer. "I am *trying* to be patient with all of these broken immortals. It's incredibly frustrating when they refuse my help."

"Not every problem can be fixed with healing magic, Apollo," Hermes said quietly.

"Clearly," Apollo muttered.

I scrubbed my hands over my face, suddenly feeling exhausted, then looked at him. "Considering what's happened, can you blame Yana for wanting to get her things herself?"

"Of course not. It doesn't change—"

"Just because she's an Ischyra doesn't mean you can control every aspect of her life," I said.

"Is she?" He raised his eyebrows in challenge. "She no longer has her powers. Can we still call her that? Is there even a reason to keep her on this damn mountain anymore?"

"You know what I mean," I said wearily. "She's still an immortal. One of us. We need to give her the same courtesy we would give each other. She's got exactly three living friends left, one of whom is locked in a cell and another who's missing. Cut her a break. And if you think she'll leave, if you think it's safe for her to leave, with everything that's going on, you're a fool."

"He's right, Apollo," Hermes said. "You need to bend on this one."

"That seems to be all I do these days," Apollo grumbled.

"How long have they been gone?" I asked.

"An hour or so," Hermes replied. "Tessa and I did some work on mindlinking, but I'll let her fill you in when she gets home. How are her shields coming?"

Hades and I had been working with Tessa each night, teaching her how to use her mental shields instinctually. She was a fast learner, and once she truly put her mind to it, it hadn't taken more than a couple of nights for her to manage blocking us out while she slept. As unfortunate as it was, the attack on Athens and the arena seemed to have given her motivation and confidence a much-needed jump-start.

"She kept Hades and me both out the last two nights, so she seems to have gotten that down," I answered. "We'll keep working with her for a bit longer, though."

"No dream walks, then?" Apollo asked.

"None."

He sighed. "And Menoetius?"

"More difficult than I'd hoped. I thought the magic that disabled his powers in the dungeon would at least weaken his mental walls, but they're more complex than I expected. I wanted to give Tessa more time to deal with Yana and Mary, but I'm going to need her help."

The door opened then, and Tessa and Yana walked in, each loaded down with luggage. With a huff, they dropped the bags just inside the door.

"What took you so long?" Apollo asked. "Did anyone see you?"

"We packed up all the recruits' things," Tessa told him. "And no, nobody saw us, so you can relax." She gave him a teasing smile, which he returned with a stony glare.

I gave them an amused look. "What's all that?"

"Mary and Anette's stuff," Tessa replied, walking over to the liquor cabinet and pouring wine for herself and Yana. "If either come back soon, we didn't want them to have to deal with going to the dorms to pack everything up." After handing off a glass to Yana, who didn't acknowledge anyone before sitting down in front of the fireplace, Tessa sat down next to me and tucked herself under my arm.

I kissed the top of her head. "I hear you were mind linking. How'd that go?"

She stared thoughtfully into her glass for a moment before responding. "Okay, I guess. I saw them all. Mary, Josh, Cronus, the missing Pleiades. They were in a stone cell with a slanted ceiling with a square cut into it that was letting in sunlight. Other than that, nothing identifiable."

"That's a good thing," I told her. "It might not have been much, but it's more than we had yesterday."

"I know. I'm sick of everything we try not working, though. There has to be *something* we can do."

"It confirms they're all alive, at least," Apollo said. "Did it seem as though they'd been draining Mary's power?"

Tessa shook her head. "No, and I was kicked out before I could find out anything more."

"Kicked out?" I frowned. "By Mary?"

"No, Josh." She traced her finger along the edge of her glass, her expression tense. "He just looked into her eyes and booted me. It was like he could see straight through her to me."

"Has Father learned anything more about Josh's origins?" Hermes asked me.

"Nothing new. We still have no clue who his parents are or what kind of power he has," I said, trying not to let my irritation at that fact show. "I think Hecate needs to question her witches again."

"She's questioned them three times," Apollo said. "None know anything about him."

"Everyone comes from somewhere," Yana muttered.

Apollo's jaw tensed at her tone. "Obviously, but we can only work with the information we have, which is minimal. Aside from the last four years in Renville, we can't get any trace on him."

Tessa pursed her lips. "It doesn't make sense. It shouldn't be this difficult to trace his magic. Scylla was able to see Josh when she examined the traces of his magic from Anette's mindlink. This shouldn't be any different."

"I'm starting to think he wanted to be seen," Hermes said with a sigh. "No witch could be as powerful as he seems, only to slip up exactly when we might see him."

"Precisely, so if one of you could come up with a brilliant idea, that would be most helpful," Apollo said.

"Has anyone checked his school records or his house in Renville?" Tessa asked. "I'm sure it's a long shot, but there might be something."

"Unlikely." Apollo stood. "But any connections in Renville are worth looking into, I suppose, so figure it out. I need to get back to the palace. I'll see you all in the morning."

Once Apollo left, Hermes stood and stretched his arms over his head, then yawned. "I should be going as well. I've got guardian duty tomorrow."

Immediately following the attack on the arena, Hestia and Hera had spent several days visiting each of the dead recruits' guardians personally to inform them of what had happened. On their return, both insisted on holding a funerary service, allowing the guardians their chance to say goodbye. After several arguments, we'd managed to convince Zeus that a funeral should be held, to which all guardians who'd lost their charge would be invited.

"What time will they start arriving?" Tessa asked quietly, slowly tracing her finger along my forearm as she carefully avoided meeting Hermes' eyes.

"Day after tomorrow, right before the services," he replied.

"Briefing first thing tomorrow," I reminded him. "This one's required."

He rolled his eyes. "So I've been told. Repeatedly."

I smirked. "Zeus isn't happy you've been skipping meetings?"

"I'm a very important person, you know." He puffed his chest out. "Battle strategy and allegiances are for you lot to deal with."

"Last time I checked, you were the only Elder in this room."

"He's got you there," Tessa remarked with a smile that didn't quite reach her eyes. "Goodnight, Hermes."

"Goodnight." He blew her a quick kiss, then disappeared.

Once he was gone, Yana tossed back the last of her wine. "I am going to bed," she announced.

"Will you be coming to the palace in the morning?" Tessa asked, watching her as she stood.

Yana set her glass down on the coffee table and didn't look at either of us as she began walking away. "I do not see a need, but if you think it is necessary, I will go."

"It might help to get out of the house," Tessa called after her.

"Uh huh."

Tessa and I watched as Yana walked down the hall toward the guest room we'd given her. When her door shut, Tessa groaned and slumped down in her seat. Of all the problems we'd encountered in recent days, I think she thought Yana's would be the easiest to address. It had become obvious, though, that wouldn't be the case.

"I wish there was *one* thing I could fix," she grumbled. "Just one."

I brushed my thumb down her temple. "No one can fix what's happened to her, love."

"I know." She rubbed her hands over her eyes then let them drop to her lap. "How did things go with Menoetius today?"

"Slowly and painfully." I propped my feet up on the coffee table and rested my head on the back of the couch. "Very slowly."

"You guys want my help?" she asked. "My Coercion isn't as powerful as yours, but—"

"It's powerful enough, so yes, Hades and I would be very appreciative of your help." I turned to look at her and looked over her face, taking in the tightness of her jaw and exhaustion that was clear in her eyes. "If you're up for it."

"The sooner we get into his head, the sooner we'll find Mary. At least, I hope that's the case." She sat up and looked at me. "And you don't need to be sitting in that dungeon all day, every day."

I gave a derisive snort. "Not according to Zeus."

She gave me a knowing look. "Even if your father didn't ask you to deal with Menoetius, you'd have offered to do it."

"I know." I laced my fingers through hers and brushed a thumb across her knuckles. "We'll go tomorrow after the briefing. Now tell me, what's your next plan for locating Mary? Did you and Hermes come up with any next steps?"

She chewed at her lower lip and shrugged. "Astral projection let me see her, but nothing around her. Mindlinking got me booted from her brain. Telepathy and dream walks aren't working, so I'm guessing whatever place they're keeping her is spelled against both of those things. Zeus doesn't seem to want to spare any actual trackers, and I've had next to no experience with that ability, so I'd probably end up wasting time if I tried, and Scylla hasn't had any luck tracing his magic anywhere past the Underworld."

"You tracked well enough when you were training with Athena and Ares," I reminded her.

"I had a solid starting point and a general idea of where they would be, plus I was only tracking them a few hundred feet at most. I have no idea where Mary would be, so no place to actually aim my tracking ability." She smiled appreciatively. "Thanks, though. I just think it makes more sense for me to focus on using the powers I'm stronger with for right now. If I'm going to keep training while all of this is going on, I want to stick with what I'm already decent at, you know?"

"I can appreciate that," I told her. "And let me handle my father. He's being stubborn about a lot of things these days, but there's no reason he can't have a tracker assigned to find Mary and the sisters, especially now that we know she and the Pleiades are being kept in the same place."

"Speaking of next steps... Now that we know they're together, I think it's time we go pay the others a visit down at Demeter's."

I nodded my agreement. "We'll talk with Demeter tomorrow, then. Atlas, too."

"Yeah." She shook her head. "Of all the ways to bond with your estranged daughters..."

"They'll have plenty of time to bond like normal gods and goddesses soon enough." I slid an arm around her shoulder and pulled her against me, thankful to finally have a few minutes alone with her. "Your family is going to almost triple in size once that happens," I said with a laugh.

"Then I guess you'd better get a bigger dining room table."

I smiled, hoping that what I said was true. The Pleiades had long been estranged from their father, and despite Atlas' absence, I didn't know how willing they'd be to give him a chance to incorporate himself into their lives. He'd be able to prove himself eventually, I had no doubt, but if they'd inherited any of his stubbornness, that was undoubtedly going to be a slow-going process. For his sake and that of his siblings, I hoped they'd be willing to try.

I suppose there was nothing like impending war to help bring a family together.

5

TESSA

Despite her seeming reluctance, I insisted Yana come with us to the first large briefing we'd had at the palace since the arena attack. In the immediate aftermath, orders had been given, and we'd all scattered to one place or another. Several had gone out on the hunt for more allies, others to track down enemies, and the rest to gather any information they could find on how two weakened Titans had managed to escape from Tartarus, regain corporeal form, and launch an attack on a heavily warded mountain.

When we arrived in the war room, it was apparent that those who'd gone out to court allies had been successful. The ornate, cavernous room was nearly bursting with occupants.

Oceanus, a tall, dark mountain of a Titan, stood alongside Poseidon at the head of the map of Earth, his wife Tethys at his side, both having just returned with Athena, who stood clad in her battle leathers beside them, speaking with Ares, Eris, and Enyo, Zeus' other war-god children.

At Poseidon's other side was Triton, his son and commander of his armies. Two small golden tridents were strapped to his waist, perfect replicas of the larger one that gleamed over Poseidon's shoulder from its sheath on his back. Standing next to Dionysus was Chiron, freshly healed from his injuries in the arena. They had both been gone for five days and had arrived the day before with representatives from the various clans of centaurs, satyrs, harpies, and griffins.

Cornelius, an original Ischyra and only survivor of the recent Telchine attack on Athens, stood in front of a large window, arms folded across his chest, staring at the gardens that extended beyond the palace. A surge of sympathy coursed through me as I watched him. The few times I'd seen him since the attack on the Athens' headquarters, his face had been haunted, his eyes distant, focusing on others only long enough to interact when necessary. He was here, though, acting as the main Liaison for all Ischyra on Earth.

And forming a small group at the opposite end of the map of Earth with my brothers, talking amongst themselves, were the remaining Titans who'd opted to get involved in the war. Hera, Hestia, and Aphrodite had succeeded in bringing in Scylla's father, Phorcys, Mnemosyne, Hecate's father, Perses, and Pallas, who, depending on who you spoke to, was considered the original war god. Hyperion, one of the two peaceful Titans who ran the farming operation in the Olympic valley, stood beside them. He and his wife Theia had taken on the task of easing the Titans back into life on Olympus, as most of them had been gone for centuries and would likely be staying for a while.

The rest, including Zeus' mother, Rhea, had chosen not to involve themselves in another war, which I was sure rankled him to no end.

Atlas and Zeus were speaking quietly but heatedly in front of the giant stone fireplace set into the rear wall. The energy between the two had been nuclear since Atlas returned to Olympus, the only thing keeping them from tearing into each other being their mutual need to destroy Cronus and his allies. I'd been trying very hard not to think too much on how things might be once this was all behind us and the only demons left to face were the ones that had been of our own making. It was becoming increasingly difficult, though, because as tensions increased, so did tempers, and theirs were unmatched.

"Are they always arguing?" Yana asked, inclining her head toward where Zeus and Atlas stood. "I have only been around them a few times, but it seems they are always angry."

The corner of my mouth twitched in amusement. "More or less."

"Morning, ladies," a voice beside me murmured.

Smiling, I looked over at Persephone. "Morning. How was Earth? Did you just get back?"

"Lovely, and a few hours ago," she replied, rolling her neck and letting out a few cracks. "My trackers and I will be heading back once we're done here to follow a few more leads, but we were able to take out a few smaller groups of empousa. Still no luck finding those bastard Titans, though." She put her hands on her hips and looked around the room. "Somber bunch, aren't they?"

"Can you blame them?" I folded my arms and followed her gaze. "Most of them are being dragged out of pretty quiet lives."

She sighed. "They won't be much happier once they hear what I've found."

"What happened?" Yana asked.

"I'd rather tell it once." Persephone looked at me, resigned. "Nothing good."

Just then, Zeus banged on the map of Olympus with one of the heavy wooden markers. "Now that we're all here, let's get to it!"

The murmurs slowly died out, and once the room was quiet, he addressed the newcomers.

"I'd like to thank those of you who've agreed to come to our aid in this trying time." He gave a small nod toward the Titans and the forest creatures who'd joined us. "War is not something I had hoped would bring us all back together, but here we are. Now, I know several of you have news, so we'll start with those updates before we get into where we go from here." He stepped to the side, giving a slight nod toward Artemis, who stood beside him, looking a bit worse for wear but in one piece.

"My archers and I have just returned from Peru, where several villages have been ravaged by crocotta in recent weeks. We believe we've wiped out the issue there, but according to the few Enyo questioned, there are several other factions scattered throughout South

America." She picked up a small stack of blue markers and began laying them across the continent. "Two in Brazil, two in Chile, another in Peru, and one more in Patagonia, on the southern tip of Argentina. I've sent teams of archers to each region, but Ischyra have reported sightings of other crocotta throughout the world," she finished, gesturing toward Cornelius.

"Cornelius?" Zeus lifted his brow toward the Ischyra. "Care to elaborate?"

Cornelius gave him a tight smile and stepped forward. "I've spoken to the lead Ischyra in China, the southern US, Sweden, and Canada, all of whom have reported bands of crocotta, and in some cases, groups of crocotta working with empousa, which, as we all know, is something unheard of." He ran a hand over the stubble on his chin and shook his head. "Unsurprisingly, it seems the Telchines have spread themselves into these groups as well, doling out various poisons. Combined with news of the Lotus Eaters across northern Russia as well as the farming attacks, it appears we have a larger issue than we first thought in terms of the poisoners."

"Lotus—" I shook my head to clear my surprise. "They don't leave their island. Ever. Last I checked, they weren't the warmongering type. They're trappers, not hunters."

"Those things change when a group is offered the promise of increased power. The lotus flowers that have been left behind at each site are deadly, their natural narcotics warped into something new." Poseidon shrugged. "The Tels are the only ones on Cronus' side who have the ability to perform such a trick."

"Indeed," Zeus agreed, nodding. "Demeter? What's the latest on those crop failures? Has the antidote been dispersed to the Liaisons?"

"It has," she confirmed. "A preventative has also been made, but so far we're only distributing that in high-risk regions where farming is a main contributor to the food source or survival. The antidote is being given out on an as-needed basis."

"I've gotten a general location on the Tels," Eris said. She gestured toward Northern Europe. "Very general, though. Somewhere in Scandinavia."

"That's hardly a location," Oceanus scoffed.

She tilted her head and narrowed her eyes. "Which is why I said 'general.' And it's better than what we had, which was nothing."

"Keep trying to narrow that down," Zeus said with a nod. "What of the Sirens? Have we any more information on their whereabouts?"

Athena shook her head. "Saia and Mila were last sighted in Athens when the Ischyra there were killed. Aside from confirmation that their curse has at least partially been lifted, there's been no word, no incidents. They've been quiet."

"And we're certain they're on the wrong side of this?" Oceanus asked. "They could be quite useful as allies."

"Do you have reason to believe otherwise?" Eris asked. "They seemed pretty anti-Olympus when we saw them in Athens."

"Just because the Potamoi have turned against Olympus does not mean their offspring have," Oceanus said patiently. "The carrot Cronus is dangling in their faces could be made far more enticing if we offered to lift their curse completely." He cast a pointed look at Demeter.

"Absolutely not!" she snapped. "We're not in the habit of removing curses here on Olympus, when there was a damn good reason for placing them in the first place!"

Persephone groaned. "There wasn't, though! You sent them after me to bring me home from the Underworld, even though I was perfectly happy there."

"I had my reasons for sending them after you," Demeter told her. "Several, actually," she added with a glare toward Hades.

Persephone threw up her hands in frustration. "None of which were valid! We should be leaving no stone unturned in our hunt for allies, and your stubbornness is preventing that from happening!"

"Let's not forget that the witch who cast the spell must also be willing," Scylla said, arching a brow at Persephone. "Which she isn't."

"The newer generations of Sirens are not as volatile as the last," Tethys interrupted. "It may be worth a conversation with their leader."

"Their leader came after us," Nate argued. "Saia and Mila tried to attack us right after we found three dozen dead Ischyra in the compound."

Oceanus arched a brow. "From what I understand, Tessa here baited her."

My eyes widened. "They came to gloat about a headquarters full of dead Ischyra, tried to attack me, and you're saying I should've been nicer? They may not be as 'volatile' as their predecessors, but they've still accepted Cronus' offer to lift their curse in exchange for allegiance."

"I'm sure if the Olympians had done or offered to do the same, we would not be having this conversation." Oceanus angled his head to the side and frowned. "That should go without saying. It's a shame you didn't learn more objectivity from your mother, Tessa. It would benefit you a great deal in a time like this."

I gestured toward Demeter. "In case you didn't notice, the Olympians *weren't* willing to do the same."

Zeus banged a fist on the table. "Enough!"

'He's angry they've been dragged away from Volos,' Nate told me. *'Try not to let him get to you. He's normally very nice.'*

'Yeah, yeah, I know.' Tensions were high and we'd *all* been put in a bad situation. I needed to remember that when tempers flared, my own included.

Yana nudged me with her elbow, jerking my attention away from the hulking Titan across the room.

"Hades?" Zeus turned to his brother. "What news from the Underworld?"

Hades stepped toward the map of the Underworld that sat on the other side of the Olympic map. "Tartarus is fully secure," he said, gesturing toward the large region in the center. "The wards have been replaced and tripled, Nathaniel and I have questioned all of the guards in depth, and only those who've shown unwavering loyalty have been kept on active duty." He jerked his chin toward Hephaestus, who stood on the other side of the table, stone-faced, as he leaned on his gleaming black cane, his dark, red-streaked hair falling across his forehead. "Hephaestus and the cyclopes will be working on weapons."

"Polyphemus and I believe we've developed a way to incorporate some of the Telchine poisons into certain weapons," the soft-spoken forger said. The last time I'd seen him was at the welcome feast the Elders held for the new recruits, where he'd worn a black suit that was cut to the lines of his body. Today, he wore dark pants and a thick, brown shirt, both clearly designed for manual labor. His face was streaked with dirt, as though he'd been pulled away in the middle of a project.

"What kind of weapons?" Ares asked.

"Powdered godsbane infused into the blades," Hephaestus explained. He slid a dagger from his waist and held it up. The metal that made up the slim blade looked black, but when he turned it under the light, small bits of blue bounced off. "It's much more effi-cient than the liquid godsbane Menoetius used in the past. We're still testing them, but so far, it appears they'll work."

Pursing his lips, Ares nodded. "How many can you forge and how soon?"

Hephaestus slid the blade back into its sheath. "I've not forged weapons in this great a number in millennia, so I'll need more powdered godsbane, steel, and leather. As it stands, I've enough supplies to make a few hundred blades, at most, within the week."

"What about arrowheads?" Artemis asked. "They'd require fewer materials."

Hephaestus nodded. "I've factored roughly a thousand arrow-heads and two hundred spearheads in, as well," he added, looking at Athena. "You'll have to make them count."

"We'll get you the supplies," Demeter told him.

"The Oceanids will supply our own weapons, so you won't need to worry about us," Oceanus said, his voice a deep rumble. "The armory in Volos is well-stocked."

"Athena, Ares? What orders are you giving your troops?" Zeus asked.

Athena stepped forward. "New surges of supernatural power have been reported in multiple regions," she began, setting purple markers in Scandinavia, northwest Russia, Australia, Iceland, and southern Africa. "All Ischyra forces in those areas are being mobilized. We're currently going over the affinities of those stationed in all regions and will be dividing them up accordingly, depending on the needs of certain areas."

"We're also bringing a handful back here to assist Cornelius," Ares added. "Mentalists, mostly, but a few who are gifted with Earth affinities will be sent to work with either Hephaestus or Demeter."

"Make sure we've got a few Psychometrics on hand," Zeus told him. "If any prisoners are taken, we'll have need of them. Enyo?"

The tall, slim goddess stepped forward, ignoring the way Athena tensed as she stopped at her side. Enyo had an ethereal beauty about her that completely belied her viciousness, something that likely made it easy for her to get a leg up on her enemies from time to time.

"I'll take my forces into Russia and the southern part of Africa," she said, pursing her full lips as she scanned the map. "We'll have the regions in hand quickly."

"I've got some news, as well," Persephone announced, stepping forward, her expression grim. "My trackers and I located Crius. Or Crius' body, I should say. It was floating in a bay just off Cancun." Low murmurs ran through the room, mainly from the Titans who still stood in a small cluster, but she ignored them and pushed on. "There was almost no residual energy left inside him, which I assume is why it took us so long to track him."

Hera frowned. "How can that be? He's only been missing a week!"

Persephone shrugged. "Your guess is as good as mine."

Hera shifted her eyes to Hecate, who stood with a small, dark-haired man with black, depthless eyes and a pinched expression. "Hecate? Do you or your necromancer have any thoughts on this?"

I felt a small chill run down my spine as I realized who the man at her side was. There were only a small number of necromancers—witches who could commune with the dead—across the realms, and Kastin was their most powerful. I'd only ever known him by reputation, and he was only mentioned in passing during my lessons in the human world.

I expected him to be taller, more imposing, but I was surprised to find his small stature made him even more intimidating.

Kastin lifted his eyes to Persephone, and when he spoke, his voice was quiet, almost soothing. "There are two potential reasons for his body to be in such a state, although I would like to keep my speculations to myself until I can examine the body." Kastin tilted his head to the side and looked back at Hades. "Out of curiosity... when was the last time you confirmed Cronus and Iapetus were inside Tartarus?"

"The day Crius went missing," Hades replied. "Why?"

Kastin arched a brow. "You entered Tartarus, then? Saw their presence firsthand?"

Hades jaw tightened as he and the necromancer stared at each other. "No, I did not enter Tartarus. When I need to confirm a prisoner's location, I send out my power and locate them."

Clasping his hands in front of him, Kastin gave him a small smile that was slightly unsettling. "Well, as I said, I'd prefer to examine Crius' body before making any assertions." He inclined his head toward me. "I would like to bring your Mimic with me if that's alright."

Zeus grunted his assent as I stared at the necromancer wide-eyed. "I can't commune with the dead," I told him, suddenly very thankful for that fact.

"No, but you have Psychometric abilities, which will supplement my own quite well," Kastin replied.

A movement from my periphery drew my attention, and when I saw Atlas take a step forward to argue, I quickly backpedaled. "I'd be happy to help however I can," I told Kastin.

'Are you sure?' Nate asked.

'No, but I'm going to try, anyway.'

Hecate cleared her throat and stepped forward. "As much as I hate to add to the...unfortunate news, we also seem to have hit a dead end finding an origin for Josh. Scylla's trace on his magic only showed her his true face, the one behind the glamour he wore in the Underworld. In addition, I've again reached out to all of my witches. Each are accounted for, their minds have been examined, and no children I was not already aware of exist."

"Fine, then," Zeus said with a huff. "We'll continue to seek out information on him, but our main focus should remain on the threats we're well-aware of. Cronus, Iapetus, their forces, and the threat of stolen power." He let his gaze travel around the room, stern and steady, before looking back toward his posse of war god children. "Athena, Ares, let's go over our numbers again."

6

TESSA

Talk continued for a few more hours, and by the time Zeus finally let us loose, all I wanted was to go home and sit in a nice, quiet room to process all we'd learned. I was glad he hadn't asked me for an update on Mary's whereabouts, although I knew Atlas would be on his way to find me soon enough to ask about his daughters.

"I feel as though my ears are bleeding," Yana remarked as we emerged onto the front lawn of the palace.

Outside the confines of the stifling war room, the crisp, Olympic wind felt fantastic. I pulled my jacket tighter around me and headed toward the rocky cliffside that overlooked the range, needing to get as much open air as I could.

"Join the club," Dionysus muttered, falling into step beside us. I looked over at him and cocked a brow at his uncharacteristically grumpy expression. Chiron was grinning mischievously from his other side.

"Rough week?" I asked.

"Dionysus seems to have underestimated just how much work it takes to lure the forest creatures into war," Chiron said with a smirk.

Dionysus grunted in response. "The only way any of those creatures agree to anything complicated is after a significant amount of forest wine. *Very* significant."

I gave him an amused look. "As the god of wine and debauchery who frequently attends college, shouldn't you be well accustomed to things like drinking to excess?"

"Have *you* ever gotten drunk off forest wine with centaurs and satyrs?" he asked me pointedly.

"Can't say I have."

"I wouldn't recommend it. Their gatherings are worse than human fraternity parties, if you can believe it, and the wine is... painful." He rubbed his eyes and yawned. "I've got to go sleep off the last few days. Come get me if the world ends. I'll see you all in the morning."

Shaking my head, Yana, Chiron, and I walked over to a rough outcropping to wait for Nate, who'd gotten held up with Apollo and Cornelius.

"It is worse than I thought," Yana said as she looked out over the mountains. She shifted her eyes to Chiron. "That necromancer thinks Crius was killed long ago, correct?"

Chiron folded his thick arms across his chest. "That would certainly be my guess."

"Do you think it was Menoetius who killed him?" Yana asked.

"If anyone can destroy another Titan discreetly, it would be him," I murmured. I looked up at Chiron, who was staring contemplatively out over the snow-capped mountains. "What's up?" I asked.

"It's all just a lot to process," he said quietly. "My brethren have been living their own lives quietly for so long now. I hate having to ask them to break that peace to fight in a senseless war."

"Is there anything we can do to help?" I asked.

He smiled down at me, his soft expression belying his wild appearance. "Not yet. I'm going to get the centaurs and the others settled in the forest, then I'll be diving into research to see what I might be able to find on our newest threat." His expression turned sympathetic. "I'm truly sorry for how things have turned out, Tessa."

"It's not your fault, Chiron. And please, let me know if you need help with research." I gave him a wry smile. "I have a feeling I'm going to be stuck on this mountain for a while."

He shook his head. "Unlikely, but even if you are, it'll be because you're needed."

Yana gave a quiet sound of agreement.

Chiron gave her an appraising look. "Yana, if you're able, would you mind digging into the archives with me? I could use the help, and we may be able to unearth some way to rectify your loss of power as well."

Scowling, Yana kicked at a few pebbles, sending them skittering over the side of the cliff and into the abyss below. I elbowed her, and she huffed out a sigh and rolled her eyes.

"Alright, I will help."

Chiron slid me a grin. "Okay, then. We'll get started once I get everyone settled." He gave us both a quick nod of farewell before galloping off down the mountain.

"No matter how many times I see him in that form, I do not think I will ever get used to it," Yana muttered as we watched him disappear into the clouds that seemed to perpetually ring the uppermost portions of Olympus. "Are you looking forward to seeing your guardians tomorrow?"

"Yes and no, considering the circumstances." I was more worried about facing Eric's guardians, but that wasn't a fear I'd yet voiced to anyone. I tried very hard to tamp down any guilt I felt over the actions my father and brother had taken against my friends, but it was very, very hard.

"It is not your fault, you know," Yana said quietly. "I have seen that look on your face since I woke, and I know what you are thinking. But none of this is your fault."

I gave her a tight smile. "My father and brother are orchestrating a coup against Olympus and have destroyed my friends beyond repair. It's hard not to feel like I should've—or could've—done more in the past, you know?"

"I do," she allowed. "But I still do not blame you."

That doesn't mean others won't.

I kept the thought to myself, not wanting to burden her with making me feel less guilty.

Instead, I gave her another smile, this time more genuine. "I appreciate you saying that, Yana. Really."

"So...why did Zeus not ask about your progress?" She spoke hesitantly, as if she wasn't sure how her question would be received.

"I think...Well, he's gotten ripped into several times now by Atlas regarding my training and what Zeus expects me to do, which feels like pretty much everything at this point. Everyone in there was so tense... I honestly wouldn't be surprised if he was talking to Nate about me right now."

"Almost correct," Nate said, coming up behind us. "We finished talking about you five minutes ago."

I smiled at him as he sat down next to me. "What did he have to say when you told him I'd linked with Mary?"

"Glad you were able to do it, less than thrilled you and Hermes weren't able to get much information." He shrugged.

"Tell him to join the club," I muttered.

"Tessa! Nathaniel!" Hades barked from the doorway. I huffed out a sigh. and Nate smirked.

"What does he want?" I groaned.

"Zeus wants you to examine Crius' body right away, then he wants the three of us questioning Menoetius," Nate explained. "I tried to tell him it was a bad idea with Hades in whatever mood he's in, but..."

The sound of boots scuffing on rock approached, and when I turned, I saw Hades stalking toward us, clearly still annoyed about his exchange with the necromancer. Apollo followed behind, hands in his pockets, an amused expression on his face.

"What is it?" I asked, trying to keep the annoyance from my voice.

He didn't bother with hellos when he reached us. "Let's get this over with," he groused. "I want Menoetius dealt with, and I don't have time to be up here much longer."

"You don't need to stay," I told him. "Nate and I can handle it."

"No, you can't." He jerked his chin toward Yana. "Get the recruit home and let's get on with it."

Yana's jaw tensed, but to her credit, she kept quiet. She'd had no qualms snapping at Apollo, Nate, or either of our brothers the last few days, but Hades' ire wasn't something she needed to be taking on right now.

'No need to be a dick, Hades.'

"Come, I'll take you back," Apollo told Yana. She looked like she wanted to argue, but before she got the chance, Apollo touched a hand to her arm and teleported away.

Shaking my head, I glared at Hades. "She's been through enough already. You don't need to be such a jerk."

"If you think I'm going to worry about hurting the feelings of a damaged Ischyra, think again," he snapped. "Now come on." Without another word, he began striding back toward the palace.

Nate took my hand as we started to walk back inside. "Ignore him. His ego is wounded, and you know how he gets."

"Yeah, well, it'd be nice if the three of us could have a united front when we deal with Menoetius," I said with a sigh. "So where's Crius' body, anyway?"

"Zeus insisted we bring it up here to be examined," Hades grumbled. "It would appear my darling brother is too good to make the trip to the Underworld."

He led us inside the palace and through the labyrinthine halls until we reached a simple, wooden door on the lower level. It bore the same color scheme as the rest of the palace—white, trimmed in gold, but where everything else was ostentatious and had a larger-than-life feel, this looked just like a regular door that had been painted to match.

Hades pressed his palm to its center and closed his eyes. A few seconds later, the lock came free with a *snick* and he pulled the door open. The thump of footsteps on stairs followed, so we made our way down the staircase to the area below.

We stopped in a basement of sorts. It didn't look like a dungeon, necessarily, but it had the dark, dank feel of one. The room was about the size of the war room upstairs, only instead of gleaming travertine and gilded walls, the floor was hard-packed dirt, the walls were made up of gray stone. Large boreholes dotted the walls all the way around, and when I looked up, I saw more in the ceiling. Bits of metal stuck out of a few.

"This was the original dungeon, wasn't it?" I whispered. "From when Cronus' palace still stood here?"

Nate slid me a look, then nodded. "It is."

"This way," Hades snapped. He stalked toward a table on the right hand side of the room where a body lay, draped in a sheet. Zeus, Kastin, Persephone, Hecate, Oceanus, and Atlas all stood waiting.

Before any of the others could speak, Kastin stepped forward and reached out a hand to me. Even though everything inside me was screaming to step away, I met his cold, dark eyes unflinchingly. I took his hand, and he covered it with his other one. He gave me a small, unsettling smile. "Thank you for coming."

"Of course. Whatever I can do to help." My eyes darted toward where Zeus stood behind him.

Kastin held out his arm, gesturing me forward toward the table. He pulled back the sheet, and I only just refrained from gagging at the sight of Crius' mottled, purple skin and the sickening, bloated mound of his torso. His face was frozen in a look of terror, and his body had become so full of gasses it was a wonder he hadn't popped on the journey here. And the stench... it took all I had not to vomit as the cloying scent invaded my nostrils, so heavy I could feel it coating my taste buds.

Realizing everyone had been awaiting my reaction, I cleared my throat and looked at the necromancer. "Have you been able to commune with him yet?"

He nodded curtly. "Briefly, although he was somewhat incoherent." His eyes flashed toward Hades. "It would seem he has yet to make passage across the Acheron."

Hades arched a brow. "Has he *tried*? Charon doesn't go hunting for stray souls who linger on the shores, nor do I. If Crius hasn't made passage, it's his own doing."

"Yes, well, regardless, I believe Tessa may have more luck using her Psychometry on his corpse. His mind has become addled, but I have my suspicions."

"Which are?" Hades growled.

"I'd prefer to wait until Tessa has done her examination before voicing them," Kastin replied coolly.

Hades opened his mouth to retort, but Persephone cut him off.

"There is no use speculating when we're still missing information, Hades. Be patient."

Hades shot a glare at his wife but remained silent.

Ignoring everyone in the room but Kastin, I stepped forward. I felt the warmth of Nate's body at my back, but before I could ask him to back off, he spoke.

'It's either me or Atlas, and I figure I'm less distracting.'

I cast a glance at my twin and sighed quietly. He stood stock still, feet spread, arms folded across his chest. The muscles in his jaw were clenching and unclenching as he glowered across the table toward me and Kastin.

'Alright,' I said reluctantly. Atlas trusted Nate to keep me safe, and I trusted Nate to give me whatever space he could. He wouldn't involve himself in this process, but he would stay close enough to prevent any who might—like my twin—from interrupting.

I looked at Kastin. "I've never done this on a dead body before, only objects. I'm assuming it'll be a bit different?"

"Not so much," he said quietly. "His energy has nearly vacated his body, so he's no more than a bag of parts now."

I bit back a gag at that.

"So he's essentially an object, then," I said, nodding. "Got it." I gave Zeus a questioning look. "Before I dive in, is there anything specific you want me to look for?"

"No." He narrowed his eyes in assessment. "You're certain you can do this?"

"Yes," I told him firmly. "I just need everyone to keep quiet and keep *back*," I said, giving Atlas a pointed look, which he returned with an angry look of his own. Seeing the exchange, Oceanus gave me an amused look and moved to stand beside my twin.

Reassured Atlas would be kept in hand if things went sideways, I returned my focus to Crius' corpse, then I blanched at the realization that I was going to actually have to touch his decomposing flesh in order to use my power.

Taking a deep breath, I gently placed my hands on his wrist. The flesh gave slightly under my fingers, and I tried not to imagine what would happen if I pressed any harder, although I couldn't seem to stop the vision in my head of water balloons exploding. Closing my senses to everyone around me, I pulled forth my Psychometry and reached out, seeking his energy.

At first, I saw nothing. A few moments passed, and I began to think I wasn't going to find anything, then suddenly, light flashed, and I began to see images in my mind. I pushed back as far as I could go, but I couldn't tell exactly how far back I was. When I hit a wall that I couldn't get past, I stopped pushing and just watched.

The images I saw were scattered, making it difficult to latch onto just one. Instead, I relaxed and tried to watch through Crius' eyes as they drifted by. Finally, I saw the face of Xander—the face Josh had worn when he visited the Underworld—in front of me, and without thinking, I reached out and latched on.

There was no sound. I only observed, all semblance of emotion having fled along with Crius' soul and energy. Josh stood in front of him, the smile he wore cajoling. Crius' head shook, and a look of annoyance flashed across Josh's face, then the memory vanished.

Frantically, I scanned around for more. I found one of what looked to be the gates of Tartarus, which by itself wasn't anything remarkable considering Crius' position in the Underworld, but this one... I could feel emotion attached to this memory.

Curiosity. Smugness.

And victory.

Just as that realization hit me, my eyes flew open, and I was back in the dungeon, standing over Crius' corpse.

"Well?" Zeus and Hades asked in unison.

I opened and closed my mouth a few times, then frowned and looked at Kastin. "Were you watching?"

He shook his head. "I felt it more prudent to keep any intrusions from your mind." He inclined his head toward Nathaniel. "And he was blocking me."

I turned my head and gave Nate a curious look. "Why?"

"Because every single person in this room was attempting to get into your head and watch," he said flatly. "I thought you might prefer some privacy." I didn't miss the annoyed look he wore as he glanced at Atlas.

Shaking my head, I blew out a breath and linked my fingers with his in an attempt to calm him. "I'm not quite sure what I saw, to be honest." I frowned, trying to glean any type of meaning from what I'd seen. "There were two main memories that stood out. The first was of Crius talking with Josh when he wore Xander's face."

Kastin eyed me curiously. "Xander, the witch?"

I nodded, then plowed on, not wanting to get into my past with Xander just then. "I didn't feel any emotions attached to any of the memories except one."

"That's not surprising," Hecate said. "Once a soul is gone, things like emotions don't linger long."

"Leaving us to interpret those memories to the best of our ability," Kastin added. "Which memory still held emotion?"

"He was outside the gates of Tartarus, and he felt... victorious. And smug. Like he'd just achieved something major." I shook my head. "I'm not sure when that was, though."

Kastin folded his arms and narrowed his eyes as he focused on Crius' body. He began to tap the fingers of one hand against his elbow.

When he didn't speak for several moments, Hades let out a low growl. "*What,* Kastin?"

Kastin let out a huff, then looked around the room. "When I first attempted to examine Crius, I had two potential scenarios in mind for the events that surrounded his death, both of which involve reanimation. The first would be that he was killed long ago and the Titan who'd been leading the Giants was nothing more than a revenant, a mindless puppet to be controlled at will."

"What would be the purpose of that?" Zeus asked. "What good would a revenant be for two imprisoned Titans? He didn't have the power to grant their freedom in life. He would be even less powerful in death."

"True, which is why I would say that option is the less likely of the two. The second reason for reanimation," Kastin continued, "would be as a vehicle for extrication." A small smirk twisted Kastin's lips, not quite sinister, but bordering on appreciative.

"Extrication?" I frowned, not sure I was hearing him correctly. "You're saying two non-corporeal Titans—two of the strongest who've ever lived—inhabited Crius' body as a means of escaping the Underworld?"

"How would he have been able to bear that much energy?" Nate asked.

"They were severely weakened, so with the right magic, their non-corporeal forms could have slipped through the smallest of fissures undetected."

Kastin looked up at Hecate and nodded, then addressed Zeus. "If Crius' body was used to remove the Titans, they would have had to regain a significant amount of power before engaging in an attack like Iapetus did last week. Based on the information you've all given me, my assessment would be that Cronus and Iapetus escaped long before last week and have been regaining their strength ever since."

"How long?" Apollo asked sharply.

"Weeks, maybe even months," Kastin replied. He raised his eyebrows expectantly at Hades. "When was the last time you questioned Crius?"

"Crius was the one who alerted me to the cracks in the walls of Tartarus," Hades said slowly. "But I examined his mind along with the rest of the guards. Nothing was amiss."

Kastin considered his response for a moment. "This was only a few days before the attack, correct?"

"Yes," Hades said through gritted teeth.

"At that point, Cronus and Iapetus would've been long gone. Crius would've been nothing more than the walking dead since the only thing keeping him from decomposing would be the power that had reanimated him, which would have nearly faded."

"There are spells," Hecate said, anticipating Hades' next question. "Spells that can glamour a mind, just like a face. *If* what Kastin is suggesting is true, and Crius was simply a revenant by the time you were informed of the cracks, then it's possible, even probable, that whatever was left of his mind had been glamoured to appear as it always had."

Frowning, Kastin shifted his gaze to Nate. "Nathaniel, you interrogated the guards, correct? Did you happen to peek into Crius' mind as well?"

Nate stiffened. "No, I was asked to question the Giants only. Why?"

Kastin shrugged. "That's quite unfortunate. Your power works quite differently than Hades'. Had you done so, you would've been able to tell us for certain whether his mind was intact."

Murmurs of disbelief fluttered through the room. Nate looked more furious than I'd ever seen him, but whether it was at Kastin's assertion or himself for not thinking to question Crius, I couldn't tell.

Several seconds went by before Hades finally found his words.

"There's no possible way you could know that," he growled, struggling to conceal his anger. I could feel it pulsing off of him, drifting across the room and connecting with my own empathic abilities. I cracked my neck, trying to shake off the tension it left behind, then exchanged a look with Persephone, who looked torn between jumping in to defend her husband and wanting to hear the rest of what Kastin had to say.

"No?" Kastin gave him an amused look. "From what I hear—" he shot a glance at Atlas "—you were unaware of multiple breaches of the walls. With the right magic, their life-forces could have been pulled through one of those breaches and into a waiting vessel. If this mystery witch used a glamour on himself, he could've easily concealed the actions of someone attempting to break them free."

Hades blinked, and the look of barely suppressed fury that he wore as he looked at Kastin would've made a weaker man fall to his knees. As it was, Kastin simply stared back, meeting Hades' dark gaze with an impassive look of his own.

In that moment, I felt bad for Hades. As infuriating as he was, as often as I wanted to kick him straight over the edge of a cliff, failure was never something he'd worn well. Something this big...it would crush him, even if he'd never admit it.

"Hang on," I said, stepping toward Kastin. "Menoetius did a dream walk with me a week before he and my father attacked the arena. The way he spoke, Iapetus and Cronus hadn't been freed yet." I looked toward Zeus then back at the necromancer. "He was expecting Zeus to use me to keep that from happening. The Sirens said—"

Kastin's eyes narrowed, his hands clasped in front of him as he assessed me. "Sirens are notoriously untrustworthy, and did you ever consider your brother could've been lying?"

Gods, this guy was looking to piss everyone off today.

"Menoetius has lied about plenty of things," I acknowledged. "But he was too...casual about the way he said it. He didn't outright say, 'Father and Cronus are still in Tartarus,' but he was pushing me for details about what our side was planning, Zeus in particular. If they'd already been out, I don't think he would've mentioned it at all."

"What did he say to you, exactly?" Kastin asked.

Frowning, I thought back, then looked at Hades. "A little help?"

He nodded, then his eyes went vacant as he deftly sifted out the memory of the dream walk. After a moment, he looked at Kastin. "He said, 'He thinks he can stop me from bringing my father home.'"

Even as he said the words, I realized that they could be interpreted in one of two ways.

"Assuming he wasn't lying," Kastin said slowly, "all that proves is that Iapetus was still contained within Tartarus. It says nothing of Cronus' status."

"Or he just cared more about getting our father out than Cronus,"

Atlas cut in. "I know my brother. He wouldn't have given a damn if Cronus was left to rot, so long as he had Iapetus back."

"I am not disagreeing with that possibility," Kastin said, sounding annoyed. "What I *am* saying is that, based on what I've been told, combined with the condition of Crius' body, the amount of time it would have taken to disable the wards and the lack of certainty in regards to their last known presence in Tartarus, I'm led to believe at least *one* of them had been released long before last week. It's more than likely both were released."

Heavy silence settled over the room as we all realized just how bad this situation had gotten. Up until a week ago, it had seemed Menoetius was our biggest threat outside the Underworld. He'd been the one in charge, perfecting spells, orchestrating my father's and Cronus' escape, gathering forces, but giving no true indication he or they were anywhere near battle-ready. In a matter of moments, those assertions had been obliterated. If what Kastin said was accurate, we were potentially weeks, maybe even months behind Cronus and my father.

"Despite this new revelation, not much has changed," Oceanus said. "Menoetius did what he does best—he deceived, misdirected. He led you to believe his side was still struggling when it wasn't." He shrugged. "It's clever battle strategy."

Zeus gave a small grunt of agreement. His eyes found Hades, then Nate, then me. "You three, get down there and question him. I want this confirmed or denied immediately."

Kastin moved to pull the sheet back over Crius' body, then paused. "Will you be taking him back to the Underworld?" he asked Hades and Persephone.

Hades nodded. "His body will be disposed of." His lip curled in anger. "I'll decide what to do with the rest of him once I get there."

"I'll take him back," Persephone murmured. She gave her husband's arm a reassuring squeeze. "Go deal with Menoetius."

"What will you do with him?" I asked Hades.

"Tessa, dear, don't ask questions you don't want the answers to," Persephone said with a smile. "Just know it won't be pleasant."

I nodded slowly. "I can live with that."

7

TESSA

With the distraction of dealing with Crius' body and the mysterious circumstances surrounding his death, my unease about seeing Menoetius for the first time since he'd been imprisoned didn't peak until Nate, Hades, and I were on our way to the palace dungeons. I'd never seen them, but I could only imagine that Zeus would've attempted to one-up his father in the dark-and-dank department.

"So what exactly do I need to do?" I asked Nate as we walked through the palace, down one vibrant, wood-paneled hall after another.

Nate scratched his head and grimaced. "It's a bit tough to describe, but essentially, you need to be able to see his shield, the components that form it, and disassemble it. It's similar in theory to how you break through my Coercion, but more complex because he's spent a significant amount of time creating very complex walls. You can't just use force, which would be my preferred tactic."

As we continued to walk, he and Hades began explaining the trip-wires that Menoetius had laid in his mental shields. After a few minutes, we reached a thick iron door with a small square of bars right at eye level. Before opening the door, Nate paused and faced me.

"I'm going to show you how to slip the threads of his magic loose, which is fairly simple, assuming you can see his magic the same way you can see mine. Once you've got that down, I'll just need you to focus on visual differences between the tripwires and regular magic and help me diffuse as I go."

I arched a brow. "It's painful, then?"

He nodded. "Like a needle prick to the brain. If you're able to focus on finding those, I'll be able to move more quickly."

"I'll do my best, then."

"Once we get in, don't focus on *anything* but his walls. I'll be working alongside you, disassembling as you go, but we both need to try to keep the spots we break down open as long as possible so Hades can get in. He'll deal with memory extraction." He paused, then exchanged a quick look with Hades before continuing. "And just try to ignore the things he says to you."

Nate must've seen the hesitance on my face because he touched a finger to my chin and tilted my face toward his. "Are you worried that you can't do this or about what you might find when we go in?"

"I'm pretty confident I'll be able to help you with his shield," I told him. "The rest...seeing what's in his mind, the things he's done, knowing he's going to make this as hard as possible... That's the part I'm not sure I can handle. My own memories of him are bad enough. Seeing things from his perspective..."

He touched his lips to mine, then smiled. "While I can't begin to imagine how those things might've been for you, I know you'll be able to handle whatever he's got waiting. Hades will be the one looking for memories, though. You just need to focus on his shields and nothing else."

I rested my head against his chest and sighed. "I know. And if we get even a little bit of information on where Mary and the sisters are, it'll be worth it."

With an annoyed huff, Hades yanked the door open. "If you two are done?"

I bit back a snarky reply and forced a smile. "Lead the way," I told him.

"Hang on," Nate said quietly, touching a hand to my arm.

"What is it?" I asked, frowning.

"We're going to pass by Anette and Andrei's cells on the way to where we're keeping Menoetius."

"Ah." I nodded. Fury spiked through me at the thought of even looking at Andrei's traitorous face. He could rot, for all I cared, but Anette... I'd come to see her earlier in the week in an attempt to boost her morale, let her know I was working to get her freed, but she'd been completely unresponsive.

"It's up to you if you want to visit her, love, but just know that she's not in good shape." He looked toward the stairs that led down to the dungeon. "She seems..."

"Hopeless?" I offered. "Can you blame her?"

He sighed and ran a hand through his hair. "We'll talk to Zeus again. He's being unnecessarily stubborn."

"Okay. I want to wait until I have something more to offer Anette before going to see her again. Telling her I'm trying isn't going to improve her morale any. She already knows that." At least, I hoped she did.

We trudged down the stairs, following Hades into the musty stone dungeon. It looked and felt exactly like I expected a dungeon to be like. Cold, gloomy, and bearing an overall sense of despair. I imagined execution would be a preferable punishment to an eternity spent in this place. The thought had me reconsidering Andrei's death sentence, wondering if life underground would've been more fitting. Unfortunately, though, it wasn't my call, and truthfully, I didn't trust myself to make an impartial decision when it came to Andrei's fate.

I could feel power pulsing off of Hades as we approached Menoetius' cell, and I had to check my own power to keep it from reacting to his. Nate gave my hand a reassuring squeeze, and I tapped into the calming power I'd absorbed from Dionysus to counteract the negativity I could feel forcing itself on me.

When we rounded the last corner in the long corridor, Hades stood, arms folded, glaring into the cell in front of him. He gave Nate and me a cursory nod before refocusing his attention.

Steeling myself, we came to a stop beside him where the heavy wood-and-iron door stood open, and I faced my brother's cell.

Menoetius looked the same as the last time I'd seen him, only a bit worse for wear. His dark hair was a bit tangled, his pants and black shirt slightly wrinkled. The magic in the walls of the dungeon was preventing him from using his power, and I had a small sense of satisfaction knowing he was finally getting a dose of what I'd felt each time he'd taken my own.

The sardonic grin he wore and the malicious glint in his eyes as they met mine, however, were wholly unchanged.

"Hey, there, baby sister," he said, his smile turning sly. "I was wondering when you'd stop by to play."

Frowning, I stared down at my brother and attempted to reach inside his head without actually acknowledging his presence. Menoetius' magic was the color of clay, a thick, ugly, muddy red. Nothing like the brilliant, comforting crimson that made up Nate's magic.

No, my brother's power was as vile as he was.

There, do you see it?' Nate asked.

"What, you won't even talk to me?" Menoetius scoffed.

Ignoring him, I gave Nate a small nod. *'Now what do I do?'*

"Still need your hand held, I see," Menoetius said, clicking his tongue as he watched us. He smirked at Hades. "It's a shame you didn't spend more time teaching her and less time fucking her back then, hmm?"

I felt Nate stiffen beside me, so I sent a bit of reassuring calm toward him. Nate tried very hard not to let his jealousy at my past with Hades show, but times like these, when emotions were already running high and the three of us were forced into close quarters, well... it was hard, and I couldn't say I blamed him. I'd assumed going into this that Menoetius would use my relationship with Hades as a means of trying to make all three of us unsteady, but none of us could afford to waste time on his petty nonsense.

"What do you see in this one, Tessa?" Menoetius eyed Nate speculatively then gave me a knowing look. "He's just another one of Zeus' whelps. Is Persephone too much competition for you?"

Hades snorted. "I have to say, I'm disappointed. Considering your pasts with one another, I expected your attempts to anger her to be much more creative, much less...petty."

"That's what happens when your toys and power are taken away," I said absently as I continued running my own power over my brother's shields, feeling for the trip wires Nate had mentioned. "He's barely more than a human in there, so words are all he has."

"Meager as they are," Hades said.

'There.' I showed Nate a spot where a thread of magic glowed just a hair brighter than the ones beside it.

'Alright, see if you can diffuse it. Carefully, *and one thread at a time, or else they'll rebuild themselves almost immediately. I'll work on the rest.'*

'On it.'

Nate gave me a slight nudge of approval in my mind, then leaned casually against the wall and quietly went back to work.

"Why are you here, anyway?" Menoetius asked Hades. "Are you hoping Nathaniel might be willing to share?" He chuckled quietly. "I'm sure Tessa—" He cut off with a snarl as I ripped the charged thread from his shield, using the millisecond the space was empty to shock him with my power.

"What were you saying about hand holding?" Nate murmured, amusement and pride clear in his tone.

'Next time you get a thread free, try to keep it open,' Hades instructed. *'I want to see what I can pull from his memory.'*

'Stay linked with me, then, because it won't last long,' I replied.

"So, Menoetius," Hades began, keeping his tone conversational. "A curious thing just happened. Would you like to know what it was?"

Menoetius smirked, then held out his hands for Hades to continue. "Alright, I'll play. Pray tell, what was this 'thing' that happened?"

Nate and I continued to shift aside bits of Menoetius' shield while Hades questioned him regarding Crius and his knowledge of how Cronus and my father had escaped. I wasn't holding out hope that he knew much, but I also couldn't dismiss the fact that he'd played his cards much more closely to the chest than we'd originally thought.

"Care to tell us how Crius managed to house not one, but *two* Titans within his single, puny shell?"

"Crius is a Titan," Menoetius said, as though that were explanation enough. When Hades' eyebrow winged up in response, I saw the wheels start turning in Menoetius' head.

'Hold that spot open,' Nate ordered. *'Hades, get in there.'*

Smirking, Hades looked down at Menoetius. "Ah. You didn't expect us to know that's how they did it, did you?"

With a low growl, Menoetius glared up at me and Nate. I gave him a small smile, just bright enough to infuriate him, then went back to work.

"We've gotten a good deal of information from Crius' body, thanks in large part to your darling sister," Hades continued. "So I suppose my lessons were quite sufficient, wouldn't you say, Tessa?"

Biting my lip, I slipped free two more charged portions of his shield, giving Nate space to pull out several threads of his own. "Quite."

I held the space open as long as I could, allowing Nate and Hades to do their digging.

"Hmm." Hades frowned. "What do you know about this *Josh* character I keep hearing about? I'm interested to know how he managed to smuggle two prisoners out of my prison in such a creative fashion and break down the wards surrounding Olympus."

Menoetius chuckled. *"Josh* has some interesting powers of his own. That's all I'll say."

"That's probably all you *can* say," I muttered as I struggled to find more charged threads. It looked like once I'd pulled one, the others had shifted, blending into the rest of his magic a shade better. "Now that our father and Cronus are out, I don't see you being terribly high in the pecking order."

I hissed as a sharp prick stabbed at my mind, a charged bit of shield I'd missed.

'I told you—'

'*Shut up, Hades!*' I snapped.

'*Then focus on what you're doing and stop antagonizing him.*'

'*Enough, both of you,*' Nate ordered.

"You know, Tessa, if you'd trained properly with Father when you were younger, those shields of yours might have been strong enough to keep me from your dreams," my brother said. "These fools who love you have gone too easy on you."

A snarl of anger slipped from Hades, but before he could respond, the thud of heavy footsteps sounded in the hall.

Menoetius' eyes widened in mock horror. "Uh oh. I think your bodyguards are coming."

I gritted my teeth as all three of my brothers rounded the corner and made their way toward us. Prometheus and Atlas walked side by side, while Epimetheus followed behind.

'*Sorry,*' Epimetheus said with a small shrug. '*I tried to keep them away.*'

'*It's fine,*' I replied, trying not to let him hear my annoyance. I shouldn't have been surprised that they'd show up, but the suffocating feeling of having so many gods—very tall, muscular gods—around me while I tried to diffuse my tormentor's magic was wearing on me.

The only satisfaction I got from their arrival was the flicker of wariness that flashed across Menoetius' face when he saw Atlas. Atlas' unmatched strength had been compounded by his undiluted hatred for our oldest brother, both for keeping Atlas prisoner for all those years and for what he'd done to me. The fact that he'd knocked Menoetius out with a single blow and tossed him in a cell didn't help, either.

Menoetius recovered quickly, the sardonic smirk once again twisting his lips. "Poor Tessa. She'd almost convinced me she could do something worthwhile without you brutes hovering over her shoulder."

With as much strength as I could muster, I yanked free another charged thread, managing to hold the space open a second longer than last time and eliciting another snarl from Menoetius.

Epimetheus let out a quiet laugh.

'Anything?' I asked Hades.

'Just more flashes of the mountains and beach I saw before.'

'Same perspective?' I asked.

'No.'

'Share it all with Persephone,' Nate told him.

"Have you gotten anything?" Atlas asked, his arms folded across his chest as he glowered at Menoetius.

"Just a few dozen unsuccessful attempts to piss me off," I replied with a sigh.

"It's almost like he was no more than an errand boy," Nate said, smiling slyly.

Hades gave a hum of agreement. "True." His expression turned patronizing. "You just did as you were told, didn't you?"

Ignoring us, Menoetius clasped his hands behind his head and leaned back against the wall. "I was just explaining to Tessa how much better off she'd have been if you fools hadn't prevented her from learning all those years ago." He gave Atlas a satisfied smile. "It's really your fault she died, you know."

"Enough," Prometheus growled.

'Don't you dare listen to him,' I told my twin when I saw a brief flash of pain cloud his features. He didn't respond, but his face shifted into a scowl, so I supposed that was something.

"*You* shouldn't have much to feel guilty about," Menoetius said thoughtfully to Prometheus. "After all, her twin was the one who was with her in that clearing." He shook his head slowly as he looked at Atlas. "So many times, I watched that scene replay in Tessa's dreams. Strong, formidable, unshakeable Atlas, couldn't even protect his precious little *Tessa*," he sneered. He angled his head to the side and tapped his chin. "I wonder how long she blamed you for her death?"

Without warning, I shoved Nate's and Hades' power aside and ripped a fistful of threads from Menoetius' shield, stabbing him with my own power as the small space opened up, wincing at the sharp shocks that hit my own mind. He roared and lunged at the bars, but Nate threw up a wall of Coercion, stopping him in his tracks.

A small smile tilted the corners of Hades' mouth as we watched Menoetius struggle.

I leveled a glare at my oldest brother as he continued to push against Nate's power. "There will never be a day I blame *anyone* but your rotten masters for what happened to me. You can try to instigate all you like, but it's wasted breath on your part."

Nate released the Coercion with a hard push, sending Menoetius flying back against the wall.

'Nice hit,' I told him.

'Get him harder next time,' Hades added.

Chest heaving, Menoetius looked up at me, his lips curled into a snarl.

"I'm going to love watching him destroy you," he growled.

"You'll never get that chance," I said coldly. I stepped toward the bars, wrapping my fingers around them as I stared down at the pathetic waste on the floor. "Even if I have to do it myself, Menoetius, I'm going to make sure you're obliterated by the time this is over."

A terrible smile curved his lips as he continued to watch me.

"Now that's something I'd love to see."

I BARELY SPARED my brothers or Hades a goodbye when I left the dungeon and teleported home to shower off the grimy feeling that inevitably accompanied any amount of time spent with Menoetius. Even dormant, his magic had a slimy feel that clung like pungent oil to everything it touched.

We'd made some progress disassembling his shields, and his lack of power meant they'd be nearly impossible to rebuild. Still, it would likely take days before we could pull anything worthwhile from his memory, especially the deeper parts of it. Precious time that we simply didn't have.

The scalding water in Nate's shower beat down relentlessly as I scrubbed my skin nearly raw with the rough loofah. Squeezing out some shampoo, I proceeded to do the same with my hair and scalp until I finally felt as though the residue of his magic was mostly gone.

I'd just stepped out of the shower and wrapped a towel around my body when Nate knocked softly, then walked in. Quietly, he stepped toward me and wrapped his arms around my waist, then kissed my temple, tugging my mind away from the filth my brother had left behind.

I leaned back into his chest and closed my eyes as he held me, my anger shifting to relief at the simple contact as I felt his heart beat against my back.

"You did wonderfully," he murmured after a few moments. "But I'm sorry you had to be there."

"I need to do these things," I said, meeting his eyes in the semi-fogged mirror above the sink. "I don't like to, but the only way we're going to accomplish anything is if we have all hands on deck." Turning my back on my reflection, I tilted my face up and kissed his jaw. "I hated it, but thank you for having enough faith in me to bring me in."

"No need to thank me, considering the circumstances." He smirked. "And, as much as I hate to say it, what you did for Hades—looking to him for assistance with your memory in front of Kastin—was a nice thing for you to do."

I shrugged, a bit embarrassed that he'd caught that. "I know I could've done it myself or asked you, but...I don't know. He looked so...devastated."

"You can be incredibly perceptive when you want to be, you know that?"

I smiled up at him. "Thank you. I try very hard to be."

He brushed his lips against mine, then pulled me against his chest, resting his chin on the top of my head as he ran his hands up and down my spine, his strong fingers calming me, erasing all the lingering feelings I had from being in that dungeon. The grimy feeling of dark magic and death was replaced by an overwhelming sense of comfort, of love that I knew I wouldn't be able to find anywhere but right here with him.

Knowing he wasn't going to take things any further unless I told him otherwise, I twined my arms around his neck. He'd come here to comfort me, but right then, I needed something to remind me that the hours I'd spent in that dungeon were long passed, that I was loved and cared for and *home*. Nearly everything about these last few days—the last few weeks, even—had been miserable, but right now, I would selfishly take a little bit of time to be happy, as fleeting as it might be.

Reading the intent in my eyes, he tilted my face toward his, molding his lips to mine in a kiss that said he'd missed me these last few days as much as I'd missed him.

"Are you sure?" he murmured.

In answer, I tugged off my towel and let it fall to the floor. Needing no further confirmation, Nate lifted me off my feet and carried me to his bed, not caring a bit that I was dripping water all over the floor.

8

MARY

Tessa knows you're alive.

I'd been repeating that same thought to myself for the last twenty-four hours, long after Josh left me in my cell alone, waiting for Celaeno, Taygete, and Alcyone to come back.

They'd been kept away for hours while I'd been left to half-sit, half-lay in my small corner of the room where they still refused to unchain me.

What they expected me to be able to do in a room that was spelled against power usage was beyond me. If someone as strong as Tessa had only just been able to poke through the magic, there was no way a simple Ischyra would be able to manage it. It helped, though, knowing Tessa had been able to get into my head. It had given me a glimmer of hope, but I wished she'd been able to contact me and tell me *something*.

Like whether or not Iapetus and Josh had been lying when they said Eric was dead. Like whether or not Menoetius had been successful in murdering Yana. Like whether or not all of my fellow recruits and mentors had actually been slaughtered that day.

I had no reason to think my captors were lying. The only thing keeping me from accepting what they said as truth was denial. I'd watched as Menoetius took whatever power he'd siphoned from the sisters and used it to suck out Yana's affinity. Her scream of pain had lasted only seconds before she'd just gone limp and slumped to the arena floor. Afterward, Eric and I had been dosed with something that had knocked us unconscious. The next thing I remembered, I was half-awake, watching as Menoetius snapped Yana's neck while Tessa and the others looked on, helpless behind whatever shield Menoetius and Iapetus had erected in front of them.

I knew next to nothing about the spell he'd used, but I knew there was a damn good possibility he hadn't been lying when he said he'd taken her immortality along with her power. If he had, she'd be dead, too, and I'd be short two friends, not just one.

Be freaking positive, Mary.

I heard somewhere just the act of smiling can cheer you up, put you in a more positive mindset, so I gave it a shot. I was pretty sure one of my guardians had told me that once. Probably Chris. He was always so damn positive.

This was the first time since we'd arrived on Olympus that I'd wished for the wisdom of my guardians to help get me through something. Chris and Alan had prepared me so well for life as an Ischyra, but there was nothing they could do to prepare me for something like this. Digging through my memories, I tried to pull up one that I knew would make me smile. The only problem I had was that most memories consisted of time with either Eric or Josh. The thought of birthdays, school dances, parties, and even family vacations just served to depress me further.

Finding nothing that would actually make me happy, I forced a smile onto my face, hoping I'd feel a little better.

I was pretty sure I only succeeded in looking like a poor impersonation of the Joker.

Giving up on false happiness, I slumped back against the wall. The sun was slowly sinking beyond where its light could reach the hole in the ceiling of our cell, casting the room in shadows. I cast a glance toward the tally marks that the sisters had been scratching into the stone. There were nineteen now, only eight of which marked the days since my capture. My eyes drifted shut, and I'd just started to doze, which was still a struggle due to the way my arms were chained to the floor, when the door clanged open and Taygete and Celaeno were tossed onto the floor. I'd barely registered their reappearance before the door slammed shut, leaving us in echoing silence.

Both sisters lay on the floor for a few moments, then Taygete—identifiable only by the small freckle above her eyebrow—sat up and placed her hand on Celaeno's back. A shudder rocked through Celaeno, then she began to sob.

"What happened?" I whispered.

Taygete's pale eyes didn't shift from her distraught sister as she spoke. "They've kept Alcyone," she said quietly.

"Why? They usually bring you guys back together."

"She's the strongest of us all, and our power is waning. When they couldn't get the amount of power they wanted from us, they kept her and had us sent back here."

My eyes widened. "But they've been draining your power for weeks!"

Celaeno sat up and wiped her eyes, then leaned against her sister, resting her head on her shoulder. "Our power is not regenerating as fast as they would like," she said. "Alcyone's is."

"So they've kept her," Taygete finished.

I closed my eyes and shook my head. "That doesn't make any sense. You guys are primordial witches. Your power should be—"

"Endless?" Taygete gave me a sad smile. "That is not how it works."

"What do you mean?"

"Our power is derived from a single primordial deity who chose to pass into the afterlife, dedicating their power and energy toward new beings." Taygete inclined her head toward Celaeno. "The power we have is from the same well and is split among the seven of us. When it senses a weakness in one, it shifts to another in order to compensate, flowing like water. It is not common knowledge, but Alcyone has always been the strongest. If we all become weakened, her power will always be the first to replenish."

"Why doesn't it divide up equally?" I asked.

She gave a small shrug. "That is a question for our progenitor to answer."

"Wouldn't that be Atlas and Pleione?"

"They are our parents, yes, but they only gave us life, immortality, strength." Celaeno took on a slightly wistful expression. "Our power —the power of all the primordial witches—is much older."

"Who is it from?"

Taygete slid against the wall, her once-white dress now streaked with grime and blood. "No one knows for certain. According to history, the Fates themselves created witches for balance, a way to keep the power of the gods and the rest of Chaos' creations in check, a response to the early years of creation."

Celaeno laid back and rested her head on Taygete's thigh, hands clasped on her stomach as she stared up at the darkening ceiling. "Most primordial deities only held a vague corporeal form, a mist, at most. When they chose to relinquish their physical forms, their magic continued to fuel the worlds. The Fates were allowed to harness the magic of a few and dispense it as they saw fit to create the primordial beings."

"Which is why you primordial witches are more powerful than the gods?"

"Some of us," Celaeno clarified. "Even in our weakened state, our sisters and I are more powerful than most of the other primordial witches because of our combined power. It's why they took us and none of the others."

"Then what's Josh? Why can't you guys deal with him?"

Taygete let her head come to rest against the stone wall and took on a dejected expression. "Josh... he holds primordial power, but there's no known record of his existence. At seven strong, we might be able to destroy him, but we've only got the power of three between us, and that's been weakened."

I tapped my fingers against my thigh, the chains just long enough to allow me that small movement. Josh clearly knew that Tessa was in my head, so I didn't think it was much of a secret. I had no idea how to contact someone who was linked to my mind, though, especially since I didn't even know she was there to begin with.

A couple of witches, on the other hand...

"Josh said Tessa was in my mind earlier," I told them. "A mind link."

Taygete's eyes widened and she leaned forward, shoving Celaeno off her lap. "Are you certain? This room is spelled against magic use. She should not have been able to get in."

"Well, she did," I muttered. "Not that it did much good."

"How did he know?" Taygete asked.

"And how did she get in?" Celaeno wondered aloud, seemingly to no one in particular.

I shrugged, then winced. "Don't know. He said she was there, though, then kicked her out."

Celaeno's eyes darted toward the door, then she sat up and slid forward a few inches. "What did you feel?" she whispered hoarsely. "When he removed her?"

"I—a weird flick, like someone tapped my brain with their finger."

"This is a good thing," Celaeno murmured to herself. "A good thing."

Taygete met my eyes. "Was she in your mind while we were here?"

I nodded. "It was right when they took you guys earlier."

"So she will know we're alive?" she asked carefully. "Our father..."

"Assuming she's keeping him in the loop, yeah, he'll know you guys are okay." I chewed my bottom lip for a moment before continuing. "So... when Tessa was training back on Olympus, Hades said that when Menoetius disabled her powers, they were still there, just trapped. Is that what's happening in here?"

"Essentially," Taygete confirmed. Celaeno had gone to sit against the wall beside her sister, now looking lost in thought. "If we were stronger, the room would not work so well on our own magic, but without our sisters contributing their power, there is not much we can do."

"If they knew where to direct it, do you think they would be able to break through?"

She shrugged. "It is possible, of course, if we knew where it needed to go. Even with Tessa's ability to access parts of your mind, we have no information to provide."

"Well, let's get some. Figure out whatever you can about this place, and let's get her some info." Hopefully, Tessa would be able to get into my head again, and when she did, I wanted to be well-armed with information to give her.

"We will tell you all we know so far," Taygete said. "Although it's not much."

"Every little bit counts, right?" I shifted my eyes to the door, realizing belatedly that anyone could've been listening.

Stupid, Mary. Stupid, stupid, stupid.

Celaeno gave me a small smile. "No one is out there. We should keep our voices down, though."

"Any ideas on how she might have been able to get in?" I asked.

"My guess would be Tessa is utilizing a god who has the ability to navigate other planes of existence," Taygete said. "Even a Titaness doesn't have the right kind of strength for that, Mimic or no."

"Other planes?" I frowned. "You mean like Hermes?"

She nodded. "Yes, he is one of the only beings who can find the cracks between planes. If he is helping her, that's likely why she's able to reach you, even if it is only for a few moments."

"Huh. I guess he really is more than just a pretty face." I tucked that bit away for later, hoping I'd get the chance to tell Tessa she was on the right track.

"What did Josh speak to you about?" Taygete asked.

I opened my mouth to respond, then frowned. "I... don't know."

Taygete gave me a surprised look. "What do you mean?"

I shook my head. "I can't remember." My heart began to thunder. "I don't remember anything after him kicking Tessa out of my head."

Celaeno let out a quiet snort. "Well that's certainly no good, is it?"

AFTER TRYING for a while to recall whatever memories Josh had hidden from me, I gave up and fell back asleep. I was awakened by the sound of a door opening, causing me and the sisters to jump into sitting positions. The sky was dark overhead, casting the room in dim moonlight and making it hard to see much of anything.

Two guards walked in with Iapetus directly behind, a torch in his hand and a cruel smile on his face.

He let the torch drift closer, the flames painfully close to my face. The fire danced in his cold eyes, giving his plain looks a harsher edge. "Good evening, Mary. I hear you had a visitor in the form of my daughter yesterday."

I glared at him, my disgust quickly outweighing my fear. "Yeah, it's a shame your minion came in before we got a chance to catch up."

He nodded knowingly. "Yes, Josh is very perceptive when it comes to power such as hers. It's quite beneficial to our cause, truly."

"Lucky you."

He gave the two guards a small nod, signaling them to move toward me. As they leaned down and began to undo my shackles, I tried not to show my fear as ideas of how I might escape started running through my head. Foolish ideas, ones that would never in a million years actually work, but those thoughts were the only things keeping me from collapsing to the floor in a panicky mess.

If the floors are damp, freeze them.

If you see water, make a weapon.

Fingers in the eye sockets. Knee to the balls.

My shoulders slumped as the guards dragged me to my feet, and Iapetus turned to walk out. Half of those ideas were dependent on my power magically coming to life outside my cell, and the other half assumed I could take on a Titan and two guards of unknown species.

I tried to shut my mind down, focus on the fact that he was almost definitely taking me to some torture chamber to take my powers, but for whatever reason, my brain wouldn't accept that. I'd known they would come for me eventually, but I'd just hoped that maybe, deep inside, Josh would try to spare me.

Fighting was useless. But I might still be able to find a way to help the others, assuming whatever they were about to do didn't kill me.

So, latching on to whatever shreds of bravery I had left, I let them drag me through the halls without incident.

"What are you guys, anyway? I know you're not human." I frowned at one as they dragged me through the door. They both had dark hair and pale skin. The one on my left had a hooked nose, greasy hair, and shit-brown eyes, while the one to my right had a nose that looked like it had broken too many times to heal properly, a pointed chin, and blue eyes that would've been pretty if they hadn't been filled with so much malice.

Iapetus let out an amused huff. "No, Mary, they are most certainly not human."

I took another look at their faces as I stumbled down the hall between them, taking in their features more closely. With the exception of their eyes, their faces were expressionless, their cheeks sunken, jaws slack. Bruise-like circles were under their eyes making them look as though they hadn't slept in weeks.

"They look like zombies," I muttered. "And where are you taking me?"

"*Revenant* is the proper term," Iapetus corrected, pulling open a wood-and-metal door and motioning for the guards to take me through. I tripped over a raised stone on the way in, nearly pulling my shoulder out of its socket when my body went down. The guards' hands tightened on my arms, and I hissed in pain as they righted me.

"Revenant? Wasn't that a movie?" We stopped outside another door, this one more nondescript, the wood the same shade of gray as the stone walls, faded with age.

"I've been locked in the Underworld for nearly three millennia," Iapetus said dryly. "Do I seem the type to know the answer to that question?"

"Why aren't they talking?" *Why am I still asking questions?*
Because you're trying to delay the inevitable.

"Because I removed their tongues," he said blandly. He lifted the latch on the door and gave me a cruel smile. "In you go."

I peered into the small room in front of me. It was dimly lit, but I could just make out a table in the center with a tall stool beside it.

Shit.

Shit.

"No!" The strength I'd tried to force on myself moments ago evaporated. I struggled backward as I tried to force my way past the guards. Panic slowly began to turn my bowels to jelly. "No, no, no!" I thrashed against him as he grabbed me by the arm and began dragging me away from the guards.

"Yes, Mary," Iapetus said patiently. "It's about time you earned your keep around here." He pulled me through the door, and before I could react, he slammed it shut behind us.

"Well, hello there."

Chills ran through me at the sound of Cronus' dark voice, a quiet boom in the small, dank room that held nothing aside from the table and stool I'd seen from the door.

Flashes of Yana's screaming ran through my mind, and I struggled harder against Iapetus' hold. I couldn't face that kind of pain. There was no way.

My breath started coming in rapid pants as tears filled my eyes. I tried to get my limbs to cooperate, to get my arms and legs to pull me toward the door, but it was pointless. This was it. They were finally going to take my power, probably kill me. I was just an Ischyra, after all. They'd need a dozen of us to get any power worth having, and that was if they drained us entirely.

"That may have been true a few days ago," Cronus said, reading my thoughts. "Previously, we would have needed five or six of your species to give us the power we need to fuel just one Titan. Significant...advancements have been made, however, so that is no longer the case."

"Advancements," I whispered. Considering how long Alcyone had been gone from our cell, I could only imagine what those "advancements" might be.

I swallowed back bile and stared at the cold floor, trying to focus on anything but what was about to happen to me.

"We've decided we've given you enough time to get acclimated," Iapetus said. "And it's no longer terribly prudent to be running off snatching Ischyra left and right, now that Olympus is fully mobilizing against us."

"And it's a special day," Cronus added with a cruel smirk.

"What's that supposed to mean?" No matter how hard I tried, I couldn't stop myself from shuddering under his gaze.

Iapetus grabbed me roughly by the arms, giving me no time to react before he slammed me down on the table and began strapping me down. I screamed and bucked uselessly against him, but Cronus' giant hands forced my shoulders hard against the table.

"Get off of me, you sick fucks!" I shot out with my foot, just missing Cronus' crotch. He took hold of my ankle and forced it back on the table.

"You're a strong one, aren't you?" he sneered. "That's good to know."

A low whimper escaped as Iapetus ran a wide leather strap across my shoulders and chest, pinning me in place.

"Did you know," Cronus said as Iapetus moved to tighten similar straps around my ankles, "that sixty-five Ischyra were killed in the arena last week?"

I froze.

Sixty-five?

"Today, while you're here with us," he continued, patting my arm, "your friends will be attending their funeral." I flinched as he brushed a lock of hair off my face, then he paused, considering. "Well, the friends who are left, anyway. It will be quite a lovely tribute if Olympic funeral ceremonies are at all like they used to be. It's *such* a shame you won't be there to pay your respects, isn't it, Iapetus?"

Iapetus made a hum of agreement. "Such a shame, truly."

And with that, the fight slipped out of me.

Eric was dead, they were *all* dead, and I would never get to say goodbye. My mentors, my friends, and anyone else who might've been unfortunate enough to be in that arena were gone.

And *Chiron*. I prayed Chiron was able to get out. He would've died for every last one of us, without hesitation, but if anyone deserved to live through that attack, it was him.

Cronus pulled a small vial from his shirt pocket, jolting me back to reality. For a moment, the swirling blue mass inside looked like godsbane, but when I looked closer, I saw that it didn't have a form. It looked almost like glowing blue air.

"This is what a witch's power looks like once drained from her body," he explained, pulling the small cork out. He tilted the vial back against his lips and took down the contents in one smooth gulp, then tossed it to the floor, the sound of glass breaking over stone echoing through the room.

"It's unfortunate, really," Iapetus mused. "Had Tessa simply come with us that day, you wouldn't be here... that boyfriend of yours would still be alive..."

I closed my eyes, refusing to let him destroy what little of my morale was left. I'd replayed that attack in my mind dozens of times and knew I would've made the same choice Tessa had.

"Tessa wasn't raised to be a martyr," I ground out. "Not that you would know that. Going with you still would've been a death sentence for everyone else." I forced a smirk. "At least with me, all you get is some puny water."

Iapetus' jaw twitched, and I took a second to cheer myself internally for pissing him off. Then his eyes flicked to Cronus. "She's ready."

I jerked my head back toward Cronus. I looked over his harsh features, the cruel glint in his eyes, the hard set of his jaw. Nothing about him had changed after taking down the contents of that vial, although I wasn't sure what I expected. Glowing eyes, power sparking from his fingers, something. But no, he looked just the same.

Angling his head to the side, Cronus grinned, then he leaned down, putting his lips beside my ear. "When we're done with you, we'll bring you back like we did Niko and Lawrence out there and put you to work."

My eyes widened, but before I could scream again, he'd clamped a hand over my throat and closed his eyes.

Immediately, I felt his stolen power stab through my chest. My back arched at the pain, and a guttural scream tore from my throat as he gripped my jaw, forcing my mouth open. I clamped my teeth shut, but a punch to the ribs from Iapetus forced a grunt of pain from my throat. As soon as my mouth was open, Cronus whispered a few words and leaned over so that his mouth was only a few inches from mine. He inhaled sharply, and my power began to slither like a thin, blue snake from my mouth to his.

Just as I'd felt my power pour itself into every cell of my body at my transformation, now it was being pulled out. *Ripped* out. It struggled and fought nearly as hard as I did, wanting to stay where it was meant to be. My power was a true part of me, another organ, and it was being pulled like a perfectly healthy tooth. I kept track of each pull, each vicious rip of pain that came from my very core, struggling in vain to keep a hold on it.

I tried to send my mind somewhere else, to convince my brain to ignore what was happening. Pain isn't tangible, it isn't a physical thing, so I could make it go away, right? *This won't kill you.*

Denial.

It'll just hurt of whole fucking lot.

No, it didn't really hurt. Each rip, each tear, each jerk of my body, they weren't real. They were tricks. Mind games I was playing with myself. It was just my nerve endings telling my brain to *feel* pain.

Keep telling yourself that.

Without meaning to, I started counting. Each pulse, each pull of power from my body forced itself to be seen.

Around one hundred, I finally started to feel numb, which made me wonder if I'd succeeded in convincing my brain that the nerve endings screaming in pain were fools.

Or maybe it just means you're dying. Maybe it means you've finally realized your friends are never coming for you.

Never coming for you.

Never coming...

Darkness closed in around two hundred.

Never...

You're going to die here.

9

TESSA

For the first time since Hades began mentoring me again, I visited him in his dreams. The look of devastation mixed with fury that he'd worn when Kastin told us all what had likely happened in Tartarus had been brief, but I saw it, plain as day. I'd seen that look once before, back when we discovered what Menoetius had been doing to me all those years ago, and his response had been violent, to say the least. An entire camp of prisoners had been obliterated in a fit of rage. Another had been destroyed after I'd died if Prometheus' story was accurate.

Regardless of our former relationship, I still saw him as one of the strongest gods I knew and a good ruler to his realm. And if nothing else, he was my friend.

Not that he'd ever admit it.

"I was just about to come to you," he said, looking around the empty white space I'd brought us to. "Is Nathaniel coming?"

"Not yet," I replied. "I wanted to talk to you first."

He arched a brow. "Sneaking behind your lover's back? That's unlike you."

I gave him an exasperated look. "I'm not *sneaking.* I just knew you wouldn't want to talk in front of him, that's all."

He glanced down at the floor, then back at me. "You could've brought some chairs."

I waved my hand, and two wooden chairs appeared in front of us, replicas of the ones that sat around Nate's dining room table. "Better?"

"Much." With a sigh, he sat down. "So? What is it?"

"I just wanted to make sure you were alright after today. After what Kastin said."

"Do I seem like I'm not?" he asked wearily. "And since when are you so concerned about my feelings, hmm?"

I frowned. "Why wouldn't I be?"

He gave me an amused look. "I seem to recall you using the phrase 'sadistic piece of shit' to describe me not so long ago."

"Which I stand solidly behind," I said with a grin. "Seriously, though. It's been a long time, but I know you well enough to know you probably wanted to shove Kastin in a cell with my brother after all he said. I just wanted to make sure you were okay."

"I appreciate the concern, truly." He ran his hands across his face, then tipped his head back and rested it on his chair, avoiding my gaze. "And I'm fine."

I narrowed my eyes when he didn't look at me. "What did you do?"

His eyebrows lifted in an unconvincing show of innocence. "What makes you think I did anything?"

I stared at him expectantly.

"Fine," he groaned. "There were a few prisoners who'd just been devoured by Scylla waiting to cross the Acheron. They'd been especially heinous in their lives, so I tossed their coins in the river and stuck them in a cage with Cerberus for a few hours." He shrugged. "Charon said he'd have one of the Hydra fish their coins out so they could cross eventually."

My eyes widened incredulously. "You sicced your *dog* on them? Did they survive?"

"It's highly unlikely their souls are still intact, so, no. Now let's get

Nathaniel in here. I'd like to get some practice in before dawn if that's alright with you. We've got a long day tomorrow."

I sighed, his words reminding me of what tomorrow would bring: a funeral for nearly seventy Ischyra, most of whom had barely gotten a taste of their immortal lives.

I rolled my shoulders and reached out for Nate, touching his mental walls and waiting for them to retract and let me in.

A few moments later, Nate appeared and we started running through the exercises Hades had given me when we first started training. Nate used his Coercion to suppress my magic, forcing me to push back Hades' power, using sheer will. Once that was out of the way, I had to break through Nate's Coercion so I could use my power to kick them both out and secure my walls, preventing either of them from returning. After we'd gone through that a half dozen times, they both began to examine the shields that my mind had finally begun to maintain without my help, pointing out weak spots here and there and helping me target my power toward those areas to strengthen them.

Between dream walks and mental training in the waking world, we'd been working tirelessly every night for the last week. I was exhausted, but in a good way—the way that tells you that you've been doing something right, working the right muscles, honing the right skills.

The knowledge that Menoetius was locked away in a place where he couldn't reach me mentally, even if I was unprotected, helped ease my nerves, but the need to protect myself had become overwhelming. I was beyond thankful that Nate and Hades tolerated each other long enough each night to help me, but I wasn't sure how much longer they were going to last.

So, I kept pushing myself. I kept doing all I could to absorb their lessons, take in everything they tried to teach me. It was exhausting, even painful at times, but each time I succeeded in keeping them out made it all worth it.

∿

LATER, after Nate and Hades had left my mind, I stared quietly up at the bedroom ceiling. The moonless night cast no light into the room, leaving only stars visible through the large skylights over the bed. I lay there for a while, watching as the constellations slowly passed overhead, unable to sleep because I was so bogged down with thoughts of what tomorrow might bring.

As if awoken by my thoughts, Nate wrapped his arm around my waist and snuggled against me, resting his face on my shoulder.

"Can't sleep?" he whispered.

"My head's a noisy place tonight," I murmured.

"Do you want to talk about it?"

"No, I'm fine," I whispered, kissing his forehead. "Go back to sleep."

He propped himself up on his forearms and looked at me. "What's wrong?"

I stared at him for a moment, then turned my face back toward the ceiling before responding.

"I'm nervous about tomorrow. About seeing all those guardians."

He took my hand in both of his and lifted it to his lips, then kissed each knuckle. "Because you think they'll blame you for what happened?"

I gave him rueful smile. "I wouldn't blame them if they did."

Irritation flashed on his face. "Then they'd be fools. Tessa, you weren't here when they attacked. There's nothing you could've done to prevent this."

I sighed, then squeezed his hand. "I know. Logically, I know. But my father and brother were here for me, so it's hard not to feel a little at fault."

"That's perfectly normal, but I can promise you that you've got nothing to worry about." He kissed my shoulder. "Nothing."

"Even an all-powerful Coercer can't promise something like that," I teased. "Unless you've suddenly become a seer, too?"

"Funny." He tugged the comforter up over us both, surrounding us in a cocoon of warmth, then rested his head on the pillow beside me. Smiling softly, he brushed a strand of hair off my face. "Worry about the things you can control, love. What people think of you, how they view this situation... those aren't in your control."

"Says the literal god of mind-control." I smirked, then took his hand. "Thank you. I know all of that, it's just hard to convince myself that I shouldn't feel guilty, you know?"

He nodded. "Of course. What I know is that this will get better. Whether people want to wrongly assign blame or not, this *will* get better."

I smiled reluctantly. "Thanks."

He kissed my forehead, then tucked his arm around my waist. "Now get some sleep. Tomorrow is going to be trying."

I sighed. "Don't I know it." I smiled at him. "I love you."

He tightened his arm around me and snuggled closer. "I love you, too."

Closing my eyes, I let the warmth of Nate's body and the heavy comforter settle my nerves and eventually, lull me to sleep.

THE FUNERAL for the recruits was something Nate, Hestia, Hera, and I had argued with Zeus about extensively. He'd wanted to simply burn the bodies and move on, but losing them the way we did, so soon after their transformations...I couldn't see not giving their guardians the chance to properly say their farewells. It was unprecedented, really.

Maybe it would've been a mercy not to deliver the news that the newest generation had been slaughtered, just let the guardians live out the rest of their lives unaware of what had happened. It was something I'd wrestled with, even as I fought with Zeus about allowing guardians onto Olympus for the first time in centuries.

It was Hera, of all people, who had been the one to finally shut him down.

"If one of our children were killed, wouldn't you want the opportunity to pay your respects, say your farewells?"

Sometimes, her place as a goddess of family made her obsessive and territorial of those she considered her own. In instances like this, though, the connections she had to the ties between families made itself evident. Regardless of how cold she might be most days, her attachment to the abruptly and senselessly severed ties had caused her to put her foot down, using her position as Queen of Olympus to her full advantage.

So, Zeus had relented, with the only exceptions being the guardians of Anette, Mary, and Andrei. He'd allowed my guardians and Yana's to come, but that was as far as he'd go. He wouldn't even allow us to tell Mary's that she'd been taken. I wasn't entirely sure how I felt about keeping them in the dark about something so important, but it was, like so many other things, not my call to make.

Sixty-five pyres had been erected on the small plateau near the foot of the mountain by the time Nate, Yana, and I arrived the next afternoon. Each wooden structure bore the muslin-wrapped body of one of the recruits or mentors who'd been killed by my brother and father. Most would be burned today, their ashes collected and either scattered here or at their childhood homes. A few guardians had chosen to bring their Ischyra home and perform their own funerals that adhered to the cultural customs they'd been raised with.

The sun was just rising over the eastern side of the mountain range when Hermes began bringing the guardians through. He'd opened a portal on the edge of the plateau to make things a bit simpler and was guiding them through in pairs. They were scattered all around the world, so it would take some time for them all to arrive.

Yana stood beside me, tense, bouncing on the balls of her feet as she watched one pair after another step through. I couldn't say I blamed her, although her excitement at seeing her guardians was much different than the wariness I felt at seeing Eric's and my own.

John and Analise had known my history. They'd been told by Hecate who and what I was. They knew I would eventually return to my former self, but I was apprehensive to know what they would think of who I'd become. There were days I felt the same as the girl they'd raised, but on others, I felt worlds removed from who I'd been.

One pair of guardians after another were led through the portal. After a few minutes, when Hermes had brought through the fifth pair, Yana let out a small whimper and took off across the grass.

Emotion welled inside me, and unshed tears burned my eyes as I watched her leap into the arms of a short, stocky man with blond hair who stood beside a tall brunette. They caught her and held her in an embrace so tight I could feel the love from fifty feet away.

Nate's hand found mine, squeezing it as we continued to wait for the rest.

Eric's guardians were the first to come through the portal from Renville. Joanne, a petite blonde, and Evan, a muscular man with brown hair who towered over everyone around him, stepped onto the grass, their expressions turning distraught as they took in the sea of death in front of them.

I wanted to run to them, these people I'd known almost my entire human life, but something stopped me.

My father and brother were responsible for his death. John and Analise knew my background, but I wasn't sure how much the others had been told.

Joanne's sharp, blue eyes found mine. She held my stare for a moment, leaning into Evan when he slipped an arm around her shoulders.

"It's fine," Nate whispered after a moment. "Go to them."

I took a deep breath, then we made our way across the grass to where they stood.

"Tessa." Joanne placed a hand on my cheek, then pulled me into a hug. "I'm so sorry," she murmured into my hair. The unshed tears from moments earlier started to fall silently down my face and onto the thin black material of her shirt as both relief and sadness washed over me. Wiping my eyes, I pulled back and shook my head.

"I'm the one who's sorry, Joanne." I shook my head. "I wish—"

"Stop right there," Evan said, his rumbly voice causing my mouth to snap shut. He gripped my shoulder with one of his strong hands and met my eyes. "You didn't do this."

Joanne took my hands and gave me a shaky smile. "John and

Analise told us everything," she whispered. "And this is *not* your fault."

"Tessa."

Nate's voice tore my attention from my relief at Joanne's words. He tilted his head behind them, toward where Hermes had just stepped through the portal, with John and Analise at his side.

Giving Joanne's hand one last squeeze, I stepped around her and Evan and stared at my guardians for a moment, not quite believing they were there.

"Tessa," Analise whispered, her face crumpling.

With a whimper, I threw myself into her arms and buried my face in her shoulder as all the emotion that had been bottled up inside for weeks came pouring out. John enveloped us both in a hug, his arms turning into vises around me as sobs shook my body.

"I have so much to tell you both," I whispered. I pulled back and wiped my eyes as I looked between them. "So goddamn much."

John pulled a tissue from his pocket and handed it to me. "There's plenty of time for that, sweetheart," he said, his voice thick with emotion. "From what we've been told, Analise and I will be here for a while."

My eyes widened, and I looked back at Nate, who'd remained far enough away to have my reunions in private. He slid his hands in his pockets and smiled. *'Apollo is setting them up at the inn in Olympia.'*

Shocked, I looked back at my guardians. "You—you're staying? On Olympus?"

Analise gave me a sad smile and nodded. "Until everything is sorted out, yes. Apollo seems to think it will be safer."

Shooting another look at Nate, I motioned with my head for him to join us. When he came to a stop at my side, I took his hand and gave John and Analise a shaky smile. "This is Nate."

John cast a surprised look at me as Nate reached out and shook his hand. "The Coercer from your school?"

A smile flickered across Nate's lips that mirrored mine. "That's the one," he replied.

Analise gave him a polite nod. "It's wonderful to meet you." Her brow drew down as she looked past us, and when I followed her gaze, I saw my three brothers standing on the other side of the plateau, watching us.

'Introductions later,' I told Prometheus. 'Please.'

I tried not to make it sound as though I was begging, but I needed time with my guardians before my two families met one another.

He held my stare for a moment, then nodded and turned to speak to Epimetheus and Atlas, no doubt to deliver my message.

"Those are your brothers?" Analise asked quietly, guilt flashing across her face.

"They are," I said. "And don't for one second think I'm angry with either of you," I added, giving them each a stern look. "We can talk more later, but just know that I'm not angry."

Analise closed her eyes and nodded as John looked away in a poor attempt to conceal his own emotion.

"Why don't you both stand with Joanne and Evan," I told them when I saw Hermes bring the last set of guardians through. "Nate will show you where to go. I need to go handle a few things before we start."

Nate stepped aside and gestured for the four of them to move forward. He gave me a quick kiss on the forehead, then they walked toward the area on the plateau where the other guardians and deities in attendance were beginning to congregate.

With one last look in their direction, I made my way toward where Zeus and Chiron stood at the first row of pyres.

"Are you certain you don't wish to speak?" Chiron asked as I approached.

We'd gone back and forth on who would be the one to give the eulogy at the funeral, until finally deciding Chiron should be the one to speak about the dead recruits. I'd only been with them for a short time, had only gotten to know a handful relatively well. He knew them all, recruit and mentor alike, and if the devastation and grief he'd worn the few times I'd seen him this past week had been any indication, he was feeling their loss the hardest out of everyone.

"I'm sure. These were your soldiers and friends, Chiron. You spent every day with them. I'm just here to send them off." I put my hand on the pyre that stood to my right, Eric's pyre, and forced back the lump in my throat. I'd allowed myself some minor hysterics with John and Analise, but I needed to keep my wits about me if I was going to get through the rest of this day. "You're the only one who deserves to be doing this."

He gave me a sad smile and patted my shoulder. When he spoke, his words sounded choked. "Thank you, Tessa. I appreciate that."

I slid my hand over his and squeezed, needing that small comfort of my friend, even if it was just for a second.

"Welcome, everyone," Zeus said, his orator's voice carrying over the crowd. Chiron and I turned to face him, both of us schooling our faces into neutral expressions. "Although it is unfortunate that we meet under such circumstances, it pleases us all to know you will be able to bid farewell to the charges you've raised to become soldiers for Olympus."

I barely suppressed an eye roll at his false sense of sympathy and waited patiently as he continued what amounted to a welcome speech.

When Zeus was done, with a small nod toward Chiron, he stepped aside and let the centaur take over.

Chiron, who looked just as wild as the first day I met him, cleared his throat and clasped his hands behind his back. He'd come in his human form today, which sent a twinge of sadness through me, knowing he did it for the benefit of the guardians.

"Today, we gather to honor the fallen," he began, his voice rough. "Forty-five recruits and twenty mentors whose lives were cut short due to the evil of others." He tilted his chin up and let his eyes drift over the mourners. For the next five minutes, he spoke of honor, strength, and the challenges all Ischyra took on when they made the leap from mortal to immortal. Each recruit brought something to this mountain, their own uniqueness, their own abilities, their own strengths, and those were things that would never be forgotten.

As he spoke, I watched the guardians, who'd spent eighteen years raising their Ischyra, absorb his words. Some, like the Andersons, were listening with rapt attention, their faces filled with pride and sadness. Others, like the guardians of the twins Dishi and Hao Tsai, wore their sadness like a veil. Their eyes were both distant and drawn, their faces ashen, and their posture that of two people who'd had their hearts trampled and set on fire.

For humans, eighteen years was a long time. A lifetime, in the case of guardians and Ischyra. In just a few moments, my father and brother had destroyed what these people had worked so hard to create.

Once Chiron was done speaking, and the only sounds to be heard were the quiet sobs of guardians and the whistle of the wind, I turned to face Eric's pyre fully. Closing my eyes, I placed my hands on the smooth, dried wood and took a steadying breath.

Mary should be here.

The thought hit me, and I gritted my teeth, biting back a sob. Tears still spilled from my eyes, tracking slowly down my cheeks.

Mary should be here. Eric should be here.

Painful, accusing thoughts stabbed at my mind, making it impossible to concentrate on the one small task I'd agreed to take on. The one I'd insisted on taking, refused to let anyone else do.

They were looking for you in that arena.

You're the reason they're dead.

It's your—

A warm, strong hand squeezed my shoulder, and I stiffened, then leaned gratefully against my twin as my galloping heart began to slow. The lump in my throat continued to force its way up, until, finally, the tears I'd been trying to hold back began to course down my cheeks.

"It's alright, Tessa," Atlas assured me, his deep voice a quiet rumble against my back. "You can do this."

"How?" I whispered thickly. "How did you do it?" Atlas had stood where I was three thousand years ago when he and our brothers had set fire to my and Clymene's pyres. He didn't know that one of us would make our way home eventually. All he knew was that, through death and discord, our family had been decimated, and he felt as though he'd played a large part in that.

"I told you and Mother we would meet again, that if I ever made it to the afterlife, I would find you both. And you will," he whispered fervently. "You *will* meet your friends again. Maybe not in this life, but you will find them eventually." He gripped my shoulders as emotion roughened his voice. "It's time to say farewell, Tessa."

My entire body began to shake, and my hands froze inches above Eric's pyre. No matter how hard I tried, my mind refused to set them down and admit that it was truly time to say goodbye.

I don't want to. I don't want to say goodbye. I don't want to never see him again.

"Together?" Atlas whispered, wrapping a hand around my wrist.

My gratitude stuck in my throat, so I nodded, then gripped his arm with my free hand and let him guide my hand to the surface of the pyre.

Forcing my paralyzing thoughts to retreat, I reached deep inside myself and pulled forth the pure searing fire that Eric had been gifted with at his transformation, fire I was still learning to wield, and spread my fingers over the wood.

I didn't bother trying to hold back my tears as the flames of Eric's magic licked across the wood, brushing against the muslin that wrapped his body, curling the edges of the photograph of him and his guardians I'd placed there just this morning. Atlas' arm encircled my shoulders, and I leaned against him, my entire body trembling with grief as I watched the fire spread. I felt his own tears dampen my hair as he shared my grief, taking on some of my pain in a way only a twin could.

Solemnly, Chiron, Athena, Ares, Nate, Hera, Apollo, and Zeus each picked up one of the torches that had been propped against a nearby boulder and touched the ends to the flames that were now crackling loudly around Eric's body. Methodically, they went up and down each row, setting the pyres ablaze, one by one, until soon, the only sounds on the plateau were the crackle and roar of flames mixed with the whipping of wind that carried the thick smoke off across the open air of the mountain range.

As I watched the ashes of my friends and mentors drift away, I forced myself to focus on the soft scent of wood smoke, of burning pine, rather than the acrid smell of burning flesh.

10

NATE

It was a struggle not to go to Tessa when she hesitated at Eric's pyre, and I was thankful when Atlas made the decision easier. If there was ever a time she needed him, it was today. Tessa hadn't spoken to me much about the guilt that had been gnawing at her over the past week, but those few times she had, I could see how much it weighed on her. I also knew I couldn't relate, at least not to that extent, but her twin could.

Apollo and I stood beside each other, both of us lost in our own thoughts as we watched the thick, gray smoke billow high above us. I'd attended the cremations of recruits and other dead before, presided over Karis' when she'd been killed, but I'd never experienced anything like this. Death was a thing that happened, but not naturally, not for our kind or the Ischyra. That fact made days like today more than sad—it made them infuriating because someone had *caused* this. The ire of the gods, both present and elsewhere, was palpable, something I felt awakening in my own mind, as well. The need for vengeance had left a bitter, but not unwelcome taste in my mouth.

"I've spoken to Reginald down at the inn," Apollo murmured. "He and Rosalind have set aside a small apartment for the Averys. If they would like more permanent living quarters, you'll need to speak with one of the Ischyra in charge of housing assignments."

"Thank you," I said quietly. "I'll bring them down after the service."

My brother and I, previously estranged and now... not, stood silently for a few more moments before Apollo spoke again.

"We will find them, Nathaniel. This isn't a slight that will go unpunished."

"Slight?" I shook my head. "No. This was a formal declaration of war."

"And it will be answered," he replied patiently. "Don't mistake Father's indifference toward a ceremony as a lack of caring for his soldiers. He is a warrior who sees no sense in sentimental things at a time like this."

"Why are you making excuses for him, Apollo?" I frowned and turned toward him. "I know why he fought us on services for the recruits. He wanted to push the attack behind us, so we can move forward. I understand that. His lack of empathy for the people on this mountain who've lost people they cared for is what angers me."

"I'm not making excuses—"

"Now is not the time, gentlemen," Athena said, coming to stand between us. "Keep your spats to yourselves until later."

"No one's spatting," Apollo snapped.

I shifted my attention back to the rows of guardians before us. Only thirty pairs had chosen to accept Zeus' invite. Some in attendance stood stoically as they said their silent farewells, others leaned against one another, wiping their eyes with tissues as their shoulders shook with grief. Once the service was over, they'd be taken to the Ischyra dorms to retrieve their charges' belongings if they wanted. Many, like the Averys, formed a parent-child bond with their Ischyra, but on a rare occasion, a set would see the child they were tasked with raising as a job, a duty to fulfill, and nothing more. The former would mourn for some time, possibly never truly getting over it, while the latter would simply move on.

I wasn't quite sure which would be harder.

ONCE THE PLATEAU became inhospitable due to the pyres that were fully blackened, the gods present began teleporting the humans down to Olympia. Tessa and I escorted John, Analise, and Eric's guardians down, coming to a stop just outside the dorms.

"I can show you both his room," Tessa offered. Joanne and Evan nodded mutely, their hands clasped tightly between them. Tessa gestured toward the gate and led them inside, leaving me to stand beside John and Analise.

There was no question as to what kind of guardians they or the Andersons had been.

The Averys and I stood quietly, waiting for Tessa to return, and I realized that, despite my age, I had no idea how to initiate conversation with my lover's parents.

"I suppose you'll both have a lot of questions," John began, turning toward me. Analise looked as though she wanted to protest, but bit her lower lip, silencing herself.

I angled my head curiously, unsure he knew how much I knew about Tessa's history. "About?"

He eyed me shrewdly, then shook his head. John Avery wasn't the type to pull punches; that was evident. He looked like the type of man who would portray a football coach and doting father on a family sitcom, tough but unconditionally loving at the same time. The way he watched me now, considering what my intentions might be with his daughter, made it clear he didn't care in the least who or what I was.

"I know Tessa's been told that we're aware of her history, and I'm sure you both have your thoughts on that. It's clear to me you two have become a bit of a unit," he said, gesturing vaguely toward where Tessa and the Andersons had walked off. "So you should know that anything Analise and I did was done solely to keep Tessa safe."

I frowned. "I think this is a conversation that should be had with Tessa, don't you?"

He nodded slowly. "And it will. First, I need to know... how is she?" He cast a glance toward the dormitory gates, then looked back at me, his dark eyes a bit softer, almost pained. "With all that's happened, and I'm sure we haven't heard the half of it, how's she doing?"

I slid my hands into the pockets of my suit pants and sighed. "There's no simple answer to that, John." I looked toward the summit of the mountain, covered in crisp snow and surrounded by a hazy ring of clouds. "Ever since she awoke, there hasn't been much time to truly address what's happened to her."

"But she seems so... calm," Analise said, looking perplexed. She swallowed hard as a grimace of grief flashed across her face. "This wasn't what it was supposed to be like for her."

I couldn't help the twist of annoyance I felt. How in all the realms had they expected things to be? No logical creature could possibly think Tessa's circumstances warranted normal reactions. From the moment her soul had returned to her body, there'd been one life-or-death predicament after another. She'd gotten her life back, her family back, then almost immediately lost her best friend and almost all the friends she'd made since coming to Olympus.

Yes, Hecate had placed an interdiction on John and Analise when she revealed Tessa's true nature, but, as with Apollo, I couldn't help but feel angry that no one had come up with *some* way to prepare her for her return to life as a deity.

I wouldn't say any of that to the Averys, though. They were already in pain, their feelings of guilt palpable. Telling them that she was anything *but* calm, that she was anything but scared for her life and the lives of those around her, wouldn't be at all helpful.

Instead, I gave Analise a gentle smile.

"She's doing wonderfully," I told them. "There are times she struggles, but she's got more support than anyone could ever ask for. You did well by her."

Analise closed her eyes and smiled, and John let out a quiet sigh of relief.

"Thank you," John said after a moment, patting me on the shoulder as he turned to face the dorms again.

"For?"

"Softening the blow."

We waited in silence for a few more minutes before Tessa reappeared, wiping her eyes as she made her way toward us. Wordlessly, Analise opened her arms, enveloping Tessa is the type of comforting hug only a mother could offer. John cleared his throat and turned away in a clear attempt to hide his emotions, and the lump in my throat had me shoving my own down as well.

Pulling back, Tessa smiled at Analise. "Joanne and Evan are taking some time with Eric's things privately. Hermes is going to be in and out, so he'll make sure they get back safely."

John frowned. "They didn't want to stay?"

Tessa shook her head. "No, they just wanted to be alone."

"I'm glad they're getting this time," Analise said. "I know this isn't a luxury the gods would usually be willing to provide."

"So," John said, changing the subject. "Will we be able to see where you're staying while we're here? I'm guessing you're not still in the dorms, right?"

Tessa's eyes widened, the expression on her face slipping into that of a mortified teenage girl who'd just been caught doing something wrong.

"Oh. I—um, well, after everything that happened, I... started staying with Nate. In his house."

I bit my lip, trying to conceal my amusement.

'You realize you're nearly four thousand years old, correct?'

'Shut up,' she snapped, clearly annoyed at her own flustered state.

Analise's eyes danced with humor as a myriad of emotions flashed across John's face. She was no fool, but John was clearly still wearing the role of father, and human fathers didn't like the thought of their daughters living with their boyfriends. The fact that Tessa and I were neither humans nor teenagers was clearly conflicting with his previous notions of propriety.

He looked back and forth between us, then, frowning, opened his mouth briefly before snapping it shut. Shaking his head, he let out a frustrated sigh before speaking.

"Well, Nate, I acknowledge that any threat I might make will be entirely empty, so I won't bother. Just know that if you hurt my little girl, I'll gladly stand by and cheer Tessa on if she chooses to whoop you to kingdom-come."

I grinned as Tessa's face flamed with embarrassment, the motion feeling a bit foreign after the last few days. "So noted, sir."

I gestured up the street toward Reginald's, Olympia's only inn. "The inn is right up here. We can get you both set up if you'd like. Hermes said your things were already brought down."

"Yes, he told us he'd have them sent there for when we arrived," Analise confirmed. "It's much appreciated."

"Of course." The four of us began walking up the hill toward the inn, which was about three blocks away.

A quiet bell made a tinkling sound as we entered the old building. Built of stone and thatch by a skilled carpenter nearly fifteen hundred years ago, the roof having since been replaced with wood, and currently bore the solar shingles that allowed power to be provided to the village. The lobby consisted of a built-in wooden desk in the center, a winding staircase to the right, and a hallway to the left that led toward the rear courtyard, where several small cabins had been built a few centuries prior.

"Nathaniel!" The cheerful voice of Rosalind, an Ischyra and wife of the Inn's owner, Reginald, carried over to us from the hall as she made her way toward us.

She smiled brightly at John and Analise. "You must be the guardians who'll be staying with us," she said, holding out a hand toward each. "We're thrilled to have you, although I do wish it was under better circumstances."

Analise gave her a grateful smile. "Thank you, Rosalind. We appreciate it."

"If you'll follow me this way, I've deposited your belongings in one of our cabins," Rosalind said, gesturing toward the rear exit.

"Thank you," John said, smiling.

Taking my hand, Tessa and I followed the three of them out back toward the cabins, waiting as Rosalind opened the door on the first one and held out a hand, beckoning them inside.

"Now, everything either of you might need can be found right out on Main Street," she explained as John and Analise looked around the small cabin. It consisted of a single, large room that had a half-wall separating the living area and small kitchen from the sleeping quarters and bathroom. "There are plenty of restaurants and a small grocery, as well as a few clothing stores. We're a completely self-sufficient village, so there's no currency required here."

"It's lovely, thank you," Analise replied as she gazed around the room.

I ran a hand down Tessa's spine and brushed a kiss to her temple. *'You three should take some time to visit. Go grab dinner. I'm going to take care of a few things before heading back.'*

She gave me a grateful smile. *'Thanks. I'll see you at home.'*

After saying my farewells to the others, I teleported up to Apollo's, realizing belatedly that it had been the first time Tessa had truly referred to my home as hers. I didn't doubt her feelings for me, but I'd watched her struggle to find her place the last few weeks, to figure out where she fit both as a person and as a deity. A sense of relief that I didn't know I'd been waiting for settled over me as I realized that she considered my home to be hers, that I held a part of her, a part that she willingly gave me. Considering the current state of affairs, that feeling of contentment was more than welcome.

11

TESSA

A short while later, I'd left John and Analise to get settled in so I could say my goodbyes to the Andersons and make sure Hermes got them home safely. When I returned, Rosalind, the tall, dark-skinned, sharp-eyed owner of the inn, was manning the front desk, writing rapidly in a small notebook. When the bell above the door rang, she looked up, then flashed me a bright smile.

"Did your friends get back safely?" she asked.

"They did." I smiled at her. "Thank you for taking my guardians in," I told her. "I know circumstances are unusual right now."

She shrugged. "It's what I'm here for," she said simply.

"Considering what's happened, are all the businesses open?" I asked.

She gave a sharp nod. "Most businesses were only closed for a day or two after the attack. Everyone wanted to get back to normal, or as normal as they could, quickly."

"Most?"

"A few owners have opted to return to the field and fight, now that the Titans are returning," she explained with an odd twist to her tone. "The rest...we've decided it's best to maintain as much normalcy as we can for those who've chosen to remain on the mountain."

"Yeah, I suppose that makes sense," I murmured. "Well, thanks again."

Giving her one last farewell smile, I made my way back to the small bungalow Rosalind had given John and Analise. It was quaint —there was really no other word for it. With honey-stained wood, an overstuffed sofa and chair, and a small fireplace, it was the kind of place you would curl up in front of a fire in fuzzy socks and drink hot chocolate while the snow swirled outside.

I smiled when I found John reclined in the cushioned chair and Analise stretched out on the couch. Both had changed out of the formal black suits they'd worn into more comfortable clothes. "You guys want a nap before we eat?"

"No, no," Analise said, sitting up and nudging John's foot with her own. He opened his eyes and sat up.

"Are you in the mood for anything in particular?" I asked.

"Just get something simple, kiddo. We don't need anything fancy," John said.

A short while later, the three of us had opted against going out to eat, instead ordering a pizza and a bottle of dandelion wine from the Italian restaurant and bringing them back to their cabin.

"So," John said as they sat down and I began to pull plates out of the cabinet. "I suppose you have a lot of questions."

Right to it, then.

I turned back toward the cabinet, deciding to stall for time by pulling three glasses out and rinsing them in the sink. I honestly hadn't thought I would get the chance to ask them all the things that were attempting to bubble out of me, not knowing whether or not I would ever see them again. I'd hoped I would, of course, but I also would've preferred they remain as far away from me and the craziness that had become my life as possible.

I poured us each a glass of wine and sat down, then stared at the golden liquid for a few moments. They both waited patiently, food untouched, as I gathered my thoughts.

Finally, I met each of their gazes. "Why? Why agree to Hecate's terms and accept the interdiction? Why on earth would you want to raise a Titaness who would undoubtedly have a target on her back the moment she was discovered?"

John leaned back in his seat as Analise took a large gulp of wine. Neither spoke for a few seconds, so I waited, trying to channel some of John's infinite patience.

"There were a few reasons," Analise began. "And, if we're being honest with one another, a good portion had more to do with being young and naïve, and less with honor."

John shot her an incredulous look, but she waved him off and faced me. Leaning forward, she ran her finger along the base of her wine glass. "As you know, guardians are told shortly before receiving their charge that he or she will be arriving. We told you that we found out just before you came to us, but we actually found out about a year before. We felt special, having been chosen to raise a baby like you."

Confused, I shook my head. "I wouldn't even have been born at that point. My birth mother dumped me off at that police station when I was barely two months old."

They exchanged a look that told me I wasn't going to like what came next.

"Tessa." John paused, his jaw tense. It was nearly painful not to just jump into his head and read his mind. He took a deep breath, then leveled a stare at me. "Tessa, your human mother... she didn't exist."

"What?" Shaking my head, I propped my elbow on the table and rubbed my hand over my forehead. "No, Hecate told me I was reborn in human form."

"Remade, would be a more accurate term," Analise said. "It's why everything about you is the same now as it was in your previous life. Your appearance, your personality, your powers."

I nearly choked on a sip of wine. Slowly, I set my glass down. "Re —remade? I assumed my soul got sent to me when my birth mother got pregnant."

"Not exactly," she replied. "Hecate came to us about a year before you were brought back and gave us the gist. She explained that she'd searched for a pair of guardians who would be best suited for the task and had eventually found us. She didn't get into *why* she chose us, other than the fact that she believed you would be just as in sync with John and me as he and I are with one another." She gave him a tight smile. "Almost immediately, John requested an interdiction be placed on both of us, which she did, then she explained your full story."

"Essentially, a corporeal form was made for you," John interjected, sounding as though he were describing how one might construct a car. "A vessel. When she recalled your soul from Chaos, it was placed inside the new body, then nature just... took over."

I arched a brow. "She made a baby. From scratch." Unbelievable. "I wasn't actually born into a human body, then?"

"No, you weren't, and don't ask for specifics, because she didn't disclose anything about how that was done." John ran a hand through his brown hair and huffed out a breath. "We were under strict instructions not to tell you anything, but we managed to get around them a bit by telling you about the people who would be in your life."

"I remember," I murmured. "It's why Taurus became our common point, right?"

"It was," Analise said quietly.

"We just wanted you to have as much information as we could give you." John gave me an amused smile. "Although you weren't exactly the best student when it came to the history of Olympus."

I rolled my eyes. "Yeah, yeah. Apparently I was a pain in the ass in all my lives."

"Aside from that, you pretty much know everything," Analise said. "There were things we had to keep from you, stories we had to fabricate, but I hope you can see why that was necessary. I don't know much of what's happened since you... came back, but I know most hasn't been pleasant."

"Now, can you fill us in on what's been going on up here?" John asked. "We knew before you left that there was a threat of rebellion, but aside from that, no one gave us much in the way of specifics."

I leaned back in my chair and took a gulp of wine. "Gods, I don't even know where to begin. There's been so much…"

"Start at the beginning," Analise suggested. "When you discovered your powers."

My lips twitched as I recalled the day Nate and Chiron had figured out why my powers seemed to be going haywire, when Chiron had pushed me into a stream, and Genevieve—my heart hitched at the thought that I would never see her again—had first demonstrated her ability to become invisible to me.

"Well, that was Nate, actually," I told them. "And Chiron, but Nate was the one who figured out something was wrong."

And so I told them about the last two months on Olympus, about how I'd gone from awestruck just at the sight of the Elders to waking up as a Titaness. I glossed over the dream walks with Menoetius and the things he'd done to me in the past, instead, giving them detailed accounts of the friends I'd made, those I'd rediscovered, and the family I now had that had been binding itself back together, day by day.

I told them about rescuing my twin, fighting the empousa that had possessed him and dragging him from that rotten hole Menoetius had trapped him in.

My words slowed when I reached the part of my story that consisted largely of death. The first time I'd been tested in the field; when I'd fought the empousa with Persephone, Athena, and Demeter; the attack on Athens, where a few dozen Ischyra had been poisoned to death in a meeting room; and, finally, the attack on the arena.

Again, I didn't go into great detail. They'd gotten the watered-down version already—there'd been an attack, recruits and mentors had been killed, Cronus and Iapetus were free and unaccounted for, and Mary had been taken. I didn't speak of Josh's involvement, Andrei's duplicity, or the mind link that had held Anette. I also didn't bother mentioning that I'd spent the entire previous day attempting to disassemble my sadistic brother's mind, taking no small pleasure in the twinges of pain that had regularly crumpled his face, or that I'd likely be doing it again tomorrow.

John let out a low whistle when I finished, and Analise just stared at me in mute horror. Feeling uncomfortable under her gaze, I picked up my glass and downed the rest of my wine.

"And what's being done to find Mary and Atlas' daughters?" she finally asked, her voice rough.

"I've been working with Hermes daily, jumping onto the astral plane, the dream realm, attempting to form mind links." I tapped my fingers on the smooth wooden table. "Zeus won't spare a tracker for them because he's got them focused on hunting down Cronus and Iapetus. I'm hoping that will lead us to them, but it would be nice if there was one dedicated to finding Mary and the sisters specifically."

"You... you're not able to track, then?" she asked.

My face flushed. "There are a lot of powers I haven't been exposed to or haven't had sufficient time to train in. I *can* track, but not over long distances, not yet. I'll learn eventually, but right now I think it's best to focus on the powers I'm more skilled with."

"I think that makes sense, sweetheart," Analise said, her eyes comforting.

"So what are they, anyway?" John asked, perking up at what he would've considered shop talk. "Which powers are you best at?"

"Mental stuff, mainly. Coercion, astral projection, psychometry. Earth and fire are the Elemental powers I'm best at."

"Still keeping up with your physical combat?"

"Properly?" I smiled ruefully. "No. I've definitely gotten some practice in, though. I'm not rusty by any means if you're thinking of challenging me," I added with a smirk.

"Wouldn't dream of it." He smiled and picked up a now-cold slice of pizza.

"So, how are things in Renville? Anything new?" I didn't want to outright ask what they may or may not know about Josh, but I *did* want to see if there was anything they might be able to offer.

"It's been pretty quiet," Analise said. "We're planning on traveling some, once we get back, do that round-the-world trip we dreamed up at sixteen," she said teasingly.

"Well, now you've got all the time in the world," I said, happy that they were finally free from the obligations of guardianship. All guardians retained their regular, very healthy salary once their Ischyra left their care, ensuring they'd be set for life. They could do whatever they wanted now.

She flashed me a smile that was tinged with sadness before continuing. "We've gone to dinner with the Andersons and the Millers a few times, trying to keep in touch. It's strange, not having the three of you flitting between houses like you used to."

A twinge of sadness caused my stomach to clench as I recalled all the times Eric, Mary, and I, along with Josh and Leila, had done just that.

I cleared my throat and attempted to look casual. "Have you seen Leila at all? She was pretty upset when we left. Do you know how she's been doing?"

"She came by a few times," Analise replied. "For coffee and to chat. She's put off college for a year, now that Josh has left. I think losing the four of you—"

"Josh left?" My tone was sharper than I intended as I latched onto her mention of him. "Do you know why?"

John shrugged. "Football scholarship to some private university. I forget which. Somewhere down south, I think?"

I arched a brow. Josh had been an average student all through high school and a half-decent football player at best. "When was this?"

"Not terribly long after you all left to come here." She shrugged. "Felt bad for the poor thing. She'd planned to go to school with him, right?"

I nodded. "She did. They were planning on going to Penn State together. I think he was going to do a few semesters at community college first."

"Those two were together for a long time," she said. "It could've just been he wanted some distance."

"Yeah, maybe," I murmured. "Still weird, though."

"I'm sure he'll be back," John said.

But now my curiosity was piqued. The impression I'd gotten from Menoetius was that Josh had been involved with their cause for some time. It hadn't just begun when the new batch of recruits arrived on Olympus, which meant he'd been working with the rebels since long before my transformation. Assuming Hecate's mind-wiping spell worked on Josh the same way it had worked on everyone else, there was no logical reason—that I could see, anyway—for him to leave Renville at the same time Mary, Eric, and I had left. Even if by some chance he knew who I was, he wouldn't have been able to follow us to Olympus. If he had, he wouldn't have needed to use Anette to spy on me.

According to Hecate, everyone's memories had been wiped of any knowledge of me. We knew her spell hadn't worked on Menoetius, but the failsafe had been that no one would believe anyone who *did* remember if they tried to tell them—it was the reason Atlas didn't believe Menoetius toward the end of his imprisonment, the only reason he'd been able to pull back some semblance of himself. That information could *only* come from the caster of the spell, which was Hecate, and only with permission from the Fates, which was how Hecate had been able to explain things to John, Analise, Apollo, and Hestia.

I'd thought Josh had just been a plant—Menoetius clearly knew who I was, so once I discovered Josh's deceit, I assumed Menoetius had inserted Josh into my life and told him to spy on me. If I'd been in Menoetius' shoes, I would've kept Josh in Renville. There were at least a dozen ways he could've used Josh to further torment me by keeping him there. It was oddly bad form for my brother.

"Well, guys, I think I'm going to head out," I told them, annoyed that I now had even more unanswered questions to ponder. "I'll try to stop by tomorrow."

"Don't you worry about us," Analise said, patting my hand. "We've got plenty to occupy ourselves with, not to mention a village to explore." She grinned. "You've really found yourself a beautiful home up here, Tessa."

"You do whatever you need to do to keep it that way, you hear me?" John said, his voice going from easy to no-nonsense guardian in one breath. "No holding back, Tessa. There's nothing up here you can't handle if you put your mind to it. Don't let the things that are out of your control—"

"Take control. I know." Smiling, I stood, accepting tight embraces from both of them. I wanted them to stay forever, to never have to go back to Earth and return to whatever their normal lives were now.

Reluctantly, I turned and left. After waving a quick goodbye to Rosalind on the way out, I teleported home.

12

TESSA

Nate was waiting for me when I walked in the door, lying on the couch with an arm across his forehead. He'd lit a fire, so the room was toasty, a nice respite from the cold air outside.

"Who ya talking to?" I asked, toeing off my shoes and walking toward the couch. He let out an *ooof* when I plopped down in his lap, then wrapped his arms around my waist and pulled me down to lay beside him.

"Apollo and Athena," he said, kissing my forehead. "We're going to talk to Zeus tomorrow about dealing with Anette and Andrei."

"And where will I be during this conversation, considering they were both technically spying on me?"

"With us, preferably. You, Atlas, and I are going down to Demeter's to meet with Sterope, Maia, and Electra. I think you're right, combining your power with theirs might help track down their sisters and Mary."

"What about Menoetius? Shouldn't we be working on him?"

"We will, but later. Apollo and I both think you might be able to get something worthwhile with the sisters that we can use when we dig into his mind." He pinched the bridge of his nose and let out an annoyed sigh. "And I'm beginning to think Menoetius may be a waste of time."

"You don't think we'll get anything from him?"

"Maybe. But all I've been doing is spending my days in the dungeon and getting nothing but scraps to show for it."

"What do you think I might find with the sisters that would help?"

"Locations. Details. Anything specific about where they are, who's working with them. Focus on those things, and we'll hopefully be able to use what we learn to find what we need in Menoetius' memory. It'll also give Persephone and her trackers a bit more to work with."

I lifted my head and arched a brow. "That's it? No 'if it's alright with you'?"

He frowned. "Isn't it?"

Grinning, I kissed his jaw. "Of course. I just haven't seen you so take-charge in a while. I like it."

"I'm not quite sure how to take that. Thank you?"

"Any time." I grinned and laid my head back down on his chest, idly playing with the buttons on his shirt. We lay there quietly for a few minutes, no sound except for the crackling fire and the driftwood clock that sat on his mantle ticking away as I ran over the events of the day.

"Hey, Nate?"

"Hmm?"

"What was it like for you? When Karis died?"

His body tensed for a moment, then he took a few seconds before answering. "It was one of the most painful things I'd ever experienced," he said softly. "As though a piece of me had been taken away."

I chewed my lower lip, debating whether I should push forward or let it be and avoid upsetting him.

"It's okay," he whispered, his lips against my hair. "It was a long time ago."

"What did you do to fill that hole?"

"Nothing, at first. I felt like I was doing her memory a disservice if I tried to refill it. Eventually, I acknowledged how foolish that was, so I focused on making stronger Ischyra and figuring out ways to address and overcome weaknesses so things like that wouldn't happen again." Slowly, he stroked my hair, something I think comforted him as much as it did me. "I pulled away from my family, lived on Earth for a long time, getting to know the humans, how they lived, thought, existed. I was fortunate enough to have parents who allowed me that freedom, even if they didn't want to allow me to leave."

"Did it work?" I asked quietly.

"It did," he replied with a sigh. "After a very long time, it did."

"How long?" I trained my eyes on the rise and fall of his chest, needing to focus on something to keep from crying again.

"That's not really something you can quantify, Tessa," he said softly. "Our circumstances are different. There are different emotions involved. I loved Karis, yes, but her death... as much as it angered me, as much as I hated Apollo for knowingly sending her into a situation where she was at a disadvantage, her death was typical for an Ischyra. I—and she—knew it could happen, just as it could with any soldier. It didn't make the loss any easier, but it did make it easier to move on." His arms tightened around me, as though he could feel my emotions starting to bubble to the surface. "What happened here to your friends was much different. Coming back from that isn't something you should try to rush."

I nodded, no longer able to form words as my arm formed a vice grip on his waist.

"It'll be okay," he whispered. He pressed his lips to my forehead and held me tighter, not saying anything more as the tears started to flow. I'd wanted this to come later, after we'd won the war and things got back to normal. I wanted to be allowed to wait to truly grieve, to *really* cry for the loss of one of my best friends, for the absence of the recruits who should still be here.

Who *would* be here if my father and brother hadn't come to Olympus looking for me.

"Stop that," he murmured, and I realized my mental walls had faltered. It was as though even my power knew it was alright for him to see the bits of me I wanted to keep hidden.

"I can't help it," I whispered.

"None of this is your fault, Tessa. This is the work of selfish, power-hungry gods, nothing more."

I took a slow, shaky breath. "I know. Just keep reminding me of that, okay?"

"Every day, if you need me to."

"Thank you." Needing a distraction, I rested my chin on his chest and smiled. "So Rosalind and Reginald...they're married?"

"For several centuries now," he confirmed.

"Did you go to the wedding?" I'd always wondered what the ceremonies were like for those Ischyra who did choose to marry. Marriage between Ischyra was incredibly rare, mainly because it was nearly impossible to guarantee placement with your spouse; meaning, couples could end up separated for decades or even centuries.

He shook his head. "Ischyra weddings... they're for Ischyra only. It's one line the gods drew years ago. We can and do insert ourselves into every aspect of their lives, but we've barred ourselves from attending private events like that unless explicitly invited. The focus is on the bride and groom. Gods in attendance, especially uninvited ones, would draw attention away from the ones who should be the center of attention."

My eyebrows lifted. "Seriously? Whose idea was that?"

"My mother's. She believes very strongly in the sanctity—and privacy—of marriage."

"Huh." Once again, Hera surprised me with her decency toward beings who were inarguably lower than her.

"Don't sound so surprised," he murmured, tucking my head under his chin. "She might be a bit obsessive and overprotective of her children—"

"A bit?" I gave him an incredulous look. "She threatened to kill me if I hurt you, Nate. She literally said she would destroy me."

He chuckled. "She takes marriage and family very seriously.

Choices were taken away from humans once Zeus and the others created the Ischyra; this was her way of making sure they maintained some semblance of autonomy."

"That's... surprisingly kind of her."

"She's not all bad, no matter how abrasive she may seem."

"Abrasive is one word for her," I muttered. "So does this mean if we ever actually get married, she's going to be more or less obsessive?"

He snorted. "I'm fairly certain the stereotype humans have for mothers-in-law is based on her."

"In other words, eloping would be out of the question?" I teased.

That got a full-on laugh from him. "Yes, that would be *far* out of the question. She's had weddings planned for all of her children for centuries." He kissed my forehead. "Sorry, love."

Grinning, I pressed my face to his chest. Any other girl would've been over the moon to hear her boyfriend talking as freely about marriage as he was.

But me? I was just happy he was talking so freely about the *future*, about things that could or would come once this war was over, and we no longer had threats of death and destruction hanging over our heads.

Right now, a future was all I could hope for.

WHEN MORNING CAME, I called for Atlas to come down so the three of us could discuss plans for visiting the sisters. I'd decided to go over everything with him, then let him decide whether or not he'd join us. He'd never been close with his daughters prior to his imprisonment, and now a few thousand years sat between them. I didn't imagine that was something that would be easy to walk back, regardless of our current circumstances.

"So what exactly do you plan to do?" Atlas asked. He stood in front of me, arms crossed, as a myriad of emotions flitted across his face. In my previous life, he'd been one of the fiercest warriors who'd ever resided on Olympus, able to intimidate anyone by mere presence alone. But as a father who'd been long-estranged from his daughters, several of whom were missing, he looked lost, which was an emotion that was foreign to him.

"I'm not sure," I said slowly. "But I was able to get through whatever magic is blocking us from them, at least a little bit. Now that we know that Mary and the rest of the Pleiades are alive, I'm hoping we can figure out some way to combine our power to reach them."

Atlas exchanged a look with Nate, clearly indecisive as to how much he wanted to facilitate my newest plan, and I had to force back a frustrated huff. Of my brothers, Atlas was the only one left who held significant doubts about my abilities, despite what he might say, and was being the most stubborn about changing those views.

Looking back at me, we stared at each other, bodies tense, as a battle of wills took place between us. After a few seconds, Atlas's shoulders loosened and he nodded.

"Alright. We can try." He glanced at Nate. "Will you be coming with us?"

"I am."

"Okay, then," I said. "Let's go."

The sun had fully risen by the time the three of us arrived at Demeter's home in the farming valley. It was a simple, albeit massive, farmhouse that sat along the woods on the edge of the valley. The wide spread of the valley was filled with rows upon rows of crops, all spread over what had to be thousands of acres. From where I stood I could see fruit trees and vines, vegetables, vibrant flowers, cotton and flax, wheat, bamboo, and along the outer edge, a few dozen boxes that sang with the buzz of thousands of honeybees.

As a soft breeze sent the smell of fresh herbs across the yard, I heard the quiet whinny of a horse from inside the stables where the stallions were kept. A soft *ker-thunk* hummed from a workshop located in one of the outbuildings, and yards of freshly dyed fabrics fluttered gently on the long rows of clothesline that stretched along the back, drying in the sun. It reminded me of being at my human grandmother's home when I was a girl, hiding between the drying sheets in summer, running my fingers along the cool, damp fabric that slowly warmed in the sun. The vivid smell of the laundry detergent she'd used flashed through my mind, too quickly to grab hold of, but enough to make me smile at the memory.

"I could stay here forever," I murmured, taking it all in. "It's so peaceful."

Nate slid an arm around my waist and kissed me. He didn't speak; just stood there with me, taking it all in.

"One day," he whispered, "if this is what you want, I'll give it to you."

Overcome with emotion, I turned my face into his chest and sighed, then looked up at him with a smile. "With a porch swing?"

He kissed the top of my head. "Sure."

"Wheat fields and flying stallions, too?"

He laughed. "I don't know about that. But the rest... absolutely."

I returned his smile, then I glanced toward my brother, who'd walked toward the farm fields and was staring up at the mountains.

"I'll go grab Demeter," Nate said.

Nodding gratefully, I went to stand beside Atlas, slipping off the leather jacket I'd thrown on—a gift from Persephone, accompanied by several pairs of sturdy leather pants—that had become stifling in the sun now that we were away from the whipping winds of the upper mountain.

"You okay?" I asked my twin.

He gave me a tight smile. "This is the first time I've seen anything but the top of the mountain or my prison in three thousand years. I'd forgotten how open it is."

I wrapped my arms around his waist and squeezed, needing to remind him that he was really here, that it wasn't another mind trick that our sadistic brother had whipped up. "It's going to be okay, Atlas. You know that, right?"

Muscular arms went around my shoulders. "I know that we'll do what we can to achieve that, Tessa, but all I can do is hope that you're right."

I wanted to contradict his pessimism, but now wasn't the time.

We'd both been locked away for thousands of years, but while I'd been blissfully unaware of my own absence, he'd known nothing but suffering. He wouldn't be bouncing back anytime soon, no matter what I said or how many times I tried to reassure him.

A few moments later, Demeter appeared before us, dusty but radiant in the morning sun, Nate trailing behind her. "Good morning," she said, smiling. "Let's head inside. The sisters have been awaiting your arrival, but Hyperion and Theia are anxious to see you both as well."

Brushing off her hands on her cotton pants, she led us inside and into the living room, a vast space with wide-planked hardwood floors smooth with age, pale gray walls, and overstuffed sofas and chairs that flanked a large, river rock fireplace.

The two Titans, some of the few who had switched sides in the last war, sat on the larger sofa. Hyperion, a fair-haired, bearded giant, was sketching in a book that balanced on the couch's wide arm. Theia, a tall, stunning brunette, was stretched out along the length of the sofa. Her head was propped on Hyperion's thigh, while her long legs rested crossed at the ankle on the opposite arm, a heavy-looking book in her hands. When she heard us approach, she rested it on her stomach and turned her face toward the door.

"Tessa," she said quietly, slowly swinging her legs around so she could plant her feet on the floor. She set the book on the table in front of her and stood to greet us, Hyperion following suit.

"Hello, Theia," I said as she stepped closer. I hadn't known Theia or Hyperion well in my last life. They'd initially stood by Cronus when Zeus, Poseidon, and Hades rebelled, only to pull back once they realized what Cronus had done to his children. When the war was over and the dust had settled, they, along with a small handful of other Titans, chose to live on Earth, adopting a much more peaceful existence than they'd had in their early years when they were under the command of the youngest of their brethren.

When Theia reached me, she opened her arms and pulled me into a fierce hug. Despite not knowing her well, she had been very close with my mother, and as she looked at me, sadness flashed across her face. When her gaze shifted to my twin, standing solidly behind me, her eyes turned wary. I stepped to the side so that I was beside him, not liking the feeling of him hovering.

"Atlas," she said with a nod. "Have you be reacclimating to Olympus well?"

"Well enough," he replied. "A lot has changed since I've been gone."

"Yes, well, that happens when you're imprisoned for a few thousand years," Hyperion said grimly, giving my brother's shoulder a squeeze. "It is good to have you back, though."

"Thank you," Atlas said. He glanced around the room. "Why have you chosen to live here and not on Earth?"

Theia sighed and gave him a half smile, then gestured toward the sofas, waiting until we were all seated before continuing.

"After the war, we all felt a bit lost on Earth," she began. "Those of us who still held favor with the Olympians were welcomed back, and eventually, Hyperion and I helped Demeter set up the farming operation to supply Olympus. It was just textiles at first, but as you can see, it's grown quite a bit," she added with a smile, justifiably proud of the work they'd done.

Atlas shifted his gaze toward Hyperion. "I was pleased to hear you both had escaped imprisonment," he told them. "That your honor hadn't been besmirched by the deeds of our ruler."

"Oceanus had fair points once the war ended, when he decided we should step back and see how the newer generation ran things," Hyperion said with a shrug. "Cronus liked to think he was all-knowing, all-powerful, but the bulk of us needed that reminder that he wasn't."

Atlas' lips twitched. "What was it he said that day in the cave? Just as the war had nearly ended. 'We're no more conquered by them than we are by Nature?'"

Hyperion nodded. "And truer words were never spoken, in my opinion."

"What did he mean by that?" Nate asked curiously.

"That the rules of nature are what allowed Zeus and his brothers to overtake their father in the end," Theia replied. "Cronus damaged our world when he imprisoned his children, when he turned to malice instead of reason. It may sound silly to you, but the older generations have always held the belief that nature wanted a balance, so Cronus was punished for killing his own father by having a similar fate handed to him."

I nodded in response, not wanting to tell her that I thought it *did* sound silly, that Cronus hadn't suffered the same fate as his father— conquest by his youngest son—because of some balance-seeking force of nature. It had happened because of his deeds, because he'd tried to thwart fate when he locked his children away out of fear one of them would overthrow him. That wasn't nature; that was paranoia at its finest.

Theia must've seen the doubt written on my face, though, because she gave me an understanding smile. "As I said, I know it may sound silly, but I grew up with Cronus. I watched him kill Ouranos and imprison his children for no logical reason we could see. That's given us a much different opinion of him than you might have."

"You mean that of a tyrant?" I asked dryly.

"Precisely," she replied, a smile dancing on her lips.

"You don't see him that way?" Nate asked.

Theia gave us a soft smile. "He's far more complex than that. Seeing one of my brethren fall as he did... he'd been disgraced, and I know that it was of his own making," she said, putting a hand over her heart. "But it hurt my heart to see how much he'd lost his way, how irrevocable the damage that had been done to him was. I comforted him in the days following the war when we were all in hiding." She brushed away a stray tear that had dripped onto her cheek. "I wanted the best for him, but sometimes, a being just can't accept that what they think is best may not align with what truly is."

"Isn't that the truth," I murmured. An uncomfortable silence followed as my and Theia's differing opinions of Cronus hung in the air.

After a few moments, Hyperion cleared his throat, breaking the silence. "So, you're here to see the witches, then?"

Atlas nodded in confirmation. "For a variety of reasons, yes."

"Then I would suggest Tessa handle her business with them first," Theia suggested. "To give you more time to handle your own."

'She's right,' I told Atlas. 'Let me get my stuff out of the way, then you'll have all the time you need.'

'Alright. Just... stay with me when we first meet? I hardly knew them back then...'

I patted his hand, knowing how hard it was for him to admit he needed help with something like this. 'You'll be fine.'

"We should go, then." I stood, then lifted my brows at Nate, who stood with me. "You coming, too?"

He nodded. "I want to be there if you manage to get in, see if I can catch anything in case you all have trouble holding things together."

A small part of me wanted to be insulted that he didn't think the witches and I could manage this, but logic overtook that fairly quickly. Mary was trapped in a place that was clearly spelled to keep us out by two powerful Titans and a witch of unknown origin or power. I would be a fool not to accept his help.

Not to mention, I'd been the one to tell him we needed all the help we could get.

"I'll take you out back," Demeter offered, stepping into the room.

I sent a smile and a small wave toward Theia and Hyperion, then joined Nate in following Demeter outside.

13

TESSA

When we left the main house, Demeter led us toward a white stone cottage that had been hidden from view behind the house when we arrived. Gauzy curtains fluttered through the open first-floor windows, and colorful flowers rioted in the small beds along the front that had been sectioned off by stones the size of footballs. A cozy, narrow porch with a few wooden rocking chairs encircled the small structure.

"I swear, this place is an artist's dream," I murmured.

As we approached, Demeter turned to face us. "Just a bit of forewarning; the sisters can be a bit mercurial at times. One never quite knows what to expect with them, so just be aware that they won't be as easy to read as others. Do *not* let them dissuade you from your purpose."

I exchanged a quick glance with Nate, who just shrugged.

"Hello, girls!" Demeter called as we entered the quiet house. "I've brought you some visitors!"

The sound of feet trotting down the stairs met my ears just before the three sisters appeared in front of me, each so identical in appearance it was a bit unnerving. I hadn't known them in my previous life; Atlas' relationship with their mother Pleione hadn't been a long one, and once the sisters were born, Pleione had taken them to live with the other Oceanids in the Gulf of Volos. As I took in their appearances, it was clear they'd gotten their identical looks from their mother's side. Hair so pale it was nearly white, light blue eyes, and skin that held just the slightest hint of a tan were all the trademarks of an Oceanid.

It was quite startling when I realized how much they also resembled my mother, who'd been an Oceanid herself.

Swallowing back that observation, I offered them a smile.

"Hi," I said. "I'm—"

"Tessa, we know," one of them said, her voice coming out strong and sure. "I'm Maia, and these are my sisters, Electra and Sterope."

The other two nodded their greetings, but neither spoke.

"We understand you would like to attempt to merge your power with ours to locate your friend," Maia said, "and our sisters, if what you say is true, and they're still alive."

"They are," I confirmed. "I saw them with my friend Mary two days ago. It was very brief. I was removed from Mary's mind as soon as the witch discovered my presence."

Sterope angled her head curiously. "How did he know you were there?"

I shrugged. "Not sure. He just acknowledged me, then kicked me out."

"You know him, then?" Maia asked.

"Yes. He's—well, he used to be a friend when I lived on Earth. I spent the last four years in school with him."

"You didn't know you were friends with someone supernatural that whole time?" Maia eyed me dubiously. "Your powers truly were concealed, weren't they?"

My back went up at her tone, but I tried not to show my annoyance. They didn't know me, so I couldn't blame them for questioning my abilities, especially considering how weak I'd been in my past life.

"There was nothing I could do about that, and I can assure you, I'm strong enough now."

Maia exchanged a look with her sisters before facing me. "When you rescued your twin, how did you do it?"

Quickly readjusting to the change in topic, I ran through how I'd done a dream walk, then astral projected first into Atlas' cave, then into his mind to fight off the empousa that had possessed him.

"So you managed to hold that projection long enough to fight off a beast in his mind?" Maia's sounded only slightly impressed by that. "Without injury?"

"Well, no." I felt my face flush. "It had been a while since I'd fought one of those things, so I didn't exactly come out unscathed."

Maia nodded. The sister next to her, Electra, I was pretty sure, eyed me speculatively before turning to face her. She whispered something in her ear, causing Maia to arch a brow.

"My sister isn't sure you're strong enough to perform a long-distance link like that," Maia explained. "She tends to be quite a good judge of these things."

"Don't be difficult, Maia," Demeter warned.

"What would the harm be to you if I fail?" I asked.

"Nothing," Electra said with a shrug. "Your disappointment and that of those around you will be the only result."

"Then it shouldn't matter whether you think I'm strong enough." I took a deep breath. "Listen, I'm going to keep trying to do this, with or without you. I would really appreciate it if I had your help, because time is a bit of the essence here."

Maia turned and had another whispered conversation with her sisters. Sterope kept shooting me furtive glances as they spoke. After a few moments, they turned to face me again.

"Alright, we'll help, but on one condition. If you cannot locate your friend, use our essences to try and find our sisters. All of our attempts to locate them have failed, including dream walks and spells. This... Josh creature has figured out a way to block us from connecting to their magic. You've got access to abilities that we do not, so you may be able to succeed where we failed."

"You won't be able to do that through me?" I asked, my hopes beginning to plummet.

"We'll likely be able to help you connect to your friend, cementing you in her mind enough for you to track her—I'm assuming you're able to track?"

"Sort of," I replied. "I've only managed short distances because my training got cut short."

She nodded slowly. "Your tracking abilities, limited as they might be, should allow you to find her."

"Alright, but why won't you be able to lend more power?" I asked.

"Our power is shared with our sisters," she said. "We'll be expelling enough joining with you. We don't know if the connection to our magic has been severed or not, but if we use too much, we risk weakening the others if we are still connected."

"Do you think you are?" Nate asked, suddenly reminding me of his presence.

"We're not sure," Electra said. "I am typically the most sensitive to fluctuations in our shared power, and I have not felt their presence in any significant way since they were taken. But whatever this new magic is that this witch has brought into our world makes things difficult to read."

"New magic?" I frowned. "I thought Josh was just a witch?"

"He is, so far as we can tell," Maia replied. "An incredibly powerful, heretofore unknown, primordial witch."

"Well, that's just dandy," I muttered. "Alright, then. How do we do this?"

"First, we need to get our other sister."

"Is Merope still on Earth?" Nate asked.

Electra nodded. "She is aware that our sisters have gone missing but has been afraid to leave her family behind. I will return shortly."

When she was gone, I looked at Maia. "Atlas is here with me," I told her. "Will you be willing to speak with him once we're done?"

She gave a small shrug. "I see no reason not to. He was no father to us before he was imprisoned, but I would like to give him the benefit of the doubt and assume he might've rectified that, had he had the chance after the war."

I let out a relieved breath. "Thank you, Maia. That means a lot. To both of us."

Seconds later, Electra returned with Merope, another mirror image of her sisters, in tow. Yet despite her identical appearance, there was something more...earthly about her. Electra, Maia, and Sterope all wore their hair loose, with similar gauzy dresses in pale shades of purple and blue, but Merope had a tougher, more rugged look to her. She wore sturdy jeans and a white peasant top, tall, scuffed-up leather boots, and her white-blond hair was pulled back in a tight French braid. If not for her face, I would've pegged her for a typical human.

'She's lived among humans for two thousand years,' Nate said, picking up on my assessment of her. *'Married an immortal demigod and started a family.'*

"Are you sure this will work?" Merope asked, not bothering with a greeting as she looked around at us.

"No," Maia said bluntly. "But nothing we've done has worked. Tessa's idea has some merit."

Merope eyed me for a moment, then nodded curtly. "Alright, then. Let's get on with it." She gestured toward the door. "I think it might be best if we move outside for this. It will be easier to connect to your friend's or our sisters' energy if we're directly connected to the Earth."

I frowned. "Why?"

"Because the Earth connects all things, even people," Electra said quietly. She looked at me, then Nate. "You should call for Apollo. We may have need of him."

"Of course," Nate said. His eyes went vacant for a moment, and seconds later, Apollo appeared beside us.

"What is it?" Apollo asked as he took us all in.

I huffed out an annoyed sigh. "We're going to try to track Mary and the other sisters. I'm assuming someone thinks I'm going to hurt myself."

"It wouldn't be the first time," he muttered, shrugging out of his pale gray jacket and laying it over the porch rail. He rolled up his sleeves to the elbows, giving me an expectant look as he did. "Well, get on with it."

The sisters led us to the middle of Demeter's back yard, a flowing grassy expanse that stretched toward the mountain.

"The rest of you will need to keep a safe distance," Maia announced, and I realized Atlas, Demeter, Hyperion, and Theia had joined us. "We cannot have anyone interfering with this link; otherwise, it will fail."

"What happens if it fails?" Atlas asked, crossing his arms.

"Tessa will either simply fail in her mission or remain stuck somewhere in between here and there, although I'm sure she's already aware of the risks." She arched a brow at me. "It all depends on her ability to maintain her hold on us."

"And you on her," Nate said, worry creasing his brow as he looked at me. *'You sure you want to do this?'*

Atlas opened his mouth to object, but I shot him a silencing look then gave Maia a quick nod.

She gestured to the ground in front of us. "Sit."

I did, and the sisters followed suit, the five of us forming a circle, with Merope and Maia on either side of me.

"Do you have something, a strong memory, perhaps, that you can use to locate her?" Electra asked. "The more meaningful, the better."

I chewed my lower lip, thinking.

"You're a Mimic, Tessa," Apollo groaned. "You've quite literally got a piece of Mary inside you."

My eyes widened. "Yes!" I looked at Electra. "Will the power I absorbed from her work? I know it's technically mine now, but do you think I could use that to help track her?"

"Certainly," she said, smiling. "I'd say it would greatly improve your chances of tracking her."

I let out a sigh of relief. "Perfect. Okay. Tell me what to do."

The four of them began to dole out instructions, one piling on top of the other until I had a general, if not muddled, idea of what I needed to do.

Taking the hands of the two sisters beside me, I closed my eyes and reached deep inside myself until I found that tiny spark of vibrant blue magic that I'd absorbed from Mary. It felt strong and willful, just like her, so I latched on and pulled it forward, wrapping my own power around it.

"Good," Maia whispered. "Now, reach for your Ttracking power, touch it to her magic."

I rolled my shoulders and nodded, then exhaled a quiet breath.

It was a little hard to find my tracking ability because I'd used it so infrequently, but once I did, my magic did all the work for me, reaching out for Mary's small kernel of power. With a jolt, it shot out of me.

"Now focus, don't break your hold on it," Merope ordered. "We're going to meld our power with yours now and attempt to guide it to our sisters. You just focus on your friend."

I concentrated on guiding my power toward wherever it was it needed to go to respond, but a moment later I felt four separate consciousnesses settle into my own. My connection to the Earth was suddenly more solid. I felt their magic holding me in place, joining my own to act as a tether, wrapping around the piece I'd sent out with one end and bolting me to the Earth with the other. The tension from the onlookers was palpable, but I forced myself to remain focused. Once the sisters were locked in, I felt a bit steadier and was able to get a solid hold on the power that was shooting out of me. I held tight to the end of it as the sisters twined their own magic with mine, combining their link to their sisters with mine to Mary, then I let it all unfurl, seeking out the other ends of those connections on its own.

Moments later, my eyes flew open, and I stared up at Nate.

"We've got them."

14

MARY

I must've still been knocked out when Cronus and Iapetus dumped me back in my cell, because when I awoke, it was to the small square of sunlight that always seemed to taunt me with dreams of the outside. Groggily, I reached for my magic, hoping I'd still feel its presence. It was there—I knew that with my entire being—but the bulk of it had been replaced by a heavy, empty feeling, as though a physical piece of me had been removed.

Frowning, I looked around for what had woken me, wanting nothing more than to go back to sleep. Then I felt it; a tiny prickling in my mind, a weird sensation that felt like fingers running through my thoughts and dreams.

I sat bolt upright, gripping the sides of my head. "What the—"

I was cut off by a sharp shushing from Taygete, who was also awake, along with Celaeno and Alcyone, who'd been brought back seemingly half-dead while I'd been asleep. Quietly, Taygete tapped the side of her head, then pointed at me.

Letting my hands drift to my lap, I nodded.

Someone or something was in our minds.

'Grab hold of whoever it is.'

I jumped, then my eyes widened with the realization that Taygete was in my mind, speaking to me.

'Use your mind,' she instructed.

Nodding, I licked my lips and closed my eyes, turning my attention inward, trying to recall how Tessa did whatever she did when she had to control her own mind.

Then I heard her. Tessa's voice was broken, like she had a crappy cell phone signal, but it was there.

'Mary! Can—ear—me?'

'Yes! Yes, I can hear you! Who's with you?'

'Oth—isters.'

'Tess, I have no idea where we are!'

'—ell me —rything and —old on. —rying to —ack you. Sisters — alking to oth—'

As fast as I could, I ran through everything I could remember, including the fact that there were things that I literally *couldn't* remember. Taygete and Celaeno's eyes were closed, their brows furrowed in concentration as they relayed their own knowledge. Shooting up a silent prayer to whatever gods might be listening that Nate had hopped on board, too, I continued to throw information at her.

'You need to get the other sisters connected to them because they might be able to break through the—'

'Yes—'

Our heads snapped up when heavy footsteps began to echo in the hall.

No, no, they can't be back already!

'Tessa, they're coming! Please, find us!'

'We will. —omise.'

The second the door burst open, Josh stormed in, and the connection was broken. Sobbing in frustration and anger, I slumped against the wall and glared at him.

This past week he'd been the same old Josh. His mannerisms, his voice, his stupid smile, the way he nudged me in what I'm guessing he thought was a playful way—they were all the actions of the Josh

I'd known for years. I was well aware that it was all a ruse to get me to let my guard down, but even still, it made his presence preferable to the random beatings at the hands of Iapetus or Cronus.

Whatever the creature was who stood in front of me wasn't the guy I knew. As he looked around the room, hands on his hips, his face looked like it'd been carved from stone. His jaw was set in hard angles, his lips pressed into a thin line, and his eyes—gods, his eyes were just inhuman.

He finished his assessment of the room, ignoring the sisters who were huddled against the wall, and stared at me.

"I have to say, I'm finally, truly impressed," he said coldly. Slowly, he stalked toward me, and I struggled not to shrink away when he reached toward my chains and unlocked them. "She managed to break through without the help of a travel god, and you managed to hold on. I suppose this newfound strength will get you a few minutes to stretch your legs."

"I—what?" Without warning, he touched a finger to each of the shackles on my wrists, causing them to release with a quick *snap*. I barely had time to enjoy the feeling of freedom before he pulled me to my feet. I swayed with the sudden motion, still unsteady after what Cronus and Iapetus had done.

"Walk," he ordered, shoving me forward.

"No more Mr. Nice Guy?" I muttered, my steps slow and aching as I moved toward the door.

I didn't look at the sisters as I left, not wanting to draw unnecessary attention to them. Alcyone needed rest, and she needed her sisters there with her.

"No one is coming for them any time soon," Josh said as we stepped into the hall. He pulled the door shut with an echoing thud, then jerked his chin down the hall. "Let's go."

"Where?" My voice shook, knowing he was probably bringing me back to the room where Cronus had taken my power the day before. I stumbled as the fear of returning to that place overwhelmed me.

Grabbing my arm, he righted me, then continued walking once I was steady on my feet, staring directly ahead. "Tessa broke through my wards, and you managed to hold on for a surprising amount of time. I'd say that deserves a reward, wouldn't you?"

"A—" I stopped mid-step, swaying a bit as my vision blurred. "What the *fuck* are you talking about?" I took several steps back and shook my head. "I'd like to go back to my cell now. There's nothing left to take, anyway." I told him in a wobbly voice. *Please don't try to take any more.*

He gave me a curious frown. "I'm not taking you to have your power stolen, if that's your concern."

"Um, yeah, it kind of is."

His lips tilted in a crooked smile as he flicked his brown hair from his eyes—something I'd seen him do a million times and had always seen as a tic that would've been easily remedied if he'd just brush his damn hair.

A sudden leaden feeling in my stomach reminded me once again that this wasn't the Josh I knew.

He turned and began to walk again. Grudgingly, I followed as he led me through the dank stone halls of wherever they were keeping us until we came at last to a narrow staircase that led up to a heavily bolted wooden door. Stepping to the side, he gestured for me to go ahead of him.

I clenched my teeth and glared at him, seeing exactly what he was doing.

My Josh knew full well that, normally, I would've stubbornly fought against putting my back to my enemy. In this case, fighting would've been stupid.

This Josh was seeing if I knew just how stupid that would be.

Rolling my eyes, I climbed the stairs, stopping at the landing and looking back at Josh expectantly. He waved a hand, and I watched in awe as the locks and door disappeared.

"So—"

He held up a hand to silence me. "You'll get to ask your questions in time, Mare Bear."

"Stop *calling* me that!" Tears of frustration filled my eyes. "Just because Leila gave Tessa and me those stupid nicknames doesn't give you the right to use them."

"I have every right to do whatever I want," he said. "Now be quiet."

Telling myself I was better off obeying him, I forced my mouth to stay shut and stop getting me in trouble.

The stone hallway on the other side of the door was wide enough for several people to walk side-by-side. Stepping beside me, Josh placed a hand on my back and led me forward. It took every ounce of will I had not to flinch away.

He wrinkled his nose. "You smell terrible."

Smirking, I fanned myself with the collar of my shirt, wafting whatever stench stuck on me after a week in a dungeon toward him. "Guess you should've let us out to shower, then."

He let out an exasperated sigh. "Immortality certainly hasn't taught you maturity, has it?" he asked as we turned a corner toward another door.

"*I'm* immature because I enjoy pissing off my captor?" I snorted. "Yeah, I don't think so. Where are you taking me, anyway? And do your bosses know you snuck me out?"

A quiet chuckle escaped his lips. "My 'bosses' are away at the moment." He opened a door; this one painted a deep red and had gold hardware.

Civilization. Great.

Sure enough, when we stepped through, we were in a hall with cream-colored walls, matching travertine tile floors, and tall, arched windows that were spaced evenly on either side every ten feet or so. Most were open, the burgundy curtains shifting slightly with the stiff breeze that blew through.

I put my senses on high alert as we began walking forward, discreetly taking in any details I could. I strained my ears for any sounds of voices or wildlife, waves crashing, or sea birds screeching, but found nothing. When I looked out, all I could see was blue sky. The air that came through the window was hot and carried a soft scent of brine and something... murky. Like tidewater.

So, we were near saltwater. That *totally* narrowed things down.

"I feel your discontent," Josh observed.

"I can tell you about it, too, if you'd like," I replied sweetly. "It's no secret."

"You'll get your chance to speak, Mary. Don't worry."

He didn't say anything else as we walked down one fancy hall after another, finally stopping at a set of ornate, black double doors. Pushing one open, he shoved me inside, then shut and locked the door behind us.

15

NATHANIEL

When the connection to Mary and the sisters broke, the four Pleiades let out gasping breaths as Tessa was sucked back into her body, shaking.

Atlas made a lunge toward her, but Merope held up a hand, stopping him in his tracks.

"Leave her be," she ground out, her voice harsh and rasping. "Give her a moment."

I cast a concerned glance at Apollo, but he shook his head.

'No injuries. She just needs to shake it off.'

I rubbed a hand across my eyes and waited as Tessa steadied her breathing. She pulled herself to a kneeling position and tilted her face upward as a light breeze blew through the yard. After a few moments, she rolled her neck and stood, then turned to face the rest of us.

"Well?" Apollo asked.

"They've started taking her power," she said, her chest still heaving with the exertion of holding the connection. "Only once, just yesterday, but it's weakened her."

"How much?" Apollo demanded.

"I don't know!" Tessa scrubbed her hands over her face and looked at him with a helpless expression. "I barely got through."

"They were able to make contact with all of them," I told him. "The sisters could hear Tessa, and Mary was able to talk to her."

"The connection was unstable, though," Maia said. "Flickering in and out."

"Yes, quite poor," Electra said. "Considering the circumstances, though, it's the best we are able to do as a group."

Merope put her hands on her hips and looked at Tessa. "Keep trying. We were able to guide you to them, now you need to continue to try and push that connection."

Tessa nodded. "Alright. Yeah, I'll do my best." She cast a glance at me. "Any thoughts?"

I grimaced. "I don't think I saw any more than you did."

"Which wasn't much," Tessa replied. "I was too focused on holding the connection."

"The room was hazy," I told them. "All four were there, although Alcyone seems very weak."

"Yes, they've likely been drawing power from her most frequently," Sterope said.

"Why?" I asked with a frown.

"She's the strongest," Atlas bit out. "Her power regenerates the quickest—"

"So they tap into her well of magic more often and more deeply than the others," Maia finished, narrowing her eyes at her father.

"Is that why Mary was saying we need to find a way to get you four connected to them?" Tessa asked.

"It is," Merope confirmed. "Together, we're far stronger than Cronus and Iapetus, but being separated by the magic they've been using to keep us apart makes us weaker as a whole. If the connection between us and our sisters can be repaired, we would—"

"*Should*—" Electra cut in.

"—be able to beat them without difficulty."

"What about Josh, though?" I asked. "With your shared power, are you seven stronger than him?"

"Of course," Maia said, sounding slightly offended that I'd even asked. "We're seven primordial witches, after all. He's just one."

"One we know next to nothing about," I countered.

"Did you see anyone else?" Apollo asked. "Guards, any of their other allies?"

"I saw glimpses of a few of the guards in Mary's mind, but I couldn't make out any more than dark hair."

"They're using revenants," Merope said. "I could feel their rot."

Apollo and I exchanged a glance before he continued questioning them. "Who has been taking her power? Did she have any memory of how it was done?"

"Cronus was the one who took it," Tessa replied. "His face kept flashing in her mind, so I'm assuming it was him."

"It was," Maia confirmed. "Iapetus as well."

"Were any of you able to get an idea of where they are?" Apollo asked, sounding annoyed as he continued to fire questions. "Were you able to use your magic to track them?"

"Apollo!" I groaned. "Give them a chance to answer."

He sent me a glare, then looked at Tessa expectantly.

"Sort of," Tessa said, wincing. "They're in Greece, I think. I couldn't get a pin on where, exactly, but it's in the general vicinity. Somewhere near water, though. The connection was cut before I could get any further."

"Well, I suppose that's better than nothing," he said, lifting his jacket off the porch rail. "Despite the fact that Greece is surrounded by water on three sides and contains several *thousand* islands."

"Not helpful," I murmured.

"I'm going to bring this to Father, see if he'll deign to spare a tracker or two now," he said.

"At this point, I might be able to do it," Tessa said. "At least I have a boundary."

"Did you miss the part about there being several thousand islands to factor in?"

"Only a fraction of which are habitable," Atlas said. "A few hundred at most."

Apollo shook his head. "No, the days it would take her to do that would be better spent elsewhere." Apollo gave a quick nod of farewell to the others, then disappeared.

Tessa stared at the empty space where he'd just stood, then looked up at me. "He's extra Apollo-y today, isn't he?"

"He doesn't like all of this uncertainty," I told her. "Being unable to fix problems sets him on edge."

"Tell him to join the club," she muttered, then turned toward the four sisters. "So, what now? Do we try again?"

"Now we rest," Sterope said, her face suddenly looking drawn. "My sisters won't admit it, but doing things like this without the other three is quite tiring."

Maia and Merope shot her identical looks of annoyance, but the weariness was clear in their eyes as well.

"Well, I appreciate the help," Tessa said, smiling at them. "Hopefully this gives us enough to be able to find them all."

"Give us a day or so to rest and we can attempt another link," Merope offered. "If the trackers have been unsuccessful."

"Okay, I'll check back in, then." Tessa shot a look at her twin, then at the sisters. "I think Nate and I are going to head out, so…"

Atlas cleared his throat. "Right. Let's hope we can find out more later," he replied lamely.

The four Pleiades eyed him speculatively, and, if I wasn't mistaken, a bit suspiciously. Merope was the first to speak.

"If you'd like to come in, you're welcome to," she offered.

Atlas' shoulders slumped a hair as relief hit him. He nodded, then smiled. "Yes, I would like that very much."

"Alright, then," Maia said brusquely. "Let's go."

Tessa gave Atlas an encouraging pat on the back as he passed, and he smiled down at her gratefully.

Once they were gone, she and I were left with Demeter, Hyperion, and Theia.

"We should get back," Tessa said after a moment.

Theia gave her an understanding smile. "I hope you find what you're looking for with Menoetius," she said. "He's a vicious creature who lacks little in the way of intelligence."

"I just want to find my friend," Tessa told her. "Atlas' daughters.

The creatures that are threatening this mountain. Once it becomes clear he can't give me any of those things, his time in this world will be done."

"Just don't lose yourself along the way," Theia replied. She looked between Tessa and me. "Either of you. It can be easy to do once vengeance takes over your mind."

I gave her a tight smile and nodded. "Thank you, Theia."

Taking Tessa's hand, I teleported us to the palace.

APOLLO HAD BEATEN us to the palace and had already given our father the rundown of what had happened when Tessa and the sisters connected to the others. Zeus was less than thrilled that we hadn't gotten more from linking with Mary and the missing sisters, although he tried not to show it. He hadn't said it outright, but the fact that his father and Iapetus had gotten such a lead on him had caused his pride—and ego—to take a hit.

I felt for him, truly. We were in a bad situation all around. Yet at the same time, I hoped it would make him more open to the ideas of the people he trusted to help advise him. The more ideas that were offered, the less receptive he became, which had been causing an added stress over each meeting we had. My mother, who stood beside him now looking uncharacteristically weary, had been trying to temper him as best she could, but even she hadn't been able to convince him to let the gods he'd delegated responsibilities to do their jobs.

"Father, at this juncture, sending out trackers in the three Grecian regions would be the best way to find a solid location for our enemy," Apollo said once we'd finished discussing all we'd learned during Tessa and the sisters' link with the captives. "Which would in turn lead us to the missing Ischyra and the Pleiades."

"I'd also like to send out feelers for a location on the Telchines," Athena added.

"Already on it," Eris interjected. "I've got a few more leads to follow, but I should have an exact location by tomorrow."

Athena clenched her jaw and nodded. "Alright, even better. Once you find them, we'll send forces in to take them out, nip any more involvement in the bud."

Zeus stared down at the map of Earth, his index finger tapping on his chin as he scanned the markers of where the various enemy factions had done damage.

"No," he said finally, shaking his head. He pointed at the various areas where empousa had been causing trouble. "The empousa are inflicting far worse damage. We need them dealt with."

"Father, there are far more of them than the Tels—" Athena began.

"Exactly my point," he said, cutting her off. "His largest force is the one we need to cripple."

"The Ischyra can handle the empousa and crocotta in their own regions," I argued. "With the Telchines' abilities, they're just as destructive as the empousa, if not more so. If they're all in one place, it would be simple to wipe them out within a day. A couple of hours, even."

"Which would then free us up to move onto the other factions with a minimized threat of further poisonings," Athena finished. "A valuable weapon would be taken from our enemy's largest group of soldiers." She threw her hands up in the air. "We've been arguing this for *days,* Father. Why won't you let me carry out the duties you've assigned to me?"

Zeus waved a hand dismissively. "Fine, fine, but I want to hear a more detailed plan for how you plan to deal with the larger forces first," he ordered. "Hecate's witches have pinpointed several regions of more highly-concentrated power use. I want those addressed."

Apollo arched a brow and exchanged a look with Athena, then me. "The plan would be to have the Ischyra handle the larger forces and investigate the areas the witches have highlighted," he said, "while we dismantle their machine by taking our their smaller and *more destructive* forces."

"And that is a plan that's full of holes," Zeus shot back.

"How so?" I asked. "We've all been in touch with the Lead Ischyra and Liaisons in every region, and forces are being shifted around to account for increased threats in Asia, South America, and the South Pacific. What else would you have us do?"

"Something other than worry about a small batch of poisoners while entire forces are terrorizing the rest of the planet!"

"We are!" Athena shook her head, exasperated. "This is what the Ischyra were created for, Father. To handle the malevolent forces that have infested the Earth. They were *your* idea, and now you're putting too little faith in their abilities to rise to the occasion. Apollo, Ares, and I have all doled out orders, and they've been fulfilling them *as intended*. You can only stretch us so thin before we break, Father."

My shoulder's slumped, and I shook my head. Zeus and Athena's arguing over strategy had become cyclical in recent days, causing many of these meetings to lead us absolutely nowhere.

Zeus gave her a challenging glare. "Do not presume to tell me what may or may not be going through my head, Athena. You are not in charge here."

Athena blinked, wide-eyed. "You put Ares and me in charge of all of your forces long ago."

"The Tels are bigger fish, and I'm giving you good intel on where they are and what they're doing," Eris cut in. "Let your soldiers deal with Cronus', and let *us* handle his special forces. Or have you forgotten the abilities and talents of your own children?"

'This isn't helping, Eris,' I warned. *'You need to calm down.'*

'Shut up.'

"No, but you seem to have forgotten your place in this family," Zeus shot back.

"My place?" She stared at him, incredulous as her power rolled off her in heavy waves. "My *place* is as a war god. You and Mother created me for this exact purpose, created Athena for the *exact* damn purpose of advising you, yet you refuse to listen to reason!" She spun to face Tessa. "And if you don't get the *fuck* out of my head with your calming magical bullshit, I will level you, do you hear me?"

I bit back a smile, happy that Tessa had taken it upon herself to try and settle my sister down, something that was almost always an impossible feat.

"Oh, by all means, let's just keep yelling at everyone, then," Tessa snapped. "Absolutely nothing productive is going to happen when you're acting like a child!"

Fuming, Eris took several steps toward her. "Don't you tell me—"

"Eris!" I barked, stepping toward her. "Enough!"

Rolling her eyes, Eris stormed out of the room with a muttered, "come get me when someone gives a shit" before slamming the door behind her.

"Keep tabs on her, Nathaniel," Hera said once she was gone. "Her temper is going to get the best of her one of these days, and she wasn't around for the last war. You're her favorite. She'll listen to you."

Athena let out a quiet snort.

I huffed out a laugh. "Clearly you haven't met her."

"I told you it was a bad idea to bring her and Enyo back in," Athena reminded them, shaking her head.

"Enyo has been quite beneficial during field interrogations," Apollo countered. "So let's not write them off just yet."

"They're not going anywhere, regardless of what anyone thinks, so figure out how to work together without fighting amongst yourselves," Zeus said, shifting his eyes to me and Tessa. "You two need to get downstairs and work on Menoetius some more. If we aren't able to get anything from him in the next day or two, I'm calling an end to it, and we'll explore other options."

"Cornelius and I will reconnect with the Lead Ischyra in the more highly affected regions and go over our plans again," Apollo said. "We'll reassess, see if there's anything that needs to be or *can* be adjusted."

"It's the best plan we've got," I told him. "Have those in the field deal with the more widespread threats while we handle the more localized ones."

Zeus grunted his acknowledgement, then shifted to examine the map of Olympus and the surrounding areas.

Tessa waited a beat before speaking. "And what about Anette and

Andrei?" She glanced at me, then met his gaze evenly. "I'd like to take Anette home."

Zeus' dispassionate gaze flicked to me, then her. Hera shifted so she was facing him, and after a moment of silence, he nodded. "One of you needs to examine her one last time first. As for Andrei..." Zeus frowned and shook his head. "His execution will be held sometime in the near future, but there are more important things to deal with right now than a single traitor who sold himself to some empousa."

"We're certain that's all he is?" Tessa asked.

"Hades and I both dug into his deep subconscious," I told her. "Selfishness and fear were his only motivation."

Apollo sighed. "And the trackers?"

"I've already sent word to Persephone," Zeus replied. "Once they finish the mission they're currently on, she's to send one to that area."

"When will that be?" Tessa asked sharply.

"Two or three days, most likely."

"Two or three *days*?" Tessa shook her head. "They could all be dead by then!"

"And until then," Zeus continued, "keep trying to link with Mary and the sisters again. You may be able to gather more information in the meantime about plans our enemies may have."

Frowning, I exchanged a quick glance with Apollo, who looked almost as suspicious as I did.

As if on cue, I heard Persephone's voice in my head.

'Do you two want me to send two trackers out tonight?' she asked.

'Doing the end run around Zeus?' I asked, amused.

'Clever girl,' Apollo murmured.

'Of course I am,' she said smugly. *'He's being overcautious and a bit conniving, if you ask me. I've got two I can spare that won't hinder me a bit. It still might take a day or two for any results, but just say the word.'*

I looked back at my father, contemplating whether or not my suspicions about his directives were accurate. Based on the perplexed look on Apollo's face, they were.

'Do it.' Apollo said before I could respond.

I shot him a surprised look before answering. *'Agreed. I'm not leaving them to waste away there just so he can potentially get a scrap of information.'*

    'Consider it done.'

16

MARY

My heart sank when I saw where Josh had brought me. After he'd led me from my cell, I'd thought for a few foolish moments that he might've been serious, that he was taking pity on me. He'd said he planned to release me eventually, and a small part of me thought that now might be the time before Cronus and Iapetus could take me away and torture me some more.

As usual, I was wrong.

"You brought me to your fucking bedroom, you sicko!" Stumbling backward, I turned and tried to open the door, but I hit some kind of invisible barrier that caused me to bounce back several steps. I beat against it, searching for a way through, but it didn't give an inch.

"You need to relax," Josh said, nudging me out of the way before striding past me.

Spinning back around, I glared at him. "Easy for you to say!"

Ignoring me, he opened the doors to a large armoire and started digging around, muffling his response when it came.

"I may be a lot of things, Mary, but I'm not a rapist, if that's your concern." He found whatever it was he'd been looking for and shut the doors, tossing a small pile of clothing at me. "I've got other uses for you, though."

I snatched the ball of fabric out of the air and held it up. Jeans, underwear, and a pale blue t-shirt. "What's this?"

He arched a brow and folded his arms. "There's a shower just in there. Go clean yourself up."

I stared at the fresh clothing, my mind bouncing between jumping at the chance to be clean and demanding he let the sisters have the same opportunity.

"Why can't you let the sisters do the same? They've been here longer than me. It's not fair." I met his eyes, then examined the clothes he'd given me more closely. "Hang on...these are mine. Where—"

He sat down at the foot of the bed, a dark wood monstrosity that would've taken up my entire dorm, then leaned back on his hands. "I made a run back to Renville when you arrived," he explained. "I figured you might need a change of clothes eventually, and your guardians still haven't gotten around to getting rid of your old things."

"Were my guardians—"

He grinned. "Chris and Alan were home. They were really excited to see me. I think it reminded them of old times, you know?"

My heart began to thump wildly. "You didn't hurt them, did you?"

His eyes widened. "Of course not. Why would I?"

I closed my eyes and clutched the clothes to my chest. "Can you please stop doing that?"

"Doing what?"

I opened my eyes and looked at him. "Sounding like the guy I thought was one of my closest friends."

He frowned. "I was, though."

"No, you were a deceitful twat," I snapped. "Did you even care about Leila? Or was she in on your scheme, too?"

"I told you that you'd get to ask your questions," he replied, all emotion evaporating from his tone. The back-and-forth between nice guy and evil douche was starting to give me whiplash. "Go shower. We can talk when you're not stinking up my room. Everything you need will be in there."

With a frustrated growl, I stormed into the bathroom, slamming and locking the door behind me. Not that it would do any good, considering he could apparently just make doors dissolve at will.

When I was alone, I leaned against the door and closed my eyes as I tried to settle my nerves. Whatever the reason he'd brought me here, it wasn't to be nice.

He's not your friend. Focus on getting information.

Opening my eyes, I looked around the room. The bathroom was tiled in warm reds and browns, with smooth marble on the floor and tiles of varying shapes and sizes making up the walls. The shower was in the shape of a square in the center of the room with half a dozen shower heads aimed in all directions. Various bottles and a wide-tooth comb were lined up on a shelf inside, and, thank the gods, a toothbrush and toothpaste sat on the edge of the counter.

Two large, wide-silled, arched windows were cut into the far wall. I bit my lip, considering what the ramifications might be if I attempted—or succeeded—escape. The sisters would be left behind, which didn't quite sit right with me, but I couldn't make this about feelings. If any of the three of them were given the chance, I wouldn't begrudge them if they took the opportunity to escape. I'd probably be more pissed off if they *didn't* try.

Silently, I wandered toward the windows, curious about their construction. They were a single panel of glass that ran the entire length of the frame. I didn't see any latch or a means of opening, so if I wanted to attempt to break free, I'd have to break the glass.

Glancing around the room, I saw a large planter in the corner that might do the trick.

I leaned forward until my forehead was pressed against the glass and looked down. What I saw caused my heart to sink.

We were about four stories off the ground, which was a flat, rocky expanse that stretched out a few hundred feet where it began a gradual decline onto the shoreline of what looked like a big lake. I could just make out some kind of structure in the distance, tall and thin. Some sort of lighthouse or radio tower, maybe.

Doing a quick risk-benefit analysis on a jump through the window—assuming I could even break it—I reluctantly acknowledged that, while the fall wouldn't kill me, it might break some bones, which for an Ischyra, would take a few hours to heal. That was going with the assumption my healing powers were anywhere near their normal levels.

Narrowing my eyes, I leaned against the window and tried to see if there were any ledges along the outside wall I could use to climb down. There were a few windows, but I'd seen enough movies and read enough books to know I'd probably end up getting caught and dragged through one of them.

At this point, Josh had been the only one of my captors who'd even hinted that he didn't plan to hurt me. I couldn't guarantee that about anyone who might catch me trying to make a break for it.

The enemy you know, right?

I shoved away all thoughts of how freaking bizarre this was, then set my clothes down on the counter by the stone vessel sink and turned on the shower. It became hot almost instantly, and the feel of it on my hand when I tested it vaporized any thoughts that didn't involve being clean. I stripped out of my clothes and left them in a filthy pile on the floor, not really caring about the etiquette of cleaning up after myself, considering the circumstances.

I took a good half hour in the shower, partly because the water felt amazing, partly because I wanted to stall and hopefully give my power more time to regenerate, and also because my long, wavy hair was bordering on matted at this point,

But mainly because I was hoping it would piss Josh off.

I took my time drying off, slathering on lotion, getting dressed, and drying my hair before finally leaving.

Maybe immortality *hadn't* boosted my maturity as much as I'd thought.

"That's better!" Josh said with a grin when I exited the bathroom.

"Care to tell me why you're being so generous?" I asked, folding my arms.

He jumped up off the bed and grinned. "Well, you see, I thought you might want to hear sooner rather than later that I plan on releasing you in the next few days, returning you to Olympus."

My heart thundered against my ribs, but I willed it to settle down because I knew damn well this was too good to be true.

"Why?" I asked calmly. "And will I be alive when you do?"

"Why not? And yes, you will be alive and in one piece." He glanced toward a table where a tray had appeared, laden down with food and a pitcher of water with some type of leaves floating in it. "Go on, eat something."

"I'm not hungry." *And I don't trust anything you'd feed me.*

"I know you're not hungry, but you've always liked to comfort-eat, so—"

"Okay, enough!" I held up my hands and shook my head. "Enough with the 'we used to be best buds' shit, seriously. I'll drink your goddamn water if it'll get you to stop."

Narrowing his eyes, he pursed his lips and nodded. "Fair enough."

With shaking hands, I poured myself a glass of water, which honestly sounded pretty amazing right then. As I lifted the glass to my lips, trying to smell if there was anything off about it, there was a knock at the door.

"Come in," Josh called absently as he plucked a grape from one of the large, crystal bowls on the table.

The door opened, and Cronus walked in, followed by Iapetus. Both froze in their tracks when they saw me.

Cronus' eyes turned to slits of fury. "And here I thought the guards were lying," he said, seething. "Why is she out of her cell?"

Josh glanced at him, then popped the grape in his mouth and went about pouring himself a glass of wine. "I had need of her," he said absently. "Is there something I can help you with?"

I stayed frozen in place, clutching my glass and trying not to draw any more attention to my presence.

Cronus stalked forward, his death stare focused solely on Josh. I flicked a glance at Iapetus and saw his eyes were trained on me, which had me taking an involuntary step back.

Josh took a small sip of wine, then turned to face Cronus and looked at him expectantly.

Wordlessly, Cronus knocked the glass from Josh's hands, scattering wine and bits of glass across the floor. "What do you think you're doing?" he growled.

Josh looked down at the shattered remains of his glass that were now scattered across the floor with a curious expression, then a familiar, insolent look crossed his face. "I told you, I had need of her."

"And you didn't think to inform us before removing a prisoner from her cell?" Iapetus asked, not taking his sharp eyes off me. "And *cleaning* her? That's highly imprudent."

"I wasn't aware your kind had the type of *needs* she might fulfill," Cronus bit out.

I swallowed back a gulp, then pressed my hand to my stomach, feeling nauseous at his insinuation.

A small smile curved the corners of Josh's mouth, and his eyes danced. "And *I* wasn't aware you expected a report of my comings and goings," he said, "but if you'd like to insist, then by all means, ask away."

A small part of me felt bad for Josh, who seemed to suddenly take on some of my own stubbornness. The other part of me hoped the three of them would end up fighting each other and forget about me entirely.

Cronus took another step toward him, his bulk taking up nearly double the space of Josh's body. Josh's face remained expressionless as he slid his hands in his pockets.

"Prisoners stay in their cells," Cronus growled. "There are no exceptions to this rule."

Josh lifted his eyebrows. "Ah, is that one of those rules you two are so fond of?" He frowned in consideration, then nodded. "Apologies. I must've missed that one."

"Insolence helps no one," Iapetus said quietly. "I think you'd do well to remember that."

"Would I?" Josh smirked, his expression almost... indulgent. "Alright, then. I will refrain from any further *insolence,* and the prisoner will be returned to her cell once I'm done with her."

"I hope you aren't planning on taking her power for yourself," Cronus said threateningly.

Josh surprised us all by bursting out in laughter.

"What in *all* the realms would I need her power for?" Bracing his hand on the back of a chair, he shook his head, struggling to get his laughter under control. "Have you forgotten—"

"We've forgotten nothing!" Cronus snapped. He jabbed a finger into Josh's chest, shoving him back a few feet. "You seem to have forgotten the rules that have been set in place for a reason!"

Josh glanced down at the spot where Cronus had touched him, then frowned when he met his eyes. The amused expression on his face vanished. "I would appreciate it if you didn't touch me, Cronus. Your hands are quite filthy."

My eyes widened, and I took a step back, not wanting to be anywhere near the middle of a fight between a Titan and... whatever Josh was. Evil Josh I could wrap my head around, possibly even logic out his actions, but the guy in front of me was slowly spiraling into batshit-crazy territory.

"My hands—" With a roar, Cronus wrapped a thick hand around Josh's throat, then squeezed. "Do not *ever* presume you can speak to me like that again. I don't give a damn who you think you are."

Josh smirked, not seeming the least bit concerned that Cronus was dangling him a good foot off the floor. "Or what?" He angled his head to the side. Immediately, Cronus dropped him, his expression stunned. Straightening his jacket, Josh stared up at him, unflinching. "I asked you a question. Or. What?"

"I suppose you're wishing he'd kept you in your cell now, aren't you?"

I jumped at the sound of Iapetus' slithery voice in my ear and scrambled to get away from him as Josh and Cronus continued their dick-measuring.

I kept backing away, trying to put the table—or at least a chair—between us. "St-stay away from me."

"What will you do?" he sneered, matching my steps. "Sic my weak-minded daughter on me? Please do, I'd love to get to know how Hades' plaything has evolved over the years."

"Iapetus!" Cronus barked.

Annoyance and fury flashed in Iapetus' eyes as he reluctantly turned away from me. "What?"

"Let's go." Without bothering to wait, Cronus stormed out of the room.

With one last glare in Josh's direction, Iapetus slunk from the room after his master, slamming the door so hard it shook the walls.

Narrowing my eyes, I looked at Josh.

"What is it now?" he snapped.

I shook my head, unsure whether I should be scared or relieved if my sudden realization was on point. "What just happened?" I asked cautiously.

He sat down and pulled the bowl of grapes toward him, then began methodically plucking them from their stems. "They don't like when things go outside the norm." He shrugged and the corners of his mouth tilted up in amusement. "Removing you from your cell and allowing you to shower does just that."

I sucked my lower lip through my teeth and narrowed my eyes. Sitting down in the chair furthest from him, I slowly slid a bowl of strawberries my way and began pulling off the leaves. "You told me you would give me answers, right?"

He grunted in response.

When he didn't say any more, I rolled my eyes. "Are you planning on letting me ask questions, or are you just going to sit there and sulk now that you got your wrist slapped?"

He lifted his eyes to mine, and it took every ounce of willpower not to shrink back from what I saw. His eyes—once a warm brown—had gone black.

Clearing my throat, I set down the strawberry I'd just picked up and held his stare. "Well?"

He angled his head to the side, the motion more predatory than I'd seen from him this last week, and appraised me, his dark eyes running over my face. I felt the unmistakable pressure of magic on my mind. Then he nodded.

"Alright, Mary. I'll tell you all you want to know."

I arched a brow, trying not to show my excitement as I pondered what to ask first. I'd thought my first question would be about our life in Renville, but, surprising myself, my first question addressed Anette.

"Why Anette?" I asked. "Why do a mind link with my roommate and not Tessa's?"

"Simple." He popped another grape in his mouth and chewed, then swallowed. "Tessa is an incredibly powerful Titaness. If I'd been linked to her roommate's mind, it's quite probable Tessa would've caught it. So, once Andrei informed his empousa contact that Anette had become close with you and Tessa, I chose her. Tessa didn't spend enough time with her to notice something like that, and you don't have the ability."

"Okay...um, then why Andrei? He seemed so gung-ho about being a fighter when we first arrived in Olympia."

He shrugged and took another grape, chewing thoughtfully. Grinning, he pointed down at the half-empty bowl. "These are delicious. You really should try them."

I arched a brow. "They're grapes. I've had them before."

He made a small "huh" sound in the back of his throat. "Andrei was a lazy pawn. He provided information in exchange for safety, even though all he needed to do to guarantee his safety was fight. Instead, he chose to be protected. A soldier gifted with the powers of the *gods*, and he wanted to be coddled." He clicked his tongue. "It's sinful."

"So that was it? He was convenient?"

"Essentially. And now he'll be nice and safe tucked away in the Underworld." He frowned, considering. "Assuming Hades allows an easy crossing. He tends to get a bit fussy when it comes to our Tessa, doesn't he?"

I snorted. Hades and fussy were two things I would never put in the same sentence.

"I considered Nathaniel, you know," he said with a sly smile. "I thought about infiltrating his mind. When I saw him at school that second time, I could tell he'd be around Tessa just enough to allow me to keep tabs." He sighed and shook his head. "I could feel his intended deceit, though, so I suppose he should be considered quite lucky, hmm?"

"Uh huh. Yeah. Lucky him." *Asshole.* "So you knew who Tessa really was before she even arrived on Olympus. How? Why didn't Hecate's spell work on you? Are you like Menoetius?"

He let out an offended huff. "I'm nothing like that mutt. No, I've been keeping tabs on Tessa her entire life."

"Her entire *life?*" My brain struggled to wrap itself around that bit of information. "You only moved to Renville a few years ago!"

"Yes, well, it eventually became easier to insert myself directly into her life instead of continuing to watch from the outside." He gestured toward himself. "A good-looking teenage male accomplished that quite easily."

I rubbed my fingers over my eyes and shook my head. "Why date Leila, then? Why not go right for Tessa?"

He shrugged and began to chew on another grape. "Too easy. Easy is boring."

"Can't have that," I muttered. "That still doesn't tell me why Hecate's mind-wipe spell thingy didn't work on you."

His smile turned smug, and he leaned forward, resting his elbows on the table. "Hecate's spell didn't work on me because *spells* don't work on me. I see them for exactly what they are. A taint on everything they touch."

"But you're just a witch. How are you more powerful than the leader of *all* the witches?"

This time, the smile that curved his lips made my blood run cold. "I guess you've still got a lot to learn about me, huh?"

I cast my eyes toward the door Cronus and Iapetus had just gone through, then looked back at Josh.

"I guess I do."

17

TESSA

As Nate, Apollo, and I made our way through the halls of the palace toward the dungeons, I continued to stew over Zeus' stubbornness. I understood the need to focus on larger factions, but there was no reason that I could see to justify not taking out the Telchines. It was a no-brainer.

"He's being ridiculous," I grumbled. "If what Eris said about the Tels is right, it would take no time at all to take them out."

"They're cocky by nature," Nate agreed. "They certainly wouldn't expect it."

"He's wasting time and doing a terrifically awful job of hiding the real reason he doesn't want them found just yet." A fact which still had me fuming so badly that I'd all but lost my words back in the war room.

"You're not wrong," Apollo muttered.

I gave him a surprised look. "Did the golden boy just contradict something our almighty ruler said?" I asked, raising a brow.

"No, he just stated the obvious," Apollo snapped. His temper had been fraying recently, far surpassing his normal snark, but this was the first time I'd heard him speak so directly against something his father said.

"Then go back and talk to him," Nate said. Then, to me, he added, *'Persephone is already sending out her trackers, so try not to worry too much.'*

I let out a quiet breath, thankful that in this instance, they'd opted to avoid further arguing and go around Zeus' orders.

"No, I've got other things to deal with," Apollo said, coming to a stop near the door to the dungeon. "Are you going to question Menoetius now or later?"

"Tomorrow," Nate said. "We need to work out a better plan for him. Just going in and picking at his shield is taking too long."

Apollo nodded absently. "Agreed." He looked at me. "Good luck with Anette, Tessa. I hope she hasn't become too damaged in her time here."

I stared at him, momentarily speechless. "Apollo... that's so... nice."

He narrowed his eyes. "Don't get used to it."

I waited until Apollo had gone, then put my hand in Nate's. I was beyond thrilled that Zeus had finally acquiesced in regards to Anette, but even though we were currently the bearers of good news, I couldn't help the wariness I felt as we walked toward her cell. She was essentially in this place because of me. I might not have thrown her in jail, but the only reason she'd been linked to Josh in the first place was to spy on me.

Nate brushed a hand down my spine and kissed my temple, a quiet reassurance that I wasn't the one to blame here. *'I'll wait out here. Call me when you're ready.'*

With a sigh, I placed my hand on the door and waited for my power to unlock it, then stuffed my guilt back into the same corner as everything else I'd deal with later.

After a few seconds, the lock clicked, and I nudged the door open.

"Anette?" I poked my head in, not wanting to startle her. "It's Tessa."

I pushed the door open the rest of the way, revealing the tiny cell she'd been put in that held nothing but a thin mattress on top of a straw-covered stone floor. It was more than what Menoetius had been given, but just barely, which infuriated me further. *She* hadn't done anything wrong, yet here she was being treated nearly as badly as the Titan who wanted to bring down the whole damn mountain.

Anette was crouched in the corner with her arms wrapped tightly around her knees. Her pretty blond hair hung limp around her shoulders, no sign of the bouncing braids she normally wore. I'd snuck her a change of clothes when I visited earlier in the week, once it became apparent Zeus wasn't going to release her right away, so at the very least, she wasn't stuck in the training uniform she'd been in when they questioned her. As it was, her clothes were still filthy.

She looked nothing like the peppy blond I'd met back when we first arrived on Olympus. This girl... she was beaten down. There were no bright smiles or laughing eyes, only a morose expression that told me she'd been, or was on the verge of being, broken.

Her eyes shifted toward the door at the sound of my voice, and the corners of her mouth twitched. "Tessa." Her voice was rough from disuse, her soft Norwegian accent somehow thicker than it had been. "I was wondering if you would come back."

I knelt down in front of her and put a hand to her cheek. "How are you doing, Anette? I've been trying hard to get you out of here, but Zeus is being so stubborn."

She covered my hand with hers. "It is alright. I do not blame him for keeping me here."

I curled my fingers in hers. "I do." I flicked my gaze toward the door. "I'm going to get you out, okay?"

"I appreciate that, Tessa, truly, but—"

"We convinced Zeus to release you," I told her. "I just need you to let me do something, first. I have to examine your mind one more time. Is that okay?"

She gave me a wary look and sidestepped my question. "What happened at the arena? I heard someone say something about an attack, but no one will give me details."

"There was an attack," I told her. "I'll give you all the details once you're released. You don't need to be dealing with that in here."

She nodded, then leaned her head against the wall and stared at the floor. "They are all dead, aren't they?"

I hesitated before responding, but she took that as confirmation.

"Is it because of me? Because of what... happened to me?"

I gripped her hand tighter and met her gaze unflinchingly. "No. Unequivocally, *no*. They were here for me. Whether that witch had been linked to you or not, they would've come for me. None of this is on you, Anette."

Her lips gave another twitch, as though she might smile. "That is nice of you to say, Tessa."

I brushed a hand over her hair and tried to give her a convincing smile. "It's the truth. Believe that, please. Now, will you let Nate and me examine you, one last time?"

As if on cue, Nate stepped into the room. She looked back and forth between us, her eyes wide, before settling on me. "It hurt last time," she whispered.

Nate crouched down beside me, and I watched her shrink away from him. "I'm sorry about that, Anette. If there had been another way... but when a link has taken hold like that one had..."

Anette straightened her back and nodded, doing her best to hold her chin high while not looking fearful of him. "I understand."

She licked her lips and fiddled with her fingers in her lap. After a moment, she wiped her tear-streaked cheeks with the back of her hand and nodded as hope sparked in her eyes. "Alright. Do what you need to do. I have nothing to hide, and I don't think I can bear this place any longer."

Tightening my fingers on hers, I shifted so I was sitting on the floor in front of her. "Just focus on me, okay?"

"Just you?" she asked suddenly, casting a furtive glance at Nate.

He nodded. "Just Tessa."

Closing my eyes, I reached out for her mind. Her thoughts were a bit scattered, mussed by her fear, confusion, and anticipation. I sifted through the emotions until I found the marks left behind by the mind link Josh had done on her. Nate had described deep, magical gouges in her mind where the attachment had been, but now, there was hardly a shadow. It was clear the link had been released, and the remnants were fading away. There was no sign of another presence, malicious or otherwise, anywhere.

As soon as I felt confident there was no lingering magic, I released her mind, then I squeezed her hands and smiled. "Alright, then. Let's get you home."

With that, she burst into tears. She fell against me, her entire body shaking in my arms as she cried. After a few moments, I gently nudged her back. "Are you alright to come stay at Nate's for a bit until we figure out more permanent arrangements? Yana is there, too."

She swallowed audibly, then nodded. "Yes, I—for now, yes, that will be fine."

Standing, I pulled her to her feet and looped my arm around her waist as Nate began to lead us away from her cell.

"We'll get Hecate up to put a block on your mind if you want," I told Anette as we led her up the stairs from the dungeon. "If it'll make you feel safer in your own head."

Her steps faltered, and she shook her head jerkily. "No, no. I do not want anything like that. If you need to look into my mind now and then to confirm nothing is wrong, that is fine, but I cannot have something so... permanent."

I patted her hand. "It's fine, Anette, really. We understand."

Nate looked like he wanted to argue, but I silenced him with a look. Not forcing the issue wasn't the wisest decision, I knew that, but we also weren't planning on letting her out of our sight anytime soon. Someone would always be with her, and she'd be getting checked on multiple times a day if need be. Worst case scenario, it'd be easy enough to keep the bulk of any important information away from her.

'We can put her on research duty with Chiron and Yana,' Nate said. 'It'll keep her busy and her mind off of what's happened.'

'Good call. I'll bring it up in the morning.'

Compared to the cells, the upper levels of the palace practically glowed. Anette squinted against the bright light when we emerged through the dungeon door. Having lived in the dungeons for the last two weeks, I imagined it must've been blinding for her.

She looked around furtively, her hands gripping my arm tighter as we walked.

Nate placed a hand on her shoulder, then let it drop when she flinched. "No one is coming," he whispered. "We'll teleport back to my house once we're outside."

Anette smiled up at him gratefully. "Thank you."

I half expected Zeus to pop up with some final words of warning to Anette, but surprisingly, we made it through the rear door of the palace unobstructed. As soon as we touched the soft grass, we teleported back to Nate's.

When we landed on the front lawn, Anette sucked in a breath and dropped to the ground, her fingers curling in the thick grass. Silently, she leaned forward until her forehead was touching the ground, then her shoulders started to shake.

'Go get Yana,' I told Nate. With a nod, he jogged up the front steps. As I waited, I crouched down beside Anette and placed a hand on her back.

"Anette, it's okay," I murmured. "You're out now. It's just us."

My words seemed to have the opposite of my intended effect, causing her to sob harder rather than settle down.

I felt Yana come to a stop beside me, then her hand joined mine as we tried to soothe Anette. Quietly, Yana began to murmur to Anette in Romanian, the words foreign to me but seeming to comfort her.

'Does she speak Romanian?' I asked. Yana gave me a brief nod.

'She speaks several languages. Six, I believe.'

I rocked back on my heels, a bit surprised I didn't know that about her.

Wordlessly, Yana scooped Anette up in her arms and carried her up the steps as I trailed slowly behind.

'Put her in the room next to yours,' I told Yana. *'It's where I put her stuff the other day.'*

Nate must've closed himself off in our room, because he was

nowhere to be seen as I walked through the house toward the guest rooms. When I got to the one that had remained empty in recent weeks, I saw that Yana had deposited Anette on the stone tile floor of the connecting bathroom. She ran a soothing hand down her back and continued to whisper to her.

"Anette?" I asked quietly. "Is there anything specific you'd like to change into? Yana and I brought all of your stuff from the dorms."

Anette startled a bit at my approach, so I slowed my steps. She seemed to be far warier now that she was out of the dungeon than when she'd been locked in her cell.

Yana said something else in Romanian, and I suddenly found myself wishing I could absorb some type of power that would let me understand all languages. Then again, it seemed like privacy was the main reason Yana had chosen a foreign language, so it was probably for the best.

'I am just telling her that she does not need to be scared here, but I think being around Nate...'

'Yeah. I get it.' This was exactly what Nate had been afraid of when he agreed to help with these things. I knew there was no possible way I could reassure Anette of her safety without making it seem like I was minimizing his actions or her fear. *'Just... keep trying to reassure her. She'll get it in time, but I think it'll be easier for her to adjust if she's hearing it from you and not me.'* Not from the lover of the god who'd just interrogated her a week ago. Her interrogation hadn't been much more than a sift through her mind, because all he could see were the remnants of the mind link, but I imagined it would've been traumatic, regardless. It was nothing compared to what he'd done to Andrei, but considering she'd witnessed Andrei's questioning, I didn't think that mattered all that much.

A thought occurred to me then. *'Hey, do you think it might help if I brought my guardians up? Analise might be a bit more soothing than me right now.'*

'Yes, I think that would be a good idea,' Yana replied.

I dragged Anette's suitcase out from under the bed and unzipped it, then pulled out some pajamas, a change of underwear, and some fuzzy pink socks that were so incredibly Anette it made me smile. I set them on the bathroom sink along with her bag of toiletries, then turned and walked out, leaving Yana with the task of helping her shower and dress.

"Tessa?"

I turned when I heard Anette call me just as I'd opened the door to leave.

"Yes?"

"Thank you."

I found Nate on the front porch, sitting on the steps and staring silently up the mountain. He wasn't stoic by nature, nor did he wallow in self-pity, but right then, the only emotion I felt pulsing off of him was misery.

Sitting down next to him, I wrapped my arms around his waist and leaned against his chest, snuggling closer when he pulled his arm out from between us and slid it around my shoulders.

"Anette settled?" he asked quietly.

"Yeah," I replied, my words muffled by the fabric of his shirt. "Yana's helping her."

He gave a small hum of acknowledgement.

"Nate?"

"Hmm?"

"You know this isn't your fault, right?"

"Whose fault is it, then?" he murmured, pulling back and leaning against the railing so he was facing me, leaving one hand resting on my thigh. "I'm the one who sifted through her head. Regardless of the *why*, I will always be that person to her." He scrubbed his hand over his face in annoyance. "This is exactly why I didn't want you to do any inquisitions. You should never be put in the position I'm in right now."

"Nate—"

"Tessa, there is quite literally nothing you can do to change the way I feel about this." I tried not to flinch at the harshness in his tone. "I did what I had to do in order to find out who was spying on you and on this mountain, but Anette is a good person." He shook his head and looked back out toward the forest. "She doesn't deserve to feel the way she does right now."

I pursed my lips, choosing my next words as carefully as I could. A similar guilt had plagued me ever since the attack, and I knew that I would one day be put in a position where I would have to do things I might normally judge others for. I also knew that most of us—god and Ischyra alike—were probably going to do things we never would've considered possible under normal circumstances.

"Nate... are you more upset that you had to look through her mind, or that Zeus had you put her in the dungeon afterward?"

"Both." He leaned forward and rested his elbows on his knees, pressing his thumbs to his temples. "I realize she was better off being held for her own safety. We didn't know whether or not whoever she'd been linked to would return, and it was best she be kept sequestered so the link could fade. Logically, I know that. But this..." He waved his hand in the direction of the house. "I *know* these things will always need to be done, but it doesn't change the fact that I feel like utter shit when I'm forced into the head of a good and innocent person. This is why I left Olympus in the first place. "

I stared down at my hands and shook my head. "And now you're back."

"No." He leaned forward and took my hands. "Don't you dare put any blame on yourself. I knew there was a possibility that Zeus would have me take up my old position once this rebellion started. Knowing that, I chose to stay here." He lifted my hands to his lips and kissed them. "My place is with you. Don't ever doubt that. Regardless of how conflicted I might feel, I plan to defend this mountain however I can."

I squeezed his hands and nodded. "I'm sorry, I know. I just hate seeing you like this."

He wrapped an arm around my shoulders and pulled me against him. "It comes with the territory, love. It's not the first time I'll have to do this, and it certainly won't be the last. Just let me have a few minutes to wallow, alright?"

I could hear the rueful smile in his words and laughed. "We're both pretty damn good at that, aren't we?"

"That's for sure," he murmured. He rested his forehead against mine and closed his eyes. "I'll be alright, Tessa."

He wrapped his arms around my waist and pulled me close, pressing his face to my shoulder. I kissed his temple, then rested my head against his. No matter how much I tried to comfort him or he, me, there would never be a point where either of us felt unburdened by the things we had to do in order to win this war. Whether the pain we inflicted was well-deserved or not, it would still take a toll because the knowledge that we *could* inflict that type of pain was what hurt.

Neither of us were cruel people, but the fact that we could demonstrate cruelty when necessary was damaging in and of itself. He'd done it before and walked away, but it had taken a long time for him to accept the fact that the god who'd caused so much pain all those years ago wasn't the god he was today, the one who held me right now.

The hand on my waist slipped under the hem of my shirt and came to rest on the small of my back. When his skin made contact with mine, the tension in our bodies melted away. I tightened my arms around him, then called on Dionysus' calming magic.

"It'll be okay, Nate," I whispered.

He nodded, then kissed my neck, relaxing a bit as my power flowed into him. "I know."

18

TESSA

Nate and I sat on the porch for a little while longer before I finally explained my plan to bring Analise up to help Anette. He agreed to go down to the inn with me and bring them both fully up to speed, so a short while later, we'd teleported down to see them. Not surprisingly, I got a mild lecture from them both for not coming to them sooner.

"I know you're busy up here, Tessa, but having a couple of guardians, even if we aren't hers, present when she was released is something you should've considered before going to get her," Analise chastised as we waited for John to tug on his shoes. "Why on Earth would you think shoving her into a house with the god who questioned her would be helpful?" She put her hands on her hips and looked right at Nate. "And for someone with so much experience with humans *and* Ischyra, *you* certainly should have known better."

My eyebrows shot up when she turned her mom voice on Nate, and I nearly laughed when I saw his cheeks flame under her verbal finger-wag. John stood beside her, an amused grin on his face.

"I won't argue with you there," Nate said after a moment of stunned silence.

Analise immediately turned her ire back to me. "And *Josh?* How could you not tell us? You know what? Never mind." She threw up her hands in defeat. "I'm just going to chalk it up to a need-to-know situation. Let's go."

I took her hand while Nate put a hand on John's shoulder, then we teleported them both up to his cabin.

"Come on in, I'll show you where they are," I told her as we ascended the steps.

"I think Nate and I'll wait out here," John said, sliding his hands into his jeans pockets. "This seems like a girl thing if I'm not mistaken."

I flashed him a quick smile. "Good call."

I led Analise through the house toward Anette's room, then knocked quietly before opening the door.

"Hey, Anette?" I stepped inside and found her and Yana sitting on the bed talking quietly. She looked up at me and gave me a questioning, hesitant look.

I gestured over my shoulder. "There's someone here I wanted to introduce you to," I told her, motioning Analise forward. "This is Analise, my guardian. I thought, well..."

Yana gave me a small smile as Analise stepped toward the bed, then stood and held out a hand.

"Hello, Mrs. Avery. I am Mariana, but everyone calls me Yana. I was Tessa's roommate when we first came to Olympus."

Analise smiled warmly and took Yana's offered hand. "It's wonderful to meet you, Yana. Please call me Analise. Tessa told us so much about you."

Slowly, Anette stood on the opposite side of the bed and wiped her eyes, then wrapped her arms around herself. Her hair was still wet and tangled from the shower and hung over her shoulders, leaving wet spots on the front of her pajama shirt. Even disheveled, she looked a dozen times better than she had just a short while ago. Her pep, the thing that had initially caused Mary to want to shun her as a roommate, was still entirely absent, though.

Her eyes darted back and forth between me, Yana, and Analise before settling on me. Her chin tilted up a fraction of an inch as she inhaled slowly. I did a quick perusal of her thoughts, hoping to get an idea of where her mind was. Her thoughts and emotions fought against each other, some telling her she was safe, others reminding her that she was in the home of the god who'd essentially had her imprisoned.

I stepped toward her and took her hands. "I know how hard this must be for you, being here in Nate's house," I whispered. "I get it, I really do, and I want you to know you're safe here—to believe it." I inclined my head toward Analise. "I may not be able to help you deal with all of this, but Analise was the best mother I ever could've asked for." I sighed. "If it was in my power to get yours for you..."

She squeezed my hands and gave me a tight smile, but she couldn't hide the misery that still filled her eyes. "I know, and I appreciate this, truly. Getting me out of that dungeon... I can't thank you enough."

"There's no need. Just let Analise mother you a bit. She's good at it," I said with a grin.

The ghost of a real smile flashed across her face. "I will be alright, Tessa, I promise. Deep inside, I know Nate is not a bad man."

"Don't feel like you have to rush into getting back to normal," I told her. "And listen, if you'd rather we set you up in the village—"

"No!" Her grip tightened around my fingers, and her eyes widened. "No, I will stay here with you and Yana. These feelings... they will pass." She shook her head and took a deep breath. "But I can't be alone right now. Please, I promise—"

"Stop!" I whispered fervently. "You have *nothing* to apologize for. You're welcome here for as long as you want. I just wanted you to know that there are other options." Smiling, I pulled her into a fierce hug. "You've got us, Anette. We're not going anywhere."

I felt Analise come up beside me, so I stepped aside and let them get acquainted. Yana followed me out into the hall and closed the door behind her.

"How much do you think I should tell her?" she asked, her voice a whisper. "I do not know what she knows about the attack or about Mary..."

I blew out a breath and leaned back against the wall. So much had happened since Anette had been locked away, enough that would set anyone's head spinning. For someone in her state of mind...

"I think..." I shook my head. "I think honesty might be the best policy right now, but in small doses. Don't dump it all on her at once, and if you want to leave some of it to me, that's fine, too." I met her eyes. "And for now, let's keep it to things that are mostly general or common knowledge."

Yana nodded slowly, understanding my implication. "I will just answer her questions for now. Anything major, I will come find you."

"Sounds good," I said, straightening. "I'm going to go catch up with John." I rubbed at my eyes, suddenly feeling exhausted. "Yana, I'm sorry we couldn't keep your guardians up here."

She shrugged. "I know if you were able, you would have. Just having that short bit of time with them was more than I could have hoped for. I will see them again soon, I am sure."

I smiled, hoping that was true. There was no way I could guarantee that one way or the other, but I knew I would do all I could to make sure she saw them again.

I found John and Nate on the porch, talking quietly. When I emerged through the front door, they stopped and looked at me expectantly.

"How's it going?" John asked.

I shrugged and dropped down in Nate's lap, his arms automatically looping around my waist. "We'll see, I guess. Anette's still really shaken up, but Analise is good with stuff like this, so I think she might be able to help."

John patted my knee, then leaned back in his chair and rested his feet on the porch railing, ankles crossed. "That she is."

"John just brought up something that we may want to broach with Zeus," Nate said. "He's suggested approaching the guardians for additional forces on Earth."

My eyes widened and I looked over at John. "Would the Elders do that? Put you guys in the field?"

He shrugged. "Why not? They handpick every guardian they put to work, developed the foundations of our training themselves. We might be human, but the guardians are essentially their creations."

I leaned back against Nate and chewed my lip. There were reasons Olympus hadn't brought guardians on before, the main one being they were mortal. There were more than fifty thousand immortal soldiers across the globe in addition to thousands of deities and demigods. Each and every one of them held supernatural powers that, in most cases, far surpassed the capabilities of human weapons. We protected the humans from the supernatural creatures who wished to harm them, and in exchange, centuries ago, Zeus and the other Elders had made an agreement with humans that they would act as guardians to fledgling Ischyra, train them, raise them as their own children, while Olympus would focus on protecting the realms. Olympus wouldn't have left the humans to suffer if they'd refused the agreement, but the fact that human guardians meant fewer Ischyra relegated to training duty was sufficient incentive. So from then on, the Elders chose the children who would become guardians, just as they chose which orphans became Ischyra.

And now John was suggesting they go back on that agreement, which, despite how much sense it made, bothered me to no end.

I didn't want my guardians put into a war where the main forces they would face would be supernaturals. No matter how hard I tried to view it optimistically, I could see no outcome where they would survive.

"I don't know," I said slowly, trying to conceal my negativity. "Wouldn't they have already asked if they wanted that?"

"Probably, but it doesn't hurt to ask," Nate replied. "My guess is that Zeus will want to keep them strictly in their current roles of training future Ischyra and not risk losing them to war, but it's certainly worth considering."

I looked at John, who appeared just as strong and fit as he had the day I'd left, not that I would've expected any different. His brown hair showed a bit of gray at the temples, but if anything, it made him look stronger, more intimidating.

But he was human, which meant breakable in the most permanent sense. There were no do-overs like there were for Ischyra or
deities. When their necks snapped, they were gone from this world
forever. Wasn't that the kind of thing I was supposed to help protect
against? Wasn't that what he'd raised me to protect?

"I know that look, Tessa Lynn, and I want you to stop whatever it
is you're thinking," John said sternly. "This may be your mountain,
but that out there is my world," he said, pointing off in the distance.
"If I can do something to help protect it, I will." He arched a brow.
"And let's not forget who trained you."

I grinned and held up my hands in defeat, even as I tried to cover
up my fear of John and Analise fighting the things that were trying to
destroy humans.

He narrowed his eyes and gave me an appraising look. "Speaking
of which... when was the last time you did any type of physical
training?"

I blew out a breath. "I fought some empousa last week. Does that
count?"

"That depends. How'd you do?"

Nate snorted, then clapped a hand over his mouth when I glared
at him.

John gave me an amused look. "That bad?"

I rolled my eyes. "No, actually. I kicked ass."

"What was it Apollo said?" Nate mused, tapping his finger to his
chin. "'You look like something Charybdis regurgitated.'"

I smacked his chest with the back of my hand and he caught it,
laughing. "So I got a bit messy," I muttered. "Like you never got hit
with blood spatter."

John shook his head. "I taught you to have better reflexes than
that, Tessa. Once you slice, you should be gone before blood has time
to spray."

"Yeah, well, I had a lot on my mind at the time," I said with a huff.
John would never, not in a million years, show sympathy for things
like getting doused in blood or even injured in a fight if it was due to
my own actions.

He made a small 'hmm' sound, then angled his head to the side. "Got any staffs lying around?"

Slowly, a smile spread across my face. Within seconds, I'd fashioned two staffs using my earth magic, silently gloating a bit at the stunned look on John's face as I did. Standing, I rested one on my shoulder then handed the other to him. "Best out of three?"

Chuckling, he took the proffered staff and stood. "Why do I think I might be eating my words pretty soon?"

I shrugged. "I suppose we'll see."

A SHORT WHILE LATER, John had thoroughly reminded me of how important it was not to slack on my training in one area in favor of another.

I was also reminded—quite painfully—that strength and durability did *not* equate to infallible skill with a weapon.

Even better, I'd gained an audience. Halfway through my second round with John, Apollo and my brothers had shown up. They'd distracted me enough with their sudden appearance that I'd faltered, only for half a second, but it was long enough for John to get the drop on me, sweeping the staff out and sending me sprawling onto my back.

I was a goddamn Titaness, and my human trainer was *still* managing to kick my ass.

That wasn't to say I didn't get my own knocks in. By the time we'd gone three rounds, John was sporting a bruised chin, bloodied knuckles, and what would very likely be a painful shoulder, after a sharp blow I'd dealt him that sent him out of our designated circle.

'You better heal him when we're done,' I told Apollo.

He snorted. *'You've got access to my power. Do it yourself.'*

I shot him a glare, then narrowly missed a knock to the head with the end of John's staff.

Breathless, he stepped outside the circle and held up a hand. "I'm tapping out," he said. Pointing a finger at me, he added, "But there's no reason I should've been able to get the drop on you like that. It's important you have a thorough understanding of your powers, Tessa, but you also need to give time to your physical abilities, as well. You always loved a good fight. Don't let immortal strength diminish that."

"Yes, sir." I loved that we'd been able to fall right back into our old training routine. I'd worried a lot about how he and Analise would react once they reentered my life, wondered whether they would treat me the same, be the same parental figures to me as they had been just a few months ago. Sparring with John and listening to him lecture me on appropriate form and how to handle myself made me happier than I'd thought possible.

"Come on," I said, inclining my head toward the porch. "You can meet my brothers."

He faltered, only for a second but long enough for me to notice. Stepping forward, I linked my arm through his, dropping my staff on the ground next to the one he'd just been using. "They're not nearly as scary as they look."

He slid me a glance and patted my hand. "If you say so, kiddo."

We made our way to the porch where my brothers, Nate, and Apollo waited. Nate and Epimetheus had taken seats on the top step, while Apollo and Prometheus stood on the ground by the bottom one. Atlas stood about ten feet away, as though he'd started to walk toward where John and I had been sparring but thought better of it. His eyes tracked John as we moved forward, eyeing him like he would a potential foe. I saw Prometheus and Epimetheus exchange a quick glance behind him.

"Atlas, this is John, my guardian," I said once we'd reached my twin. I arched a brow at him. "He raised me. For the last nineteen years."

A muscle feathered on Atlas' jaw as he took in the only true father-figure I'd ever really had. Despite what Iapetus had allowed to happen to me, I knew exactly what Atlas saw when he looked at John: a replacement for what he considered my real family.

John, to his credit, met his gaze unflinchingly.

'Feel free to break the tension, you two,' I said to the twins.

Prometheus stepped forward so that he was beside Atlas and held out a hand to shake John's. "Mr. Avery, it's good to meet you," he said, his soft baritone voice carrying a soothing edge.

Epimetheus hopped down off the steps and followed suit, shaking John's hand and even going so far as to give him a one-armed hug. "Thank you for everything you've done for her," he said, stepping back and gripping his shoulders. He jerked his chin toward where we'd been sparring. "What you've taught her, what that means to us... That's not something that will be easily repaid."

I flicked a look toward Atlas and realized that probably wasn't the best thing for Epimetheus to say, considering Atlas' somewhat half-hearted attempts to truly train me in my past life. Sure enough, Atlas' jaw had tensed, and his thick arms were now folded across his chest.

John gave Epimetheus a nod and a tight smile. "Thank you, I appreciate you saying so."

Just then, Analise and Yana stepped outside. Analise paused when she saw us, while Yana came to a stop beside Nate at the top of the stairs.

"Analise!" My voice came out a touch more shrill than I intended. "Come down here and meet my brothers."

Let Atlas give *her* the cold shoulder.

With a warm smile, she walked down the stairs and took John's hand. "It's so wonderful to finally meet you all," she said, giving them each a look so full of love and appreciation, my eyes burned.

Catching her off guard, Epimetheus pulled her into a tight hug. "Thank you so much," he whispered fervently. "For everything."

Smiling, she patted him on the back, then put her hands on his biceps and stepped back. "She was always your sister, Epimetheus. We just did what we could to get her back to you safely."

"Something we will always be appreciative of," Prometheus told her quietly.

Once again, my twin remained silent, watching this meeting of my two families in a shroud of stoicism.

Rolling my eyes, I grabbed his hand and jerked him forward. *'Will you stop it?'* I snapped. *'You're acting like a grumpy ogre.'*

With a sigh, I introduced him. "Atlas, this is Analise. Analise, Atlas."

He shot a disbelieving look at me, then shook his head. Giving Analise a forced smile, he held out his hand. "It's lovely to meet you, Mrs. Avery."

Ignoring his surly behavior, she squeezed his hand in both of hers. "And it's wonderful to finally meet you, Atlas." Her voice was so wrought with emotion, I wondered if she was recalling all those times we'd gazed up at the stars, seeking out the constellation that held the stars named for him, his daughters, and their mother.

He cleared his throat, then looked at John. "It appears you've trained her well. Why the staff?"

John shrugged, looking a bit more at ease now that my twin had thawed out a bit. "It was the first weapon Tessa picked up when she was a girl. We've trained her in all forms of weapons fighting, but that was always her preference."

Atlas made a surprised sound. "Interesting," he said, glancing at me. "I suppose some things stuck with you, after all."

"I suppose so." I arched a brow in challenge. "I've still got some energy to burn. Wanna see how much I remember?"

Prometheus chuckled. "Don't get him riled up, Tessa."

Epimetheus smacked his twin's chest with the back of his hand. "Shush. Did you see her just now? I want to see him take her on."

Atlas' lips twitched, threatening to turn into a smile as he stared down at me, his eyes twinkling. "You think you can take me?"

"I used to hold my own just fine," I told him. "I think I remember laying you out on more than one occasion."

He snorted. "I let you win, dear sister."

Epimetheus sucked in a breath. "Ouch," he muttered.

My mouth dropped open in outrage. "I'll have you *know*, you big oaf, that I am quite capable of kicking your ass."

He wrapped an arm around my shoulders and gave me a loud kiss on the top of my head. "Maybe later."

Frowning, I looked at my other brothers and Apollo. "What are you guys doing here, anyway?"

"We haven't seen you in a few days, and we aren't heading back out until tomorrow," Epimetheus said. "So we figured we'd come visit."

"We didn't know you had company, otherwise—"

I held my hand up to stop Prometheus. "No, I'm glad you're here." I gave Apollo a curious look. "Did you miss me, too?"

"No," he deadpanned. "You've just brought a prisoner home. I thought it might be prudent to see if any type of healing was necessary."

"That's oddly benevolent of you, Apollo," I said.

"Don't take it personally," he muttered.

'He's drawn to broken things,' Nate explained, his words tinged with an unmistakable bit of sadness. *'It's very hard for him to stay away when someone he knows needs healing.'*

I pursed my lips, suddenly wishing I could take back my ribbing. If Apollo naturally sought out those who needed to be fixed, he was certainly getting a fair dose of it with our little group.

"I will take you in to see her," Yana told Apollo, appraising him as though he might try to shove Anette back into the dungeon the first chance he got. "Although I think she is fine."

Apollo let out a suffering sigh. "Then my visit should be brief. Hopefully you can withhold your disdain until I'm gone."

Not deigning to respond, she turned and strode through the front door.

"Be nice, Apollo!" I called after him, shaking my head. One of these days his snark was going to get him smacked. Hard, if Yana had anything to do with it.

He gave me a dismissive wave before disappearing into the house.

Plastering a smile on my face, I turned toward John and Analise. "So. You guys want to stay for dinner?"

19

MARY

Josh was called away not long after we began talking, putting an unfortunate end to my questions. There was so much I wanted to know, so many questions I wanted to ask so I would have more to give Tessa if she was able to reconnect with me or the sisters, but with the exception of the knowledge that spells didn't work on him, and he was clearly more powerful than any other witch in existence, not much of what he offered was terribly shocking.

When he dropped me in my cell and I saw the sisters' dirty, disheveled states, I immediately felt a bit of shame about my clean hair and clothes. It wasn't fair that I'd gotten a taste of the outside world while they sat in there wallowing in misery.

Then again, maybe feeling shitty about being clean was just another form of punishment.

Wary eyes followed me as Josh slammed the door shut behind him. Running my hands up and down my arms, I slid to the floor in my normal seat against the wall, thankful that he hadn't chained me back up.

The four of us sat in silence for a few moments before Alcyone spoke. She was finally looking marginally better, although her strength didn't seem to have returned in any significant amount.

"Where did he take you?" she asked quietly. I saw her eyes run over me, but she thankfully didn't comment on my appearance.

I pulled my knees to my chest and wrapped my arms around my legs, resting my chin on top. "To his room," I said. "And before you ask, I don't know why."

Taygete arched a brow. "He didn't say anything at all about why he chose to take you?"

I shrugged, uncomfortable under her stare. "He said something about how I deserved a reward because Tessa was able to get through to us, and I was able to hold on."

"So he gave you a bath?" she snorted.

"He didn't *give*—you know what, never mind." I huffed out a breath. "He offered a shower, and I took it. You would've done the same," I muttered.

An awkward silence followed.

"Sorry," I murmured. "I don't really know what the point of him taking me was unless it was some stupid psychological bullshit to make you guys resent me."

"It's alright," Celaeno said quietly. "Do not let them fool you. If any of us had been taken, we would've gladly accepted a hot shower." She gave me a small smile when her sisters harrumphed. "Now tell us all he said."

I leaned my head back against the wall. "Not much, really. Cronus and Iapetus showed up, they all argued, then before Josh could tell me much more, he got called away somewhere."

"What did they fight about?" Taygete asked.

"They were pissed Josh took me out of my cell, said something about how he should be informing them when he takes prisoners or whatever."

Alcyone frowned. "How did Josh respond?"

"Like a petulant teenager," I said, rolling my eyes. "So he's either really stupid or—"

"Knows they can't hurt him." Celaeno sat up a bit straighter, her eyes wide. "What else?"

I wrinkled my nose, thinking back to our conversation. "The only other thing that stood out was that spells don't work on him. He said he could see them for what they are. Basically, since he could see spells, he could avoid being affected by them. Does that sound familiar?"

Celaeno gave me a curious look. "Similar to Menoetius, then?"

I shook my head. "No, he said *no* spells worked on him. There are some that work on Menoetius, just not ones that affect memory, right?"

She nodded, a considering look filling her features.

"That is an odd gift, indeed," Alcyone said. "I've never heard of a being, gifted with primordial power or otherwise, who could manage such a feat."

"Yes, this means he must be incredibly powerful," Taygete agreed.

"Yeah, but we already knew that, didn't we?" I asked.

"No, not necessarily to what extent," Taygete replied. "Primordial witches are powerful, certainly, but even we have our limits. Our power can be taken, just like any other deity. If weakened, we can be overpowered easily."

I held up my hands in question. "Again, nothing new."

Alcyone rolled her eyes. "Does Cronus strike you as the type who would let a powerful primordial witch work *for* him? Especially one who is immune to spells? Or would he be more likely to try and take that power for his own?" She arched a brow when I didn't respond. "Is he the type who would allow himself to be anything other than the most powerful being in the room, if he can help it?"

"The spell to take the power is still a spell," Celaeno said slowly. "It's possible Josh's power can't be taken."

I bit my lip as I thought. "Even if it could, if a witch that powerful agreed to fight with or for him, why would he bother taking his power? It's a pain in the ass, from what I can tell." I tried not to think back on my own memories of having my own power sucked out. Cronus had made it look easy, that's for sure, but it still took time, and he'd eventually have to come back for a refill, something I also franti-cally tried to ignore.

"Cronus isn't the trusting type," Taygete said, shaking me from my thoughts. "Neither is Iapetus, but it seems he's little more than Cronus' lapdog. No, if Cronus had the option of thieving that witch's power, he would do it. He wouldn't drag the three of us into his little cell every other day."

I grimaced. "Eh. I don't know. My money is on him not wanting to waste the energy."

Celaeno arched a brow. "Then I'll ask you this. When you saw the three of them interact, who appeared to be in charge?"

I opened my mouth to respond, then frowned and let it drift shut. "I mean, Cronus was definitely giving Josh a verbal bitch slap." I ran back over the memory of my time in Josh's room. "But I don't know. Josh pushed back fairly hard."

The three sisters deflated. "Well, I suppose we'll have to wait and see, then," Taygete said with a sigh, not looking entirely convinced. "Although I'm not quite sure what difference it will make if Cronus turns out the be the underling."

"It will mean every single being fighting against him has been aiming their efforts at the wrong enemy," Alcyone snapped.

"No, if Tessa knows Josh is involved, I can guarantee they've been looking into his history," I told them. "They know what Cronus can do, especially now that they've confirmed he can steal power. Josh is an unknown, so they'll want to know all they can about him. They aren't entirely in the dark."

"Hopefully they know what they're looking for, then," Taygete said. "Because we've certainly never heard of him. If there was a written record, Hecate and the others would have found it."

"Only if they had a place to start," I countered. "'Really strong witch we've never met before' isn't exactly a great starting place."

"It is if they look in the right place," Taygete argued.

"Which would be where?"

She narrowed her eyes in thought as she stared up at the small square of sunlight above our heads. "I don't know," she finally said.

I slumped back against the wall in defeat. I was annoyed that she didn't have a better answer and that I hadn't gotten much at all from my interaction with Josh, aside from speculations about his level of authority. Which, if any of us were being honest here, really didn't matter much. Whether Cronus was in charge or not was irrelevant. Whether he and Josh were working side-by-side was irrelevant. All I knew was that both of them were working to take down Olympus, the place that had become my home over the last few months. They'd worked together to kill nearly all the friends I'd made since arriving and locked me and the sisters in here like animals. It didn't matter who was in charge. They both needed to die.

I closed my eyes and tried to let my thoughts drift toward more pleasant things, like thoughts of home and the people who had become my new family: Yana, Anette, Tessa, Nate, and all of their siblings. No matter how intimidated I might've been when I'd first started spending time with the gods and goddesses Nate and Tessa were related to, they'd all quickly become beings I could spend time around without feeling like they might kick me off the mountain if I annoyed them.

Well, except Apollo. And maybe Atlas. Those two were freakin' scary.

The rest—Dionysus, Hermes, Athena, Prometheus, and Epimetheus—had quickly become acquaintances, if not friends. I'd never pictured myself joking around with Dionysus or Hermes, sharing weapons talk with Athena, having simple conversation with Prometheus and Epimetheus. I'd thought fitting into Tessa's new life would be impossible, that I'd lost my best friend to a previous life where Ischyra would be considered far beneath her. Heck, I'd thought I was losing her when she ended up dating Zeus' son.

Instead, she'd shown me that we could all have a life together, one where my best friend wasn't pulled from her new life by her old one or vice versa. She'd shown me I was still her family, no matter how powerful or what kind of being she was.

As my thoughts continued to veer away from the awful situation I was in, I slowly began to drift off to sleep, crossing my fingers that I might hear from Tessa or the other sisters again soon.

20

NATHANIEL

Knowing they'd be insulted if they weren't included, I called Hermes and Dionysus to invite them to join us for dinner. Not long after they arrived, Tessa, Atlas, Prometheus, John, and I found ourselves shunned to the living room while a massive dinner was being prepared. Somehow, Analise had taken over cooking, while Epimetheus, Hermes, and Dionysus practically perched on her shoulders, stealing bits of food as she cooked and asking questions about her recipes. The picture of patience, she answered their barrage of questions with a smile on her face, and at one point, even letting Epimetheus take over sautéing onions for her sauce.

"This is disturbing," Tessa whispered to me from the sofa, taking in the smooth rhythm the three of them had fallen into.

"How do you think I feel?" John asked. "I'm watching my wife cook dinner with three gods."

Hermes laughed. "Dionysus has never been one to take his position all that seriously."

"I heard that!" Dionysus called over his shoulder.

"Where'd you guys get all the food, anyway?" Tessa asked.

"Demeter," Hermes replied around a mouth full of shredded cheese.

"We raided her stores," Dionysus added, "so it's real—what is it you humans call it? 'Farm to table?'"

Tessa laughed and shook her head. "Yep. That's it." She shifted her attention to John and lowered her voice. "You think she'll leave me a stash of blueberry pancakes?"

Epimetheus held up a now-empty basket of blueberries. "Already done!" he announced.

John smiled fondly. "You should've known better than to ask."

Atlas had been observing everyone's interactions since he'd arrived and found Tessa sparring with John, her attention so heavily focused on her guardian that he'd watched for nearly twenty minutes before she noticed his presence. Tessa had told me before that he tended to be naturally suspicious of outsiders, but it was hard to tell whether his sit-back-and-watch behavior was due to suspicion or unease around the people Tessa viewed as her parents.

Footsteps in the hall alerted me to Apollo's presence, followed by Yana. Tessa and I exchanged a look as Yana took a seat across from her.

"How is she?" Prometheus asked.

"Fine, physically," Apollo said, rubbing a hand across his brow. "There's little I can do to help heal the mental scarring."

"Did you truly expect to be able to do anything?" Atlas asked, a frown carving his features. "She was violated in one of the worst ways a person can be. No amount of magic will remove what was done to her."

Silence followed, broken only by the various sounds of cooking coming from the kitchen. I rested my head on the back of the couch and tried very hard not to think about my contribution to that violation. Logically I knew that if I hadn't searched her mind, the link could've gone permanently undetected. Even still... I'd entered her mind under orders from someone else and without her permission. Regardless of the outcome, it was likely Tessa's friend would never come to fully trust me again.

Tessa slipped her hand through mine. "Then what do we do for her?"

"There is nothing we can do," Yana said, sounding annoyed. "Except leave her be."

"She may want to talk eventually, but for now, the best thing you can do for her is to let her come to you," Apollo said, finally sitting down.

"He's right, kiddo," John said with an apologetic smile. "I know you might feel a bit responsible, unreasonable as that is, but this isn't something you can fix by force."

"If it is any consolation, I do not think it will be long before she wants to talk," Yana said reluctantly. "She has already been asking questions."

"Well, that's good," Tessa said hopefully. Her eyes darted to John, then her twin. "But I won't push."

Conversation was light but tense as we waited for the others to finish cooking. Tessa and Hermes had set the dining room table while we waited, something that hadn't been done in decades. It was an odd sight to see, with plates and cloth napkins and a long, white table cloth I'd forgotten I owned. Dinner guests, or company in general, really weren't something I entertained often, and it seemed my home was suddenly becoming home base for everything we did lately.

After Analise and Epimetheus had set the food on the table, we all took turns piling our plates full of chicken parmesan, garlic bread, salad, and pasta. There was a lull in conversation as we all ate, a testament to Analise's cooking. What conversation was had mainly involved Dionysus peppering her with questions about how and where she learned to cook.

Once everyone was settled in and had eaten their fill, Prometheus stood and, waving Analise off, began clearing the table. She smiled up at him thankfully, then turned to Tessa, indecision clear on her face as she looked around the table.

"So, Tessa, I was wondering." She cleared her throat. "Have you considered going to Renville to hunt down any information on Josh?"

Tessa wiped her mouth and set her napkin down, leaning back as her brother took her plate from her. "We haven't gone yet, but the idea's been brought up. Why?"

Analise shrugged and picked up her glass of water. "Even the smartest beings can't cover their tracks completely, right?"

"It's unlikely he left a forwarding address when he left," Atlas said dryly, then scowled and ducked when Tessa tossed her napkin at him.

"Was there something specific you thought we might find?" I asked.

"No," Analise replied. "But I find it very hard to believe that he didn't know who Tessa was the entire time he was there. If he did end up there by coincidence, he may have left some hints as to where he was previously. If he was there intentionally, well, there still might be something to be found, at least at his house."

John inclined his head toward Tessa. "Considering Tessa's new arsenal, I would imagine you'd be able to find quite a bit in the places he frequented the most."

"That's been our thinking as well," Apollo agreed. "Tell me, did the two of you know him well? Or his parents?"

Analise shook her head. "Only as acquaintances. His parents never had much interest in socializing, it seemed. Josh was never anything but polite and respectful when he was at the house."

John blew out a breath and sighed. "He and Leila... well, they weren't around as long as Eric and Mary, obviously, but the five of them clicked like a puzzle when he moved in."

Hermes angled his head curiously. "How long did Leila live there?"

"She moved in third grade," Tessa said. "Long before Josh showed up."

"Well, you and I both know that it's possible she was in on whatever ruse he had going on," John said reluctantly. "I hate to say that, but if he was able to pull one over on us for that long, she could've done it, too."

"She was eight when she moved to town, so I find that highly unlikely," Analise said with a slight scoff.

"Why?" Atlas asked. "She was his lover, correct? He could have easily indoctrinated her."

Analise met his steely gaze with a hard one of her own, not backing down from the gruff edge to his voice. "Yes, she was, and if you'd seen her even once in recent weeks you would see that duplicity is the last thing on her mind."

"It's worth looking into," I said, cutting off Atlas' retort. "Although I'm more inclined to agree with Analise. If she's been so distraught that she's barely left the house, she'd be pretty useless as a spy."

"Agreed," Apollo said with a sigh. *'Nathaniel, take Tessa and two others and go to Renville tomorrow,'* he ordered. *'Get it done now before Zeus decides to send in someone who's a bit more lacking in morality.'*

As conversation continued around us, I arched a brow. *'Suggestions?'*

'Eris needs to get off this mountain. Bring her. Epimetheus, too. He'll temper her a bit.'

I tried to hide my incredulity that he wanted me to bring Eris, of all my sisters, to speak with a human girl who was likely too distraught to function.

'Just trust me.'

'Alright, but if she makes this worse, I'm blaming you.'

'I'd expect nothing less.'

TESSA and I were up at dawn the next day with plans to head to Renville a short while later. Taking the time-change into account, that would put us there in the early afternoon in Pennsylvania, which Tessa thought best since Leila's parents would be at work. The sun had almost crested the summit of the mountain when Tessa and I went out onto the porch to wait for the others.

"Remind me again why Eris is coming?" Tessa asked as she hopped up on the porch railing opposite where I sat in one of the chairs. "Isn't she kind of the worst person to bring with us for something like this?"

"Eris needs a purpose," I explained, patting her ankle when she rested her feet on my knees. "She's not so bad, as long as she doesn't get riled up, so giving her a purpose, something to do, helps with that. It's part of the reason she's so adamant about dealing with the Telchines." Despite her mercurial disposition and questionable methods, Eris was, at her heart, a good person. She tended to struggle with any question that had an uncertain answer—like how long it would be before Zeus gave her the go-ahead to take out the Tels. His caginess set her on edge, which didn't bode well for her or anyone involved in her plans, so giving her a set task, keeping her busy and avoiding too much idle time, was best for everyone just now.

"So basically, we're just keeping her occupied?" She arched a brow. "Was this your idea?"

I shook my head. "Apollo's. Eris and Zeus can barely stand to be in the same room together right now, so she needs as many off-mountain missions as we can give her. This one is minor, but she'll be good to have around if we run into trouble."

"That's fine and all, but Leila is... sensitive. She took it hard when we left." Tessa ran a hand through her hair, then began twisting it up in a hair tie. "Losing Josh had to have made things a hundred times worse." She let her hands drop to her lap. "I don't want to upset her any more than she already is."

I held out my hands for hers and gently tugged her into my lap, letting her rest her head against mine. "Are you planning on telling her about Mary?" I asked after a moment.

"I don't know," she said quietly. "I don't think it's fair to lie, but at the same time, there's no reason for her to know other than the fact that Mary is her friend."

"You wouldn't be lying to her, necessarily," I said slowly. "You'd be withholding information, which I suppose some might argue is just as bad—"

She sat up and gave me a pointed look.

The corner of my mouth quirked up, then I brushed a strand of hair from her eyes that had slipped free of her ponytail. "As I was saying... Yes, sometimes withholding information is a bad thing. In this case, though, I don't necessarily think it is. Don't mistake me. I'm not saying you should keep things from her. But... as much as I hate to even say this, there's no guarantee that any of us will be able to get back to her with an update on Mary's status any time soon. If she's truly as damaged as you say, total honesty in this case may make things more difficult. Only you can make that call, though, Tessa. She's your friend, you know what kind of person she is."

"She's a worrier." Tessa leaned back against me. "Her mind goes to worst-case scenarios when bad things happen. I don't want to tell her, but at the same time I feel like I should, you know?"

"People can be more resilient than you think, love. If you think she'll be alright and that it won't make circumstances worse, then give her the chance to show you that."

"She just doesn't have a huge support system in Renville. She's got her parents and her little sister, but they don't really have any other family in the area. All of our friends from school are either off to college or on their way by now."

We sat quietly for a few moments as she mulled over her options, then I patted her thigh. "Whatever decision you make, I'm sure it'll be with her best interests at heart."

The door opened behind us, and Yana emerged onto the porch with Anette just behind her. Now that she'd been cleaned up and given her own clothes, a real bed to sleep in, and fresh air, Anette looked to be bouncing back fairly quickly. There was still a sense of unease around her whenever she looked at me that I tried not to let get to me too much. I hoped that, in time, she'd be able to forgive me for what I'd done, but until then, I just wanted her to do all she could to bring herself back to normal.

Tessa sat up and schooled her features into a neutral expression. "Anette! How are you feeling?"

Anette sat down gingerly on the chair beside Tessa while Yana leaned back against the railing across from her.

"I'm... well. Yana tells me you are going to investigate Josh in your hometown?"

"We are," Tessa confirmed. "Yana will be helping Chiron with archival research, and short of scouring Earth for his hideout, Renville is the only place I can think of to start."

Anette gave us each a skeptical look. "You don't think you will find anything, do you?"

"I honestly don't know," Tessa replied. "But he lived there and was a part of Renville for four years, so if nothing else, maybe I can use my psychometry to get some information on where he was before he moved there."

"Do you know where he moved from?" Yana asked.

"Somewhere down south," Tessa replied with a shrug. "Deep south, I think, but I forget where, exactly."

Anette began twisting her hands nervously in her lap. "Tell me what I can do to help. I cannot just sit here. I've done nothing but sit for nearly two weeks."

Yana's eyes darted toward me, then Tessa, before she spoke. "You can help me and Chiron if you would like. I am going to meet him in the library archives today, and they are large enough for the three of us."

Anette gave her a grateful smile. "Yes, I'd like that." Turning back to us, she asked, "What starting points do we have for Josh?"

"Not much," I told her. I gave her a quick rundown of everything, little as it was, we'd learned about Josh and what we knew about primordial witches. Her face reflected the frustration we'd all felt when she realized just how little we had to go on in our search.

"Will you attempt to form a link with Mary again?" Anette asked.

"I've tried several times since the sisters and I connected with them," Tessa said with a frustrated huff. "I haven't even been able to touch her."

Anette's lips tightened for a moment, then she straightened in her seat. "Alright, well, we will do our best then," she said, her smile seeming slightly more confident than her words. Fear clouded her eyes seconds later. "But please... be careful. If he was able to get through the wards and link with me for so long without being detected..."

"We will," Tessa assured her.

Just then, Epimetheus appeared, followed quickly by Eris.

"Morning," Epimetheus greeted us all. He nodded at Anette. "Anette, how are you feeling?"

"A bit more like myself today," she replied, smiling. "Thank you."

"Can we go?" Eris asked, sounding surlier than normal.

"Good morning to you, too," I said, smirking.

She sneered at me, then flipped her hair over shoulder. "It's not. Our father is an asshole. Can we go?"

Yana's brows shot up. "Okay... um, would one of you mind taking Anette and me down to the village to meet Chiron?"

"He can't be bothered to come get you?" Eris muttered.

"He's on his way here now," I told them, ignoring Eris' snark. As if on cue, Chiron emerged from the woods behind my house, snapping the buttons on the sides of his breakaway pants as he walked.

I shot him a questioning look, and he shrugged. *'My human form is more normal for Anette, who I'm guessing is still skittish.'*

'She's seen you in your centaur form before, though.'

'Yeah, well, something tells me she's going to have to be eased back into our version of normal, considering. I'm just trying to make sure she's comfortable. Not to mention the archive stairs are a pain in the ass to get down in my other form.'

I let out a huff of laughter as he ascended the stairs and greeted everyone.

Tessa eyed me curiously, but I just shook my head.

"Are you ladies ready?" Chiron asked Yana and Anette. When they nodded, he held out a hand to each, then looked over at me. "Let us know when you return, and we'll get together for an update."

I nodded, and we all said our farewells.

When they were gone, Eris turned to me. "What's the plan?"

"We'll hit Leila's house first, I think," Tessa said. "Then the school and Josh's old house."

Eris arched a brow dubiously and tilted her head. "And we're expecting to find..."

"Anything," I told her. "Anything at all that can give us a hint to his past. Or recent past, at the very least."

"Let's get going, then," Epimetheus said, casting his eyes up the mountain toward where the sun was continuing to climb.

Standing, I held out a hand to Tessa, then the four of us teleported to her hometown.

21

TESSA

The woods at the end of Leila's street were quiet when we stepped into Renville, the only sound the quiet symphony of buzzing insects and the gently lapping waves of the lake just through the trees. The late-summer heat had settled over everything like a sticky, weighted blanket, giving the air a suffocating feel. I immediately regretted not making the choice to arrive in Renville in the cooler morning hours as opposed to the sweltering afternoon.

"Ugh," Eris groaned, pulling at the neck of her T-shirt. "How did you live in this humidity? It's like a damn swamp."

I smiled wistfully. "It's home," I said with a shrug.

"Are we sure we want to do the girlfriend's house first?" Eris asked.

"Yes," Nate said. "See what she has to say, then check out wherever it was he lived."

"Is she going to be okay to see you?" Epimetheus asked me.

I shrugged. "I think so. John and Analise said she's been sad since we all left, so maybe it'll perk her up a bit."

"Most of her friends left, followed by her boyfriend," Eris said, sliding out of her denim jacket and tying it around her waist, revealing a bright red tank top the same color as the streaks in her hair. "I guarantee she needs more than perking up."

I slid her a look but didn't answer. Leila had always been very dependent on her relationships. Her friends and her boyfriend were part of what defined her, no matter how much she tried to express her individuality by getting involved in extracurriculars. That she had Josh to lean on when we left was one of the main reasons I knew she would be alright losing us.

Now, with all of us gone, I couldn't imagine how she must be feeling.

"You're nervous," Nate said quietly, putting a hand on my back. "She'll be thrilled to see you."

I took a deep breath and nodded. "You're right. Hopefully." I hadn't even considered the possibility that she might *not* want to see me, that I might be a painful reminder of the doting boyfriend who'd left her.

When we stepped through the trees onto the sidewalk, the hum of insects merged with birds twittering away in the cherry trees and in shady corners of porches of the ass-to-elbow houses that lined the street.

The four of us made our way up the street toward the small, white, clapboard house that Leila had lived in most of her life. It was a bungalow style, with a deep porch furnished with a wide bench swing, several ladderback rocking chairs, and a few small, glass-topped tables. I thought back to all the days and nights we'd spent hanging out right here, fighting over who got the swing, and sneaking the occasional wine cooler from the basement refrigerator. And if you were a storm-lover like Leila, Mary, and I were, it was the best place to watch one come through without getting soaked in the process.

"Cute," Eris commented as she assessed the house. "Very 'American Dream.'"

I'd just lifted my hand to knock when the door swung open, and Leila's ten-year-old little sister Josie was grinning up at me.

"Tessa!" she squealed, launching herself forward.

"Hey, Josie!" I laughed as she latched onto me like a baby monkey. "How ya doing, kiddo?"

Her face fell, and she shook her head. "I'm okay, but Leila..." she winced.

Frowning, my eyes drifted past her toward the dark wooden stairs that rose up to the second floor. "Is she here?" I asked.

Josie sighed. "Yeah, she never comes out of her room anymore. As soon as Mom leaves for work, it's hard to get her to do anything with me," she said sadly.

Concerned, I looked back at her. "That bad, huh?"

She nodded solemnly, then peeked her head around me. "Who are your friends? Are they gods?" Her blue eyes grew round, and she lowered her voice to an excited whisper. "Did you bring *gods* to my house?"

Leaning down so we were eye-level, I smiled and tapped her nose. "I sure did." I gestured for Epimetheus to come forward. "Did you know that I have a big brother?"

Her mouth formed a small O of surprise. "You *do?*"

I nodded. "This is Epimetheus," I told her.

He crouched down in front of her and extended a hand. "Hi, Josie," he said, giving her a thousand-watt grin. "It's nice to meet you."

Still wide-eyed, she took his hand and gave it a small shake. "H-hi. How come I never met you before?"

His smile faltered briefly. "I haven't seen Tessa for a very long time." Resting on his heels, he folded his arms across his chest. "Do you think I could hang out with you for a little bit while my sister and yours catch up a bit?"

She nodded quickly and blushed, immediately succumbing to my brother's charm. "Doyouwannaseemytreehouse?"

Epimetheus cast a glance up at me, then flashed Josie his dimples. "I'd love to see your treehouse, Josie." Pursing his lips, he looked at Eris. "Do you mind if my friend comes with us?"

Fortunately, Josie didn't see Eris' mouth fall open in outrage at Epimetheus' suggestion or the glare she shot at Nate, who was looking at her sternly.

With a sigh, she stepped up beside Epimetheus, bending at the waist to see Josie. "Hey, kid. I'm Eris."

Josie bit her lip in excitement. "Your hair is so cool!" she exclaimed, reaching out and grabbing one of Eris' fire-red streaks.

Eris stiffened, but to her credit, didn't flinch away when Josie gave her hair a tug. Instead, she patted Josie on the head and gave her a tight smile. "Thanks."

Josie's eyes drifted to Nate, then me, and she wrinkled her nose. "Is he your boyfriend?"

I laughed. "Yes, he is."

Narrowing her eyes, she gave him an appraising look. "He's cuter than your other boyfriends," she observed.

"A lot cooler than them, too," Nate stage-whispered.

Josie preened, then looked up at Epimetheus expectantly.

Epimetheus gave me a wink, then held his hand out for Josie to take. "Let's go see this treehouse. I bet if you ask Eris nicely, she'll show you how high she can climb."

Eris narrowed her eyes and jabbed him in the side with her elbow. Then she smirked, and a wicked glint filled her eyes. "Hey, Josie, I'll come play, but I have one favor to ask," she said, holding up one finger.

Josie's eyes widened. "What?"

Eris' smirk turned into a full grin. "You have to tell Epimetheus and me *all* about these 'other boyfriends' Tessa's had."

My mouth popped open in protest, but before I could react, Josie was tugging on Epimetheus' hand, dragging him toward the backyard where her dad had built a miniature version of their house in the tall oak tree in the center of the yard. He'd built it for Leila when she was around Josie's age, but now it was mainly used by Josie and her friends.

Nate touched a hand to the small of my back. "Go on up and see your friend. I'll go outside and make sure Eris stays out of trouble."

I wrinkled my nose in annoyance, then gave him a brief smile. "If there are kids and toys involved, Epimetheus might be the one you need to worry about."

He kissed my temple and laughed. "Good luck."

Once he was gone, I squared my shoulders and faced the staircase that led up to the second floor. Given the level of Josie's excitement, I had no doubt Leila had heard her call my name. Slowly, I climbed the stairs, each step echoing hollowly. When I reached Leila's door, I hesitated.

I wanted to see my friend. Badly. At the same time, I was scared to see what Josh's absence had done to her.

I knocked quietly before pushing open the door and sticking my head inside. The light scent of body odor hit me almost immediately, along with the sour scent of something stale, like moldy food.

"Lei?" I called softly. The shades were drawn, bathing the room in darkness, and the only light was from her laptop, where the sounds of Winchesters fighting demons floated from the speakers.

"Tessa?" Leila's voice came from the old rocking chair in the corner of her room where she was wrapped up in her pink-and-blue mermaid blanket, a half-full glass of water on the small table next to her. She leaned forward and tapped a button on the keyboard, pausing the show.

"Hey," I said, smiling as I shut the door behind me.

She stood slowly, her eyes wide as she watched me step forward. Her blanket slipped to her feet, revealing a wrinkled blue t-shirt and matching cotton shorts. A moment later, she launched herself at me, twining her arms around my neck in a vise-grip.

In seconds, she was sobbing. I let her cry, stroking her hair as her tears soaked through my shirt. Her once-shiny, bouncy brown hair felt greasy and unwashed under my fingers. Between that and the body odor, it was clear that whatever Josh had said or done when he left had damaged her far more than I'd expected.

After a few minutes, I gently pushed her back and met her eyes. "Leila, what happened?"

"He left!" she cried, not bothering to wipe away the tears that were still coursing down her cheeks or the snot that glistened on her nostrils. "Josh—he just got up one morning and broke up with me," she said as a fresh torrent of tears began to flow.

"Shit, Lei, I'm so sorry," I murmured, pulling her in for another hug. Any hope I had that Josh might've taken pity on her when he left was slowly dwindling. I motioned toward the bed, then sat down on the edge, gently pulling her down to sit beside me. "Tell me exactly what happened."

She sniffed, then pulled the collar of her T-shirt up to wipe her tears. "That's the thing," she moaned. "I don't know! We were *fine* one day, then the next we weren't. I don't know what changed overnight, but he woke up one morning and decided to take some scholarship he'd never even *told* me about—god, we were supposed to go to college together!" Her brow furrowed as anger seeped into her voice. "We were supposed to go together, get an apartment, and then he just *left!* He said—"

A series of hiccuping sobs stopped the words from coming out. Finally, she sucked in a sharp breath and continued. "He said he didn't *need* me anymore." She dropped her face in her hands and shook her head as she took several deep breaths. When she looked back up at me, her eyes seemed nearly lifeless. "Was I a bad girlfriend all this time, and I just didn't know it?"

"No! Absolutely not," I told her firmly, taking her hand in mine. That Josh had not only left her but been so damn cruel about it nearly had me spitting. "You were the best goddamn girlfriend he could've asked for, and don't you ever doubt that!"

"Then why?" Her eyes searched mine. "Why would he do this?"

I bit down on my bottom lip, wondering if it would help or make things worse if I told her the truth. I needed to ask her questions about his past, anything she might know, and there was no real way I could see to accomplish that without also revealing he wasn't the guy she thought he was. He'd shown himself as cruel, but I didn't think I had it in me to tell her he was simply evil on top of it all.

"I don't know, Lei." I gave her a sympathetic smile and smoothed a hand over her hair. "Where did he go, anyway?"

She shrugged. "He didn't say exactly. The scholarship is to LSU, but I don't know if he planned to live on campus or not. His parents left, too. Just, poof." She did a half-hearted jazz-hands motion. "All gone."

"Huh. He had family down south, right? Maybe that's why?"

"Yeah, I guess." She twisted her hands in her lap as she stared down at the floor. "I don't know how he managed it," she said morosely. "He wasn't that great a football player."

"No, he really wasn't," I agreed.

"I bet you think I'm pathetic," she said, sniffling.

"I absolutely don't," I assured her. "Far from it."

"I just don't understand why I can't move on," she said, her voice breaking. "Why is this so freaking hard, Tess?"

I put my arm around her shoulders and pulled her in for a one-armed hug, resting my cheek on top of her head. Leila and Josh had been one of those rare high school couples who never faltered, not once. There was never a period of doubt or a time when they were on-again, off-again. They'd met the first day of school freshman year and had been inseparable ever since. I couldn't blame her for feeling so blindsided.

"You can move on, Lei. It just hurts. I think it's just how it is with these things."

"I guess," she muttered. She sighed, then dragged her hands through her hair, her fingers snagging slightly at the ends. "What are you doing here, anyway? Shouldn't you be off being all immortal and what not?" She attempted to smile, but the forced curve of her lips resembled a grimace more than anything close to amusement or happiness.

"I had some business in the area, and John and Analise told me about you and Josh, so I wanted to come see how you were doing."

"Well, I'm glad you came," she said. "I feel like I don't have any friends left these days."

"Don't think that way." I gripped her shoulders and turned her to face me. "I know how much Josh must've hurt you, but he is not worth this. You've still got friends. You just need to reach out." I picked up a lock of her hair, the once-shiny chestnut color now dull and tangled with grease. "This isn't you, Lei."

She brushed my hand away and sniffled loudly. "I know. I *know* that. I just can't—I don't know, Tess, I just can't let it go. It's like he died, you know? Only it's worse because he's still out there some-where doing whatever it is he's doing because he doesn't *need* me anymore."

"I know, sweetie, but it'll get better," I told her. "You have to want it to get better, though. Otherwise, it never will."

"How?" she whispered. "The only thing I want is for him to come back. That's not going to happen, though, and I don't know where to go from here. I want to feel better, but—"

"You've gotten so used to him, that you don't know how to do it for yourself?"

She clenched her jaw. "I wasn't going to be so blunt about it, but yeah, I guess."

"Sorry," I murmured, silently chastising myself.

"It's okay," she muttered. "I have to pee. I'll be right back."

I waited until she'd closed the door of the small Jack-and-Jill bathroom she shared with Josie before reaching out to Nate.

'Would it be the worst idea ever to use a bit of Coercion on Leila to help her get over Josh a little quicker?'

His was response was a few seconds in coming. *'I... don't really know. Is she that bad?'*

'It's bad,' I confirmed.

'And you want to, what, erase her memory of him? That's not a good idea, Tessa.'

'No! I want to make her feel better, make her believe she can move on without him easily. She's wallowing, and I think she's headed toward a scary place.'

'Emotional manipulation, then?'

'I guess? I don't know. It sounds awful when you put it that way. More like a confidence boost?' I winced. That didn't seem quite right, either, but I couldn't just do *nothing*, and I knew once I left, she would spiral right back down.

'It's your call, Tessa. Just be careful. If you don't think you can do it, call me. Do not *call Hades. Even though he could do it effectively, he'll—'*

'*Enjoy it too much? Yeah, I know.*' If anyone could alter Leila's mind-set, it would be Hades, but intentional or not, the fact that he'd get enjoyment out of her pain rankled me. '*I'll be careful.*'

'*Alright. Let me know if you need a hand.*'

'*Will do.*'

I tapped my fingers on my knees as I thought over how to handle Leila. It wasn't my job to clean up after Josh, to repair the emotional carnage he'd left behind, but Leila was one of my oldest friends. I couldn't, and wouldn't, take away her memories of him, because he'd made her happy for a very long time, regardless of his intentions. What I could do, though, was help her take her first steps forward.

The bathroom door opened, and Leila sat back down next to me. "So am I allowed to ask how things are going on Olympus?" she asked meekly when she settled on the bed again.

"They're going," I hedged. Zeus and the Elders had made the decision to leave the dissemination of information to the citizens of Earth up to the human governments, and as far as I knew, they'd yet to come to an agreement on when and how much information would be given.

I ran my gaze over her face, my heart squeezing a bit as I saw how small and broken she seemed. In that moment, I knew there was no way I could tell her about Eric and Mary. Not yet. There was also no way I could leave her like this, and frankly, I was a bit sick of only using my powers to handle the creatures I was fighting. I needed to help, not harm, for once.

"Hey, Lei. Look at me for a sec?"

She lifted her brow in question and met my eyes. "What's up?"

I touched a finger to her chin and held her gaze. "You know you can do this, right?"

A frown flickered across her face. "What do you mean?"

Lacing my words with a bit of Coercion, I continued. "Get through this. Move on from Josh. Yeah, you guys had a great run, but why not take this chance to figure out who *you* are?"

Her brown eyes cleared a bit. "How, though?" she whispered. "He was here with me for so damn long. How do I move on from that?"

I pushed a bit more power toward her. "You sit down at that computer over on your desk and start looking up schools and majors. Figure out what *you* want to do with your life, what career *you* want, where *you* want to go. Don't base your future on anyone but yourself, you hear me?"

"What if it doesn't work?" She shook her head. "What if I can't find anything—"

"You will," I stated. "Because no matter what Josh Harper did for you in the past, you are what matters in the here and now."

Her body relaxed a bit, a tension I hadn't realized she was carrying slowly seeping out. "It's just so hard," she whispered, slumping. "I had all these plans, then everything was just... flipped."

"No one likes surprises like that," I told her. "Trust me, I get it. You just need to figure out how to take that shock and turn it into something you can work with."

"Tessa... are you telling me to find the silver lining?" she asked with narrowed eyes.

I nearly sagged with relief at the humor in her voice. "I am," I said. "I am absolutely telling you to find the goddamn silver lining because you are worth more than this. Josh doesn't deserve to get the best of you. Not like this." I gestured around her room. "He doesn't deserve the satisfaction of knowing he did this to you."

Tears filled her eyes again as she looked around and took in the state of her room. "I'm scared," she admitted. "I miss him so much, but Tess, I'm scared. I feel like I'm floundering, you know? Like I got tossed in the ocean and left behind."

"So, be scared," I said simply. "Be terrified. But, Leila, *please* try to look through all this grief and figure out who you are. You were never just 'Josh's girlfriend.' You're Leila Malone, cheer captain and math whiz. You had the confidence to get your team to follow you, to *want* to follow you. You may not believe it or realize it, but no one did that but you." I gently poked her shoulder and smiled. "Figure out how to be that person for yourself."

"Okay," she said, sitting up a bit straighter. "Okay, I'll do my best."

A mild feeling of guilt nudged at me, but I forced it away. I'd spent too much time using my power to hurt others, either in training or in the field, and this time, I knew deep down that what I'd done for Leila would help her in the long run. As much as I wanted to have confidence in her, after seeing her like this, I knew she wouldn't be able to pull herself out of this without help. She needed to move on, and she wasn't going to do that unless she had a slightly clearer head. I would never take away her memories of Josh, but taking away a little bit of her pain so she could start the process of healing... that was something I would do for anyone I loved, a hundred times over.

22

NATHANIEL

If ever I needed a pick-me-up, I knew all I needed to do was drag Eris down to Renville and set her up with Josie Malone and her treehouse hair salon. The look of suppressed agony on Eris' face as she sat cross-legged on the pink flower-shaped rug on the floor in the Malone's tree house while Josie braided her hair, was quite possibly the most entertaining thing I'd seen in centuries.

"You know, kid, I thought you'd have way more interesting stories about Tessa," she grumbled as Josie began braiding a third section of her hair. "These guys sound kind of boring."

"Eh." Josie shrugged, then slipped a small tie off her wrist. "They were. Caleb was okay, I guess, but the others were kind of dumb."

I bit back an amused smile when Eris glared up at me.

"You know, Josie, I'm a bit of a braiding pro myself," Epimetheus said. "I used to braid Tessa's hair all the time when she was younger."

Not taking her eyes off the handful of red streaks she'd gathered, Josie let out a quiet snort. "Tessa could *never* braid her own hair," she told him. "If you'd come back from wherever you were sooner, you could've taught her."

There was a brief tightening around his eyes at her words before he responded. "Well then, I should probably teach her now, huh?" He grinned down at Eris. "Maybe she can practice on Eris."

Eris sneered and flipped him off, keeping her hand low enough that Josie didn't see.

The muffled thud of feet sounded on the treehouse's wooden ladder, and a moment later, Tessa appeared in the doorway. "Hey, guys," she said, casting a bemused look toward Eris.

"Hi, Tessa!" Josie exclaimed. "Look!" She pointed at the half-dozen small braids she'd put in Eris' hair, alternating between the dark brown and red streaks. "Your brother said you still can't braid, but Eris said she'll let you practice on her when you guys get back."

Eris' eyes flashed indignantly. "I—"

"So how'd it go with Leila?" I asked, cutting her off.

Tessa sat down on the floor and leaned against the wall by the door. "Not great, but it seems like she might be headed in the right direction. She's in the shower now."

"Finally!" Josie groaned. She stepped away from Eris and sat down beside Tessa. "She showers, like, once a week and smells *so bad.*"

Tessa smiled fondly and ruffled her hair. "She'll be okay, kiddo. Try not to worry."

"Thanks, Tessa," Josie said, leaning into her. "I miss you," she said quietly.

Tessa wrapped her arms around Josie and rested her chin on her head, then closed her eyes. "I miss you, too." She held her for a few more moments as she collected herself, then cleared her throat and gently nudged Josie back. "Listen, Jos, we have to go, okay? But I promise I'll come back soon and check in. Sound good?"

Josie sighed quietly. "Yeah." She scrunched up her nose and looked at Tessa. "She'll really be okay?"

Tessa flashed her a smile. "She will. I promise."

ERIS, in a rare show of niceness, waited until we'd left the Malone house and teleported inside Renville High School to pick the braids out of her hair.

"Damn kid," she groused as she yanked at the strands. "It's all tangled now."

I smirked. "I don't know, Eris. You looked like you were enjoying yourself back there."

"Blow me," she snapped.

"Seriously, though, that was really nice of you," Tessa told her. "Josie looks up to Leila, so I think she enjoyed having a grown up to, ah, play with."

Eris glared at her. "Since I think that was a compliment, thank you, and don't ever mention it a-goddamned-gain." She looked around the dimly lit science class we'd landed in. The shades were drawn, and the faint smell of disinfectant lingered in the air. "Where do they keep records in this place?"

Tessa stepped toward the desk where a desktop computer sat, its screen dark. "Oh. We need a password to log in. Shoot. Nate, can you—"

"On it." I sent out my Coercion through the building until I hit an area that was more heavily populated, presumably the main office, and searched until I found myself in the mind of a secretary. I took a swift look through her head until I found what I needed, then pulled my power back in. "Username is MDougherty, capital M and D, and password is..." I frowned. "Sniffles?"

Tessa grinned. "Mrs. D *loves* her cat. Apparently, it sneezes a lot, so... yeah." She pressed the power button, then tapped her foot, waiting for the old machine to boot up. Once it did, she typed in the login information and navigated to school records.

"What exactly are we hoping to find here?" Epimetheus asked quietly. "I can't imagine he would've given valid information when he moved here."

I shrugged. "We've got nothing to go on except the places he's been. Chiron is working on the historical part, so this is where we start our bit."

"Waste of time," Eris murmured, hopping up on one of the desks. Almost immediately, her knee started bouncing impatiently.

"We're going to his house next," I said. "But we're in Renville, so it doesn't make sense not to come to a place he spent most of his time."

She rolled her eyes but didn't respond.

"Hmm." Tessa folded her arms across her chest and straightened up.

"What is it?" I asked, stepping around behind the desk to look at the screen.

"It says he moved from New Orleans," she said, frowning. "I remembered he was from down south, but I wasn't sure where until Leila told me he got a scholarship to LSU." She sent me a concerned look. "Kinda weird, huh?"

"What's so special about New Orleans?" Eris asked.

"It's where Tessa was born," I said, moving to stand beside her. Looking over her shoulder, I quickly read through the rest of the information on the screen. Nothing else seemed terribly interesting.

"Well, where they *said* I was born," she amended. "I was always told I got dumped off at a police station not long after I was born."

"But it is where you came from," I told her. "I know the Liaison who contacted Olympus personally."

"That's an odd coincidence," Epimetheus said, frowning. "That you both ended up here."

"It is," Tessa agreed. "Renville is about as small-town as you can get. The population is barely two thousand. Josh said his family moved here because his grandparents were nearby, which is really the only reason anyone would have to come here."

"What do you think it means?" Eris asked, her brow furrowed in curiosity as she looked at both of us.

"I don't know," Tessa said, shaking her head as she turned off the machine. "Whether this information is accurate or not is beside the point."

"The fact that it's the same as your reported birthplace is a bit unsettling, though," I said. "It's entirely possible he knew you'd eventually find these records."

Her expression turned doubtful. "What purpose would that serve?"

"He could've been following you," Epimetheus suggested. "We already know he can conceal his identity." He inclined his head toward the computer. "Something like this... it could be his way of letting you know he knew who you were."

"I'd say that's pretty freaking obvious by now," Eris muttered.

"Following her." I ran a hand over my jaw as I realized what he was saying. I let out a muttered curse. "He could've been watching you your entire life."

"It doesn't make sense," Tessa said quietly. She waved a hand toward the computer. "This doesn't make sense."

"Considering what we know about him, there's literally no reason at all to have provided *any* information, much less accurate information," Eris argued. "He's a witch. It would've been simple enough for him to just cast a spell and bypass school admins entirely."

"Then why wait until I was in high school to insert himself into my life?" Tessa's voice wobbled a bit. "It's more likely he just knew where I came from."

"No." Eris hopped off the desk and put her hands on her hips. "Your humans like their consistency. You probably had plenty of people in your life before he showed up who were always around. Friends, your friends' families, teachers, coaches. In a town like this, I bet people weren't banging down the door to move in."

"No, they weren't," Tessa murmured.

"Then I'd *also* bet he's been here just as long as you," Eris said.

"Who else was there?" I asked. Not for the first time, I was struck with the urge to take Tessa and hide her away until this was all over. "Who else was a big part of your life before you became friends with him?"

"Gods—I don't know. I'd have to think back, maybe talk to John and Analise." She shrugged. "Either way, it doesn't really matter now, does it? He's Josh. I'm sure he's had plenty of different names if he makes it a habit of changing faces all the time, but we know who he is now. We just have to work our way back to find out where he came from."

"Did Mary say anything at all about Josh knowing your true identity before you broke Hecate's spell?" Epimetheus asked. "I assumed he was just joining Cronus' cause as an ally, but I honestly can't see any other reason he would've intentionally placed himself in the same town as you if he didn't know who you were."

"She didn't say, but the connection was spotty, and we weren't able to hold it long," Tessa answered.

"Menoetius could've stationed Josh here," Eris said. "We already know Hecate's spell didn't work on him. He might not have been able to explain the specifics about why he was stationing Josh here, but that wouldn't really have been necessary. All he'd need to do was tell Josh to keep an eye on her."

"No, we would've gotten word of the rebellion far sooner if that had been the case," Epimetheus said. "It's barely been a year since we found out."

"He's right," Tessa agreed. "The amount of detail that would've gone into all of Menoetius' planning... no, I don't think Josh would've been idle this whole time if Menoetius was involved."

"We'll call the Pleiades when we get back to the mountain," I said. "See if you can get another link going."

Tessa nodded. "For now, let's go hit Josh's old house, see if there's anything there."

We teleported away, and a few seconds later, we were standing on the front lawn of Josh's former home, a single-story, wood-sided rancher set back in the woods on the outskirts of town.

I looked around warily, my senses going on high alert. There was an odd feel to it, something that hung in the air that made it feel off. As if in confirmation, the woods surrounding the house were silent. There was no twitter of birds or incessant buzzing of insects, no crunching of leaves under the feet of small animals.

"So what exactly are we looking for?" Eris asked, putting her hands on her hips. "I don't see us coming across anything damning in an empty house."

Tessa rubbed her hands on her jeans and took a deep breath, then looked at me. "You feel anything alive in there?"

I sent my power out through the house, searching for any signs of life. "None that I can feel. You?"

"Nothing."

"Let's get going, then," Eris said. "I don't want to be here all damn day."

We spent the next few minutes circling the house, seeking out any indication that the property might be booby-trapped or rigged against intruders. The weeds and vines that surrounded it were so overgrown and tangled that Tessa had to use her Earth power to retract them so we could get a better look at the grounds. In the heavy silence around us, the sound of our feet crunching the parched grass seemed to double in volume.

Frowning, Tessa stepped toward the side of the house and placed her hands on the wood siding. She closed her eyes in concentration for a few moments, then pulled back and frowned.

"It's like the history of this place was just... erased," she said, shaking her head. "I don't see anything but emptiness when I try to see its past."

We made our way up the front steps and into the house. The front door opened onto a hall that stretched toward the back of the house. To the left was a living room, to the right, a dining room. Square spaces were visible on the walls where the sun had bleached the blue floral pattern of the wallpaper, leaving nothing but the outline of picture frames that had once hung there. The carpet in the living room was a dark teal, faded and flat with age. The wood floors were scuffed and scratched as though they'd never seen a fresh coat of floor wax, and a thick layer of dust had given anything with color—the carpet, the dark wood floors, and the blue curtains that still hung in the windows—a muted look.

My wariness intensified.

"Tessa...he was still living here when you left for Olympus, right?" I whispered.

"He was," she confirmed. "He had a goddamn graduation party here the night before." She shook her head in confusion. "But this.. "

"This place hasn't seen a good cleaning in years," Eris said, looking around the living room.

"Decades maybe," Epimetheus added.

Tessa continued to look around the room, her eyes wide. "He must've had this place glamoured the whole damn time."

"Spread out," I told them. "See what you can find."

Silently, the four of us went off in different directions, our footsteps echoing loudly away from each other. Making my way into the kitchen, I began opening and closing drawers and cabinets, searching for anything that might give an indication as to who'd lived here last. The only thing I found was newspaper lining one of the drawers that was dated thirty years prior, which, considering the state of the rest of the house, seemed about right. The only other sign of age I found were mouse traps under the sink that held the skeletal remains of long-dead rodents.

Turning, I saw a narrow wooden door with dark metal hardware on the other side of the room. When I opened it, I found a set of stairs leading down into a darkened basement.

'Tessa, can you come give me some light?' I asked.

'Yup.'

A moment later, Tessa appeared at my side. "You're going into the creepy basement alone?"

I gave her a disparaging look. "We're gods, Tessa. We don't get creeped out by basements."

She eyed me dubiously. "You say that now, but I've actually been in that basement," she said, peering down into the darkness. "It's creepy." With a sigh, she touched her fingers to the light switch and sent a small shock of electricity into the wires. A few seconds later, a single bulb at the bottom of the stairs flickered to life. "There you go."

"You're more than welcome to join me, you know," I told her, grinning as I began to descend the stairs.

"Nope." She started backing away, smiling. "I'm heading up to check the attic. It's where Josh's bedroom was. Just call me when the monsters attack, and I'll come save you."

She blew me a kiss before walking off in the direction she came.

When I reached the bottom of the basement stairs, which were so old and creaky I was surprised I didn't fall straight through, I looked around the large, cold space. It was completely empty, save for a few pale green cabinets that had been shoved in the corner that looked like they'd once been in the kitchen and had been relegated to basement storage after a remodel. On the wall beside them was a door sitting slightly ajar that matched the one that led down to the basement.

I started going through the cabinets and drawers first, finding nothing but old hardware and a few broken light fixtures. Moving on to the door beside them, I pushed it open and found myself in a dimly-lit concrete root cellar. Orienting myself, I realized I was under the front porch. Crude but sturdy-looking wooden shelves had been built against one wall, and several large hooks hung with threadbare fabric bags were screwed into the wall across from it.

I did a quick scan of the space and, finding nothing amiss, stepped back out into the main room and finished my perusal. I'd just set my foot on the bottom stair when I felt a burning sensation in my nose. Sniffing, I turned to face the room.

Immediately, my breathing began to labor and black spots clouded my vision.

Seconds later, I was hit with the unmistakable odor of godsbane.

23

NATHANIEL

I barely had enough energy to teleport out of the basement and back up to the kitchen. Wheezing, I braced my hands on my knees as I tried to force the poison from my lungs.

'Everyone out!' I roared, my lungs burning too much to form words. *'Godsbane in the basement!'*

Tessa appeared in front of me, a look of panic on her face that lasted only seconds before she latched onto my arm and teleported us outside. As soon as the fresh air hit me, I sucked in a hard breath, hacking violently as my lungs began to clear.

"I'm fine," I wheezed as Eris and Epimetheus appeared beside us. Clearing my throat, I stood upright. "You two go do a lap around the house," I huffed at her and Eris. "Epimetheus and I will check the woods."

"What are we looking for?" Eris asked.

"This, I'm assuming," a dry voice said from behind her.

Eris spun, and when I saw who—what—had spoken, I instinctively stepped in front of Tessa. Saia, leader of the Sirens, stood at the edge of the porch, her skeletal legs appearing half broken.

Her hand was wrapped around the throat of a Telchine.

"Sirens," Eris groaned. "Color me surprised."

"What are you doing here?" Tessa demanded.

Saia shoved the Tel to the ground in front of her. "I got word that a few of Olympus' finest were sniffing around these parts." She sneered down at the small, pale male on the ground in front of her. "Imagine my surprise when I found this creature around back sliding a tube through a hole in the wall." She nudged him with her toe, and he hissed up at her.

"Stupid bitch," he spat, his facial features transforming from mostly human to monstrous.

Saia smirked, then bent at the waist until her face was inches from his. He shrunk back at her proximity, then when she quietly began to hum, his hands flew to his ears, and he began to scream.

"Saia!" I snapped, wincing as her voice pricked at my eardrums. "What are you doing here?"

The steady hum she'd been emitting stopped, and the Tel slumped to the ground. She looked over at us and gave me a small, feline smile. "Why, waiting for you four, obviously."

I cast a cursory glance around the property for any signs of a potential ambush but saw nothing amiss.

"You expect us to believe you weren't just trying to poison us?" Epimetheus asked.

She gave him a level glare. "I'm not the enemy you perceive me to be, Trickster."

"You sure about that?" Eris asked. "Last I checked, fighting for the opposition generally makes you an enemy."

"I came to warn you. One of my sisters got wind that you were seeking information on our newest threat." She inclined her head toward the house. "When I discovered your whereabouts, I came to investigate."

"And why is that?" Tessa asked, exasperation clear on her face.

Saia narrowed her eyes at Tessa, then folded her arms tapped her fingers on her elbow. The Tel at her feet attempted to crawl off, but she let out a quiet hiss and pressed a foot to his shoulder, shoving him back to the ground. "As I said, I'm not the enemy."

"Hang on," Epimetheus held up a hand. "What do you mean 'our' newest threat?"

She arched a narrow brow. "What threatens your world also threatens mine."

"And yet you've made a deal with them," I said, pointedly looking at her legs.

She wrinkled her nose and looked down at the frail appendages. "I thought I did. As it turns out, I may have made the wrong one."

"What do you know?" I asked. "You must have figured out why we're here, so what do you know?"

The Tel began struggling again.

"Oh, for the gods' sake," I muttered. I hit him with a blast of Coercion strong enough to knock him out, then looked back at Saia questioningly. "Well?"

Stepping away from her unconscious prisoner, she sat down on the steps and stretched out her legs. "I know that having these legs has not been as advantageous as I'd thought."

Tessa eyed her cautiously. "You're working with an incredibly powerful witch. Why hasn't he fully broken the curse?"

Saia waved a hand in annoyance. "He babbled on about the rule of Nature. The Fates won't allow it."

Epimetheus shook his head. "He's lying."

"Try telling him that." She arched a brow down at the Tel. "You may want to tie this one up. They can get quite feisty."

Tessa quickly summoned up two heavy vines and used them to wrap up his body from shoulder to ankle. "What do you want from us?" she asked when she was done.

Saia shrugged. "Demeter requested the curse that was placed on us. The only way the Fates will allow it to be broken is if the witch who placed it is the one to lift it."

"Who placed it?" Tessa asked.

Saia tilted her head, confused. "Scylla, of course."

"Scylla?" Tessa gave me a shocked look. "I guess that's why she was so confident the witch wasn't willing to break the curse."

"I thought everyone knew that," Eris said. "Isn't she your friend?"

"Yeah, she is," Tessa murmured.

Saia chuckled darkly. "Of all the witches out there, wouldn't you agree Scylla would be the best for the job?"

"Regardless of who placed it, you haven't given us a compelling reason to plead your case to her *or* Demeter," I said. "You've given us a sob story, nothing more."

Her face was blank as she looked up at me. "You seem different, Coercer. It's been some time, but I haven't seen you so cold in centuries."

"It's funny how an attack on my home has changed my outlook on things," I deadpanned.

Her lips curved up in a sly smile. "And your father? How does he feel about this change in demeanor?"

"Can we get back to the point?" Eris grumbled.

"Which was what, exactly?" Epimetheus asked.

"I want the Sirens' curse lifted," Saia said. "In exchange, you'll have my allegiance and that of my sisters." She lifted the Tel by his collar and shoved him toward us. "Take my saving your life as a show of good faith."

"His poison wouldn't have killed us," I said.

"Are you certain of that?" She kicked a small metal box with a hose attached toward us. I bent and picked it up, then immediately dropped it back to the ground when the poison residue near the tube seared my fingers.

"What is that?" I asked. I slid my sleeve down over my hand and picked the box up by the tube.

"The newest of their creations," Saia said with a shrug. "Take it back to Hecate and Demeter, have them perform their tests. Maybe then you'll believe me."

"How do we know you didn't stage this whole thing?" Tessa asked. "How do we know you didn't bring that with you?"

Saia held out a hand toward her. "You've got the gift of Psychometry, correct?" She looked down at her hand then back to Tessa. "Go on. You'll see everything, even the things I don't remember myself."

'Bad idea, love,' I told her.

'I don't really think we have a choice.'

A moment later, Tessa's shields dropped, and I felt a gentle tug as she pulled my mind into hers. Slowly, she walked toward Saia, ignoring Epimetheus' shout of warning. When she was a foot away from the Siren's outstretched hand, Tessa reached out and touched the tips of her fingers to Saia's palm, then I watched as she replayed the most recent of Saia's memories.

When the Siren had first arrived at Josh's house, she'd waited in the woods, watching as the small Telchine had circled the house, poking past bushes until he found his point of entry for his poison. Not long after, the four of us appeared on the lawn, and Saia began to sneak through the brush toward the Telchine. Seconds later, she had him by the neck as he thrashed and struggled against her.

Tessa's dubious response matched my own, so she immediately went back further until we came to a conversation between Saia and her second, Mila.

"Who told you they were there?" Mila asked.

"No one," Saia replied evasively. *"I've been watching them."*

Immediately, I started to dig through her memories as Tessa continued to watch her interaction with Mila.

Mila scoffed "And you believe they'll help? After what they saw in Athens?"

"They may believe us to be murderers, but that doesn't change the facts. We are weakened, and the Olympians are the only ones with the power to get us to our former state."

Mila snorted quietly. "Best of luck, then. I'll watch for your wings to show up on our doorstep when they rip them from your shoulders."

Releasing her hand, Tessa left Saia's mind but remained connected to mine. *'What do you think?'* she asked me.

I eyed Saia suspiciously. Nothing about the memory seemed falsified, but that didn't mean it wasn't. If anything, recent events had demonstrated just how much we couldn't trust the memories of others.

"You've been waiting here for weeks." I raised my eyebrows. "Why? Why not question us when we saw you in Athens?"

"You had it set in your mind that Mila and I were responsible for the attack on the Ischyra headquarters. You wouldn't have listened. Had you looked into my mind then, you would have seen that."

"Memories can be faked," I said flatly.

She gave me a surprised look. "Not to you. I'd venture to say you're one of the few who can see straight through false memories, at least in a creature such as myself."

"I trust very little of what I see in the minds of others these days," I told her.

She shrugged. "Regardless, my offer still stands. We will offer allegiance in exchange for removal of our curse. *Complete* removal." She huffed out a sigh when she received nothing but impassive looks in response. "I am not my mother," she said wearily. "I am not the one who tried to kill you, Mimic, nor am I the one who killed your lover," she said to me. "I'll admit to my own missteps, but I would ask that you not place blame on me for the crimes of my predecessors."

When neither of us responded, Saia shook her head. "I blame neither of you for the deeds of your fathers. I wish you would do the same in return." She glanced down at the Tel. "I'd get him back to the mountain before he wakes. He's probably got a good deal of information to offer." With a final, curious look in our directions, she spread her large green wings and shot skyward, becoming a distant speck in the sky within seconds.

"So what do we think?" Eris asked once she was gone. "Do we buy it?"

Tessa shook her head. "I don't know. She's not lying." She looked at me and raised her eyebrows. "Right?"

"No, she's not," I agreed. "That says nothing of her future mindset, however. She could feel differently by tomorrow."

Epimetheus picked up the unconscious Tel and tossed him over his shoulder. "We should finish this conversation at home, and you two need to question this one." He jerked his chin toward Eris. "You can carry the poison," he said with a smirk.

Yanking her sleeve down over her hand, Eris glared at him and picked up the small box. "I am *never* coming on a mission with you three again. First, I'm getting my fucking hair braided by that little ankle-biter, and now you have me lugging around poison. Assholes."

"It was either us or Zeus," I told her. "You go on ahead. I want to take one last look around."

"I'll stay with you," Tessa offered.

"Alright, then," Epimetheus said, adjusting the body of the Tel when it began to slide down his arm. "Be careful."

When he and Eris were gone, Tessa and I did another lap around the house before deciding to do one last check of the interior. None of us had been able to do a full search before the Tel had arrived.

As we walked along the side of the house, Athena appeared, hands on her hips, still clad in the battle leathers she'd been wearing on all her off-mountain missions recently. Her spear was strapped to her back, and a dirk hung from her left hip.

"Hey," Tessa said, smiling. "You look battle-ready. What's up?"

Athena shot me a glare, then smiled at Tessa. "Eris came back grumbling about you lot nearly getting poisoned to death, so I thought I'd come offer some backup while they got your prisoner settled." She gave me a pointed look. "It would've been nice to have been included in the first place."

"Eris needed a break from Zeus, and you've had missions elsewhere," I told her. I gave her a curious look. "Are you angry?"

She shifted uncomfortably, then shook her head. "No."

'Liar,' I said.

"Tell me what happened," she said, ignoring me. "Hecate and Demeter will be examining the poison Eris brought back, but I want to hear it from you both."

Tessa and I gave her a quick rundown of what had gone down since arriving in Renville, showing her the memory of our conversation with Saia. By the time we were done, she was staring at us, eyes narrowed, lips pursed.

"What is it?" Tessa asked.

"Something Oceanus said," Athena replied, tapping her fingers against her arm. "He seemed to think the Sirens may be worth looking into as allies."

I sighed and raked a hand through my hair, annoyed at the shift the day had taken. "You know my reservations, but talk it over with Ares and Apollo. If you three go to Father with a united front, he may listen."

"You, as well," she said.

I shook my head. "I'm not one of his advisors."

"Unofficially, you are. You're also a Coercer and his son, not to mention you were here when Saia arrived. He trusts you, so you should be there when we meet with him, too."

"Fine," I acquiesced. "Let's just get this done, so we can get back."

She gave a curt nod. "Where did you leave off?"

"I was in the basement, and Tessa was in the main house," I told her.

"I was going through Josh's bedroom," Tessa clarified. "Not that there was much to see."

"We'll start there, then," Athena said as she motioned us inside.

Tessa led us through to the rear of the house and up the stairs to where Josh's bedroom was located. Like the main living areas, Josh's room looked as though it hadn't seen a good dusting in a few decades. The windows were foggy with grime, the curtains nearly threadbare.

"Does anything seem off as far as energy goes?" Athena asked as she walked around the room, examining it.

"There *is* no energy," Tessa grumbled. "That's the problem."

Athena stopped and gave Tessa a surprised look. "None at all? Your psychometry—"

"Nothing works," I told her.

Tessa leaned against the wall and stared around the room morosely. "Whatever this place's history was, it's gone."

Athena turned and stared out the window, drumming her fingers on the dusty sill as she thought. A moment later, she turned, and Hermes appeared beside us, looking confused.

"What's going on? I was—"

"I need you to jump on the temporal plane," Athena interrupted. "Look into this place."

"You can *time travel*?" Tessa squeaked.

Hermes grinned at her. "Of course I can."

"How come you never told me?"

"Because it's incredibly dangerous," I told her, then held up a hand when her face became indignant. "And before you can even mention the word 'coddle,' I'll save you the hassle and tell you that's not what I'm doing." Annoyed, I looked at my sister. "Is this really necessary?"

"Yes," she said flatly.

"And Nathaniel is right," Hermes told Tessa. "Even with your powers, the skills you need to navigate the temporal place take much longer than we've had to perfect. You can't use another being as an anchor, for one. And it's incredibly exhausting, which is why I avoid it at all costs."

"Then how do you do it?" she asked, shifting her irritated gaze from me to him.

"I'll essentially be anchoring my own consciousness into different areas of the past," he told her, then shook his head. "No, it's more complicated than that. We'll get to it, though, I promise," he added when he saw her expression.

"Tessa's psychometry isn't giving her any history to this place," Athena said. "This is where Josh lived, but as you can see, there's no indication anyone has lived here in the recent past."

"Hmm." Hermes tapped his fingers to his lips as he did his own assessment of the space. "Interesting. Alright. But you two owe me a bottle of wine *each* when we return to Olympus."

"Or you could just get your satisfaction knowing you're helping locate information about our enemy," Athena snapped.

Hermes gave her an easy grin. "This trip will put me on my ass for the next two days. Wine will be my bonus."

Tessa gave him a concerned look. "Will you be able to talk to us while you're gone?"

"Only mentally, so all three of you need to be reading my mind the entire time." He shot a finger at her in warning. "Do not even *think* about hopping on board."

She held up her hands and shook her head. "I'm not trying to get stuck in nineteen-fifty or wherever it is you're going."

He narrowed his eyes and looked at me. "Keep an eye on her while I'm gone?"

"Already on it." I shifted my gaze to her. "Tessa, love, let down your shields, please."

Outrage was clear on her face. "You don't trust me?"

I winced, then shook my head. "Not with this."

Scowling, she pulled back her shields and let me latch onto her mind. *I guess I wouldn't trust me, either,* she muttered. *That's the only reason I'm letting you do this.*

"All settled?" Hermes asked.

I nodded.

"Okay, then." He wiggled his brows at Tessa. "Onward we go."

24

TESSA

I tried very hard not to be annoyed—no, pissed—that Nate, Hermes, and probably Athena didn't trust me to not join Hermes as he reversed the trajectory of his timeline to move around on the temporal plane. If I'd been in their shoes, I probably wouldn't have put it past me, either, but it still rankled a bit.

Once Hermes started to move backward in time, though, I fully understood where they were coming from. As soon as he started moving, I felt as though we'd been set adrift, floating away with no trace of a tether. It wasn't like when I'd used astral projection before, where I was visibly on a separate plane. This time, I was *there*. I stood in the middle of each scene, each event, and my surroundings showed no indication that I wasn't sharing the space with the people around me.

I watched as, in rapid succession, the events of the last four years at Josh's house sped by. I'd spent so much time there with him, Leila, Mary, and Eric, and the urge to drag Hermes to a halt so I could see myself and my friends in simpler, happier times was nearly overwhelming. We'd only gotten as far as Josh's graduation party when I felt Nate's hold on my mind tighten, and I realized it was because I'd started to drift forward. My friends, everyone I graduated with, were all around us, laughing in a way that was so carefree it hurt to watch. Kellan, who'd been Mary's date to prom, was doing a keg stand, and my heart twisted when I saw that Eric and another friend of ours were the ones holding up his ankles while our other classmates cheered him on. Mary and Leila were snuggled up on Josh's couch, whispering as they passed a bottle of tequila back and forth. And Josh...

'Watch him,' Hermes instructed. 'I'm going to pause here. Do not try to move on your own.'

I felt myself nod, then I focused on Josh's movements. He sat beside Leila, idly tracing small circles on her back as his eyes drifted out over the room. In that moment, he didn't look like my friend or a loving boyfriend to Leila. Instead, he looked... calculating.

'Can you move us behind the sofa? I asked, my curiosity piqued. 'I want to see something.'

Slowly, I felt Hermes shift us forward until we were standing over Josh, Leila, and Mary.

'What is it?' Nate asked.

'Watch his hand,' I murmured. 'Does that look like he's tracing a pattern to you?'

There was a moment of silence as he and Hermes watched the slow, gentle movement of Josh's fingers across Leila's back.

'It sure does,' Hermes said. 'Commit that to memory. We'll show Hecate and Chiron when we get back.' Slowly, I felt us drift backward as Hermes began to move back again. 'If you see a spot where we should stop, just holler.'

I watched, eagle-eyed, for a few more moments until another scene caught my eye.

'There!'

Hermes slammed to a halt as we began to pass by a movie night that we'd had here the year before. The five of us were spread out in his bedroom, our eyes glued to the TV in the corner where some action movie was blaring.

Without prompting, Hermes took us to where Josh and Leila had situated themselves on the bed. Josh sat against the wall with his knees up, and he had Leila pulled back against his chest. Her head rested on his shoulder as they watched the movie, their hands linked in front. Josh's thumbs were drifting slowly across the back of her hands, the movement so casual it seemed no different than the random touches Nate and I would give each other. A sign of affection, an acknowledgement of closeness. On closer inspection, though, it was clearly different.

'He's doing it here, too,' I said. 'The same pattern.'

'Okay, let's keep going, then,' Hermes said. 'I want to get back to when he first moved in, at least.'

'See if you catch any other instances of him doing the same,' Nate added.

We continued traveling back toward the day four years prior when Josh had moved in. Altogether, we counted eight instances of the weird patterns he was tracing on Leila's body, sometimes on her back, other times on her hands, but each time seeming innocent and affectionate.

The biggest shock of all came on the day Josh moved in when we were able to see exactly how he'd transformed the house from its current, dusty state to the spotless house I'd spent so much time in. One moment, the house stood as it was now, empty and lifeless. The next, Josh appeared in the middle of the entryway. He slid his hands in his pockets and slowly looked around the space, an appraising and thoughtful look on his face. Then, everything began to shift. The teal carpet was replaced with gleaming hardwood and Oriental rugs, the yellow formica counters became shiny black granite, all appliances and light fixtures were updated, and the wallpaper disappeared, replaced by basic eggshell white paint. Furniture and decor materialized out of thin air, magazines were strewn on the coffee table, wood was stacked in the basket by the fireplace, and a few other knick-knacks were scattered about, giving the house a lived-in feel.

There was one thing that was noticeably absent, though.

'Where are his parents?' I asked.

'Excellent question,' Hermes replied. 'I'll take a wild guess and assume they never existed.'

'We should meet up with Hecate and Scylla as soon as we get back,' Nate said. 'We've got more unanswered questions now than when we left.'

'Do we keep going?' Hermes asked.

'Can't hurt,' I told him. 'Let's just go back to when the place was built. If we don't find anything else, we'll head home.'

For the next few minutes, the three of us watched as the decades sped past, as various owners came and went, as renovations and remodels were completed, and finally, we saw the house as it was being built, back when it was no more than stacks of lumber and roofing tiles waiting to be put together. A part of me had hoped we might see some inkling as to why Josh had chosen this spot in particular, but there appeared to be nothing out of the ordinary.

'It's secluded,' Hermes said when I voiced my thoughts.

'So?'

'You know how we are,' Nate said. 'Gods and witches... we like our privacy.'

'Most of us, anyway,' Hermes joked, his voice strained. 'Hold on tight. I'm taking us back.'

Seconds later, I was flying through time, watching all the events I'd just seen zip past at lightning speed. I felt Hermes detach his consciousness from various points in the past, rerouting it so he was set back on his previous course. By the time we reached the present day, all three of us were left gasping for air.

"Well?" Athena barked the moment we were back.

"A moment to rest, dear sister, if you don't mind," Hermes wheezed, falling back on his rear and leaning on his arms. He looked as though he'd just been hit with a nasty bout of motion sickness. Which, considering the way I was feeling, was probably the case.

Ignoring him, she arched a brow at me and Nate. While Hermes continued to catch his breath, Nate and I ran through what we'd seen.

"So we think he may have been putting some kind of spell on Leila?" she asked, her brow furrowed in confusion. "For what reason?"

I shrugged. "I don't know. We need to talk to Hecate, show her the memory, see what she thinks. If you guys want to go check in with

Eris and Epimetheus, I'll go see Chiron and see if he can do some digging in the meantime."

Athena nodded absently. "Alright. Let's get back." She jerked her chin toward Hermes. "He's about to keel over." She clicked her tongue and shook her head. "Father is going to be so angry I've put him out of commission."

Nate gave her an amused grin. "It was worth it if it means we got some usable information."

Athena gave him a dubious look. "That's a big 'if,' baby brother."

WHEN WE RETURNED TO OLYMPUS, Nate and Athena left to check in at the palace. Epimetheus had dumped the Telchine in the dungeon, and Nate wanted to be there to begin questioning him as soon as he awoke. After promising to call me the moment the Tel woke up, I made my way down to the archives, which were housed in the basement of the library in Olympia.

The library was one of the few places I hadn't explored when I lived in the village, having had no real need for books or research. But when I entered the large, cavernous space, I suddenly wished I'd made time.

The building was a large, gray stone structure with columns along all four sides and a giant, dome-shaped roof. Frescoes adorned the ceiling in the main entryway, which also housed a shiny wooden circulation desk. Beyond the desk and through a towering archway was the main hall. From where I stood, I could see rows upon rows of bookshelves that stood at least ten feet high, each shelf crammed to the brim with books. Long wooden tables ran the length of the room, each with a few small lamps in the center. The handful of shelves I could see showed spines of various colors, both bright and subdued, waiting to be explored. I'd never been a big reader in either of my previous lives, but there was a peacefulness that hung over this place that made me want to go up and down the rows, dragging my hands along the spines, examining the collection that had accumulated over the centuries.

Tearing my gaze from the reading room, I refocused on the task at hand and approached the circulation desk. A female Ischyra sat behind it, typing away on a computer.

The sight of the machine drew me up short. Olympia was fully powered by solar panels built into the roofs of every building, but I hadn't seen any type of electronic device—computer, phone, television—since my arrival. The other things that use electricity were lights and appliances mainly, which were things that tended to remain inconspicuous, hidden in the background of day-to-day life, unnoticed even by those who were using them.

When the woman at the desk heard me approach, she looked up and greeted me cheerfully. "Hi! Can I help you find something?"

I returned her smile with one of my own. "I'm actually meeting someone in the archives. Could you tell me how to get there?"

"Of course! You must be here to see Chiron." She gave me a knowing grin and shook her head. "He's been here almost daily for weeks now."

"Well, hopefully I can help him find what he's looking for," I replied.

"Fingers crossed," she said. She inclined her head, motioning for me to follow. "The stairs are just over here." She frowned when she heard the confused sound I made.

"Sorry," I told her. "For some reason I was expecting an elevator."

"Ah. No, the Elders insisted on stairs." She sighed. "They felt an elevator would 'ruin the ambiance,'" she explained. "Getting that laptop in here was a feat in itself. The *forms* I had to fill out..." Another head shake. "It took forever to convince them that electronic catalogues are the way to go."

I laughed as we reached the top of a wide staircase. "That doesn't surprise me in the least. When did you go through your transformation?"

She tapped her chin as she thought. "Um... about three centuries ago? I've been with the library for nearly fifty years. It's kind of the perfect place to recharge after being in the field."

"I can imagine," I murmured, casting another wistful glance at the quiet reading room. Glancing over the railing, I saw that the stairs wound downward a few floors. "I'm guessing the archives are all the way down?"

The librarian grinned. "You got it. You'll find Chiron and the others in the back with the oldest records." She tapped her head. "My name is Shelly, so just give a holler if you need help."

"Will do. Thanks, Shelly."

"Oh!" Shelly stopped mid-turn. "I forgot to tell you—you won't be able to teleport into or out of here." She smiled sheepishly. "It's our way of protecting against theft."

"Got it." I smiled. "Thanks."

Once she'd walked away, I descended several levels into the basement below. A short corridor led from the bottom of the stairs to the archives room. When I stepped through the doorway, I stopped, stunned at how big the room was. I'd expected a cluttered, low-ceilinged room packed with shelves of boxes and artifacts. What I found was a warehouse-sized space with shelves stretching out in all directions. Stainless steel tables ran down the center of each row, each boasting clear, plastic boxes with arm holes that were attached to gloves meant for examining the more delicate artifacts that were housed here.

Despite the cavern-like feel of the room, a heavy quiet hung over it. If I wasn't mistaken, I could feel the slight tinge of magic in the air, telling me someone had likely put a muffling spell over the entire place. I reached out to Chiron mentally, not wanting to disturb anyone else who might be working.

'Hey, I have some news. Where are you?'

'Row six, all the way in the back,' he replied.

I scanned the numbers written in gold script on the end of each row of shelves in front of me until I found row six, then started the long trek toward where he, Yana, and Anette were doing their research.

I found the three of them poring over ancient-looking books and fragile papers that were spread out over the surface of one of the tables.

"How'd it go?" Chiron asked, not looking up from the book he was hovering over.

"So-so." I dropped down into one of the chairs and pulled a book toward me. "A Tel showed up and tried to kill us all, then Saia popped in and incapacitated him so we could bring him back here for questioning. Josh apparently had his home glamoured for the last four years to look like someone actually lived there, and the parents I *thought* he had don't seem to have existed. Oh, and we think he might've been casting spells on his girlfriend this entire time." I gave him a grim smile as I noticed the shocked expressions on everyone's faces. "Which is why I'm here."

Chiron cleared his throat and exchanged a look with Yana and Anette, whose eyes were wide. "Are you alright? No one was hurt?"

I shook my head. "Nate smelled the poison before it could do more than sting."

"And the Siren?" Yana asked. "What did she want?"

I set the book I'd been flipping through back on the table. "Cronus isn't the master she thought he was. She seems to think we can give her what he can't."

"Which is what?" Anette asked quietly.

"She thinks we can convince Demeter to have their curse fully removed."

Chiron huffed out a laugh and shook his head. "Good luck with that."

I drummed my fingers on the table and thought back over our conversation with Saia. "Do you think I can get Scylla to lift it without Demeter's permission?" I was still annoyed that Scylla hadn't told me she'd been the one to place the curse, considering we'd just talked about it not two weeks ago.

"You know her," Chiron said. "What do you think?"

That would be a big fat *no*, then.

"Demeter had Scylla curse the Sirens because they were unable to bring Persephone back from the Underworld, correct?" Yana asked. When I nodded, she gave me a confused look. "But Persephone is happy. Why are they still being punished?"

"Have you met the Elders? They're the most stubborn bunch of gods out there," I muttered. "But anyway, back to why I'm here." I looked up at Chiron. "Have a pen?"

He sifted through the papers and books on the table and produced a small pencil and a blank piece of paper. When he offered them to me, I shook my head.

"I'm going to show you a memory. I've got to focus on what I saw, so I need you to try and draw the pattern Josh is making with his hands."

Once he was seated in front of me with the pencil poised over the paper, I sent the memory to him, focusing all my energy on the move-ment of Josh's hands. As I did, Chiron had me go back over each memory several times before he was satisfied with what he'd drawn. When I released the memory, I leaned over to see what the symbol looked like.

It was a simple design of three concentric circles with a small X in the center.

The four of us leaned in further to examine it. After several moments, Yana straightened up and shrugged. "I have never seen it before."

"Nor have I," Anette said.

Chiron was still frowning at the symbol.

"Chiron?" I asked. "Do you recognize it?"

Perplexed, he slid his gaze my way. "I'm not entirely sure. Has Hecate seen this?"

"She's my next stop. I just figured I'd hand it off to you since you three are already in research mode." Narrowing my eyes slightly, I gave him a questioning look.

He just gave me a small head shake in return.

'I don't want to expound on any theories just yet, Tessa,' he explained. He sighed and ran a hand through his wild hair and looked at Yana

and Anette. "For now we'll add it to the growing pile of things we don't know."

I smiled apologetically. "I'm sorry. I didn't mean to make things harder."

"No, no, it's fine," he said, sitting back down. "If anything, it might help narrow things down a bit as we go." He gave me a tight smile. "Let me know once you hear from Hecate."

"Will do." Raising my eyebrows, I looked at each of them. "Do you guys need anything?"

Yana tilted her head from side to side and several loud *cracks* emanated from her neck. "A massage?" she joked. "A week's vacation?"

"In time," I told her. "Don't worry. Once this is all done, we're taking the mother of all vacations."

Anette gave me a hesitant smile. "Where will you go?"

"*We*," I told her. "And I'm not sure," I said, standing up. "I've never been to Disney World."

Yana barked out a laugh, one of the first I'd heard from her in days. "After saving the planet from near destruction, you want to go to a theme park?"

I shrugged. "Why not? It's supposed to be the happiest place on Earth, right?" I grinned wickedly. "And I bet Apollo would look fantastic in mouse ears."

Chiron laughed. "I think Disney World sounds perfect."

25

NATHANIEL

A pollo met me and Athena on the front steps of the palace, heading us off before our father could get to us. His annoyed expression told me all I needed to know about Zeus' current state, making me thankful I'd be avoiding him for the time being.

"Father is furious you went to Renville without notifying him first," he told us.

"Did you tell him you were in on the decision?" I asked. "Or is he suddenly questioning your choices, too?"

"In case you haven't noticed, Nathaniel, he's become quite the micromanager lately," he said dryly. "All of our decisions are being called into question."

"You don't say," Athena muttered.

"Now tell me what happened," he demanded. "Eris and Epimetheus mumbled something about Sirens before dumping a bound and gagged Telchine in the dungeon and rushing off to find Demeter."

I gave him a quick recap of the events leading up to Athena's arrival in Renville, then she chimed in here and there as I explained our trip through time with Hermes.

"Saia just *gave* him to you?" Apollo narrowed his eyes. "I found it odd when Eris explained it, but if what you're saying is true..."

"It is," I said. "They want the curse removed in exchange for their allegiance."

Apollo let out a sigh. "That's a discussion best put aside for now. We need to get this Telchine handled. I've already called for Hades, so let's get this over with."

We followed behind, making our way quickly through the halls to the entrance to the dungeon.

"He was still knocked out when I was down there," Apollo said, "but it's probably time to wake him up."

I nodded. "We'll need to get Hecate up here, as well."

"Epimetheus has already sent for her." He indicated toward the hallway that stretched off to the right in the opposite direction of Menoetius' cell. "He's down this way."

We came to a stop outside the cell where Epimetheus had deposited the unconscious Telchine, who'd been unceremoniously dumped in the corner of the cell, still wrapped in the ropes Tessa had bound him in.

"Hades will be here momentarily," Apollo said, then looked down at the prisoner. "Shall we wake him?"

"I'm not sure." I sent out my Coercion, forcing myself into his mind, pressing against the elastic shell of magic that surrounded it. "His shields are strong," I told them, pushing against them a bit harder. "Surprisingly so."

"How do you mean?" Athena asked.

"They've been reinforced magically, just like Menoetius'," I explained. I let my power drop and frowned. "They aren't quite as strong, but he's got a few dark spots that I can't quite reach."

"Hades should be able to help with that," Apollo said, continuing to eye the prisoner speculatively. "He doesn't look well, does he?"

I looked more closely at the prisoner and saw that he'd taken on a clammy sheen. His pale skin was beginning to glisten with sweat, and his breathing had taken on a labored sound.

Seconds later, Hades came strolling down the hall, his face unnervingly calm.

"This place is becoming quite popular," he commented as he came to a stop beside me. He stepped closer to the bars and peered down at the unconscious prisoner. "What have you done to him? He looks ill."

"Nothing," I told him. "He doesn't seem to be taking to the Olympic air well."

"Altitude sickness?" Hades suggested glibly.

I arched a brow. "Altitude sickness? Really?"

He shrugged. "It could happen."

"No, it couldn't," Apollo said. "Get on with it, already."

"Are we waking him up for this interrogation?" Hades asked.

"See what you can get from him while he's knocked out," Athena said. "If we need to wake him, we will."

Slowly, I unfurled my power and brushed it against the Telchine's mind again. The shield was thick like heavy rubber, flexing under the pressure of my power. I split my Coercion into thin whips of magic; then, with a flick, I sliced through his shield, instantly shattering it and the magic that bound it. Once I'd cleared the remnants of magic out of the way, Hades' and I combined our magic and drifted toward the dark concealment spots.

Hades examined the areas for a few moments, his magic poking and prodding them as he tried to glean information.

'He certainly didn't create these himself,' he said after a few moments. *'They're loaded with protective magic. Whatever information was put in these areas is heavily protected.'*

'Great.' I sighed. *'Alright. Let's wake him up.'*

We pulled out of the Tel's mind then in unison, we hit him with twin blasts of power, jolting him awake.

Immediately, he began thrashing around on the floor, straining against the bonds. When he saw where he was and took in the four of us standing over him, he froze, then his eyes narrowed into slits of fury.

"Olympians," he hissed. "You shouldn't have brought me here."

Hades slid me a look, then gave him a vicious smile. "Really? I've found our powers of persuasion to be quite effective."

"You'll get nothing from me," the Tel growled.

"We haven't even tried," I told him. "What makes you think you won't break?"

Slowly, he dragged himself up into a sitting position and smiled humorlessly. "Because I am a weapon for my ruler, and a weapon who cannot be wielded must be destroyed."

"What—"

Before I could finish my question, a loud *snap* sounded in the room, and a choking sound came from the Tel's throat.

"Shit!" Shoving Hades aside, I slammed my palm to the lock of his cell to release it. The door swung open, but by the time we'd rushed inside, the Tel had begun to foam at the mouth. Seconds later, his body went still, his eyes frozen and lifeless.

Silence hung over the cell as the four of us stared down at him, frozen.

Athena blinked, dumbfounded. "Did that really just happen?" she asked quietly.

Leaning down, I gripped the Tel's chin and forced his mouth open, then let out a muttered curse and shoved his body away. "Poison tooth." I shook my head and gripped the back of my neck. "We should've known he'd do something like this."

"There's no way we could've anticipated this, Nathaniel," Apollo said.

"They're goddamn poisoners, Apollo! We should've searched him before bringing him back!"

"And what, given him a dental exam in the process?" Apollo snorted. "You're smarter than that, brother."

Athena touched a hand to my back. "Apollo's right."

Just then, footsteps sounded in the hall, and a moment later, Tessa appeared in the doorway. When she saw our expressions, her eyes shot to the Tel's body.

Brows lifted, she looked at each of us in turn. "What happened?"

"Contingency plan," I bit out. "He was fitted with a poison tooth. Once he woke up, he broke it."

She sighed and slumped against the wall. "Well, that sucks."

Athena gestured toward the body. "Someone get the tooth, take the poison to Demeter and have her test it."

"This is becoming tiresome," Hades grumbled as Apollo pried open the Tel's mouth and began picking out tooth fragments.

"What is?" Tessa asked.

"A dungeon full of useless prisoners," he replied.

"Well...hang on a sec," Tessa said. "Let me examine the body, see if I can get anything." Without waiting for a response, she crouched down beside the Tel's body and laid her hands on his chest. She closed her eyes and went still as she let her power drift into him.

When she opened her eyes, her expression was grim. "Nothing.'

"What do you mean?" Apollo asked.

"I mean, there's nothing there." She stood and put her hands on her hips, scowling down at his lifeless form. "Whatever memories and events may have been attached to him are gone. He's a blank slate. Wiped clean, just like Josh's house."

"May I go back to complaining now?" Hades asked blandly.

"By all means," Apollo said, stuffing the broken tooth in his pocket as he began to walk back toward the exit. "I'll be at Demeter's. Let me know if you find anything," he called back.

"I suppose this means we're back to where we began," Athena said, slumping against the wall. "With nothing."

"Not necessarily," Tessa said. "We know the Tel's are prepared to kill themselves if caught."

"And that helps us how?" Hades asked. "Or do you have plans to go out and round up every single one of them?"

Tessa frowned. "No, of course not. I'm just saying, it's information we didn't have before. We may be able to use it." She shrugged. "Or not. I don't know."

She turned and began walking away.

"Where are you going?" I called.

"To see my brother," she replied. "Come on."

The three of us followed her through the halls until we came to Menoetius' cell. When we stopped in front of the door, a sly smile spread across his face. "Ah, Tessa. And here I'd thought you'd forgotten about me."

"We just captured a Telchine," she told him, forgoing any type of acknowledgement. "He's dead."

"Ah." He nodded knowingly. "Those little poison capsules in their teeth are quite ingenious, wouldn't you say?"

"What kind of poison is it?" I asked.

He shrugged. "I can't say. I was never stupid enough to get near it." He eyed us curiously. "Might I ask how you came across this unfortunate poisoner?"

"Oddly enough, he was trying to kill us," Tessa said.

Menoetius leaned his head back to rest on the wall, clasping his hands together in his lap as he eyed her. "That *is* odd, isn't it?"

Tessa glanced at me, a question in her eyes, before answering. "I suppose it is."

"Well, it's not, really," Hades said. "It's quite genius, actually."

It took everything inside me not to tear open the door and slam Menoetius against the wall as I realized the conclusion Hades had just come to. Instead, I took a measured breath, then looked down at him. "'A weapon that can't be wielded must be destroyed.' That's what the Tel said. Are you saying he came after us to *kill* Tessa?"

Menoetius looked smug. "It's quite possible. She clearly won't fight for our cause, and at this rate, accessing her and successfully taking her are unlikely, correct?"

"Highly," Hades said quietly.

"Well, then, there you have it," Menoetius said.

Rage, mixed with a painful need to protect tore through me. It was one thing trying to prevent them from taking Tessa. Knowing they no longer had any qualms with killing her completely changed things.

"Any other questions?" he asked, smirking up at us. "I'm feeling a bit chatty today."

I narrowed my eyes and tried to quell my curiosity. "Why?"

He shot me a look. "Perhaps I'm simply tired of having my mind poked at."

"No." Tessa shook her head. "What game are you playing now, Menoetius?"

Athena tilted her head to the side and gave him an amused look. "You've gotten bored in here, haven't you? Has the silence finally gotten to you?"

"How is the investigation into *Josh* going?" He grinned knowingly. "Have you figured out how to kill him yet?"

Tessa stiffened, and I could practically feel her desire to question him humming off of her.

'Don't take his bait,' I told her.

She pressed her lips into a thin line but kept her curiosity to herself.

"If you're feeling so chatty, why not share a bit of what you know?" Athena asked. She looked around the hall and into Menoetius' cell. "It's not like you're going anywhere."

"Alright." Menoetius held up three fingers. "I'll give you three guesses as to Josh's true nature. If you guess correctly, I'll tell you the truth."

"We already know what he is," Tessa said.

He chuckled darkly. "Trust me, baby sister, you don't."

Hades arched a brow. "Menoetius, I have to know something. Why in *all* the realms would a powerful primordial witch bring you, of all creatures, into his inner circle? Aside from your taste for violence, you've really got nothing to offer."

Menoetius glared up at him.

"He's right," Tessa said quietly. "Why you?"

Menoetius shrugged. "I suppose that's something you'll need to ask him yourself."

Hades barked out a laugh. "Oh, believe me, if we find that cretin, *your* role in all of this will be the last thing on my mind."

Menoetius gave him a self-satisfied smile. "You know, I'm not even sure our father or Cronus knows what Josh is," he said. "I don't know that they ever will."

"What's that supposed to mean?" I asked. I tried to tamp down the curiosity that I'd just been telling Tessa to keep hidden.

Closing his eyes, his smile turned wicked. "It means the Olympians truly have no idea what they're up against."

26

NATHANIEL

A short while later, the four of us, along with Epimetheus and Eris, were gathered in the war room to give my father an update on the day's events.

"So aside from Menoetius' assertion that Josh is *not* a witch, you're telling me we've got nothing new to go on," Zeus said flatly once we'd finished.

Eris let out an annoyed groan. "No, Father, we're telling you quite the opposite."

"A new brand of poison, a suicidal Telchine, and strange symbols being traced on the back of some human does not equate to anything useful, only somewhat expected and marginally interesting." He turned to face me, Athena, and Apollo. "Tell me again what happened to the Telchine you managed to let kill itself."

Hades snorted. "Unless you regularly examine your prisoners' teeth, little brother, I would save the judgment for someone deserving."

Zeus glowered at Hades. "Do not—"

"Demeter is examining the poison as we speak," Apollo interrupted. "Along with the poison Epimetheus and Eris brought back from Earth."

"She seems to think it's a derivative of godsbane," Epimetheus explained. "Modified, both genetically and magically to be more catastrophic for deities and other immortals."

"The poison in his tooth and the poison that was released into the house are likely one and the same," Athena said.

Zeus grunted his agreement, then picked up two markers from the edge of the map of Earth and placed it over Pennsylvania, one indicating the presence of the Tels, the other, the Sirens. "I'm going to meet with Oceanus and discuss furthering an alliance with the Sirens," he said after a moment.

"You think you can convince Demeter to lift the curse?" I asked skeptically.

"Demeter doesn't rule this mountain," he said quietly.

We were silent for a few moments, the lull in conversation interrupted when Persephone and Hecate came through the door.

"I've got bad news," Persephone said, forgoing any greetings. "My trackers and I have been all over Greece. There's no sign of your missing Ischyra or witches anywhere." She looked at Tessa apologetically. "I'm sorry, Tessa."

"What do you mean there's no sign?" Zeus asked. "I thought I told you to wait to seek them out?"

"I mean I used the information I was given along with the trace of power Tessa provided to try to track down her friend. Nothing came up, so she's either not in Greece, or my trackers are suddenly shit at their jobs." She preened at Zeus. "And I must've mistook your meaning. I assumed there was urgency behind your command, seeing as the lives of Olympic immortals were at risk."

"I would go with the first option," Hecate told her, ignoring Zeus' look of outrage. "They could have the location cloaked or disguised."

"Hello, square one," Athena sighed, dropping into a chair. "So lovely to see you again."

"You'll need to try to reach Mary again," Hecate told Tessa. "Your best—only—option now is to have her provide as much information as possible about where she is."

Tessa nodded. "Understood."

I took out the piece of paper on which Chiron had drawn the symbol that Josh had been tracing on Leila and slid it across the table. "Hecate, have you any idea what this symbol might mean?"

Frowning, Hecate picked up the paper and examined the drawing curiously. "No, it doesn't look familiar, but then we witches stopped using symbols long ago. They're too easy to mar," she explained when she saw my questioning look. "A few of the primordials still use them from time to time, but for the most part, they've become obsolete."

"How long?" I asked.

"Millennia," Hecate replied. "Before your time, certainly."

"You have no idea what it is?" Tessa asked. "Chiron mentioned a protection spell."

Hecate pursed her lips and drummed the fingers of one hand against the edge of the table. She tilted her head this way and that as she turned the paper, examining the symbol from all angles. Finally, with a sigh, she set it down.

"Yes, I can see why he might think that." She pointed to the three concentric circles. "The object of the spell would be the X in the center, and each ring *could* represent a layer of protection." She gave the drawing another considering look as Tessa told her how Josh had traced the symbol on Leila.

"It always seemed like one of those tiny, affectionate gestures that guys do," Tessa told her, frowning. "I never paid much mind to it until now."

Hecate held up the paper. "May I take this with me? I have a few resources I can tap for information."

"Take what you need," Zeus ground out. "Get us some goddamn usable information already."

With a small nod, Hecate left. Once she was gone, Zeus glanced over at Tessa. "Go try and contact your friend again," he ordered. "See if you can get through."

"I'll do what I can," she said with a sigh.

'I've got a lead to follow up on,' Eris said, keeping her eyes trained on our Father.

'Where?' I asked.

'*Up north. I'll meet you back at your house in a bit.*'

I looked over at Athena, whose gaze followed Eris' retreating form as she left the room.

Eyes narrowed in suspicion, she looked at me. '*What's that all about?*'

'*Not sure. I'm assuming she's following up on the location of the Telchines.*'

Zeus threw up his hands in annoyance when he saw Eris sneak out. "Where is she going?"

I shrugged. "Following a lead. I'm sure she'll be back soon."

He grumbled something unintelligible under his breath, then went back to studying the map.

BY THE TIME we got home, the sun was just setting, casting a soft, orange glow over the yard. After being cooped up in the palace for so long, neither Tessa nor I were in any rush to close ourselves inside the house, so we decided not to go in right away. Sitting down in one of the wide wooden chairs, I tugged her down onto my lap and wrapped my arms around her waist. I sat quietly for a moment, breathing her in as she ran her fingers through my hair.

"You were amazing today," I whispered.

"You weren't so bad yourself," she replied, shifting so she was straddling my hips. Touching a finger to my chin, she tilted my face toward hers. "I love you, Nate."

Leaning forward, I slid my hands up her thighs and around her hips, then kissed her. "I love you, too."

"Hey, lovebirds!"

Tessa groaned at the sound of Eris' voice on the lawn.

"Oh, don't look so disappointed!" she exclaimed when she saw us. Taking a seat in the chair next to me, she wiggled her eyebrows and grinned. "I've got news that you'll both be quite interested in."

"Oh?" I quirked a brow as Tessa moved back into a sitting position. "What kind of news?"

She grinned mischievously. "The kind I should be telling Father first."

"Then why aren't you?" Tessa asked.

"Do you want to know or not?"

"What did you find, Eris?" I asked, annoyed that she'd interrupted one of the few quiet moments I'd gotten with Tessa in days. But then, I shouldn't have been surprised. My siblings seemed to have a knack for interrupting.

"Tels." Eris propped her feet up on the rail, legs crossed at the ankles. "Their whole damn headquarters," she said. "They've set up shop in a small village in Iceland that had been cleared out by crocotta a couple of months back."

Tessa's eyes widened. "An entire village?"

I eyed her suspiciously. "I thought you said they were in Scandinavia."

"Did I say that?" She frowned, then shrugged. "Oops. Anyway, seeing as you two have some nifty tricks up your sleeves, I wanted to talk to you first." She smirked.

I arched a brow, confused. "About what? And why?"

"Well, you've said multiple times we need to take the Telchines out. Father keeps hedging, wanting to go for the bigger fish, stick with the more complex plans, even if they're a waste of time."

"I'm not the only one of our family who's suggested that," I pointed out.

"Ah, yes, but none of *them* would even think about circumventing one of Zeus' orders."

Ignoring her satisfied smile, I shook my head. "And you think I will?"

"If anyone could get away with it, it's you," she said with a cheeky grin.

"And you'd get a nice dose of feuding family members to feed from, right?" Tessa muttered.

"Just a bonus," my sister said, her eyes alight with mischief.

I drummed my fingers on the wide arm of my chair, torn between hearing her out and sending her away. Tessa and Eris both sat quietly, waiting as I deliberated internally.

Finally, I shifted his eyes back to Eris. "What did you have in mind?"

She pulled a small brown bottle out of the pocket of her leather jacket and set it on the arm of her chair. "This is the poison Hecate and the others extracted from the Tel we brought back from Renville."

Tessa gingerly picked up the bottle and turned it this way and that, watching the thick liquid swirl around. "How did you get this?"

"Ah... it's better if you both don't know."

"Unsurprising," I murmured. I held my hand out for the bottle, taking it when Tessa handed it over. "Again, what are you thinking?" I held up the bottle. "I'm assuming poison, but how?"

"Give them a taste of their own medicine, literally."

Slowly, a grin spread across Tessa's face, even as I frowned, torn between consideration and doubt.

"Hang on." Tessa sat forward on my lap and faced Eris. "Do you remember what Hades said, about how you and I could do some major damage—"

"...if we were sent into enemy camps together?" She grinned. "Not quite where I was headed, but the thought's crossed, trust me."

"Wait." I held up a hand and shook my head, desperately trying to avoid going down a road that involved Tessa and Eris teaming up to do anything. "Answer the damn question, Eris."

"I found the place where they like to hang out," she explained, slumping back in her chair. "A little hole in the wall bar they took over from the humans. Bunch of partiers, those Tels." She wiggled her eyebrows then reached for the bottle, but I held it just out of reach, waiting for her to finish explaining. Scowling, she rolled her eyes. "Lotus Eaters, too, from what I'm told. And—" she held up a finger before I could speak— "my sources tell me that humans have been seen frequenting this place, so I'm guessing..."

"There's a new party drug going around?" I said grimly. The

Telchines were almost as good at creating narcotics for humans as they were at creating deadly poisons in war, so the fact that they'd opted to dip into the human drug trade in the midst of all this turmoil was unsurprising. It wasn't the first time, and it likely wouldn't be the last if history served to repeat itself. I wouldn't have put it past them to start a new drug pandemic in the middle of a war just to cause more chaos around the world.

"Alright." I inclined my head toward the bottle in my hand. "How much can you have made by tomorrow?"

Eris smacked my knee with the back of her hand. "That's the spirit! Give me 'til this time tomorrow, and I'll have all we need." Her eyes shifted toward Tessa, then drifted up and down her body, taking in her jeans and blue and white flannel. "You have something a little more... feminine than that?"

Tessa lifted my eyebrows. "Sexy feminine or just girly?"

"Sexy. Hot."

"Ah... I don't know, actually."

'The dress you wore to the welcome feast,' I said. *'That purple one.'*

Smirking, she slid me a glance. *'You remember what I wore that night?'*

I kissed her shoulder. *'I'm pretty sure any male with eyes would remember that dress. Wear the shoes, too.'*

Her cheeks flushed, and I took a small amount of pleasure in knowing I'd been the reason for it. She nodded at Eris. "Yeah, I have something."

Eris clapped her hands and jumped to her feet. "Perfect. On. Tessa, how are you with illusions? Or glamours?"

"Um... I've never done glamours, but I can manage illusions well enough. Why?"

"Appearances may need to be altered," she explained, wincing.

"Coercion might be better for that," I told Eris. "We can both work that, and she's got more experience with it."

"Whatever." Eris waved a hand dismissively. "Just make sure no one recognizes us."

"We'll do what we can," I told her.

"I suppose that'll have to be enough." With a grin, she blew us each a kiss. "Night night, kids."

27

TESSA

Twenty-four hours after Eris talked Nate and me into joining her on her mission to take out the Telchines, I'd pulled my plum-colored pencil dress and gold stilettos from the back of the closet and laid both on the bed. I eyed them warily, then looked up at Nate, who was wearing slim-fitting jeans with a white button-down, and scowled.

"It's really not fair that you basically get to wear the same thing you wear every other damn day." I touched the hem and wrinkled my nose. The dress was made of a slightly stretchy jersey material, so I'd be able to move in it well enough. It wasn't nearly as versatile as the leggings or jeans I normally wore, though.

He slid his hands in his pockets and shrugged. "Such is life," he said with a grin.

I sneered at him, then shooed him away. "Can you go get Yana? I need her to do my hair," I told him.

He stepped toward me and lifted a lock of hair off my shoulder and frowned. "Your hair looks fine."

"Eris said sexy. Hot." I gestured toward my air-dried hair that was mostly straight but with a very subtle wave. "This is *cute*." I looked at the piece of hair in my hand and frowned. "Ish."

His eyebrows lifted in amusement. "Well, my apologies." He slid his hands around my waist, then his eyes drifted toward the dress. "Need a hand getting that thing on? It looks difficult."

"Nathaniel, whatever you're thinking will *not* get us out of here in a timely manner," I teased.

"Oh, but it would be fun." Smiling wickedly, he kissed me gently, then rested his forehead against mine. "Do you have any idea what was going through my head when I saw you in this dress the first time?"

I preened up at him. "Good things, I hope."

He gave me a slow smile. "I think that would depend on your definition of 'good.'"

I shook my head and grinned. "Well, once this is all said and done, you might have to elaborate."

He kissed me on the forehead, then brushed a thumb across my cheek. "I'll hold you to that. I'll go grab Yana for you."

Once he'd left, I stripped down to my underwear and slipped the dress over my head. When it settled, I shifted uncomfortably. After two months of wearing jeans or leggings—I'd yet to venture out in the leather pants Persephone and Athena had forced on me—it felt strange to have my legs bare and fabric clinging to my body from my chest down to my thighs.

I let out a small groan when I looked at the four-inch heels, wondering how painful it was going to be to wear them after all this time. They'd been brand new when I'd come to Olympia, and I'd had only one night, a few hours, to break them in.

"Suck it up, Tessa," I muttered.

"Talking to yourself?" Yana asked, stepping into the room, curling iron in hand. "They say only crazy people do that, you know."

I snorted. "Anette still with Chiron?"

"Yes. The research seems to help keep her mind off of things. I think it makes her feel useful." She held up her pink-handled curling iron. "Curls again or straight?"

"Straight, please. Poker straight, if you can manage."

While we waited in the bathroom for the iron to heat up, she began pinning up sections of my hair with long pink clips. When she was done, she stepped back and scrutinized my outfit.

"What?" I asked curiously.

"What exactly are you all doing?" She picked up the iron and gave the metal a quick tap, then, satisfied with the heat, gestured for me to turn around. "You look like you are going to a club."

I turned to face the mirror and held still as she began slowly straightening my hair, one small section at a time. "Paying a visit to a Telchine village, hopefully wiping out a large chunk of them if we can. Eris will have more details when she gets here."

"Which I am," Eris said, coming up behind us, causing Yana to jump.

"Warning would be nice," she muttered. "Unless you want Tessa to lose a bit of hair."

"Yeah, yeah." Eris hopped up on the counter next to me and watched as Yana curled my hair, turning my wispy waves into soft, shiny curls that flowed over my shoulders and down my back. "So, why aren't you coming with us, Yana?"

Yana quirked a brow but didn't meet Eris' inquisitive eyes. "Because I do not want to. And I was not asked."

"Well, that's shitty," Eris said, sending a chastising look in my direction. "I think you should come, help distract those nasty little Tels. I bet you could rock a minidress."

"No," Yana said flatly, slipping a clip from my hair and sliding it into her pocket.

I gave Eris an amused look and shrugged. "I didn't ask for a couple of reasons. One, I knew she wouldn't want to go," I began, meeting Yana's eyes in the mirror. She gave me a small smile in return. "And..."

"You do not know how well-equipped I am to defend myself," she finished, setting the iron down and facing Eris directly. "I do not like it, but I agree that it is not smart for me to be out in the world, especially since there are some who believe I am dead."

"Nice try, though," I told Eris with a knowing grin. "But no arguments to start here."

She gave me a quick sneer and hopped off the counter. "Fine, fine. Let's get this show on the road, shall we?"

"Yep. We'll be out in a few."

Yana finished off my hair with a hefty dose of flowery hairspray, then unplugged the iron, then smiled at me.

I looked in the mirror and grinned. "Thanks, Yana. It looks perfect."

We made our way out to the living room and found Dionysus waiting with Nate. Dionysus let out a low whistle when we walked in. "Someone cleans up nice," he commented. He twirled a finger in my direction. "Immortality certainly changes the way that thing looks on you, Tess."

I rolled my eyes but couldn't help but smile. "I take it you're coming along?"

"You know I can't miss a good bout of revelry, and Eris was right. Those Tels love to party."

Nate came over and kissed my temple. "And we'll want him there in case we need to relieve tensions. You need to be focused solely on Coercion and illusions."

"Got it." I took a deep breath and looked around at them all. "We sure we want to do this? Go behind Zeus' back like this?"

"It's a good plan and needs to be done," Eris said. "Considering the Telchines' allegiances, it's entirely possible we'll find other enemies there, as well."

"So we could potentially kill two birds with one stone," Nate finished.

"Or find yourselves in a bigger heap of shit than you are expecting," Yana said, shaking her head slowly.

"Gotta love your positivity, Yana," Eris said with a wry grin.

"We'll call for help if we need it," Nate told Yana, seeing the concern she was trying hard to mask. "But try not to worry." He looked at me expectantly. "Tessa?"

I flashed him a quick, hopefully convincing smile, then sent out my illusion magic, letting it flow across the room, willing the appearances of me, Nate, Eris, and Dionysus to shift. It was uncomfortable, like trying to stretch a balloon over a basketball, but once I managed to snap it into place, the illusion seemed steady enough. I added a touch of Coercion, hoping it would be enough to hold the illusion in place until we were done.

When Yana's brow drew down, and she looked back and forth between us, I knew it had worked.

"This is not normal," she muttered. "Red hair does not suit you, Tessa. And why did you make me do your hair if you were just going to change it?"

I snorted as Nate tugged gently on a lock of the red hair I'd given myself. "It's still the same, just red and a little longer."

She grunted in response as she continued to look over the others.

Nate's sandy brown hair had been transformed to smooth, glossy black, his eyes, light green, and his height a good six inches shorter than normal. I'd given Dionysus a magenta faux-hawk and altered the shape of his nose, then broadened his shoulders a bit to add some bulk to his lean frame. Eris had gotten a boost in height, bringing her about even with my five-foot-eight, and I'd changed her brown-and-red hair to a platinum bob. Her pert nose was shifted into a longer, more aristocratic version, her athletic build made more curvy.

"You know, I think I might have to give this a shot for real," Dionysus mused as he examined his new hair in the mirror on the wall beside the door.

Nate nudged his brother out of the way to look at his own reflection, then shot me a disparaging look in the mirror.

I covered my mouth and giggled.

"Is everyone clear on their role?" Nate asked, turning away from the mirror.

"I think so," I replied.

"Well, no time for thinking now," Eris said. "Let's go."

We teleported into the woods about a hundred yards from our

destination on the edge of the small village the Telchines had overtaken. The quiet thump of dance music flowed through the open
door of the bar that beckoned to passersby with the promise of a
good time. It was more than the hole-in-the-wall Eris had described
but still small enough to be easily overtaken if the opportunity
should present itself. With the four of us posing as humans looking to
gain a fix from the Tels within, we'd have no problem getting—and
hopefully fitting—in.

Getting out, on the other hand...

Nate slipped his arm around my waist and tugged me toward the
door. *'Let's get this over with,'* he murmured. *'I don't want my memories
of you in that dress ruined by what we're doing.'* He gave my hair a
teasing tug. *'Or by that hair.'*

I leaned up and placed a quick kiss on his jaw. *'I can always get a
new dress.'*

'I like this one.'

Eris and Dionysus skipped ahead, fingers linked, as they
approached the bouncer. He was a tall, burly human who looked like
he'd thrown a customer or ten out on their ass at some point in his
lifetime. Something told me he wouldn't hesitate to do the same if he
thought we were attempting to gain entrance for nefarious purposes.

Nate rattled off a few words in Icelandic, then I felt a hint of his
power slip toward the bouncer. A moment later, the guard's eyes went
blank, then he simply angled his head toward the door for us to
enter.

'You speak Icelandic?' I asked Nate, curious.

*'Learning foreign languages is probably one of the more entertaining
things about living among humans for two millennia,'* he said. *'I can teach
you a few if you want.'*

My fingers tightened in his as interest and jealousy feuded in my
mind. Pushing it all back, I smiled up at him. *'Thanks.'*

He stopped and turned me to face him. "I'm sorry, that was—"

"It was nothing," I said. "I may have missed out on a few years, but
I've got all the time in the world now, and that's what matters, right?"

He leaned down and gave me a soft, heated kiss. "Right."

Grinning, Eris spun and grabbed my hand, jolting me from my conversation with Nate. "Let's dance!" she shouted over the music. Before I had a chance to argue, she'd tugged me away from Nate and dragged me out on the dance floor. The music—loud, thumping electronic dance—thudded painfully through the speakers as Eris tugged me forward.

'Let off some steam now,' Eris said, taking a hand and spinning me. *'And keep an eye out.'*

'We'll be in the back,' Nate told us. *'Keep an eye on things on your end. If you see anyone suspicious—'*

'Start dancing on the bar?' I teased, laughing as Eris began to mime a pole dance in the middle of the dance floor.

'I'm always up for a good striptease,' Eris joked.

'Focus, both of you,' he scolded.

For the next four songs or so, Eris and I danced like two drunken lunatics. Every so often I would feel the brush of Dionysus' magic as he fed off the emotions of the partiers around us. Now and then, there was a gentle tap on my mind, Nate's way of reassuring himself I was okay. Once in a while, I felt his Coercion flow through the room, touching on any humans present and mentally ordering them to leave.

As Eris and I danced, we did our best to inconspicuously watch the faces around us. Most were Telchines, but there were a number of other immortals present, most of which I couldn't place by sight, although I noticed a few of the white-haired and dark-skinned Potamoi, Oceanus' river-god children, as well as some that bore the pale skin of the shape-shifting crocotta. The rest of the bar's occupants seemed to be human, all in various states of inebriation, and that number was quickly dwindling thanks to Nate's power.

Suddenly, I froze, my breath catching in my throat as my eyes landed on a raucous group of Tels that had just walked in.

'Keep moving!' Eris snapped, giving my arm a hard tug, covering up my faltering dance with another spin.

Covering up my shock with a laugh, I reoriented myself on the dance floor, so that I was facing her and started dancing again. I watched over her shoulder at the small group of Tels that had just taken up residence at the end of the bar and were now waiting to order drinks.

There, seeming to hold court over the whole group, was the short, pale Telchine I'd seen when I'd used my psychometry to examine the meeting room in Athens.

The same one who'd released airborne godsbane into the room, killing nearly three dozen Ischyra.

And just like that, my plans for the night shifted.

'What is it?' Nate asked, noticing my change in mood.

'At my three. Look familiar?'

Moments later, I felt Nate's warm hands slide across my waist. Dionysus had taken Eris' hand and was twirling her around the dance floor, checking out the rest of the area.

'You've got conniving on your face,' Nate said, brushing his lips against my neck as he began to move with me. 'You're not going rogue on me, are you?'

I smirked up at him. 'I may have just come up with a better plan than poisoning them,' I admitted. 'We should still do that, though. Well, you should.'

'Supplementary plan, then?' He took my hand and spun me away, then pulled me back into his chest. 'Show me.'

Casting a glance at the group of Tels who'd just gotten their round of drinks at the bar, I quickly ran through my plan, which even I could readily admit was crazy. To his credit, Nate's face didn't falter once as I told him my idea.

'So?' I held out my hand to Eris, who'd just danced back over to us, laughing. She pulled me away from Nate and started grinding on me.

He gave me a mocking bow, then he and Dionysus wandered off, laughing.

'Do it,' he said after a moment. 'He's very high-ranking, if I'm not mistaken, which means very well-connected, so he'd be a good option. But be careful. We'll take care of the rest. Call out to me if you run into trouble. I'll meet you in a few.'

Eris and I danced to a few more songs, waiting as Nate continued to coerce the humans into leaving.

Taking Eris' hand, I leaned toward her. "I'm running to the bathroom!" I shouted over the music.

She gave me the thumbs up, then gestured toward the dance floor. "I'll be here!"

I blew her a kiss, then, flipping my hair over my shoulder, I sauntered off in search of the restroom.

When I reached the end of the bar where two hallways stretched off at a ninety-degree angle, I paused and bit my lip. With a sigh, I turned toward the group of Telchines nearby, their pale skin an odd yellow in the neon lighting of the bar.

"Hey, um, guys?" I held up my hand and smiled meekly. "Do any of you know where the restroom is?"

Taking a gigantic gamble, I touched the Tel from Athens with my Coercion. Instantly, he smiled, the same cruel, slimy smile he'd worn as he fed poison into the Ischyra headquarters in Athens, one that spoke volumes about the thoughts in his head.

"Of course." His smile widened as he gestured behind me.

Ugh. Even his *voice* was slimy.

I gave him a simpering smile and did my stupid hair-flip again, trying hard to see his face and not the lifeless eyes of the thirty Ischyra he'd slaughtered a week ago. "Thank you *so* much!"

He held out his arm toward the right-hand hall—the one illuminated with all of one working light fixture and clearly didn't end at a restroom.

"I don't know," I said hesitantly. "Are you sure?"

"Oh, I'm sure," he called over his shoulder. "I come here all the time. They should really fix the lights, don't you think?"

"Yeah, totally!" My heart started to thud as we neared the end of the darkened hall, far past the point where other patrons might notice us. I began to have serious second thoughts about my new plan.

Suddenly, he stopped, and before I could speak, his hands were on my neck. He slammed me against the wall so hard my head snapped back, and I heard the crunch of plaster beneath my skull. I was momentarily stunned that a creature who was a good head shorter than me and more than a little waifish was able to put so much force into his attack.

I guess poisons aren't their only strength, after all.

"I know exactly who you are *Mimic*," he sneered. "So you can lose that pretty red hair."

I swallowed back my revulsion as his rotten breath invaded my nostrils and tried to force a threatening tone. "If you know who I am, why'd you come down here with me?" I slammed my foot down on his instep and brought my knee to his groin. He let out a loud grunt and went down, grabbing a fistful of my hair as he fell and pulling me down onto the filthy, sticky floor beside him, where he immediately tried to flip me onto my back. I heard the quiet slip of metal on leather, but before he had a chance to get his blade to my throat, I'd flipped him over and slammed his head into the hard, cracked tile. The knife sliced along my thigh in the process, causing me to falter almost long enough for him to regain the upper hand.

Wincing against the burning pain in my leg and cursing the stupid dress for not having a slit, I straddled his waist, pinning his arms to the floor.

Realizing he'd lost his advantage, he froze. Narrowing his cold eyes up at me, he scowled. "What do you want?"

I put more pressure on his wrists and gritted my teeth, letting all the anger that had been building inside me take over. "Funny you should ask."

Footsteps sounded, then Nate came to a stop beside me.

Leaning down so his face was beside mine, Nate smiled at the Telchine. I expected him to speak, make some kind of taunt, but instead, he merged his power with mine and tore into the poisoner's mind, obliterating every shield he had in place. The Tel cried out, but his words were choked off when Nate used his power to silence him, holding his mind wide open and preventing him from acting on his own.

I drew on my Splitter powers and dove into his head, then tapped into the minds of all the Telchines he shared blood with, confirming the moment we connected that Nate was right in his assumption that this one was high-ranking.

Once I felt their connections—hundreds of minds suddenly open to my own, pricking at mine like needles—I sent out one, single command.

"I want you to go ahead and break that tooth of yours."

28

NATHANIEL

Chaos erupted in the main bar as cries rang through the building, echoing down the hall to where Tessa and I stood over a now-dead Tel. Foam bubbled up out of his mouth from the poison he'd just ingested, and if the panicked shouts from the main room were any indication, he wasn't the only one.

Quickly, I pulled Tessa to her feet and helped her adjust her dress and hair, which had both become disheveled in her scuffle with the Tel, then leaned down to examine the wound on her leg. Prodding it lightly, I saw that the skin was beginning to stitch itself back together.

I glanced up at her. "How bad does it hurt?"

She winced at my touch. "Pretty bad, but it's fading, so I think it's just regular godsbane." She looked past me toward the main room. "We should probably go."

Tugging the hem of her dress over the healing wound, I took her hand and hurried us down the hall, foolishly hoping I could get her out before the gravity of what we'd just done hit her.

The shouts had almost died out when we stepped back onto the dance floor. The music still thudded painfully throughout the room, but instead of bodies writhing on the dance floor and tossing back liquor, they were prone on the floor or slumped against the bar. The Tels who'd shared a blood connection with the one Tessa and I dealt with were all foaming at the mouth due to the poison in their teeth. The rest of the patrons had dropped dead at the hit of poison they'd gotten when they accepted the shots of absinthe Eris and Dionysus had so generously bought for the entire bar.

Dionysus was sitting on top of the bar, his eyes hazy and his legs swinging as he uncorked a bottle of wine, nearly drunk off the pleasurable emotions he'd been siphoning since we'd arrived. He grinned when he saw us and held up the bottle in greeting. "That went *splendidly,* brother, wouldn't you say?"

"Where's Eris?" I asked as Tessa, wide-eyed, took in the damage we'd just caused. "We need to get to and destroy any stores they might have and get back home."

Frowning, Dionysus glanced around the room. "She went to get the DJ," he said. He took a swig of wine, then gestured toward the DJ booth just as the music stopped. "Unlike the rest, he did not care to partake in our generosity."

Turning, I watched as Eris dragged the DJ's limp body from the booth. Tessa sucked in a quick breath at the sight, and her hand tightened in mine.

"Hey, baby brother!" Eris jerked the unconscious Tel to his feet and smiled, then held up her onyx-handled dagger in the other hand. "What do you think? Kill, maim, or torture?"

Tessa made a small sound that came out like a cross between a gag and a laugh.

Eris gave a single nod. "Kill it is." Yanking the Tel's head back, she whispered in his ear. He jolted awake just in time to feel her blade slice deep into the flesh of his neck. Eyes wide in panic, he thrashed against her as dark blood spurted from the gaping wound. Her nostrils flared as she drank in his fear and pain, then she tightened her grip, pulling his head back and widening the wound.

Tessa's entire body tensed as she watched the life slowly slip from him.

'Turn away,' I whispered. *'She tends to enjoy these things too much.'*

'I just helped kill several hundred Telchines,' she said stubbornly. *'I can handle this.'*

"He's getting blood all over your shoes," Dionysus observed, shaking his head at Eris. He hopped down from the bar and assessed Tessa's expression, then handed her his bottle of wine. "Here, drink this."

Not tearing her eyes from where Eris had just killed the Telchine, she swallowed hard, then took the bottle and downed a healthy swig. When she was done, she handed the bottle back to Dionysus and wiped her mouth with the back of her hand.

"Thanks," she whispered hoarsely.

When Telchine stopped its struggling, Eris tossed him to the floor beside the rest. Wrinkling her nose, she looked down at the black stilettos she'd worn that were now spattered with blood. With an annoyed huff, she sheathed her knife. "Let's get out of here before any surviving locals get curious."

I nodded, then tugged Tessa's hand, needing to get her out of there as quickly as possible. I hated that I'd agreed to her plan, but I hated it even more that Eris or I hadn't thought of it earlier. It was a good plan, but if we'd thought of it sooner, we could've planned better and avoided the need for Tessa to go off alone.

No. I'd promised Tessa I wouldn't fall into the same overprotective patterns as her brothers, and I needed to keep to that.

"Hang on," Tessa said when we stepped through the door. "We—well, I should probably—we need to get rid of the bodies, don't you think?"

"Go for it," Eris said grimly. "Burn it all down."

I wrapped my arm around Tessa's shoulders and felt her lean into me as she looked at the building that had just been massacred—that *we* had just massacred. The act of taking lives was never one I would take pleasure in, not like some of my relatives.

And yet... I couldn't help the slight sense of relief that sparked in my heart when I considered the outcome of our actions.

Stepping away from me, Tessa conjured a ball of fire in her hand. Jaw set, she drew her arm back and threw, sending the ball sailing onto the roof. She repeated the process several more times until, finally, the entire building was ablaze.

The four of us stood and watched the flames climb higher, staring as they tore through the old wood of the building.

"It's going to get big," Tessa murmured. "We should get out of here."

Eris smirked up at me. "Father is going to be *pissed.*"

"Pissed" was an understatement.

One might have thought Zeus would be pleased that such a significant enemy faction had been all but annihilated in the span of a few moments, but apparently they would be wrong.

"I told you to wait!" he roared, pacing furiously in front of his fireplace. "I would have expected you, Nathaniel, of *all* of my children to obey me!" Disappointment colored his features as he looked at me before switching his gaze to Dionysus, who was leaning casually against the wall beside the door. "And you! What were you thinking?"

"It was my idea, Father," Eris said before either of us could respond. "And it needed to be done."

"You're lucky I don't ship you back to Earth!" he roared. "Back to whatever hole it was you were torturing things in! I should probably blame you for your brothers' actions tonight!"

"Send me back, then!" she shouted, throwing her hands up in annoyance. "All you do is hem and fucking haw about every goddamned decision we make! Those bastards were single-handedly winning this war for Cronus, and you wanted us to fucking *plan things!*"

"For good reason!" He stopped his pacing and advanced on her. "The four of you just *completely* exposed our hand!" He jabbed a finger in Tessa's direction. "The entire *world* will now know exactly how powerful she is!"

"Good!" I shouted. "Tessa nearly destroyed the main faction we've been chasing our tails over for months in *seconds*! They *should* know! "

"Zeus—" Tessa began.

He rounded on her, furious. "The only reason you're not getting a reaming of your own is because—"

"Tessa!"

We all jumped when Atlas bellowed from the door. Before she could respond, he was in front of her, checking her over for injuries. When he was satisfied she wasn't hurt, he stepped back and glared at her, his hands still clenched around her arms.

I glanced at Zeus and shook my head, furious when I saw the grim satisfaction on his face at Tessa's chastising.

"Real nice," I muttered.

"What were you *thinking*?" Atlas hissed.

Obviously angry, she jerked from his hold. "I was *thinking* that it was time to stop sitting up here waiting for something to happen!"

"You should've—"

"What?" Tessa took another step back, fury rolling off her. "Asked permission? Checked to make sure it was okay with you first? I'm not a child, Atlas!"

"Then stop acting like one!" he roared. "You could've gotten yourself killed!" He rounded on me. "Was this your idea? So help me—"

My eyebrows shot up. "And if it was? This was her decision to make, Atlas, not yours."

Tessa stepped in front of me and glared up at her brother. "Don't you dare try to blame Nate! I'm not just going to sit up here picking at Menoetius' mind and doing fuck-all to help the people who are out there actually *risking their lives* to save this place!"

"And for the last time, it was *my* idea," Eris groaned as her discord began to seep across the room. "Give a girl some credit, for crying out loud."

'If you can't reel your power in, you may want to leave,' I told her as I watched Tessa and Atlas' tempers spike.

Her lip curled in annoyance, but I immediately felt her power retreat.

"I don't care whose idea it was," Atlas growled, stepping toward Tessa. "Under no circumstances—"

"Choose your words carefully before you finish that sentence, Atlas," Tessa warned.

Atlas' eyes widened in disbelief. "Are you *threatening* me? After you just—"

"Atlas."

He stopped when a large hand touched his arm, then he turned to face Epimetheus, who'd just entered the room with Prometheus.

"What?" he snapped. "Have you come to defend her again?" His eyes shot to Prometheus. "And you?"

"This doesn't need to turn into a fight," I said. Stepping forward cautiously, I held up my hands in an attempt to placate the brothers. I shot a look at Dionysus, who sent out a light wave of calming magic.

Atlas glowered down at me, the full extent of his rage swirling in his eyes. "You put her in danger," he growled.

I clenched my jaw and tried to rein in my own temper. "No, I didn't. I went into the field with three skilled deities and took out an enemy. Effectively."

"Against explicit orders from your leader!" Zeus yelled.

"Ugh!" Tessa threw up her hands and groaned.

"Did you at least remember to destroy their stores before you left?" Atlas demanded.

"Of *course,* we did," Tessa snapped. "It's really pissing me off how little you think of me!"

"Alright, that's enough!" Zeus barked. He looked back and forth between me, Tessa, Eris, and Dionysus before finally landing on me. "I want a full report. Now."

With a sigh, I detailed the events of the last hour, starting with Eris' knowledge of where the Telchines had been living and leaving out the part about her somehow acquiring illicit poison.

"We—Tessa, really—saw an opportunity," I told him. "So we took it. Tessa has been working on her Mentalist abilities, so when she suggested using her Splitter powers to supplement poisoning the tavern's liquor, we all agreed it was the best course of action."

'You mean you agreed,' Eris muttered, clearly still irritated we hadn't cleared that part with her ahead of time.

Atlas pressed his fingers to his eyes as Epimetheus and Prometheus shared a quick look of pride. Prometheus schooled his features almost immediately, but Epimetheus' smile widened as he looked at his sister.

"You're saying you and Tessa joined your powers and killed off nearly every Tel in existence?" Epimetheus asked, barely managing to hold back a grin.

"Yes," I replied. "The one she chose was also the one who killed the Ischyra in Athens," I said, looking at my father. "He was old, second generation. His blood connections were incredibly high."

"How many?" Zeus asked quietly through gritted teeth, quickly realizing what I was saying. There had only been a handful of Telchines in the first generation, so any who still remained from the earlier years of their existence could almost always trace their blood to the bulk of the entire population. "How many did you manage to Coerce into killing themselves?"

Tessa and I shared a quick glance. She took a deep breath, then looked at him. "Seven hundred and sixty-four."

My lips twitched at the stunned silence that ensued, and pride surged in me for what she'd accomplished. She hadn't just defeated an enemy; she'd also proven to her brothers, three of her biggest obstacles at times, that she was more than capable of holding her own, protecting herself, and defending this mountain and Earth.

Tessa's brothers and my father were staring at us, dumbfounded.

"Seven... *hundred?*" Atlas' face went slack, and his hands fell to his sides. "At once?"

Epimetheus' smile turned into a gleeful grin.

"How?" Prometheus asked sternly.

"I had tapped into my Splitter powers when the sisters and I reached out to Mary and the other witches, so I just... expanded on that. It wasn't easy, but with Nate using his Coercion to hold the Tel's mind open, it wasn't much harder than forming connections with human minds."

"But... *seven hundred.*" Atlas shook his head. "You shouldn't be strong enough for that."

"She is, though," I said quietly, arching a brow at him. "She absolutely is."

"Adrenaline and vengeance may have been contributing factors," Tessa said.

Dionysus barked out a laugh and took a swig from the bottle of wine he'd brought back with him. "I felt your power slam into all the Tels around me. There was nothing weak about it."

The flush that had colored Zeus' face retreated a bit. "Prometheus, let's send a few scouts out to assess the full damage Tessa and my children did. We need to know if Tessa's number is accurate."

"It is," I told him. "I felt them all."

"What was the total Tel population?" Epimetheus asked. He bit back a smirk. "Before tonight, that is."

Zeus gave him an exasperated look, then pulled a large, leather-bound ledger from a shelf beneath the map of Earth. Flipping toward the back, he ran a finger down a page, then gave a small tap with his index finger. "At last count, which was about two weeks ago, they were at just over eight hundred."

"Meaning we're left with a few dozen at most," Prometheus murmured. He arched a brow at Zeus. "Regardless of how we may feel about their rash decision-making this evening—" he sent a scolding look at Tessa "—I think we should call it what it is. A win."

29

MARY

The brief taste of freedom I'd had when Josh took me from my cell had given me a temporary morale boost, small and unreasonable as it might've been. Now, as I watched myself begin to fall back into the filthy state I'd been in when he'd taken me, my mood began to plummet along with my appearance. My clean, soft hair had become greasy, the fresh clothes he had given me, grimy. Each time I looked down at the pale blue shirt I wore, I grew more angry, and my previous thoughts about the new clothes being a punishment returned.

But even though I was unable to touch my power, I could feel it slowly replenishing, which was both reassuring and disappointing.

After scratching out another tally mark on the floor three days later, Taygete slumped back against the wall and gave me a tired smile. We'd been waiting for hours for them to return Alcyone, but it seemed, just as before, they were keeping her longer than the others.

"I'm beginning to think we may not get out of here," she said. "Or that we might not all survive."

Celaeno shushed her. "Negativity won't help our circumstances, sister."

"She's not wrong," I muttered.

Celaeno gave me a chastising look but didn't contradict me.

The three of us were silent for a few moments, each lost in our own thoughts. It had been days since I'd had any inkling of Tessa's presence in my mind, and I was beginning to lose hope I'd hear from her again.

"Have either of you heard from your sisters?" I asked.

Taygete shook her head. "No. Hopefully they and Tessa will attempt to make contact again soon. It seems together is the only way they can."

I leaned back against the wall, resting my head against the cool stone as I thought over just how unlikely it was that Tessa would be able to get back through, especially since it didn't make sense that she'd gotten through in the first place. Josh seemed crazy powerful, and Tessa, Titaness or not, was three thousand years out of practice

As it had done several times over the last few days, my mind drifted back to the day in Josh's room when he told me he planned to release me soon, something that made almost as much sense as Tessa getting through his wards.

I'd just closed my eyes, not really caring to ponder to complexities of whatever the fuck was going on, when the door slammed open. The four of us jumped, but I'd barely had a chance to turn my head to see who it was, when a heavy hand yanked me to my feet and slammed me against the wall.

My entire body jerked, and I cried out when Cronus backhanded me across the face. Pain, hot and sharp, pierced through my skull, and spots began to dance in my vision as he tossed me to the floor. Wincing, I managed to look at him, gingerly touching the spot he'd just hit. He was leering down at me, his face more furious than I'd seen since I'd arrived. There was no trace of the smug bastard who'd stolen my power days ago.

No, this guy was *pissed* and about to take it out on me.

"Your little friend thinks she can pull one over on us," he seethed, his teeth bared in a snarl.

"Leave her alone!" Alcyone cried. "She hasn't—"

Her words were cut off by a kick to the gut from Iapetus.

"My daughter, it would seem, is far more powerful than we first thought," Iapetus mused, delivering a hard kick to Taygete's side. "I'm almost... proud."

Eyes wide, I stared at where Taygete and Alcyone lay, arms wrapped around their middles as they whimpered in pain.

A small part of me was dying to know what Tessa had done to piss them off this much, but at the same time, it also seemed like he was about to take that out on me, which I wasn't exactly in a rush to experience

Cronus crouched down in front of me and touched a finger to my chin. The expression on his face was calming, almost soothing, which kicked my fear up about ten notches. "Your dear friend has taken out a very important part of our army," he said quietly. "Using powers that, until now, we were unaware she'd become so skilled with."

I jerked away from his touch. "Maybe you should've gotten a better spy, then," I snapped. "Clearly, Andrei sucked at his job."

"Hmm." Iapetus leaned down and smiled cruelly. "Perhaps." He grabbed a chunk of my hair and pulled, then snapped my head back against the wall. "I'm not prepared to discount our misstep there. As it stands, however, it's time we delivered my daughter another message because it's become clear that slaughtering the majority of her friends was insufficient."

"No!" I beat against him as he dragged me to my feet. I barely had time to get a solid kick out before Cronus' big, meaty hand wrapped around my throat, pressing so hard I couldn't get enough air in to scream. The sisters were on their feet in an instant, eyes wide with fear, but when they tried to rush forward, they hit an invisible barrier. They beat against it, and I watched as tears began to flow down their faces as they realized just how bad this had gotten.

"Iapetus, which do you think would be more *impactful*?" Cronus asked, accepting a glittering blue blade from his partner. Iapetus was quiet for a moment as Cronus began to drag the poisoned blade down my cheek.

My panic increased as the searing pain of godsbane burned

across my skin. My vision wavered, and I was hit with the terrifying realization that I was only one slice from a painful death.

A death like the one Eric had experienced.

A sob escaped as I pushed against Cronus' hold, dragging forward every ounce of strength I could muster, but Cronus pressed the full weight of his body to mine, pinning me to the wall.

"I would go with dismemberment," Iapetus said thoughtfully, pulling out his own knife. He grabbed my hand and slammed it painfully against the wall. "Perhaps hands first? But save the head for last."

The corner of Cronus' mouth curled, and he touched his knife to my ear. "I'm partial to ears, myself. First one..." He touched the edge of his knife to the thin shell of my ear, drawing a painful whimper from my lips as he lifted the blade and touched it to the other. "Then the other." He gave me a wide smile. "We'll give your body time to heal between amputations, of course."

Bile rose in my throat, and my vision began to go dark. A voice inside my head started screaming at me to stay awake, to fight, to not fucking give up.

There was a strange thump. Iapetus' eyes went wide, and he slumped to the floor in a heap.

Cronus took a startled step back, dropping me to the ground in the process. Rising to my knees, I rubbed at my bruised throat and stared at the blood pouring from a wound on Iapetus' back and the thick black blade that was embedded there.

I skittered back as Cronus spun to face the new threat.

Hands on his hips, Josh grinned down at Iapetus, watching with glee as his mouth opened and closed as if attempting to speak.

"What have you done?" Cronus grabbed Josh by the collar and shoved him against the wall. I scrambled across the room and launched myself at the sisters. Taygete pulled me down with them and wrapped her arms around me as we continued to watch in stunned silence.

With an easy grin, Josh wrapped his hand around Cronus' wrist and twisted. Cronus hissed, then released Josh and stumbled back several steps, looking at Josh in stunned fury.

"He's been on my nerves for weeks now," Josh said as he adjusted the collar of his shirt. He angled his head to the side and smirked. "Come to think of it, Cronus, you've become quite tiresome, too."

Cronus' eyes widened, and I thought I saw a flash of fear there. "You wouldn't *dare*! I've done *everything* —!"

Josh's expression turned curious. "Wouldn't I?" He frowned. "Why not?"

When Cronus opened his mouth to respond, Josh waved a hand. There was a sharp *crack*, then Cronus' head fell at an odd, unnatural angle, and he slumped to the floor beside Iapetus.

With a satisfied nod, Josh turned toward me and the sisters and rubbed his hands together excitedly. "You girls ready for a road trip?"

My lips trembled as I stared at the two Titans on the floor, unable to drag my eyes from Iapetus' lifeless stare and Cronus' grotesquely bent neck.

"What... the fuck," I whispered. Taygete's arms tightened around me protectively as Alcyone and Celaeno shifted, pressing against their sister.

Josh looked down at me, perplexed. "I think what you're looking for is 'thank you.'"

"What did you do?" I choked out, finally meeting his gaze. "Why?"

He gave me a chastising look. "I know you're not that dense, Mary." He gestured toward the floor. "One is dead, the other will wake up spitting mad shortly." He nudged Cronus' head with the toe of his shoe and laughed. "He's going to be so angry. This floor is filthy."

Celaeno cleared her throat. "And that doesn't worry you?"

He snorted. "Of course not! They've been needing a reminder about who's in charge for a while now."

Alcyone eyed him curiously. "And that would be you?"

"Yes, that would be me." He snapped his fingers, then some unseen force dragged us all to our feet. "I told Mary I planned to release you all, and I've recently gained incentive to keep my word."

"So does this mean you're finally going to tell us what you are?" I asked.

"That's highly unlikely." He glanced down at our hands. "Come on, hold hands. We want to hurry."

Taygete took my hand in hers, her grip painfully tight. "You're quite powerful, then? If you're in charge of these two?" she asked, gesturing toward Cronus and Iapetus.

He chuckled darkly. "You could say that."

I cast one last look at the bodies on the floor, hoping wherever Josh was taking us, it was better than here.

30

TESSA

We teleported back to Nate's a short while later, leaving Zeus and my brothers to discuss what our next steps would be now that we'd eliminated almost an entire enemy faction.

I couldn't help smiling to myself as we made our way across the front lawn. I'd never done anything in either of my lives that gave me a sense of accomplishment like this, but right then, I was really damn proud of myself. Something had unleashed inside me tonight; something that had started to shift when I'd fought the empousa and again in the arena.

I knew without guessing that that 'something' was knowledge—the knowledge that I was strong, that I was valuable, capable, *useful*. The knowledge that I could be a freaking warrior if I wanted to be, no matter what kind of doubts my twin or anyone else might have. The fact that this threw any previous notions Atlas had about my powers out the window also helped.

And yet... something still tugged inside me, something that repeated the words Theia had said a few days earlier.

"Just don't lose yourself along the way. It can be easy to do once vengeance takes over your mind."

It didn't take a genius to know the other thing that was tapping relentlessly at my mind was my conscience questioning my actions.

As if in answer, Nate took my hand and tugged me to a stop at the top of the porch steps. I looked up at him curiously.

"What is it?" I asked.

He wrapped his hand around the back of my head and pulled me against him, then just stood there quietly, holding me.

"I absolutely hate what you just did," he finally said.

"Nate—"

He pulled back and looked down at me. "I'm not going to ask you to stand back, Tessa. I will never do that. But I will also *never* be okay with knowing that you carry the burden of taking lives, no matter how deserving your victims might be."

The other small thing that had been nagging at me waved its greeting.

Yes, the Telchines were deserving of what had happened to them tonight. Like the empousa, they'd facilitated the deaths or injuries of thousands, human and immortal, alike, so there was no mercy deserved on their part.

But unlike the empousa, I'd wiped out hundreds in one fell swoop. Hundreds who'd been nowhere near me, far out of sight and unsuspecting. The empousa I fought in Atlas' mind and in the field had been engaged in a vicious, hand-to-hand battle with me. Tonight, I only fought one but had killed hundreds.

That selfish sense of accomplishment I'd felt just moments ago diminished, just a bit.

"Don't mistake me, Tessa," Nate whispered. "What we did tonight was the right thing to do. Just know that, once the adrenaline rush passes, once the high of winning is gone, your feelings might shift."

I nodded, then slipped my hands into his and looked up at him. "I know."

He lifted one hand to his lips and kissed my knuckles, then did the same with the other hand. "But let yourself be proud, alright? Regardless of how you might feel about this in the morning, you deserve to be proud of yourself."

I smiled. "I suppose we'll see how I feel in the morning then, hmm?"

He slid an arm around my waist and kissed my temple. "Hopefully, you'll able to re-link with Mary so we can get some more information."

I sighed. "Yeah, I hope so." I didn't want to say it outright, but I was fairly certain our luck with reaching Mary and the sisters had run out. After finding the odd bits of information left by Josh in Renville, there was no doubt in my mind that he'd been anticipating me or the other Pleiades getting through his wards. Whatever game he was playing, there were certain things it seemed he wanted us to know.

"Come on," he whispered. "Let's get some sleep."

I hit the barrier first, bouncing back into Nate the second we walked through the door.

"What the—"

The light flicked on. As my eyes adjusted to the brightness, I froze.

Josh sat on top of Nate's liquor cabinet, a glass of wine in his hand. Yana sat at his feet, her back against the couch, her eyes wide with terror as she stared, unmoving, at the two of us.

"Yana!" I lunged to run to her, but I was stopped by the invisible barrier Josh had thrown up and Nate's grip on the back of my dress.

'Don't even think about going near him,' Nate snapped.

With an amused expression, Josh followed my gaze to Yana, then hopped down from the cabinet. "Don't worry. That will wear off once I'm gone." He gave me a smile, one so boyish and *Josh,* it caused my heart to clench. "I'm just here to... chat."

'Nate, can you do anything about this?' I asked desperately.

'No, I can't push through his power. I'm calling Apollo.'

So, we were stuck.

"I thought it was time I brought Mary back to you." Josh took a quick sip of wine. "She's been in my possession long enough, and, well, now that you've accomplished your goals, I don't really need her anymore."

Whatever that means.

I cast a cursory glance around the room. "Then where is she?' I ground out.

A confused expression flickered across his face as he looked at the floor near his feet. "She's around here somewhere," he murmured.

Nate and I exchanged an incredulous look.

"Ah!" Josh waved a hand, and Mary appeared, gagged, and filthy on the floor beside him. The moment she saw us, her eyes widened in panic, and she began thrashing violently against some unseen bonds, screaming against the gag in her mouth. My heart leapt at the sight of her. A small whimper escaped as I really took her in. Her eyes were wild, rolling in her head as she tried to buck herself away from him, but whatever he was doing kept her from moving more than a few inches.

I tried to quiet my thumping heart as I focused on Josh and not how desperately I wanted to go to my best friend. "What about the sisters? Have you returned the Pleiades, too?"

The look he gave me suggested he thought I might be dim. "Of course. They've been left with their sisters."

"Great. You can go now," Nate growled.

He snapped his fingers, and Mary disappeared again. "Not just yet."

"Where did you send her?" I cried, stepping forward, my eyes riveted to the spot where she'd just been.

He sniffed. "I just popped her into another dimension for a bit. Don't worry, she'll be fine."

"Another— Bring her back!" I shouted. A million panicked thoughts ran through my mind, most of which centered around how simple it was to get lost in a foreign dimension.

"Why are you here?" Nate asked, his voice full of suspicion. "You aren't doing this out of the kindness of your heart."

"I'm not here as a decoy if that's what you're thinking." Josh smirked and poured himself another glass of wine. Lifting the glass, he gave the red liquid an appraising look. "You know, Nathaniel, this stuff is pretty good. You'll have to give me the name of your supplier."

When Nate didn't rise to the bait, Josh rolled his eyes and set the glass down. "Fine, fine. I came here to bestow a gift." He smiled at us. "My way of congratulating you."

"And what is it you're congratulating us for?" Nate asked. "Killing off your minions hardly seems like something you'd be thankful for."

"Ah, on the contrary!" Josh brushed his dark brown hair from his eyes, then slid his hands in his pockets. "You've achieved more tonight than your foes have since this war began! I'd say that warrants a pat on the back, wouldn't you?"

Dumbfounded, I shook my head. "You're insane," I whispered.

"Eh." Josh scrunched his face and bobbed his head from side to side. "Not so much, no. I'm just happy to acknowledge a job well done."

Nate ran a hand across his jaw. *'I've got nothing,'* he said.

'Keep trying.'

"I'm still a bit confused as to why you're rewarding us for killing your soldiers," I said, eyeing Josh a bit more warily. I'd known he was powerful, but I hadn't factored "completely unhinged" into the mix, too.

"Let's just say I'm a fan of a level playing field." He stepped closer, now only inches away, separated from us by whatever barrier he'd put up. "When Cronus and Iapetus managed to get free in *such* a glorious way, I'd hoped you'd find a way to do something equally as impressive." He gave me a conspiratorial wink. "Your potential to do such great things is why I made sure you came back, after all."

"Came back?" I frowned, momentarily sidetracked. "Back where?"

He chuckled and walked back toward Yana, then leaned against the cabinet with his arms folded. "I have to say, the most disappointing thing about this whole ordeal is that only *two* have deduced my true nature."

'What is he talking about?' Nate asked.

'I don't know!'

"Who knows your true nature, Josh?" I asked carefully. "What are you?"

"There have been a few over the years." His brow drew down as he swirled the wine in his glass. "None who knew for certain, but there were a few who wrote about me. Not extensively, of course. None would be able to do that." He sent me a smirk. "And, despite his more animalistic nature, your tormentor has some impressive powers of deduction. Vicious as he may be, he's quite smart, that Menoetius." He frowned, then angled his head to the side. "Would you like me to kill him for you, Tessa?"

I cursed my stupid heart as it started to race. He might as well have asked if I wanted him to end the war right then. The way he asked was so casual, as though he simply wanted to know whether or not I would like the gift he was offering.

The thought of Menoetius being dead, of no longer living in the same world as me, was more than a little enticing, and there was no question Josh could hear how badly I wanted that to happen. "If I thought it would come without strings, certainly," I replied. "We all know that's not the case."

'We still need Menoetius for information,' Nate warned.

Josh gave me a surprised smile. "Of course, it would come without strings." He narrowed his eyes, then tilted his head to the side. "Done. Oh, and I took the privilege of dealing with your father, as well. Odious old creature, that man." He clicked his tongue and shook his head. "The worlds are better off if you ask me."

I blinked furiously and tried to will my emotions back down. If what he said was true... No. There was no way.

"That's very generous of you," I said through clenched teeth. "But you didn't need to do that."

He shrugged, then picked up his glass and eyed the contents inside. "What can I say? Menoetius would have been of no further use to either of us, and, if I'm being honest, Tessa, I grew quite fond of you in our years together."

"Years—" My eyes narrowed. "What are you talking about? Who *are* you?"

He let out a quiet laugh, then swallowed back the last of his wine and placed the glass on the cabinet. He snapped his fingers, and Mary appeared at his feet, her entire body shaking in terror. Josh eyed her for a moment, then faced us. "I'm quite certain you'll figure it out soon enough. Take a peek through Mary's memories. You'll find most of what you're looking for there—including the things you were hoping to get from your brother's now-addled mind."

The door flew open, and Apollo rushed in, followed by Athena, both slamming to a halt against my back.

"Ah!" Josh grinned and made a quick fist-pumping motion at the sight of them. "The healer and the warrior! Perfect timing!!" He nudged Mary with his foot. "She'll certainly need your assistance, Apollo. It's been a rough week."

Athena and Apollo both stood, speechless, as they stared at the scene in front of us.

Josh gave me a quick wink. "I'll see you soon, Tessie Bear."

"Wait!" I tried to step forward, but the barrier hadn't fallen yet. Josh lifted his eyebrows in question. "What did you mean, *our years together*?"

The corner of his mouth drew up in a teasing smile. "Now, Tessa, if I gave you all the answers, I'd be taking all the fun out of our game. Figure it out yourself."

Before I got a chance to react, he was gone.

The barrier fell, and the four of us tumbled to the floor.

PART II

31

TESSA

The moment the barrier fell, Yana toppled over, her chest heaving as she sucked in air. Athena and Nate ran to her, as Apollo and I scrambled to get to Mary.

Mary's eyes were closed when we reached her, her entire body shuddering. "Check her for injuries!" I touched a palm to her cheek, then immediately drew back. "Gods, she's freezing!"

Apollo crouched down beside me and tilted Mary's face toward him. "Mary! Look at me!"

Her body continued to shake as she struggled to focus. Suddenly, she sat bolt upright, her wild eyes scanning the room. Apollo and I gripped her by the arms to steady her, and she immediately began screaming and thrashing against us.

"Goddamn it, hold still!" he scolded, grabbing her by the arms and holding her in place.

"Get off of me!" she screamed, her entire body bucking as the two of us tried to lay her back down so Apollo could examine her.

"Apollo, use your damn magic!" Nate snapped. Leaving Athena to help Yana, he ran over and tugged me to my feet. "Let him check her for injuries first," Nate whispered. "He'll use his magic to settle her, don't worry."

Biting my lip, I nodded.

I took a few tentative steps back with him, wrapping my arms around myself as I watched Mary continue to struggle against Apollo's hold. Athena had helped Yana to her feet, and both were now leaning against the back of the couch, wide-eyed.

My leg began to bounce impatiently as I waited for Apollo to work his magic.

Pinning Mary's back against his chest to stop the bulk of her thrashing, Apollo moved one hand up her arm, releasing a soft trail of healing light and whispering quietly as he went. When he pressed his palm to her cheek, the effect was instantaneous. The light grew brighter, then within seconds, her eyes fell closed, and she slumped into his arms. Deftly, he lifted her up and laid her down on the couch.

"She'll need to be cleaned up," he muttered as we hurried over to join him.

I knelt down on the floor beside her and began combing my hands through her messy hair. "Just make sure she's alright," I whispered. My eyes ran over her face in search of any kind of pain, but I saw nothing. I gnawed on my lip, waiting impatiently as Apollo did his examination.

Nate knelt beside me and ran a comforting hand up my back. *'She'll be fine,'* he said quietly. I could hear the doubt in his words. *'Apollo is good at what he does, Tessa. If she needs to be healed—'*

'Not all injuries can be healed with magic,' I bit out.

"She seems to be alright physically," Apollo said, pulling his hand back from her face. "I'm going to wake her up now."

I nodded, clutching Nate's hand as the light Apollo sent out slid from yellow to white. It pulsed briefly, then Mary's eyes fluttered open.

She sucked in a heavy breath and groaned, then rolled to her side, gripping Apollo's arm like a drowning swimmer would hold a life vest. Sobs shuddered through her body, deep, heavy cries that brought more tears to my own eyes.

Tentatively, Apollo placed a hand on her back, switching back to his healing magic. Gradually, her body began to still and her breathing became deep and even.

"She's asleep," Apollo said, jaw tense as he slowly extricated himself from her grip. "Her mind is moving too quickly for her to process where she is. Nathaniel, cut off her dreams, please."

I jerked my head around to look at Nate. "What? Why?"

"She needs rest, Tessa," Athena said softly. "Nathaniel is just going to make sure her head stays clear while she sleeps." She gave me a small smile. "In other words, no nightmares."

Apollo hoisted himself up onto the couch and looked at the three of us expectantly. "Now, would anyone care to tell me what just happened here?"

"How did he get in your house?" Athena asked as she helped Yana around the large sectional to sit down. "I just came from an inspection of the wards around the Olympic realm. There were no flaws or weak spots to be found."

I slumped back on the floor, my head coming to rest against the edge of the coffee table. Helplessly, I stared at Nate. He leaned back to sit beside me and wordlessly slipped an arm around my shoulders, then looked at Yana. She still looked a bit shaky, if not majorly pissed off.

"Tell us what happened," Nate demanded.

She sneered and shook her head. "I was in my room and heard a noise out here," she said, looking at each of us in turn. "I assumed you had returned, so I came out to see how things went. He was here, sitting on the sofa. When I stepped into the room, I was hit with a blast of magic, and the next thing I knew, I could not move."

"How long ago was that?" he asked.

Her eyes flicked to the clock on the mantel. "About an hour, I believe."

"Gods, Yana, I'm so sorry we weren't here," I said.

She waved off my apology. "He did not hurt me, and even if he did, you were doing important work."

"What did he say to you?" Apollo asked, casting a wary glance at Mary.

"Not a lot," Yana replied. "He babbled a bit about his 'true nature,' although none of what he said made much sense. The same things he said to you about how others have written about him, or at least mentioned him—he said that to me, as well. We should tell Chiron."

"I don't suppose he gave you any indication as to *who* these mysterious authors might've been?" Apollo muttered.

She quirked a brow in his direction but didn't answer.

I looked at Nate to tell him to contact Chiron.

"Already done," he said. "I gave him a run-down and will follow up with anything else we come up with."

Frowning, I went back over the entire brief exchange with Josh. Very little of what he'd said seemed logical. "What do you think he meant when he said we spent years together?" I asked. "The way he said it..."

"I was wondering the same thing," Yana said. "It sounded like he was talking about more than just the few years you knew him as a human. Do you—do you think you knew him in your past life?"

"Maybe?" I wrinkled my nose, then closed my eyes and took a deep breath before voicing the conclusion I'd come to just before Josh vanished. "Do you think he was in the Void with me? Could another soul have been sent there?" I silently prayed they would say there was no way, that it was insane to even think it, because the thought of being trapped in the Void with a creature like him for so long...

Frowning, Athena sat down beside Yana. "If there was, I've certainly never heard of it. I don't see any other explanation, though."

"Based on what Hecate told Hestia and myself when she placed her interdiction, if someone else had been in Chaos when she sent Tessa there, she was unaware of him."

"Agreed," Nate said grimly. "So we need to speak with her. Something isn't sitting right. She said she's the one who recalled Tessa's soul from the Void at the behest of the Fates, right?" He lifted his eyebrows at Apollo for confirmation.

"Yes, that's what she said," Apollo replied.

"Did you ever get the feeling she wasn't being fully forthright?"

Athena asked. "Considering the circumstances, is it possible she withheld information from you?"

"You mean, is it possible she found out how badly she screwed things up, then lied to cover it up?" Apollo shook his head. "No, I don't believe that's the case."

Athena drummed her fingers on her chin and narrowed her eyes thoughtfully. Finally, she shook her head. "I don't know."

"Join the club," I murmured. I inclined my head toward Mary. "He said the answers to our questions were in her mind."

"And knowing you, you'll want permission before diving in, correct?" Apollo barely attempted to conceal the contempt in his voice.

"Yes, I'd want permission before digging into my best friend's mind, Apollo." I rolled my eyes. "Why is that such a hard concept for you gods?"

"I only ask," he said patiently, "because you might not be the best one for the job. These are likely to be incredibly unpleasant memories, Tessa." He gave me a pointed look.

There was a beat of silence, then Nate blew out a breath.

"You want Hades to do it," he said grimly.

The five of us were silent, the only sound that could be heard was Mary's light, even breathing.

"It might be the best option," Athena said carefully.

"He's got the capacity—desire, even—to handle the kinds of things that we might find in her head," Nate added.

I gave him a sharp look. "You don't think I can handle it?"

"I don't think you *should* handle it," he said simply. "Whatever memories Josh is referring to..." He stared down at Mary, filthy from nearly two weeks stuck in a cell, her hair dingy, skin and clothes gray with dust and dirt. "Tessa, we don't know what he did to her. It seems very clear that whatever she went through isn't something we all need to see."

"He is not wrong, Tessa," Yana said quietly. "Why put yourself through that?"

"All he said was the answers were there," I said, shaking my head.

"I'm her best friend. I should be the one to do it. And...maybe they just talked."

"Maybe," Apollo said. "I'd even venture so far as to say probably, at least where Josh is concerned." His jaw tensed as he stared at Mary. "As for your father and Cronus, well, I'd say it's quite the opposite. We already know they took her power. Considering your past experiences with a similar spell, my gut tells me that isn't something you need to or should see. Hades will be willing and able to go farther."

My heart sank. He was right. I knew he was right, and selfish as it was, I agreed with what they were saying. I didn't want to see what they'd done to her. I'd lived through Menoetius' torment, relived it when Hecate and Hades pulled the memories forward and again when Hades did the same just a few weeks ago. The thought of watching something similar happen to Mary...

But on the other hand, I needed and wanted to be strong for my best friend. I couldn't pat her on the head when she woke and tell her it would be alright, not knowing what I was truly comforting her for. Had they taken all of her power? Beaten her? Tortured her?

The thoughts set my stomach rolling.

No, I couldn't let her bear those memories alone.

"We'll ask her what she wants," I finally said, "when she wakes. She may not want Hades to do it."

"I'm fairly certain you can convince her it would be the right choice," Apollo said.

"Shit!" I jumped to my feet as realization slammed into me. "Josh —he said he killed my father and Menoetius! We need to get to the dungeons!"

"Ah." Apollo looked pointedly at Mary. "How about Nathaniel and Athena go check on our prisoner and report back? It will only take a minute."

"We should probably report to Zeus while we're there," Nate said. He didn't bother to hide the annoyance that laced his tone.

"No." Athena shook her head. "We need to give that a bit more time."

"I concur," Apollo said with a quick nod. When he noticed my surprised expression, he sighed. "Unless you want this girl to spend the foreseeable future at the palace being poked, prodded, and questioned, you'll keep quiet about it for now. We'll get all the information we can, then report to him once we have a concise picture of what occurred over the last week. He'll want to confirm things for himself, of course, but if Hades is the one to retrieve the memories, there'll be no logical reason for Father to deny their legitimacy."

Nate, Yana, and I sent him identical looks of shock.

Athena smirked at her older brother. "You see, Apollo? Being nice isn't so hard."

He shot her a withering look. "Logical, Athena. I'm being logical."

"Apollo showing compassion for an Ischyra." I gave him a considering nod. "I'd say the end is nigh."

32

NATHANIEL

After convincing Tessa that the best course of action for her was to remain with Apollo, Mary, and Yana in case Anette returned, Athena and I made our way to the palace dungeons, using the palace's more discreet rear entrance to avoid running into anyone in the halls.

My sister and I stared, perplexed and in shock, into Menoetius' cell.

Now all it held was the non-responsive body of a Titan depleted of his energy. His eyes stared vacantly ahead, his chest rose and fell in short pants, and his skin had taken on a sickly pallor.

"How is this possible?" I whispered. I stared grimly down at what had been the last potential source of information of our enemies' plans. Josh hadn't completely destroyed Menoetius' body, but he'd addled his mind beyond repair. When I attempted to look at his thoughts, all I found was the feeble sparking of neurons, bits of light that flashed with no meaning. Nerve endings responding to stimuli, nothing more. The shields I'd been struggling to disassemble for more than a week were nothing more than shreds of dying magic. He was, for all intents and purposes, dead. "There's hardly anything left."

Athena touched a hand to her lips and shook her head. "I have no idea, Nathaniel, but this is not good."

"Let's just hope Mary can provide some of the information we would've gotten from him," I murmured.

"I hardly expect they were planning battle strategy or divulging secrets in her presence," Athena said. "It's unlikely she even knows where she was held."

'Nathaniel!'

I jumped at the sound of Demeter's voice in my mind. I'd completely forgotten that Josh had said the sisters had been deposited at her home.

'Demeter, are the sisters with you? All of them?'

'All but Merope, but she's on her way. What is going on?'

'I'll explain shortly, but Apollo and I have something we need to handle urgently. Just—'

'Keep quiet? Yes, I know.'

I let out a quiet sigh of relief. "Demeter has the other sisters. She's keeping it quiet for now, but at the very least we'll have to inform Atlas." I looked down at Menoetius. "What should we do with him?"

"For now?" Athena stared at him grimly. "Put him to sleep. Dealing with the sisters and Mary are the more pressing concerns at the moment. Once we have more information from them, we'll come back."

I hit Menoetius with a small touch of Coercion, far less than I would've expected to need. Seconds later, his eyes drifted shut, and his breathing became more even. I gave Athena a quick nod, then we made our way back to my house.

Mary was still unconscious when we returned, Tessa and Yana sitting vigil at her side, Apollo staring silently out the window. Tessa and Yana both jumped to their feet when we walked in.

Tessa took a step forward. "Well?"

"Have you ever seen *One Flew Over the Cuckoo's Nest*?" Athena asked dryly.

"Um... no?" Tessa frowned. "Why?"

"He's not dead," Apollo deadpanned, then turned to look at me. "Correct?"

Tessa's face fell.

"Correct," I said. "He's as good as, though. Whatever Josh did shredded his mind to bits. Lobotomized him."

"What do you mean?" she demanded. Hope mixed with wariness, filled her eyes.

"There's nothing left," Athena said. "His energy has been depleted far past the point of regeneration. There is no recovering from what's been done to him."

"It's unlikely even your psychometry will find anything," I told Tessa when she opened her mouth to ask. "We can try, but I don't think it will make a difference."

"So anything we might've been able to get from him..." she raked her hands through her hair and let out a frustrated groan. "It's gone. All gone."

Athena inclined her head toward Mary. "As of now, Mary and the sisters are the only hope we have at retrieving any form of information."

She shot me a look. "You've spoken with Demeter, then? He wasn't lying about returning the Pleiades? Have you told Atlas?"

I shook my head. "No, he wasn't lying, and we thought it best to hold off on informing anyone else that they've been returned."

"We'll examine Mary first." Apollo turned from the window. When Tessa and Yana both started to argue, he held up a hand to silence them. "It's best that we get the information now and go to Zeus together. We'll bring Hades up, he'll do what he does, then we'll inform the necessary parties."

I stepped to Tessa and took her hands. "Atlas is their father, so if you think it's best to tell him now, we will. But right now, their sisters have them. They're safe."

She stared up at me, indecision clear in her eyes. A moment later, Yana spoke.

"You should wait," she said. Frowning, Tessa spun. "Not for long," Yana hurried to add. "But he is only their father by blood. Despite his reconnection to Maia and the others who were already here, he does not know the ones who went missing, nor they him. The decision of whether to see him should be left up to them."

"I'm not going to lie to my twin," Tessa ground out. She looked around at all of us. "You can't ask me to do that."

"No one is asking that," I told her. "But answer me this. If you were to call him up here right now, what would happen?"

A muscle clenched in her jaw. "He'd want to go down there immediately."

I lifted a brow. "And?"

She let out a heavy sigh. "And... he would insist on taking me with him because Josh was just here, and my life was in danger." She gave me a determined look. "I would refuse, you know. He wouldn't take me without my permission."

"Which would then turn into an argument that we don't need to be having just now," Apollo said wearily. His eyes went distant for a moment, and I was about to question him when, seconds later, the door burst open, and Hades stormed in, making a beeline for where Tessa and I stood.

"What the fuck happened?" he shouted, yanking her from my hands and pulling her to a stop in front of him. "Are you alright? What did he do to you?"

"Hades, get off me!" She swatted him away as he turned her around, looking for any sign she'd been hurt.

"She's fine, Hades! Back off!" I tugged her back toward me and glared at Hades, then I sent an irritated glance at my brother.

"I'm fairly certain this is the antithesis of avoiding arguments," Athena said with a pointed look at Apollo.

He shrugged, then moved to the cabinet and pulled out a bottle of brandy. "We're not going back and forth on this. I'm going to wake Mary, she's going to consent to his examination, then we're going to call your blasted twin up here and tell him what's happened."

Hades, his eyes still locked on Tessa, let out a low growl. "I'm not going to ask again."

Tessa huffed, then accepted the glass Apollo handed her. As she explained the events of the last half hour, Hades' furious face turned even angrier, startling even me in its intensity.

"You should've called me," he said flatly. "The moment you saw him, you should've called me."

"Well, we didn't, but here you are, anyway," Tessa muttered. *'He needs to calm down. His power is borderline painful right now.'*

"Right now, we just need to know what Mary knows as painlessly as possible," I told him, struggling to keep my voice calm.

The poisoned looks he shot at me, Apollo, and Athena did little to conceal the fury—the *fear*—that was written all over his face, and I almost felt bad for snapping at him when he'd arrived. Considering the last time a primordial witch had gotten ahold of Tessa, she'd died,, I could only imagine the memories this had brought back.

Still seething, his lip curled. "Then you may not want to wake her just yet."

"You're not going in without permission," I told him.

He narrowed his eyes at me. "This is hardly the time for acknowledging boundaries, Nathaniel."

"It's not happening," Tessa said. "And I'll kick your ass if you try." She looked at Apollo. "Wake her up."

With a nod, Apollo set his glass down on the coffee table and crouched beside Mary. Just before he touched his hand to her face, he looked up at Tessa. "You may want to come over here. Her reaction isn't likely to be pleasant."

I brushed a hand down Tessa's spine, then she squeezed my hand before walking toward her friend. She knelt beside Apollo and gave him a quick nod.

Quietly, he touched his hand to Mary's cheek. There was a quick flash of white light, then her entire body gave a jerk. Her eyes flew open, and she let out an ear splitting scream, then immediately started thrashing around.

Apollo gripped her arms and attempted to hold her down as Tessa whispered soothing words in her ear.

"Let her sit up," I told my brother. "She's panicking. Pinning her down isn't helpful."

He lessened the pressure on her arms and helped her up into a sitting position. I felt the touch of Dionysus' calming magic that Tessa sent out mix with Apollo's healing power, and slowly, she stilled. Her fingers wrapped around Apollo's forearms as her breathing began to steady. Warily, she lifted her head, looking first at him, then Tessa.

"Tess?" Her voice wobbled as she took in the face of her best friend, then Yana, who stood just behind Apollo, and finally onto Athena, Hades, and me. As she looked around the room, registering our presence, her face crumpled, and she burst into tears. Hades let out an annoyed groan. Tessa and Apollo caught her just as she began to fall sideways, the force of her sobs making it hard for her to hold her weakened body upright.

Apollo pressed his hand to her cheek again, letting out a bit more of his healing magic as Tessa ran a soothing hand up her arm. Slowly, I stepped forward and knelt beside her.

"Mary?" Athena whispered. "What do you need?"

She dragged her eyes, still wide with disbelief, up to look at us all. "I—I don't—" She dropped her face to her hands and shook her head. "I don't know," she mumbled.

Apollo stuck out an arm and caught her as she started to tip over again.

"Ah ah, girl. We need to talk before you go back to sleep," he said. Despite the calm he forced into his voice for her benefit, I could tell his mind was going a mile a minute trying to deduce all that had just happened.

"Am I really here?" she whispered, her words thick with disbelief. She lifted her eyes to his. "This isn't a dream?"

My brother glanced at me, then let out a short laugh. "I'm fairly certain you'd consider my presence more of a nightmare than a dream."

She huffed out a quiet breath that sounded almost like a laugh. "Yeah. True."

Apollo arched a brow at me. *'Any time now.'*

"Hey, Mare," Tessa said quietly, taking Mary's hands. "Do you remember what happened?"

Mary took a deep breath and sat up straighter. "A little." She cleared her throat, then smiled gratefully when Yana handed her a glass of water. After drinking down half its contents, she set it on the table. "The last thing I remember before Josh brought us here was him killing Iapetus and breaking Cronus' neck."

"He did *what?*" Hades snapped. "Are you ill, girl?"

"Shut *up,* Hades!" Tessa rolled her eyes. "Keep going," she told Mary.

Mary eyed Hades warily, then looked back at Tessa. "He dumped the sisters off somewhere, some farm or something, then brought me back here. He kept going on about how you deserved a reward for doing... whatever, I don't know. But then Yana came out, and he did some whammy thing on her, and then I just... disappeared." Her brow furrowed slightly. "Tess, I have no idea where I was."

"Describe it," Tessa demanded. "Exactly what you saw, what you felt. Anything."

Mary rolled her shoulders and nodded. "It was dark. And cold. I could feel my memory kind of... fading?" She stared absently at the glass of water in front of her. "I guess that's the best way to describe it. My thoughts were there, but I was—"

"Fading away?" Tessa asked quietly.

Mary looked at her questioningly. "Yeah. Exactly."

Tessa paled at Mary's confirmation. In the span of a single breath, I realized exactly what Mary was saying.

When Tessa spoke, her words were barely audible. "Did you feel like you were falling?"

Mary nodded, and her eyes filled with tears. "Gods, Tessa. Did he send me—"

"Chaos," Hades spat. "He sent you to Chaos."

"What, he just opened the Void and popped her in for a few minutes?" Athena asked. "Like a goddamn holding cell?"

"The only memory I have of Chaos—" Tessa's eyes slid to mine. "—is the one Nate pulled from my head before my transformation. It was dark, cold, and I just kept falling and falling." Her jaw tightened, and she closed her eyes. "Mary, Josh said something right before he left. He said he gave you a lot of information, that the answers to all our questions would be in your memories."

Mary nodded. "Good to know. He wiped my memory at least once that I know of."

"Would you consent to let Hades pull your memories?" Apollo asked.

Shock colored her face. "What? No. Tessa—" She looked at Tessa, brow furrowed. "Why can't you?"

Tessa bit her lip. "I can, but Hades is far more suited for this than I am. He won't... shy away from the bad parts like I would. And— well, he did it for me, and I'm still grateful for it."

"You don't have to do this," I told Mary. "There are other ways—'

"That are far less efficient," Hades grumbled. He sighed and sat down on the coffee table across from Mary. "Look, I understand your disinclination. I or Nathaniel, or even Apollo, if you're more comfortable, can put you to sleep, so that you won't have to relive whatever it was that happened."

"You want—you want to knock me out?" Mary started shaking her head rapidly. "No. No! Absolutely not!"

"I can make it so you won't dream if that's your concern," I said quietly. "If you're worried about what you'll see when you close your eyes, I can make it so you don't see anything."

I almost hated to suggest it, knowing for a fact the Mary of two weeks ago would've likely thrown something at me for even hinting she needed help.

"Are you sure?" Her voice was small and childlike.

I nodded and took her hand. "I'm sure. You've got nothing to worry about, alright?"

She sniffed, then her eyes widened, and she leapt to her feet. "Wait! The sisters! Are they—"

"They're fine," I assured her, putting a hand on her shoulder and guiding her back down. "I spoke with Demeter not long ago. Once we get you settled, I'm going to run down and check in on them."

"So that farm, it was Demeter's place?" she asked.

"It was."

"I've already sent Persephone down to assist," Hades said. "She's waiting for our go ahead to let the others know of their return."

Mary looked at Apollo, surprised. "Seriously? You haven't told Zeus?"

Tessa smirked. "Golden boy has hit a slightly rebellious streak."

Apollo's lip curled in annoyance. "Can we get on with it? Contrary to what some of you think, I *would* like to keep our ruler abreast of information if possible."

"Okay." Mary sat up a bit straighter and rubbed her hands on her knees. "How does this work?"

"I'll put you to sleep," I explained. "Once you're out, I'll keep your mind clear, so you won't have to worry about dreams or nightmares. Then Hades will go in and... retrieve the memories." I gave her a tight smile. "But, Mary, it's up to you whether or not you want those memories there when you wake. I can keep them suppressed for a bit longer if you want. I don't know what we'll see when we go in."

"No, I want them back," she said firmly. "Whatever happened, I want to remember." She swallowed audibly and nodded, then forced a false bravado. "Do your thing, boys." She sent Tessa a wobbly smile. "If Tess can do it, so can I, right?"

Eyes brimming with tears, Tessa took Mary's hands and smiled. "You're damn right."

33

TESSA

There was no question that Hades was the best choice for pulling Mary's memories. He'd done it for me back in my previous life, and I'd been forever grateful, because in doing so, he had saved my life. However, it didn't make me feel any better knowing that it needed to be done for my best friend.

After convincing Hades and the others that I would be fine joining them in Mary's mind—on the condition that I would leave if things got to be too much—Hades, Nate, Athena, and Apollo started looking through her memories.

It was simple at first. All her memories were there on the surface, easy for them to look through and discard. Hades shoved aside all the ones of her time leading up to the arena attack, letting his own power draw him directly toward the more recent negative memories.

As if in answer, Mary flinched. I shot a look at Nate, and he shook his head.

'Just a physical reaction to his presence. She's out cold, I promise.'

Releasing a quiet breath, I went back in, hovering just behind where Nate and Hades were riffling through her memories.

The moment we reached the attack on the arena, I was glad for their presence.

The recruits had been practicing, completely unsuspecting, when blue marble-sized balls of powdered godsbane began flying into the arena. There were a few moments of painful screaming as the poison touched exposed skin and was inhaled into the lungs in panicked breaths.

Just before they started dropping, Iapetus and Menoetius appeared and dragged Mary, Eric, and Yana out of the fray and away from the clouds of poison that were quickly killing our friends. Mary was barely conscious, her awareness of her surroundings hanging on by a single thread. I felt her fight for it, to force herself to stay *there* because being unaware would almost certainly mean death. So she went still and watched as their captors waited patiently until the screams died down, and every single body in sight was motionless on the ground.

I felt Nate's hand tighten in mine, and someone put a comforting hand on my back, but I refused to pull out of her mind.

Methodically, Hades continued his search, tossing aside memories that didn't interest him and pausing at the ones that did.

The first time Mary saw Josh was heartbreaking. I felt her pain and betrayal as if they were my own. She'd wanted to kick and scream and *hurt* him, but even if the chains they'd put her in hadn't prevented her from doing so, she'd been stunned into frozen silence. When his warm, familiar face floated in front of her, she'd been hopeful, then simply devastated, her fear and sadness an overwhelming force that immobilized her.

'It's going to get worse now,' Hades warned.

'It's fine. Just keep going.' I gritted my teeth and prepared for the rest.

Josh hadn't come to her for days. In that time, Cronus and Iapetus each took turns beating her. Sometimes it was a hard cuff on the ear, others, a kick to the ribs or broken finger. I felt it all, each crushing injury, each spark of fury that flared in her as she felt her power beat against the cage that it had put it in.

The worst part was when I felt her begin to fade. The things that made her Mary—her snark, her sass, her unrelenting and brutal honesty—all began to dim. I could feel her frustration and anger as she struggled to remember herself, to keep some small semblance of who she was intact.

I was shaking with fury when Josh finally appeared. His first visit happened to coincide with the one instance I'd managed to astral project into her cell. I'd been sucked out the moment he touched the door, but I could tell by the knowing and slightly annoyed look on his face that he'd sensed my presence.

Hades sped through the next few days' worth of memories, brushing past each instance of the sisters being taken and their eventual return where they looked drained and beaten down. Mary's constant fear that her captors were going to come for her next grew each day.

'Pause there,' Nate ordered.

We'd just gone past the memory I'd already seen when I'd mind linked with her a few days prior. I was surprised to see Josh stop Cronus' continued beating of her and Cronus' subsequent obedience.

My body tensed, and I felt Nate's hand stiffen in mine.

'That's odd,' Hades remarked.

'Keep going,' I told him. 'This might be where she said he took her memory.'

Sure enough, we watched as Josh saw and removed me from her mind.

"It's quite fascinating that Tessa has been working so doggedly to infiltrate your mind," Josh commented thoughtfully. "Why do you think she hasn't opted to go for someone else? Say, myself?"

"Probably because she doesn't know who you are anymore."

I winced as Mary's anger began to bubble to the surface.

"Plus, I didn't betray her. She actually knows me."

Josh shrugged. "She actually knows me, too." He frowned, as though trying to reason something out. "But... it doesn't seem she remembers. I was hoping that would change after she got the bulk of her memories back, but something went wrong."

"We spent almost every day together all through high school. Of course, she remembers you."

Josh waved a hand impatiently. "No, no, before that!"

"What—what are talking about?"

Josh tilted his head to the side curiously. "I've known Tessa for quite some time, Mary. I just need her to remember."

In her memory, I felt Mary push back a snarky response, instead forcing her features into a neutral expression. *"Are you sure you don't have her confused with someone else?" she asked carefully as she silently questioned his sanity.*

"I am sane," Josh told her. "I don't understand why you would question that."

"I didn't—never mind." Mary huffed and slumped against the wall.

"You think very loudly, Mary. You should get some lessons on proper mental shielding when you return home."

For a moment, all I could see was the wall of the cell across from her as she stubbornly refused to look at him and tried to ignore the hope his words sparked inside her.

"It was a long time ago," he said slowly. "When I found her, she was... broken. She wasn't the girl she'd been in her previous life. Or the one she is now, I suppose."

"Okay... Who was she?"

"Fiery." He grinned. "She was this ball of furious fire burning with this insatiable need for vengeance."

"That doesn't sound like Tessa. Maybe you were mistaken?"

Josh chuckled darkly. "Oh, believe me, Mary, I wasn't. Tessa and I...we bonded over time. I could tell that what she wanted aligned quite closely with my own wishes."

"Which are?"

He sighed and leaned his head back, then turned his face toward her. "A new world. A better one that renewed the original state of order."

Even locked away, Mary's mind kept going a mile a minute, and I smiled as I felt her begin to connect the dots.

"So... you started a war? How does that make things better?"

"Isn't that always the point of war, Mary? To rid the world of oppressors, of creatures who harm, who do little more than destroy?"

The anger that had stirred in her moments earlier reappeared, shoving past all her fear and pain as she realized just how unstable Josh was.

"Fine. *Then what exactly was it those Ischyra did in the arena to deserve what happened to them? Or the ones in Athens?"*

He sighed and tapped his fingers against his bent knees. "It's about balance, Mary. Significant numbers were being destroyed on Cronus' side, so I needed to ensure one side didn't come out the sole victor."

A sick feeling pulsed through me as I realized what he was saying.

"You took down the wards, so they could attack unsuspecting recruits... to create balance?*"*

"It could've been worse," he said coldly. "I could've encouraged them to aim their efforts higher up the mountain. Instead, I chose the smaller fish, the less impactful victims."

"Less—are you kidding me?*"*

I winced as she instinctively tried to jump to her feet, only to hiss in pain when the chains pulled her back down.

I watched as he stared at her impassively. *"Between the empousa that Tessa and her friends killed, and the crocotta Artemis slaughtered, it was only fair to balance the scales."*

Mary snorted a laugh. "You really have no idea how war works, do you?"

He lifted a brow. "And you do?"

"I still don't understand. If this is war, why don't you want a winner?"

Josh closed his eyes and smiled wistfully. "Because I want to destroy it all."

"Oh, is that all?"

"Essentially."

Mary's voice wobbled as she tried to force bravado into her words, and I nearly smiled as she cursed herself for letting her fear and weakness show. She'd felt herself begin to slip away, but she hadn't gotten to the point where she'd completely lost sight of who she was. I could only hope that held out.

"And you, uh, think Tessa wants to help you achieve that goal? She's never really struck me as the apocalyptic type of girl."

"She might not know it yet," Josh conceded. "It was a long time ago, so I guess her perspective could've changed by now."

"I see." Mary stared at the floor, then turned so she was facing him. "You still haven't answered my question, though. How do you know her?"

Josh leaned forward and looked at her, considering for a moment. "When Tessa was sent to the Void—"

"You were in the Void? In Chaos? How—"

Her shock mirrored mine.

He touched a finger to his lips and smiled. "I was drawn to her fear. It was palpable, calling to me across time and space." His expression turned inquisitive. "Why do you think it is that she doesn't remember her time there?"

Good question.

"Her soul wasn't attached to her body. If a soul doesn't have a life force—"

"False. A soul is a life force. The energy that is given to a being by their progenitors—in Tessa's case, her parents—is what makes a physically living thing. It is a life-force in its own sense. But a soul... that's what makes a being truly alive." His smile turned soft, his eyes distant. "It is a beautiful thing to behold."

A noise sounded from the hall, breaking Josh's reverie.

"Well, I suppose it's time I go." He stood and dusted off his pants. "Try not to worry, Mary. The rest of your questions will be answered soon enough. For now, though, I think it's best this conversation is kept between us." Gently, he touched a finger to her cheek.

An instant later, she was asleep.

I SNAPPED out of Mary's head, gasping. Shoving off Nate's hands, I stood and paced to the window. Shaking my head, I dragged my hands through my hair, then braced my hands on the sill as I went back over everything I'd just seen.

"What happened?" Yana asked. "What did you see?"

"Not possible," I whispered. "Not fucking possible."

"That you were stuck in the Void with him, or that the two of you apparently wanted to destroy the world?" Hades asked dryly.

Furious, my eyes snapped to his. He folded his arms across his chest and cocked a brow.

"Tessa," Nate said, stepping toward me. "Let's talk about this before you get yourself too worked up."

"Talk about what, Nate? You heard what he said!"

"I don't care what he said!" he shouted. "That's not you, Tessa, and you damn well know it!"

"Tell me what's going on!" Yana stepped forward, her expression concerned.

"He's right," Apollo said as Nate gave Yana an abbreviated version of what we just saw. "And now is not the time to be having breakdowns over things we can neither confirm nor deny."

"Especially things we know aren't true," Athena said pointedly.

I took a few steadying breaths. "So you want to go back in and see if you can find more proof that I was plotting with... whoever he is, about *destroying the goddamn world?*"

Yana rolled her eyes. "Tessa, if you truly believe any of us think that is possible, you are fooling yourself."

"And he didn't actually *say* you were plotting," Athena pointed out. "Just that he believed you wanted the same things he did."

"Why don't I remember?" I turned to look out the window, trying again to calm myself down. I knew what Josh said wasn't true, at least not now, and Athena was right. Logically, I *knew* that. The last thing I wanted was to destroy worlds. I knew that as surely as I knew myself.

But a small bit of doubt pricked at my mind. If we'd been in the Void together all that time, and I'd been as angry as he said, what if he was telling the truth about the rest? What if I'd felt so betrayed by my family, the people who smothered me to the point of incapability, that I actually let him think I wanted to destroy it all? It sounded ludicrous when I put it that way, but so soon after my death, after being stuck in a place that was dark and desolate, not knowing when or if I'd ever escape, was it possible I'd fallen into a place *that* dark?

"If you don't shut down the pity party, I'm leaving," Hades snapped.

I wanted to bite back at him, but Nate's calming hand on my back stopped me.

He wrapped his arms around me and rested his chin on my head. *'Stop.'* I felt a small touch of Coercion, his attempt to calm me down.

'I know that's not me, Nate. But what if it was back then? What if I'm the reason he went through with starting this war?'

'He said he'd wanted to do this no matter what,' Nate replied. *'Your pain was an excuse to follow through.'*

I closed my eyes and leaned back against him, accepting his help in willing my nerves to settle. Then, taking his hand, I turned and faced everyone else. "This is big. We should probably go to Zeus now."

"Absolutely not!" Hades and Nate said in unison. Frowning, Nate stared down at me. "It's not happening."

Apollo gave them an amused look, then shook his head. "No, Tessa, as much as I hate to agree with these two, they're right. Going to my father with what we've just seen will only make him question your allegiance and your purpose. We need more information."

I inclined my head toward where Hades and Nate stood. "Hades is the ruler of the Underworld, and Athena is one of the leaders of Zeus' army. You're second in command of the whole damn mountain, Apollo! Wouldn't your word carry some sway with him?"

"Not if that word goes against whatever notions he's conceived in his mind once we tell him what we know. Even if Nathaniel is there to back up their accounts, you know how my father can be." He sighed. "Tessa, validity aside, it's quite possible Josh has given us this new knowledge in an to attempt to drive a wedge between us. If our allies think your loyalty might waver, they'll second-guess their own places in this war as well."

"You're barking mad if you think we're letting Zeus anywhere near you right now," Hades said flatly.

I dropped down on the sofa and rested my elbows on my knees, then steepled my fingers in front of my mouth. Every meager ounce of happiness I'd gained since having my best friend returned slowly began to evaporate.

"You think he's pulling a Trojan horse?" Nate asked. "Send Mary home with information that could damn us hidden in her mind?"

"I think we would be foolish to discount the possibility," Apollo replied.

"He's right, Tessa," Nate said, meeting my eyes. "Both of them. Until we know more, it's safest for you *and Mary*," he added when he saw me start to protest, "to stay here. We'll finish sorting through her memories—"

"You'll need to check mine, too," I interrupted. I looked at Hades. "When you gave me my memories back, you wouldn't have gone deep enough to touch whatever memories Josh may have hidden, I'm sure of it."

He, Nate, Athena, and Apollo shared a quick look, one that almost definitely involved a quick, internal spat between the four of them.

"We'll consider it," Hades said. "But I'm telling you, if there were hidden memories there, I would have seen them, even if I couldn't access them."

"Consider it? Don't you think we should know?" I asked.

"Tessa," Athena began, "I think, considering the circumstances, those memories may not prove all that useful."

"What? Why?"

"For one, your thoughts wouldn't have been terribly objective," Nate told me. "Also, if Josh had given you any information that would lead us to a means of killing him, he wouldn't have let us know you were with him that whole time."

I looked around at each of them. "Do all of you feel that way?"

"It was a long time ago, Tessa," Apollo pointed out. "And while there may be a slight chance there could be some useful information there, it's more likely we'll see the reaction of a girl in terrible pain."

A girl who'd been betrayed by the world she lived in.

My shoulders slumped as I realized how right he was.

They wouldn't see *me*. They'd see a girl who'd just watched her mother die, who'd just spent months being tormented by her brother at the behest of her father. A girl who'd just exorcised a demon from her mother's mind, nearly killing her in the process. A girl who was floating, alone, scared, in a cold, empty place devoid of light or life, who would probably have promised anything if it meant she could get out.

But that wasn't my world anymore. That wasn't *me* anymore.

I met Hades' eyes. "Alright, we'll wait. But if it needs to be done, I want you to do it."

His jaw tensed, but he nodded his assent.

"Should we update Chiron again?" Yana asked hesitantly. "We have a bit more information now—"

"Yes," Apollo said with a quick nod. "Tessa, take a quick break, send Chiron everything you saw in Mary's mind. We'll continue without you for now."

I started to argue, then thought better of it when I realized what they were likely about to witness. Sending the memories to Chiron would give me a few minutes of reprieve and distract me from the fact that Hades and Nate were probably going to watch Mary as my father and Cronus siphoned her power. With the state I was currently in, I couldn't have that blurring my thought process.

Selfish maybe, but I also knew that, just like I wouldn't want anyone else to bear the weight of the memory of my torture, Mary wouldn't want that for any of us, either. So, turning my back on them, I called out to Chiron.

'Chiron, you there?'

'Hey, Tessa. Is everyone alright?'

'Yeah. Well, sort of. We're going through Mary's memories now, and I wanted to send you what we got so far. But Chiron—'

'I'll keep it to myself until you all tell me otherwise,' he said solemnly. 'Right now I just need as much as you can give me. Based on some information I've found already, I have a pretty solid theory of what we're dealing with, but I still need to confirm a few things.'

'I have a feeling that's what I'm about to do,' I said grimly. I sent him everything we'd gotten from the conversation between Mary and

Josh. I couldn't bring myself to send him her memory of the arena attack. That wasn't a hurt he needed to relive right now.

'Gods, Tessa.' I could practically feel his shock through the connection. *'Are you alright?'*

'I am,' I told him. *'Now. I wasn't before, but you know how it goes.'*

'Whatever may have happened while you were gone, Tessa, that isn't you. Just remember that.'

I smiled at his reassurance. He was truly one of the most amazing beings I'd met since coming to Olympus. *'Thanks, Chiron. I really appreciate you saying that.'*

'If it wasn't the truth, I wouldn't say it. I'm going to get back to work. Let me know if you get more. I'll probably be up shortly to discuss my findings with you all, and I think a trip to the palace may be in order sooner rather than later.'

'Agreed. We'll talk soon.'

Once I closed the connection with Chiron, I turned and faced everyone else. "I'm going to get John and Analise up here for when she wakes up. I think having them here will help keep her calm."

"Will you take me to the library?" Yana asked. She cast a cautious glance at Mary. "I think I will be more help if I am working with Chiron and Anette."

"Of course." I smiled. "But don't think you have to leave."

She shook her head. "No, that is not it. I am just no use here, but I can be useful there."

"Do you need me to come with you?" Nate asked me. His expression told me that he was trying very hard not to go with me, whether I wanted him to or not, but I appreciated his restraint.

I shook my head. "Just keep going with Mary. I'll be back in a few."

"Be careful and hurry back," he told me. *'I love you.'*

I gave him a tight smile. *'I love you, too.'*

34

NATHANIEL

As soon as Tessa and Yana were gone, I looked between Hades, Athena, and Apollo. Before I could speak, Apollo voiced my own thoughts.

"I don't think I can express how not good this is," he said as he eyed Mary where she slept on the couch.

"Did you gain that level of intelligence from your father or mother?" Hades muttered, shaking his head.

Apollo scowled at him. "We could sling barbs here, or we could discuss the fact that Tessa apparently has memories that are still repressed despite your assault on her mind. Quite distressing ones if what Josh says is true."

I wanted to agree with Apollo and toss blame at Hades for missing whatever memories still lurked in Tessa's subconscious, if they even existed, of which I still wasn't entirely convinced. I also knew there was no way Hades would've known or even thought to dig past the magical barriers that had still been protecting Tessa's mind once she'd awoken. At the same time, blank spots in a being's memory were typically simple to see. They weren't always simple to access, but their presence was hard to hide from a god with powers like Hades'.

I raked a hand through my hair and sighed. "Fighting isn't going to help anyone," I said wearily.

"Agreed," Athena said.

"Let's get on with it, then," Apollo said.

I tightened my hold on Mary's mind to ensure she was unaware of the memories being sorted through, then nodded a go-ahead to Hades.

He sped through the next few days of memories, pausing only long enough to observe the process Cronus used when siphoning her power. As I watched him and Iapetus strap her down and suck her power, watched as she slowly counted down the moments until she fell into unconsciousness, I was incredibly glad Tessa wasn't around to witness it.

She'd lived that kind of pain once. She didn't need to live it again through the eyes of her best friend.

"We'll need to speak with the sisters," Apollo murmured as he watched the process. "See if they can elaborate any further on this process."

Hades grunted quietly then began pulling forward the memories that elicited the most fear, pain, and other forms of stress. Smaller beatings she took when Cronus or Iapetus decided to make a visit, the shouts and grunts of pain when one or all of the sisters were taken by Cronus' silent guards, and the constant pain in her shoulders from where they'd refused to unchain her... all were recurring stressors.

When Hades felt her adrenaline spike as Josh took her from her cell, he stopped.

He tapped his fingers on his chin. "This obsession he seems to have with Tessa is... bizarre. I don't quite understand it."

"It doesn't make sense," I agreed. "Even if what he says is true and she was trapped in Chaos along with him, he has to know that she isn't the person she was when she went in." Reluctantly, I looked at Hades. "After you all discovered what Menoetius had been doing to her, did you ever get the sense she wanted more than just revenge on him?"

He shook his head, surprising me by not shooting some biting remark my way. "She wanted his balls in a vise, but no, Tessa was never a vengeful person, not in the way he described. Certainly not in an apocalyptic sense."

Frowning, I nodded, then waved for him to continue. He started pushing through the memories again, and we watched as Josh led Mary through the halls of wherever they had been kept.

"Stop there!" Apollo said. Hades obeyed, then Apollo focused his attention on a window Mary was looking through. "Do either of you recognize that body of water?" he asked. "It looks like there's some kind of structure there."

Hades held the memory still, and the three of us focused in on it.

"Definitely a lighthouse of some sort." I arched a brow. "Are either of you well-versed in lighthouses of the world?"

"Not particularly," Apollo conceded. "Although I can tell you it's certainly not Grecian. But it's a landmark, regardless, though. If we figure out where it is, we might be able to find his base of operations."

"Or, like everything else, he could've intended for Mary to see it," I countered. "Sanity aside, he doesn't seem particularly stupid. I can't imagine he'd put her directly in front of something that could easily identify their location."

Athena nodded. "True. I'll ask Dionysus. He's traveled far more than most of us. He may be able to offer some help."

Without waiting for a cue, Hades pushed forward, replaying the time Mary spent in Josh's room that ended abruptly after Cronus and Iapetus showed up. Then, he watched the altercation between Josh and Cronus, and the seeming indifference Josh had toward the Titan who, until now, we'd thought to be the leader of their entire operation.

The sardonic grin on Josh's face as Cronus wrapped a hand around Josh's neck made it abundantly clear that Cronus was not the one in charge.

If there had been any doubts, the simplicity with which Josh killed Iapetus and disabled Cronus squashed them.

"What in all the realms was on that knife?" Apollo wondered as he watched Iapetus bleed out on the floor of the cell, his eyes wide and lifeless as the energy that kept him alive was slowly leached away.

"Poison or magic, most likely," Hades muttered. "Possibly both." He quickly skimmed through the rest of Mary's memories. Then, seeing nothing of note, withdrew from her mind. "Whatever it is, it can take down a god as easily as a human."

"Not only gods," I told him. "Titans. They have far more energy within them than the younger generations of deities."

"Or Iapetus wasn't up to his full power yet," Apollo countered. "Regardless, a single weapon that can kill deities so efficiently has never existed."

"This is all assuming he's actually dead," Athena pointed out. "Can we trust what we're seeing here?"

"I don't—"

Before I could finish, the door burst open, and Tessa ran in with her guardians hurrying behind. When John and Analise saw Mary, Analise shouldered Tessa aside, and they both rushed forward, shoving both Hades and Apollo out of the way to get to her.

Hades' brow winged up, and his face turned indignant as he took them in.

"Why is she still asleep?" Analise demanded, looking up at me. "Can you wake her now?"

"We were just about to wake her," Apollo replied.

"Apollo." John stood. "Apologies, we didn't—I—"

Apollo waved off his apology and tilted his head toward Mary. "I've healed any wounds I've been able to find, and we've just finished an examination of her memories."

Analise, who hadn't moved from her crouched position beside Mary, didn't shift her gaze from Mary's face as she spoke. "Can you wake her?"

"In a minute," Tessa said, looking at me, Apollo, and Hades in question. "What did you guys find?"

Hades shot a pointed look at her guardians, and Tessa huffed a sigh in response. "John and Analise can take Mary in the other room and get her cleaned up. Wait, hang on... Is she going to remember everything you just saw?"

I nodded. "She wants to know what happened to her."

Tessa pressed her lips into a thin line, seeming to fight the urge to tell me to ignore Mary's request. "Alright. Just keep the dreams away, okay?"

Slowly, I released the hold on Mary's mind, returning her to consciousness first but leaving the command inside her to suppress dreams for the time being. A solid night's sleep was something she desperately needed right now, and she didn't need bad dreams preventing that from happening.

Her eyes fluttered open, and her entire face crumpled when she took in Analise's worried expression.

"Oh, honey," Analise murmured, tears spilling down her face as she pulled Mary into a hug. Mary's hands gripped Analise's arms as she began to cry, huge, wracking sobs that shook her entire body. Wordless cries tore from her throat, her pain hitting me like a punch to the gut.

"I'll show you both where to go," Tessa said quietly. "We already have a room set up for her."

John lifted Mary into his arms and followed Tessa down the hall toward the room where she and Yana had deposited her belongings a few days prior. They'd already unpacked everything and set the framed pictures she'd had in her dorm on top of the small dresser.

When they were out of sight, Hades glared at Apollo. "A human pushed you, and you didn't reprimand him."

Apollo picked up his abandoned glass of brandy and took a small sip. "Yes. Believe it or not, Hades, I do care about the pain of others. They're hurting because of the actions of *our* species. Whether we're directly responsible or not is beside the point," he said when Hades opened his mouth to argue. He paused with his glass halfway to his mouth and looked down at me. "What's on your mind, Nathaniel?"

I rubbed the back of my neck and let out a heavy breath. "Things just escalated very quickly, and I have no idea what our next steps should be. We've got to go to Zeus with everything we just learned, but I don't know how to do that while also protecting Tessa from what his temper might lead him to do."

"Which would be what?" Tessa stepped into the room and gave me a questioning look. "What do you think he'd do?"

Hades and I shared a look before I responded. "That depends," I said slowly. "If we're looking at extremes, he's just as likely to toss you in a dungeon for questioning as he is to sit down and discuss this all rationally."

She wrapped her arms around herself, then pursed her lips and nodded. "Then we need more information."

"With the exception of digging through your mind, how do you propose we do that?" Apollo asked.

"Exactly that," she said. Indecision was written clear on her face, and based on Hades' dubious expression, he saw it as clearly as I did. She didn't want those memories and I didn't blame her, but I also understood why she felt so conflicted.

"Tessa, when I pulled your memories forward, I saw no indication that there was anything hidden there," Hades said cautiously. "If Josh has repressed certain memories, I—" A muscle twitched in his jaw, and he huffed out a breath through his nose. "I don't think I can access them."

"So we try," she said. "You and Nate, together."

"Alright." He tilted his head toward me. "*If* you'll let Nathaniel block your awareness, while I search."

"Hades!" I stared at him, stunned. "You can't just offer something like that without consulting me first!"

"Are you so eager for her to see what happened to her there?" He gave me a genuinely curious look. "Don't forget, I know what she went through in her previous life."

"That's the last thing I want! But if she wants to know—"

"Ever hear the expression 'curiosity killed the cat,' Nathaniel? Sometimes it's best to remain ignorant of certain facts." Hades gave Tessa a pained look. "I think you should seriously consider letting this be, Tessa. Please."

Athena held up her hands and stepped between us. "How about

we table this for now? You've each got your valid points, but there's no sense fighting about it." She sighed and let her hands fall to her sides. "But can we all agree to keep an open mind about whether pulling those memories is worthwhile? I'm not entirely convinced it is."

"Yeah," Tessa murmured. "I'm not exactly in a rush to see what my life was like back then."

Pained, I brushed a thumb along her cheek, then enveloped her in my arms. This night had taken a turn I'd never seen coming, and the idea that Tessa had memories of the three millennia she'd spent locked in the Void lurking in her mind was what upset me most of all. I knew, without question, that whatever might be hidden there, if anything, wouldn't be a reflection of who she was now. I'd wait for Hades to confirm that before voicing my opinion, but I held no doubts as to who Tessa truly was.

I thought of Atlas, who was still struggling to regain his life on the mountain after being imprisoned in a cave and tormented all these years. He was on the road to recovery, but the pain, the distrust, the wariness of the outside world was clear in his eyes each time I saw him. He'd spent that time knowing the world was changing, spinning on without him, and could do nothing to stop it. Now we knew Tessa's circumstances may not have been much different. The only upside was that she had no memory of her imprisonment.

It didn't take a genius to question whether it was foolish to change that.

"Before we do anything," Athena said quietly, "I think it's time we reach out to Atlas. We need to go speak with the sisters at Demeter's, so I'll get Hermes and Dionysus up here to stay with Mary and your guardians, Tessa."

"You need to come down there, anyway, Tessa, to help us… handle Atlas once we tell him the news," Apollo added.

Tessa nodded, knuckling away a tear that had escaped. She slipped her hand into mine and turned to face him. "Yeah, okay. I'll call him when we get down there."

Seconds later, Hermes and Dionysus walked in.

"This better be good," Hermes grumbled, rubbing his eyes. "I'm still sleeping off my trip down memory lane."

"Josh was here," I said flatly. "He returned Mary and the sisters. We need you two to stay with Mary and the Averys while we go down to Demeter's."

Hermes' hands slowly fell to his sides.

Dionysus blinked, wide-eyed. "We killed off almost an entire faction of their forces, and he brought her *back? Alive?*"

"And the sisters. Unharmed." I looked at Tessa. "Mostly."

"Start from the beginning," Hermes said. "What happened?" Then he stopped, freezing as he looked at Dionysus. "What do you mean 'killed off almost an entire faction?'" He sent a confused glance toward me. "What have you all been up to tonight?"

"You go on ahead," I told Apollo, Hades, and Tessa. "I'll fill them in and meet you there shortly."

Tessa leaned up on her toes and gave me a quick kiss. "Be quick and be safe. We'll see you in a few."

35

TESSA

Demeter's house was buzzing with activity when we arrived. The main house was ablaze with light, and the sound of harried voices filtered through the open first-floor windows. The noise level increased when we opened the door, the voices breaking into mostly female, with the occasional booming timbre that belonged to Hyperion.

The sight of all seven Pleiades beside each other was a bit disorienting, but I shoved the feeling away. Shaking off my frazzled nerves, I followed Apollo and Hades inside. Conversation paused briefly, then one of the sisters who still bore the filth of being locked in a dungeon rushed forward and grabbed my hands.

"Where is Mary?" she asked. Her voice held an edge of hysteria, and when I glanced at the other two who'd just been returned, I saw similar expressions of concern on their faces.

"She's fine...um?" I winced, unsure which sister I was speaking with.

"Celaeno." She shook her head and blew out a breath, then relaxed slightly when the other two who'd been with her each placed a hand on her shoulder. "I'm sorry, but when Josh left us here and took her..."

"Where did he take her?" one of the others asked. She had a small freckle just above her right eyebrow.

"Nathaniel's house," I told her. "He was waiting for us when we got home."

The third sister's eyes widened. "Everyone is safe, then?"

"Yes." I glanced around the room until my eyes landed on Maia. "I'm going to let Atlas know they've returned."

She gave a small nod.

"Atlas?" Eyebrow freckle asked.

"Yes." I did my best to sound reassuring, but I could only imagine how strange it must be for them, returning to find that their long-absent father had been waiting for them. "He's been really worried about you."

Maia stepped closer to her sisters and placed a hand on the back of the one who'd spoken. "We've already spoken with him at length, Taygete. We can get into more detail later, but for now, he should know you've returned."

Taygete looked at me warily, then at her sister. "Alright, I'll follow your lead, then."

I sent out a call to all my brothers, knowing the twins' presence might help temper Atlas' emotions before they got the best of him. I told Atlas to simply come down but gave Prometheus and Epimetheus a quick rundown before they left.

Moments later, all three burst through the door.

Atlas homed in on me first, not noticing that there were now seven of his daughters before him instead of the four he'd seen a few days prior. He was immediately flanked by our brothers, both of whom looked to be trying to rein in the panic that had formed when they'd heard the news.

"Are you alright?" He gripped my shoulders and ran his eyes over me. "What's happened?"

"Atlas, I need you to stay calm, okay?" I pulled his hands from my arms and held them. "Promise me?"

"I—" His eyes drifted over my shoulder. His face went slack as he took in the rest of the room's occupants, realizing that all of his daughters were present. "You—you're back." He frowned at Maia. "How?"

Maia glanced over at me, then gave me a small nod.

Taking a deep breath, I met my twin's eyes. "Josh brought Mary and the rest of the Pleiades home a little while ago."

Atlas jerked back and frowned. "What do you mean, he 'brought them home'?"

The third sister, Alcyone, cleared her throat. "She means he delivered us here not long ago, just before taking Mary to Nathaniel's."

Atlas' eyes flashed to Nate, who'd just walked in. "He was in your *house*?" he hissed. He glared at me. "Why am I just hearing about this now?"

"It doesn't matter." I met his gaze unflinchingly as Nate came to stand beside me. "We're not going to argue about timing or when you should've been told, because it doesn't matter. We're telling you now."

"Tessa, are you alright?" Epimetheus asked carefully. "He didn't hurt you?"

"It might be best if you all took a seat," Apollo said. "Now."

No one argued against the command in his voice. Somehow, the seven sisters managed to squeeze themselves onto one of the sofas, while my brothers sat opposite. Demeter, Hyperion, and Theia stood in front of the fireplace while Apollo, Nate, and I took spots facing them. Hades and Persephone stood behind the sofa where the sisters sat.

"A little while ago, Tessa and I returned home to find Josh inside," Nate began. "He had Mary held in what we now believe was the Void while he spoke with us."

There was a collective intake of breath, but no one spoke, likely due to shock or simple curiosity as to what might come next.

"Do you think that's where he's had her this whole time?" Theia asked.

"It would certainly explain why I wasn't able to track her," Persephone said. She glanced down at the sisters. "She was with you three the whole time, though, correct?"

Celaeno nodded. "Yes, she was, so that wouldn't have been possible."

As concisely as he could, Nate relayed the events of the previous hour, including the bulk of memories he and Hades had gotten from Mary and everything Josh had said about me.

As he told them what Josh said about my time in the Void, I looked around the room, taking in everyone's faces as they absorbed what he was saying. Even I had to admit it sounded just as damning as it did far-fetched, but no one present seemed to show any suspicion of unease at his words.

When I reached Hyperion and Theia, I saw them taking in my own reaction.

"And you don't recall any of this?" Theia asked curiously. "Your time in Chaos after your death. Nothing?"

I shook my head. "The only clear memory was right after my death, when I was first sent there. I have no memory of anyone else in there with me."

"Alright, so to clarify, this creature, who claims he spent three thousand years in the Void with Tessa, is also the reason she was sent back with no memory of being there?" Persephone asked.

"According to him, yes," Apollo said. "Although, Hecate told us that the Fates were the ones who decreed it was time to bring her home or risk losing her permanently." He looked across to Demeter, and the two held eyes for a few moments before he gave a short nod. "We're going to call Zeus in now," he said. He held up a hand amid the shouted protests from Nate and my brothers. "We've gotten as much information as we can from Mary. Chiron is still working in the archives. Anything else we discuss here will be mere speculation. At this point, we need more minds, and I'm not willing to bring more deities into this and ask them to keep secrets from their ruler."

I bit my lip and looked up at Nate, whose eyes were shooting daggers at his brother. When he felt my stare, he looked down at me. "It'll be alright," he murmured.

Apollo went quiet, his eyes distant as he called out to Zeus and relayed information. Based on his occasional clenched jaw and gritted teeth, he was getting a mental reaming that would likely only get worse once Zeus arrived. Finally, with a sigh, he refocused on us.

"He wants us up there."

"No," half the people in the room said in unison.

"We're not leaving," Maia said sharply. "My sisters have only just returned. I won't subject them to Zeus' inquisition up at the palace. If he wants to speak with them, he can come down here and do it."

"I'll go up and get him," Nate said, resigned.

"No need," Hyperion said. "He's on his way."

Hades let out an amused snort. I quirked a brow at Hyperion.

"Are your powers of persuasion that impressive?" Athena asked.

He gave a small nod. "You could say that."

Moments later, Zeus stormed through the front door, outrage and incredulity coloring his face. "What is the meaning of this?" he roared.

"Zeus, calm down," Prometheus said, holding up his hands in a placating gesture.

"I will not calm down!" He glared down at the Pleiades. "Prisoners of war have been returned, and I'm just finding out *now*?"

"We didn't want to involve you until we had solid information to go on," Nate said. "Now we do."

Zeus shook his head, and his lip curled as he looked at his son. "Of all my children, Nathaniel, you have been surprising me the most in recent days."

"Sorry to disappoint," Nate said flatly.

Zeus' eyes scanned the room, taking in all the occupants before coming to a stop on Hades. "Explain."

Hades looked at him amusedly. "Is that an order, dear brother?"

"Enough, children," Demeter said, rolling her eyes. She looked at Apollo expectantly. "Apollo?"

There were a few seconds of silence as Zeus and Hades continued their stand off before Zeus turned to face Apollo. "Well?"

If circumstances hadn't been so dire, the range of expressions that crossed Zeus' face as he listened to everything Apollo told him would've been comical. When Apollo reached the part where Josh said he'd been with me in the Void, Zeus switched his gaze to me, his furious eyes turning suspicious as he continued to take in recent events. Noticing his expression, Nate shifted so he was standing slightly in front of me.

When Apollo finished, and the room went silent, I shifted uncomfortably, not liking the way Zeus continued to stare at me, suspicion still clear on his face.

There was a movement to my right as Hades took a few steps closer, followed by my brothers.

"Are you telling me that this girl—" Zeus pointed at me, his voice a deadly calm, "—spent three millennia with this creature, and we're just now finding out?"

"I don't remember any of it," I said quietly. I absolutely despised how small my voice sounded as I tried to defend myself.

"It doesn't matter!" he roared, taking a menacing step toward me. As he moved, all three of my brothers shifted to block him.

"Zeus, let's be reasonable about this," Demeter said. "Logical. You knew Tessa in her previous life, and you know her now."

"I knew her better than anyone, brother," Hades said. "Do you think I'd allow her on your mountain if I thought she was out to destroy it?"

"Yes, quite frankly, I do," Zeus snapped. "I want her memories examined *now*." He shifted his gaze to me. "No negotiations."

"Hang on," Nate said, holding up a hand when Hades' lip curled in anger. "Let's look at this objectively. Father, we're talking about sifting through three *thousand* years worth of memories."

"Even scanning that length of time could take days," Hades said. "And Josh was quite clear that he was basing his assumptions on her emotions, not her words."

"Then you'll look early on, when she would've still been most aware," Zeus said matter-of-factly. "When he first learned of her... feelings."

Something inside me shifted at that, and the confusion and fear attached to those memories started to lean toward logic and anger as Zeus calmly suggested forcing me to submit to an interrogation.

"I can already tell you what you'll find," I told him evenly, stepping past my brothers so I could look at him directly. "The exact same thing you would've found in *your* mind when you were freed from your prison." I pushed forward, ignoring the fury on his face. "You wanted to kill the person responsible, overthrow him, make him pay, correct? Well, so do I." My heart started to pound at the rightness in my words. "Hecate may have sent me there, but Cronus, Menoetius, my father—*they* were the reasons she did it! Their desire to hurt me, *use* me is what caused her and my mother to seek out extreme measures of protecting me." I pointed at him. "You didn't do that. Not a single person on this mountain did that! So, no! I won't let you dig through my head and pass judgment on me based on feelings that any sane person would have! I don't *want* to know what I experienced in there and I'm damn well entitled to that choice!"

When I finished, my chest was heaving in anger, but my mind felt rock-steady. The self-doubt that had gnawed at me back at Nate's house slowly disappeared, giving way to clarity.

"And really, Father," Apollo said, "if he wants her to see those memories, then it's highly unlikely he divulged information that might be damaging to himself."

Seething, Zeus gritted his teeth. "Then how do you expect to go about figuring out who he is?"

"I might be able to help with that."

Chiron stepped into the room looking harried, exhausted, and slightly stunned. A sheath of papers was clutched in his hands.

"What are you talking about?" Zeus demanded. "Please tell me you have good news, Chiron."

"Nathaniel said Josh told them there had been men who attempted to write about him," Chiron said without preamble. "I think, based on what information I've got, I might've figured out who —what—we're dealing with." Chiron held up the papers. "Keats, Ovid, Hesiod, among others. They all wrote of the major events in our existence, wars, lineages. Their writings all have things in common as you would expect, the things we all know, but there's one thing present in their works that could be easily interpreted in a number of ways."

"And you think your way is the correct one?" Theia asked.

Chiron shrugged. "It could be a stretch, of course, but it's the best I've got." He let out a long breath, the kind one does when they're about to reveal something big.

Zeus snatched the papers from his hands and began scanning over them. "What am I looking at? These are poems, Chiron."

"Ovid might be the most illuminating here." He slid a small book from the pocket of his pants and held it up. The cover was made of worn, brown leather, the title—*Metamorphoses*—was done in gold leaf and barely legible. "According to his writings, the worlds, all the dimensions, existed in a state of disharmony, complete disorder, a ball of unusable elements that held potential, but no purpose in the state they were in. Light canceled out dark, cold warred with hot, and the earth, sky, and sea, were all devoid of life."

"Yes, we know all of this," Zeus said impatiently.

"Yes, but it's his interpretation of that pile of building blocks that caught my eye. He speaks of a god who was given nature's blessing, or assistance, depending on the translation, to pull the universe from that original state of disorder into one of harmony." He opened the book and read a line from one of the early pages. "'So into shape whatever god it was reduced the primal matter and prescribed its several parts.'" Chiron closed the book with a snap and inclined his head toward the papers Apollo was now looking through. "Similarly, Keats attributes the Titan's loss in the last war to Nature. It was nature's way of clearing the way for the next generation of leaders. Hesiod writes of the first deities being born from Chaos. In some translations, as well as other works, Chaos is referred to as female." He looked around the room, eyebrows raised expectantly. "Anyone want to take a guess as to where I'm going with this?"

Silence hung over the room as we all processed his words, sorted out the few bits of evidence he'd given us to back his theory that, on any other day, would've made him seem just as crazy as Josh.

But if what he was implying was accurate...

My brain was still struggling to catch up with the implications of his words. By the silence that hung over the room, I could only imagine the others were in similar states of shock.

"Chaos," Nate whispered. He sounded surprised, as though someone had just popped into the room that he hadn't seen in ages. "You're saying—"

I lifted my eyes to Chiron. "You're saying Josh *is* Chaos."

He gave me a grim smile. "The Creator. And I think he's come to return the worlds to their former state."

36

MARY

I couldn't sleep.

Each time I tried to doze, all I could feel was cold stone at my back, a heavy boot to my ribs, the burn of godsbane at my wrists, and the vicious yank of my power being siphoned away.

Analise hadn't left my side, and John, angry and scared but not quite knowing what to do, had been out in the living room talking with Hermes and Dionysus most of the time they'd been there.

Hesitantly, I reached for my power, but it felt as though it were recoiling from my touch.

I suppose neither of us are used to being free just yet.

I'd just shut my eyes for what felt like the hundredth time when I heard the door open. Awake now, I watched as Dionysus strode in, a sympathetic smile on his face. He sent a quick look to Analise, then she stood and kissed my forehead.

"I'll be out in the living room." She gave Dionysus a tight smile as she left.

Once the door was closed, Dionysus held up his hands and wiggled his fingers. "I can feel your misery all the way out there, so I'm here to help."

"Sorry to be an inconvenience," I muttered, rolling to face the wall. It wasn't fair, I knew that. Of all of Nate's siblings, Dionysus and I got along the best. He was the most easy-going and least pretentious, which I guessed was part of his appeal as a revelry god. I also knew he wouldn't be here to help if he didn't want to.

I felt the bed dip as he sat down. "If you were an inconvenience, I wouldn't be here." He nudged my shoulder, and when I turned to look at him, he tilted his chin toward the other side of the bed. "Scooch over."

Gritting my teeth, I slid over a foot and rolled onto my back.

"Head up," he instructed as he laid down next to me.

I lifted my head just high enough for him to get an arm underneath. When I'd settled against his shoulder, he let his other hand come to rest on my arm. "Now close your eyes," he said quietly. "This might feel a little weird at first, but it'll help."

"I'm snuggling with an Elder," I muttered. "This is already weird."

He chuckled. "Close your eyes, Mary."

I sighed, then did as I was told.

As soon as my eyes were shut, I felt the first tendrils of his magic. Tessa had explained how it felt when he'd used it to help keep her calm during her dream walk with Atlas, but this had to have been far more powerful, because I literally felt like I'd been hit with a sedative. Within seconds, I felt everything inside me relax. My mind became clearer, sorting out the bad thoughts and tossing them away. The fear I'd been feeling was turned to logic. I felt the knowledge that I was right here, safe and sound and far away from the creatures that had been holding me the past week. The magic settled in like an old friend, easing away the mild panic I'd been staving off since I woke.

And warmth. That kind of warmth you feel when everything is just... right. When there's nothing that needs to be changed, because where you are in that very moment is *exactly* where you need to be.

Home. I was home.

"You in love with me yet, doll?" Dionysus whispered.

I snorted groggily. "Almost. Until you said that."

He laughed quietly, then patted my arm. "Try to sleep. Nathaniel made it so you won't dream just yet, so now that you're relaxed, you should be fine."

"Thanks, Dionysus," I murmured against his shirt. "I appreciate it."

"I live to serve."

I FELT like I'd only been asleep for minutes when the bedroom door banged open, and three Ischyra burst in, all wearing the white uniforms of the palace guards.

I scrambled off the bed and tried to back against the wall.

Whoever they were, they were here to take me. For whatever reason, they were here for me.

I could *not* get taken again.

As if in response, I felt my power shift, as though it were peeking over my shoulder to see what was happening.

Dionysus was on his feet in front of me, using one hand to shove me behind him as he drew himself up to his full height and stared down the guards.

"Can I help you gentlemen?" he asked, his voice taking on a tone only an Elder of Olympus could carry.

One of them, a burly blond man with piercing blue eyes, stepped forward. The other two remained stock still behind him, blocking the door. All three looked completely at ease, not seeming to care that they had an angry god in front of them.

Blond guy gestured toward me. "We're here to take the girl."

Dionysus folded his arms. "On whose orders?"

"Zeus'," Blond Guy responded.

There was a beat of silence, and in that small moment, I understood exactly what was happening.

Zeus knew I was back, and these men were here to drag me to the palace for questioning.

No. No, no, no!

Dionysus came to the same realization and laughed. "Well, if that's the case, I'll be going with you." He shrugged. "In case things get... tense."

Not once since Tessa had started dating Nate had I been so goddamn thankful for one of his stupid brothers as I was right then.

'Stop calling me stupid.'

I clutched the back of his shirt and rested my head against his back, needing to reassure myself that someone in this room actually gave a shit about my current state.

Blond Guy held Dionysus' gaze for an impressive amount of time, considering their vast difference in rank. Finally, he gave a sharp nod. "Alright."

There was a flash, and the next thing I knew, we were in the dungeons.

In a cell. A dark, stone cell.

"No!"

Before I got more than a glimpse of my surroundings, Dionysus wrapped me in his arms, enveloping me in warmth. I curled my fingers into his shirt and pressed my face to his chest as I focused on calming my breathing.

"Are you three *insane?*" he bellowed. "She just got out of one of these things!"

"Zeus' orders," one of them deadpanned.

Dionysus laughed, and this time it was dark, far darker than I would've expected coming from him. "You boys are going to be in *so* much trouble when we get out of here."

"Apologies, Dionysus, but Zeus—"

"Get the fuck out of here," Dionysus snapped, cutting off which-ever one had tried to play nice. "And if my father isn't down here in five minutes, I'm taking it out on all three of you."

I didn't see Blond Guy's response, but I felt Dionysus' body tense against me. A moment later, their footsteps retreated down the hall.

Once they were gone, Dionysus pulled back and brought his face level with mine.

"Mary," he whispered. "I don't have my power here, so I need you to try and stay calm. Stay with me, okay? We'll get this sorted."

I shook my head frantically. "I can't be here," I rasped. "Dionysus, you *need* to get me out of here!"

"Shh." He pulled me against his chest. "I sent out a call to Apollo just before they brought us here. He'll be here soon, don't worry."

I tried to find comfort in his words, the soft tone of his voice, and the memory of the calming magic he'd used earlier. That comfort didn't come, though. Each time I tried to open my eyes, I was faced with stone walls, the memory of brutal slaps and hits and kicks, of my power being yanked from my body—

He let out a sharp sigh. "Stop," he ordered. "You're not there anymore."

I tried to stop, to focus on the steady sounds of his breathing, the thump of his heart, the smell of his cologne, but I couldn't stop trembling. The harder I tried, the faster my heart beat, and the closer I got to simply losing it.

"Look at me."

I could barely hear him over the blood rushing through my ears.

"Breathe," he whispered, his breath warm on my ear. "Nothing is going to happen to you. Apollo will be here soon." He stroked his hand up and down my spine as he spoke, the gesture just as soothing as it was unexpected. "Focus on me and nothing else."

I can't, I can't, I can't.

"Yes, you can." Gently, he picked me up, then sat down cross-legged with me in his lap, keeping all parts of me away from the offending stone around us.

Still trembling, I adjusted my head so that my ear was against his chest. I focused on his breathing, then pushed to get my own to fall in sync. Slowly, after a few minutes, I started to feel a bit calmer. The walls that felt like they were closing in retreated.

"Leave it to my little brother to find himself locked in the dungeons."

I jumped, then, glancing up, saw Apollo standing on the other side of the cell bars wearing an amused look.

Dionysus lifted me off the ground and set me on my feet. "If Zeus expects her to answer any of his questions, shoving her into a cell that's nearly identical to the one she was just tortured in wasn't the best idea."

"As it happens, I agree with you," Apollo said, pressing his hand to the door of the cell. A moment later, there was a quiet *click,* and it swung open.

I looked at him warily, my fingers clutching Dionysus' shirt again. "Does Zeus know you're letting us out? Because I really don't think I can handle being thrown back in here."

"Let's just say he's been, ah, persuaded to release you." He arched a brow at his brother. "Especially since a member of the Elder's council managed to get himself locked in here with you."

"Someone had to give a shit," Dionysus muttered, taking my hand and dragging me out into the hall.

Behind us, Apollo let the door swing shut with a *bang.* "You'll be pleased to know that there are quite a few upstairs who 'give a shit,' Dionysus."

I let the two brothers lead me through the palace, barely taking in the ostentatiousness of it all. The sheer amount of gold on the walls would've made a dragon jealous.

Dionysus let out a quiet laugh, and Apollo shook his head.

"I wouldn't compare our father to a dragon anywhere in his presence if I were you," Apollo said.

"Yeah, well, maybe if you people weren't so keen on reading minds without permission, he'd never know," I retorted.

A minute later, we reached a large, gilt-framed set of French doors. Apollo shoved them open, and I winced as my ears were assaulted with the sounds of gods arguing at top volume.

Tessa, Nate, Zeus, Hera, Prometheus, Epimetheus, Athena, a tall, dark-skinned giant of a god I didn't recognize, and a bleary-eyed Hermes all stood shouting at each other, one's words piling onto another's so there was nothing discernible about it.

"Quiet down now, all of you!" Apollo yelled over the din.

One by one, they all went silent.

"Mary!" Tessa cried, breaking away from her brothers and Nate to run to me. When she reached me, she put her hands on my shoulders. "Are you alright? When Apollo got Dionysus' call—"

"Yeah, I'm fine," I told her. "Kind of."

She sucked in an angry breath through her nose and turned to face Zeus, who stood beside a furious-looking Hera. "What in *all* the realms were you *thinking*?" she yelled.

"*You* do not get to come in here and holler at me, girl," he warned. "Not after what you've all just told us. You're lucky I haven't thrown you in the dungeons, too!"

That set off a whole new round of yelling.

"Enough!" Hera yelled, her voice surprisingly loud. Once again, the room slowly quieted. Hera turned her icy gaze on me, and I was suddenly reminded of how obsessively protective she was when it came to her family. When Zeus opened his mouth, she held up a hand to silence him. "Your impetuousness is going to get you in trouble, husband," she snapped. Looking at me, she sighed. "Mary. Are you aware of why my husband had you tossed in the dungeons?"

I cleared my throat and nodded. "Y-yes, I am."

"Mother—" Nate began, but she held up a hand to cut him off, too.

"Do you think there's a reason you should be locked up down there?" she asked.

"N-no, I don't."

Zeus scoffed. "She was needed for questioning," he spat. "That's all."

"So you thought it wise to imprison her in a cell that is presumably like the one she'd likely been held in this past week?" Hera asked coolly. "Kept away from the people who have come to be her family? Those who could help her better handle the pressures you'd like to put on her?"

I shot Nate an incredulous look, but he just shook his head.

Zeus' lip curled, and his eyes went cold. "That creature was in her head. He's still there, for all we know."

"Your own brother examined her," the Titan who stood beside

Epimetheus said with a smirk. "And your sons. Are you saying you trust none of them to complete their duties to your expectations?"

"Considering recent events? No, Oceanus, I can't say that I do," Zeus shot back.

Oceanus—I didn't even have it in me to be awestruck by his presence—chuckled. "No offense, Zeus, but Hades' ability to pull memories surpasses yours by quite a bit." With a sigh, he shook his head. "You've tasked your children and other family members with advising you and leading forces to protect this mountain and the people of Earth. Be angry if you wish, but it's foolish to take it out on the girl, weak as she is."

"Hades had nothing to do with our trip to Iceland if that's what you're angry about," Nate said. "Ignore my opinion if you'd like, but you can trust his."

"But he had everything to do with keeping me in the dark!" Zeus roared.

"For one goddamn *hour*!" Nate shot back. "One hour that *we* used to gain as much information as possible so that we didn't just come to you with speculation!"

"I should've been informed the moment the prisoners were returned!"

"Well, you weren't!" Nate held out his hand toward me. "And this is why! You out of *anyone* should understand why putting Mary in a dungeon would be the epitome of counterproductive!"

The room went quiet. I took a small step closer to Tessa as Zeus took in the barb Nate had just flung at him.

"He's right, you know," Oceanus said, turning to face Zeus fully, towering over him by a good six inches. "If you start tossing anyone you believe might cause you harm into the dungeons, ignoring your advisors because you think only you know what's best, you're no better than your father."

Zeus' face turned an odd shade of purple, as about a dozen versions of pissed off crossed his face.

He took a menacing step toward Oceanus. When he spoke, his voice was a deadly calm. "Do not *ever* compare me to my father."

"Alright, gentlemen, we've gotten far off track," Athena stated, stepping toward them. "Let's get back to the matter at hand." She found me on the other side of the room and lifted her eyebrows. "Mary?"

Cringing—gods, I *hated* that I was cringing—I looked around the room at all the gods who were staring at me.

"Yes?"

She gave me an apologetic look. "We need to question you. *I'll* do it," she said, glaring at her father.

"Why?" Tessa demanded. "You've already gotten all there is."

"Hades was doing a general sweep of her memories, homing in on the negative ones," Athena said. "I'm going to search them all." She inclined her head toward Nate. "With Nathaniel's help, of course."

I cleared my throat. "Oh. Um, okay."

This was so not okay.

'Say the word, Mare, and we're gone,' Tessa said. Her tone left no room for argument.

Tessa turned and looked up at Dionysus. "I want you there. If things get bad, you're better equipped to help her emotionally than I am."

"You're not the one giving orders here," Zeus growled.

Hands on her hips, Tessa faced him and sent him a challenging look. "What exactly do you object to? I may not be savvy in interrogation etiquette, but I would *think*, considering the circumstances, that having someone present who can calm her down would be a good thing." She shrugged. "I mean, unless you're considering scaring her into talking, which I can guarantee is *not* going to happen, not after drugging my guardians and having your goons kidnap her."

"And me," Hermes muttered, his face telling me he was clearly still pissed off at that fact.

Zeus blinked, and if circumstances hadn't been so dire, I would've laughed. Based on his reaction, I could only assume he hadn't gotten the full brunt of Tessa's sarcastic side yet.

Epimetheus made a small sound and ran a hand over his mouth, then turned away, barely concealing his amusement.

"Hold on." Prometheus held up a placating hand before Zeus could retort. "Arguing like this is incredibly counterproductive. We've gotten some useful, if not dubious information tonight that still needs to be sorted through. So before we all lose our heads over this, let's focus on that instead of snipping at one another."

Lose our heads.

Prometheus' words started to fade away, replaced by a steady roar.

Save the head for last.

When Tessa turned and said something to me, I took several stumbling steps back.

"Just...need..." *Air. I need air.*

"Mary!"

Someone's voice slapped at my mind.

I took another unsteady step away as ringing filled my ears.

Save the head for last.

Cold, rough stone pressed against my back.

Save the head for last.

A loud *thwack* as my hand was slammed against the wall.

Perhaps hands, first?

Someone was calling my name, the sound barely audible over the whooshing in my ears and the throbbing in my head.

...Time to heal between amputations...

Save the head for last.

I'm partial to ears, myself.

Shouting followed, but I couldn't focus. All I could feel was poisoned metal on my skin, burning pain, and the paralyzing fear that I was about to be slowly cut apart, piece by piece.

The world tilted, then I felt cold wind on my face, the quick rush of teleportation.

"Mary? Mary!"

"Someone put her to sleep!"

Save the head for last.

"Is there *no one* in this house who can properly handle a prisoner of war?"

"Not helpful, Apollo!"

First one...

"Mary?" Tessa's voice was in my ear, barely a whisper. "We're going to put you to sleep now, okay? But don't worry, you're safe, and we're not going anywhere."

Just don't let me dream, I silently begged.

"We've got you, doll, don't worry."

I felt the twinge of magic, then the world began to fade away.

37

TESSA

As I sat on the couch watching Dionysus carry Mary back into the bedroom, I let my face fall to my hands.

I was sick and tired of my friends and family being unconscious. Hurt. Broken.

First Atlas, then Yana, now Mary.

Mary. Sarcastic, sassy Mary. The girl who never backed down from a fight and didn't hesitate to speak her mind, regardless of who was on the receiving end of her ire.

The girl who'd just had a panic attack because a simple phrase my brother used triggered the memory of my father and Cronus discussing the most amusing way to dismember her.

I couldn't remember—chose not to, maybe—if I'd had similar reactions when I found out what Menoetius had done to me. If I had, maybe I'd be able to help.

As it was, my twin was the only person I knew who might be able to empathize. I couldn't pull him away from his daughters, though. He'd waited far too long to build a relationship with them, and in the last week, he'd almost lost three.

No, I couldn't take that time away from him.

I felt the sofa shift beside me as Nate sat down and slid his arm around my shoulders.

"What's on your mind?" he asked quietly.

"I don't know how to help her," I whispered. "At all."

He pulled me against him and pressed his lips to my hair. "She'll tell you when she's ready, love. But like with Anette, I think you need to let her come to you. She's been back all of three hours and has hardly gotten a moment's rest, which is what she desperately needs. For now, give her that, then wait for her to tell you what she needs."

"I know. It's just hard." I recalled the smothering feelings I'd felt when I'd been returned to my brothers. Even though they'd been the product of love, they were smothering, all the same.

"Trust me, I know." He sighed and rubbed a hand over his face. "Zeus is asking for an update. He's threatening to come down here if he doesn't hear from us every half hour."

I pulled back and looked at him in surprise. "What's keeping him from doing that?"

"Hera. What she said about Mary being pulled away from her new family was true."

"Seriously?" I paused, momentarily sidetracked from my upset. "I thought she only felt connections to family bonds?"

He shook his head. "She feels closest to the bonds between married couples and those between parent and child, but she also acknowledges that family is about more than simple blood relations."

"Huh. You know, now that you mention it, she's been very non-Hera this past week. Is that because of all of us?"

His mouth curved into a smile. "This mountain is usually full of strife between family members, for one reason or another. The last couple of weeks, families have been stitching themselves back together left and right. New ones have been forming." He nudged me with his elbow. "People have been falling in love. There are dozens of new ties for her to connect to."

I smiled ruefully. "So basically, me and my brothers have given Hera the fix of a lifetime?"

Nate laughed. "Between your relationship with them and Atlas' reconnection with his daughters, yes."

That made me smile. Hera had been terrifying, bordering on crazy, when I'd met her as an Ischyra. It was kind of nice knowing my friends and family and I had such strong ties to one another that we'd actually altered the level of strife on the mountain.

I jumped when the door opened, and Nate and I both got to our feet as Yana, Chiron, and Anette walked in.

"Did you find anything new?" I asked.

"Possibly," Chiron said. He jerked a chin toward Yana and Anette. "They wanted to come check on Mary."

Yana arched a brow and took in the room. Epimetheus had just finished a telepathic conversation with Prometheus and Dionysus was pouring himself a glass of something amber-colored from Nate's liquor cabinet, looking uncharacteristically angry. Epimetheus had come back with us because it had been decided—despite my protests —that one of them would be with me at all times, something I fully intended to ignore at first chance. Dionysus came because his calming power seemed to be the only thing that was working on Mary right now. Nate was keeping her mind clear while she slept, but the happy juice that Dionysus produced actually altered her emotions and gave her clarity.

"What happened?" Anette asked quietly.

"Mary had a slight... panic attack," I told them. "She's sleeping now."

"Why?" Yana asked. "She seemed fine when I left."

"Our astute and fearless leader thought tossing her in the dungeons to await questioning was an immediate necessity," Dionysus said dryly, shutting the door to the cabinet closed with a *thud*. "So she was already upset, then Prometheus said—"

"That part's not important," I told them, silencing him with a look. "For the time being, we're holding Zeus off. Athena will talk to her, examine her memories, but not right away."

Anette's mouth tightened. "He put her back in a dungeon cell?" she asked.

I nodded.

"I see." She looked toward the hall that led to the guest rooms. "I will wait with her if that is alright."

"No, Anette, you don't need to upset yourself so soon—"

"I need to help," she said simply. "This is a way for me to do that."

Yana and I shared a quick look, then she shrugged. "I cannot imagine Mary will mind, but if it gets to be too much…"

"I'll leave," Anette said firmly. "But it won't."

"Okay." I smiled at her. "She's in her room."

Chiron watched her walk off, shaking his head. "I was hoping to speak with Mary, confirm a few things before going back to Zeus. I'm guessing that won't be an option for a while?"

I looked at the clock over the mantle, then shook my head. It was nearly two in the morning. "Not tonight. She needs to rest. Her mind's has been poked at way too much already."

"I understand. I'm going to get back to it, then." He smiled wearily. "I've got a few more threads to pull before I shut off for the night."

"Zeus called for a meeting tomorrow morning," Nate said. "I'm guessing you'll be expected to attend."

Chiron sighed. "I am, so get a good night's sleep because we'll be covering a lot."

Once he'd said his goodnights, Yana, Nate, Dionysus, Epimetheus, and I sat down on the couch. No one spoke, and I assumed it was because, like me, their minds were still reeling from the last few hours.

Chaos. The Creator. The being that wasn't a being, only a place, or so we'd always been taught. Now, here he was, trying to destroy the worlds he'd created.

"We need more information," Epimetheus said after a few moments. "I'm struggling with the idea that the being who created every damn thing has suddenly decided he wants to kill everything he's made."

"After Chiron realized who we were likely dealing with, we were able to guide our research a bit better," Yana told him. "We found a fair amount but nothing on how to destroy a creature like Josh. He is compiling it all now to present to Zeus and whoever else in the morning."

"And you and Anette?" Dionysus looked at her curiously. "Won't you be there?"

"I—" Yana cast a nervous glance at me. "Chiron knows all we know."

"Yes, but wouldn't it make sense to have all three of you present?" Dionysus asked.

"You do not need that many cooks in the kitchen, as they say," Yana said with a wry smile.

Nate nodded. "It's probably for the best. I'm not sure who'll be in attendance, but if we thought tensions were high at the last briefing, trying to convince our allies that the 'witch' we've been dealing with is actually Chaos in the flesh will make that seem like a damn tea party," he grumbled.

Yana looked at me. "Have you made any decisions regarding your own memory?"

I shook my head. "My head's a bit clearer now that I've had some time to process what Josh said, but no, I haven't decided whether I want the memories of my time in Chaos." I frowned. "Gods, saying I was 'in Chaos' sounds far dirtier now than it did a few hours ago."

There was a beat of silence, then Dionysus snorted, and Epimetheus grinned.

"Ah, we have reached the 'hysterical joking' portion of the apocalypse," Yana said with a shake of her head. "Things are worse than I thought."

I gave her a rueful half-smile. "Delirious is more like it." I looked up at Nate. "I need to go to bed."

Nate tightened his arm around me and kissed my temple. "So do we all." He looked at his brother and at mine. "We're out of beds, gentlemen. If you're staying, it'll be on the couch."

"I'm going to head home," Dionysus said, standing and stretching his arms above his head. He looked down at me. "If Mary wakes up and you can't calm her down, call me."

"I will." I smiled up at him. "Thanks for everything, Dionysus. You rocked it tonight."

He gave a mocking bow. "It's what I do."

Zeus' spirits were marginally better when we arrived at the palace the next morning. He'd called a meeting with the witches, the war gods, the rest of the Elders, and the Titans to discuss what we'd discovered over the past twenty-four hours.

"Alright, everyone," Zeus said, pounding his fist on the table to call for silence. "Now that we're all here, I would like to update you on a few developments." He inclined his head toward Apollo. "Apollo, if you wouldn't mind?"

"I'd prefer to turn this portion over to those who carried out the mission in Iceland first if that's alright."

Nate stepped toward the map of Earth and addressed the room. "A few days back, we brought a Telchine who'd attacked us during a mission on Earth back for questioning. Before we could, he activated a poisoned tooth that had been implanted in his mouth, releasing a highly concentrated dose of godsbane. Last night, I, along with Dionysus, Eris, and Tessa infiltrated a Telchine establishment in Iceland under the guise of humans looking for a narcotic fix. Once inside, Eris and Dionysus poisoned their liquor, and Tessa and I captured a high-level Telchine, then joined our powers to Coerce him and all of his blood connections into breaking those same poisoned teeth."

"Coerce? *How?*" Ares asked.

"Splitter powers," Nate told him. "After I broke down the Telchine's shields, it was just a matter of Tessa connecting to those he shared blood with. As I said, he was very high-ranking, second generation, which was part of the reason we chose him."

"What was the other reason?" Hestia asked.

Nate cast a look toward Cornelius before responding. "He also happened to be the one responsible for the attack on the Ischyra compound in Athens."

"So, vengeance, then." Scylla gave me a wry grin as a somewhat satisfied look came over Cornelius' face. "You should've called, Tessa. My wolves would've had quite the feast."

"How many did you manage to kill?" Hecate asked.

"About seven hundred and fifty," Nate replied.

Several sets of appraising eyes fell on me. It was a struggle not to squirm under their stares, but I forced my chin high and my expression neutral. I wouldn't give anyone a reason to think I was anything *but* capable.

"That's quite an accomplishment," Ares said with an appreciative nod.

I gave him a grateful smile. "Thank you, Ares. You and Athena are the main reason I was able to manage it. Without your help..."

He waved off my thanks. "It was all there in your head, Tessa. You just needed to unlock it, that's all."

"Which she clearly has," Athena said with a grin.

"That's not all there is," Hecate said, looking back and forth between me and my accomplices from the night before. "What haven't you told us?"

Eris frowned and stepped forward. "Did something happen after we got back last night?"

Dionysus huffed out a laugh, and Apollo shook his head.

Eris sent a questioning look at Nate.

"After debriefing here, Tessa and I returned home to find Josh, the primordial witch who'd been working with Cronus and Iapetus, waiting for us." He launched into a detailed explanation of the subsequent events, supplemented now and then by Apollo's, Athena's, and Hades' own recollections. I stayed out of it for the time being, listening to what they said and turning it all over in my mind, hoping to glean some new bit of knowledge from their words. As they spoke, Persephone sidled up beside me.

'I didn't get to speak with you last night before Zeus took your friend. How are you holding up?'

'Well enough, I guess. It's just been a crazy few days and I don't see that changing.'

'I think that's a safe assumption to make.' She paused. 'Tessa, I'm sorry I wasn't able to find Mary. I need you to know that my trackers and I tried our damnedest, but—'

'I know. We're facing a threat that's far bigger than we thought, so I don't think any of us should be surprised when things like this happen.'

'We'd still like to try and find out where he held them,' she said. 'Hades said there were some memories of hers that showed potential landmarks, so I'm going to take a look, see if I can track based on her own memories.'

'Alright.'

"Hold on." Hecate's stunned, raised voice stopped my response. "Are you telling me he was *in there with her* that whole time?" She turned to me, aghast. "Tessa—I—I don't know what to say. I'm so sorry."

I took a deep breath, collecting myself before responding. My emotions since finding out I hadn't been alone in the Void had been all over the place, ranging from fear to a general state of pissed off that Hecate hadn't known or even considered the possibility that another being, even another soul, could've been sent there.

"Hecate, you know my thoughts on the decisions you and my mother made for me," I said calmly. "I can only hope if you knew there was something else in there with me, you would've refused Clymene's wishes."

"We're going to revisit that aspect of this shortly," Atlas said, not bothering to hide his contempt.

'Ease off,' I told him. 'She didn't do it intentionally.'

'She still did it.'

Hecate's mouth still hung open in silent shock, the expression in her eyes unfathomable. After a few seconds, she cleared her throat and turned back to Apollo, who'd taken over speaking. "What else have you learned? Do we know who Josh actually is?"

"And why he's so insistent that Tessa wanted to be his accomplice?" Poseidon asked. He flashed me a quick, reassuring wink.

"Possibly to the first question, and we're going to assume a miscommunication for the second," Apollo said, ignoring the glare Zeus shot in his direction. "Chiron is on his way right now to explain his findings."

"Why are we *assuming* a miscommunication?" Aphrodite asked, looking at me suspiciously. "If she was truly stuck there for three millennia, wouldn't he know her mind better than any of you?"

"No," Hades snapped.

"There are plenty in this room who know what forced isolation can do to a mind," Oceanus said. "And plenty who know the daughter of Clymene wouldn't hold that level of anger in her heart."

I gave him a surprised look. Having the support of one of the most influential Titans we'd mustered was reassuring, to say the least.

"There are also some who would point out that the *son* of Clymene seems to have no qualms about destroying whatever he can get his hands on," Aphrodite shot back. "Perhaps Josh destroyed Menoetius' energy because he knew he didn't need him anymore." She sniffed in my direction. "Now that Tessa has *returned.*"

"The mean girl look doesn't suit you, Aphrodite," Dionysus grumbled. "Back off."

She shot him a surprised look. "Are all of my brothers suddenly enamored of her?"

I raised a hand. "Um, standing *right* here. And considering the fact that I just helped off one of their most dangerous factions, I'd think that would tell you enough about my intentions."

"Unless this creature has returned to change your mind," she countered.

"For fuck's sake, Aphrodite, shut *up!*" Hermes groaned, surprising me with his hostility.

Narrowing my eyes, I scanned the room, then rolled them when I saw Eris leaning against the wall smirking. I arched a brow at Nate and inclined my head toward where she stood.

With a huff, he shook his head. A moment later, she jerked, then glared at him. Slowly, tensions started to recede.

"I'm sorry, but this is all very distressing," Aphrodite said, her voice turning slightly whiny.

"That's completely understandable," I told her. "But trust me when I say that I know my own mind. I'm all for a good dose of vengeance on those who are deserving—Menoetius, my father, the Telchines, Cronus... the list goes on. But I want to help save our world just as much as the rest of you. There are people and beings that exist here who I love and want to keep safe. So please, don't question my intentions."

"Speaking of Cronus, what does this mean for him?" Artemis asked. "Is he still in play?"

"I think so," I replied. "The way Josh spoke... it sounds like he's using Cronus to lead the rebellion since he can't do it himself."

"Based on the memories we saw," Nate said, "Cronus is aware of what Josh is. It's unlikely he'll disobey, if not impossible."

"We should expect to see movement from him soon, then," Athena said. "If this is about balance, Josh just tipped the scales our way. It's safe to assume he'll instruct Cronus to tip them back."

Artemis nodded. "And Menoetius?" She looked at Zeus. "Is there any way to revive him?"

"I've told Charon to alert me the moment he arrives on the shores," Hades said. "If he reaches the Underworld, we'll know."

"It's likely you won't, actually." For the first time, Kastin spoke up. "I've been down to the dungeons to examine him. His soul hasn't just been taken, it's been broken down. Sent back into the aether as natural energy. The only thing keeping his body alive are the natural electrical connections that exist within it."

"His soul is *gone*?" Hestia asked.

"Yes." He sent her an even look. "Not a trace remains. It, along with all of the energy and power within him, are gone. For all intents and purposes, Menoetius has been unmade."

38

NATHANIEL

"What are you saying, Kastin?" I asked slowly.

"I am *saying* I will not be able to commune with him," Kastin said brusquely. "Tessa's psychometry will not reveal anything." He looked at Hades. "Your ferryman could wait a thousand years, but Menoetius will never come to cross over."

"You can't—"

"Yes, I can know that," Kastin said, cutting off Hades response. "It's what I *do*. I can tell you, without question, that every part of his soul is now on its way to giving life to something else. He will never get the chance to cross over because he no longer exists."

The room was quiet for a few moments before Hyperion spoke.

"While death is not something I am keen to wish upon a being, I believe, in this case, we can agree that justice has been dealt." He looked at Zeus. "You were hoping to get more information from him, but that would never have happened."

Before my father could answer, I heard the door open behind me. When I glanced over my shoulder, I saw that Chiron had just walked in.

"What have you got for us?" Zeus asked, instantly shifting the discussion away from Menoetius and what had become of his soul.

Chiron stepped forward, his face drawn. With a sigh, he set down a stack of papers on the map of Earth and rubbed his eyes. Bracing his hands on the edge of the table, he looked around the room.

"After reviewing the memories Nathaniel shared of Mary's mind, I added that information to the pile we'd already begun to gather. Her memories gave solid validity to a theory I had. After further, more directed research, I'm certain my conclusions are accurate."

"Have you found more?" I asked. We'd hardly gotten past him explaining his suspicions the previous night before Apollo got the call from Dionysus that he and Mary had been taken.

He gave me a quick nod, then straightened up to address the room. "Based on all I've uncovered, I am certain that the primordial witch we thought we were dealing with is actually Chaos. The Creator, in the flesh." He held up a hand to silence the stunned murmurs. "From what I gathered from his talks with Mary, he's looking for a do-over. He seems to be using this war as a means to achieve that goal."

"Ludicrous," someone muttered.

"What proof have you got, other than an Ischyra's memory and speculation?" Scylla asked suspiciously.

"Writings based on ancient historical sources, mainly," Chiron said. "But also this." He held up an aged piece of paper with the symbol Josh had been tracing on Leila's back. The ink was a faded, reddish brown, but the symbol looked to be identical.

"Is that—" Scylla held out a hand. "We haven't used symbols like this in millennia," she said, taking the paper from him. "Where did you get this, Chiron?"

"While he was living in Renville, Josh had a lover," Chiron answered. "During a visit on the temporal plane, Tessa, Nathaniel, and Hermes witnessed him tracing this pattern on her back and hand multiple times throughout his time in Renville. I've done some digging, and it seems to be a containment spell, not protection, as I'd originally thought. Its origins are unclear, but based on what I've gathered, this specific type of spell is much older than we thought."

"How old?" Hermes asked.

"Ancient," Chiron replied.

"Older than ancient," Scylla added, frowning at the symbol.

"What's it meant to contain?" I asked.

"A deity," Chiron replied. "Persephone and I took the liberty of taking a trip to Renville." My eyebrows shot up, and I was about to question them both when he plowed ahead. "Persephone managed to track the symbol to nearly twenty locations around the outskirts of the town. We found it on trees, buildings, even a mailbox."

"Then what was the point of Leila?" I asked. "If he put up a damn containment ring around the whole town, why involve a human at all?"

He pointed at the innermost ring. "This represents an anchor, the first measure taken to keep a deity contained in a place. If my assumptions are correct, he used Leila as Tessa's anchor."

"A human as an anchor?" Scylla gave him a dubious look. "I think you've been in the books too long, friend."

Chiron shook his head. "He couldn't use Mary or Eric because of their dormant powers, not to mention they and their guardians would have been under the watchful eye of Olympus. So I think he somehow inserted a human friend into Tessa's life." Frowning, he looked up at Tessa. "Did Leila ever leave Renville? Vacations, anything like that?"

"No," Tessa said quietly. "Her parents were homebodies for the most part. Sometimes they would take trips, but she'd always have to stay home to take care of her sister."

"That's shitty," Eris grumbled.

"Yes, but it further proves my theory," Chiron told her. "By tracing this symbol on Leila, he was anchoring her to Renville, which therefore anchored *you*."

"But I took tons of vacations," Tessa told him. "John and Analise took me places every year."

"But you always came home," Athena said. She looked at Chiron. "This spell would've ensured she never left permanently, right?"

He nodded. "Probably unnecessary, since guardians tend to stick to the same place with their charges, but if he wanted to ensure Tessa stayed in a small area where he could easily monitor her, linking her magically to a human who would never leave would be one way to do it."

Hecate held out her hand for the paper Chiron was holding, then she and Scylla examined it more closely for a moment.

"When I saw this last night, I assumed it was a protection spell of some sort," Hecate said quietly. "But yes, containment is certainly feasible."

"It could be both," Scylla murmured. "The other rings would represent additional layers of containment or protection, depending on your take. We know Menoetius was aware of Tessa's identity, yes?" She glanced at Zeus for confirmation. "Alright, then if I'm reading this correctly, I think—and Mother, correct me if I'm wrong—but I *think* these outer rings may have been protection against potential locating spells."

"I cloaked the Averys' home when I brought Tessa to them," Hecate said. "Even Menoetius wouldn't have been able to see through it."

"But Josh would," I said. "He told Mary he can see spells, remember? And he'd be aware that Menoetius could eventually find Tessa, especially if he started using the siphoning spell again."

"And since Josh has it in his head that Tessa wants to burn the world to cinders alongside him, he would have wanted to ensure her safety," Athena finished.

"Which begs the question, if Josh is the all-powerful Creator, why go through the hassle of casting spells and keeping Tessa safe?" Poseidon asked. "Why not simply destroy his creations and be done?"

"Well, that's the thing," Chiron said. "I don't think he can. I'm not quite sure *why*, but it's the only logical conclusion I can come up with for why he hasn't just blown it all to bits by now."

There was a collective and heavy silence throughout the room as everyone absorbed all Chiron had just divulged. Even though it was the second time I was hearing it, it didn't change the level of shock I felt inside. The daunting feeling of working blind had been growing by the day in recent weeks, so having a starting point, knowing who we were facing, should've helped.

If anything, it made things worse.

"As you can see, this is a setback we did not anticipate," Zeus said, keeping his voice firm. "But it changes nothing. Regardless of who he is, Josh, Chaos, whatever you choose to call him, is just another enemy. We can and will defeat him, but first, we need to know how, which is where you all come in." He nodded at Chiron. "Tell us what you need."

"Information," Chiron said. "Anything you can find. The archives here are extensive, but with a creature this ancient, we need more. Records, personal notes, even stories handed down through generations can contain useful information. Also..." He sucked in a hard breath. "We need to start reaching out to the older gods, the ones who are still living. The first generation of primordials, if possible. As the oldest and more... personable, Nyx would be ideal, but there are others."

Scylla's father, Pallas, chuckled. "I wish you the best of luck with that. Nyx doesn't see anyone." He smirked at Zeus. "And she's not so fond of your ruler, either."

Zeus, for once, had nothing to say.

"Well, convince her," Chiron said irritably. "If Josh is who he says he is, then that makes them his first generation of offspring. They may know something, they may not, but they need to be contacted."

"And if she doesn't respond to our call?" Pallas asked.

"We contact the others. Hypnos still dwells in the Underworld, and Hemera was residing in the Urals, if my memory serves," Chiron replied.

"Which is all well and good, but you still need permission from the Fates to make contact, Chiron." Pallas shook his head. "They'll never grant that to you."

"We still have to ask!" Chiron shouted, banging his fist on the table. "We are talking about taking on the Creator, Pallas! Not some deity who can be killed with spells or siphoning!"

Zeus cleared his throat and held up his hands for order. "We can all agree that this situation is... unprecedented." He nodded at Chiron. "That requires unprecedented solutions. So, for now, we're going to break off and figure this thing out."

Zeus began to dole out orders, sending deities off to one corner of the world or another to search for any information to be found on Josh and weapons that might destroy something like him. The biggest question we needed answered, though, was why? Why couldn't he just smash the toys he'd made and create new ones? Clearly, something had gone wrong with the worlds he'd built, at least in his eyes, but it made no sense that he would start a war when he literally had the power of creation at his fingertips.

A hand came down on my shoulder, and when I turned, I found Chiron standing beside me, his face drawn and weary. Everyone else were making their exits with orders to regroup in three days, with or without new information.

He jerked his chin toward where Tessa stood speaking with Persephone. "How's she doing with all of this?" he asked quietly.

I rubbed a hand over my chin and shook my head. "I don't know. So many things got piled on her last night that I don't think she quite knows which to tackle first."

He gave me a sympathetic smile. "Well, I could use a drink then a brainstorming session. How about you?"

I nodded slowly. "Yeah. I'll check in once I find out where Zeus is sending me. If you need to hash anything out, feel free to use my house as a base with Yana and Anette. Get yourselves out of that dusty basement. And sneak Dionysus out with you. He'll be too distracted on Earth, and I'd rather have him nearby if Mary has trouble."

"That sounds like a wonderful plan." A true grin played on his lips. "I'll make sure he doesn't do too much damage to your wine collection." He touched two fingers to his forehead in a small salute, then turned and strode from the room.

"Nathaniel."

I stiffened at the sound of my father's voice behind me. Schooling my face into a neutral expression, I turned to face him.

It was a struggle not to show him how angry I still was for what he'd done to Mary the night before. If the room had held less occupants, I might have actually let him know. As it was, there were still about ten other deities fine-tuning plans.

"Yes?" I asked.

"There have been reports of attacks on Earth," he said. "I'm sending you, Athena, Ares, Apollo, Atlas, and Prometheus out to lead teams to assess the damage. The others can handle research for now. Chiron seems to have that aspect well in hand, so we need to focus our efforts outward." His tone held no room for question.

A muscle in my jaw clenched and unclenched as I debated how to respond. "Where?"

He gestured with his head toward the map of Earth, so I followed him over to it.

"Levees and dams have been released on multiple waterways." He pointed toward the northern hemisphere. "Japan, the United States, the Netherlands, and about half a dozen other countries across Europe and Asia have all reported major flooding."

"Are you thinking Potamoi?" I asked as I examined the placement of the attacks. "They haven't been very mobile so far."

"Yes, the river gods would be my guess," he agreed. "Millions are without power currently due to flooding, so we'll be sending in additional assistance to aid the Ischyra who are there. Poseidon and Triton have already sent out their own forces, so I'll need you and your siblings on the ground to counter any other attacks. With that many humans vulnerable, I have no doubt there will be a secondary or even tertiary attack."

"Alright." I turned to face him, meeting his eyes evenly. "I'll leave right away. But can you assure me that Mary and the others will be left alone until we return?"

His brow drew down angrily. "Nathaniel, if I see fit to bring that girl in here to question her myself—"

I shook my head. "Your tactics won't work, Father. Not with her and not if you expect to keep any peace around here."

The muscle in his jaw worked furiously as he reined in his

temper. "Take Eris and Epimetheus," he bit out. "Go to the Nether-lands and see what you can find. That is the only thing you need to be concerned with right now."

"Understood," I said with a sigh, unable to keep the annoyance I felt from seeping out. Turning, I began to walk toward where Prometheus and Epimetheus were talking with Tessa and Atlas, but I paused when Zeus spoke.

"I'm trying very hard to be patient with you, Nathaniel," he said quietly, his tone a warning. "I've always given you plenty of leeway to live your life because you've always made good decisions. Don't make me regret that."

I hesitated as a dozen responses came to my lips, then I just shook my head a let out a quiet chuckle. "I'll report back when I return."

"Be certain you do."

39

TESSA

After the majority of deities had left the war room, each off to one place or another to help find any other source of information that might help us defeat Josh, I was left alone with my brothers, Nate, Eris, Zeus, and Hera. The tension between Zeus and Nate was thick, and it didn't take much to know Nate wasn't thrilled about the idea of leaving the mountain for any length of time while there was still so much uncertainty.

"Before you all leave," Zeus said to my brothers and me, "I'd like to ask if you four want to see Menoetius one last time before Hades and Persephone dispose of him."

I shared a look with the twins and Atlas. I didn't know about them, but the only thing I'd felt since discovering Josh had essentially killed Menoetius was relief. Kastin's assertion that my oldest brother would never make it to the Underworld, that he now ceased to exist, had even more weight taken off my shoulders.

Although an eternity in Tartarus also would've been nice.

But I needed to see for myself, and I think my brothers did, too, so I appreciated that Zeus was giving us the opportunity.

Atlas nodded. "Take us to him."

Leaving Eris and Hera to finalize some plans, Zeus led us quickly through the halls of the palace, down the dungeon stairs, then to Menoetius' cell. My mind barely focused on anything as we went, not registering details as I moved on autopilot, following the others underground. Hades and Persephone waited outside the cell doors, watching as we made our way toward them.

As I stopped in front of the doors, Hades took my arm and pulled me aside, ignoring the sharp looks from my brothers. "Are you sure you're alright with this, Tessa?"

I glanced at the door, then met his dark eyes and nodded. "I am. I need to see—I need to know that he's really gone."

He took a deep breath. In his eyes and in the tension of his jaw, I could see he was holding back an argument. "Okay. I'll make sure his body is disposed of... properly."

I quirked a brow. "I couldn't ask for more than that." I sighed. "Let's get this over with."

When I looked through the bars of his cell, my heart skipped, then clenched. Menoetius had never been a good man, had never shown an ounce of goodness toward anyone or anything in his life. Each decision he made was selfish and based only on his own desires. I'd never been able to look at him without disgust peppered with fear, because in my eyes, he'd never been anything more than an animal.

And yet as he lay on the floor, looking as though he'd just dozed off, he looked peaceful. His face was smooth; no signs of his normal leer or scowl. The violence that normally pulsed off of him was entirely absent; instead, all I felt was the residual magic that hung in the room from Kastin's examination.

I felt my brothers at my back, pinning me in place with their presence. They stood just as silently as I did, watching as the shell of our brother took slow, halting breaths.

Putting a palm to the door, I waited for my magic to unlock it. When I heard the click of the lock slipping free, I opened it and stepped inside. The power the room had been surrounded with, preventing magic inside the cell, had been briefly lifted so Kastin could do his work and so that Hades and Persephone could teleport the body to the Underworld without having to carry it through the palace.

"Tessa—"

I held up one finger, silencing Hades when he called my name. Part of me wanted to let him come in with me. This was hard for him, too. In my memories, he'd watched each and every thing Menoetius had done to me, felt everything I'd felt. My brothers and I weren't the only ones here today who needed closure, but Hades would have his opportunity in the Underworld.

I had to do this alone.

I stood over my brother's body, curiously watching the automatic movements that kept it from desiccating. Nothing of the Titan he'd been remained. He, and his power, were gone.

The thought made me smile.

I heard the shuffle of feet as I crouched down beside him, then Zeus' barked order for whoever it was to stop.

Ignoring him, I put a hand to Menoetius' cheek and closed my eyes. I just needed to see, needed to be sure, that there was truly nothing left.

When I touched his mind, all I found was emptiness. Swirling, black nothingness resided where there had once been a mind teeming with hate, anger, and a desire to destroy.

The last dregs of fear that had weighed me down lifted from my shoulders, giving me a freeing feeling that I hadn't realized I was missing until now.

Opening my eyes, I looked him over one more time. I hadn't gotten the opportunity to kill him myself, which was, realistically, probably not a bad thing. But I could finish him.

With a sharp jolt, I sent a stream of electricity pulsing through his corpse. His body gave a single jerk, then went still as the smell of scorched flesh filled the room.

His chest didn't rise and fall, and his heart no longer thumped out its rhythm.

He was gone.

I sat there for a few more moments as shock and relief fought a battle inside me. My brother was dead. Really and truly destroyed. He would never hurt me or anyone else again. The poison that was his soul would never touch another living thing because it—he—had been unmade. Now the shell he'd worn for thousands of years would die along with it.

There was a heavy silence as I processed what I'd just done. No, what I'd just accomplished. I would've preferred a harsher death for my brother, but I could only hope that, as Josh's power had torn through Menoetius' shields and shredded his mind, his awareness remained intact. He deserved nothing less than to bear witness to his own destruction, especially one as painful as that.

Menoetius told me once that he thought his own fondness for inflicting pain on others ran through my veins, too. Josh's insinuation that I'd been vengeful enough during my time in the Void to want to help him destroy the world lent some credence to that notion.

The relief and elation I felt as I watched over Menoetius' corpse did as well.

Quiet footsteps sounded behind me, then a gentle hand touched my shoulder. Tilting my head, I looked into the pained face of my twin.

"He's gone now, Tessa," he said hoarsely. "It's time to go."

I felt my face crumple at his words, at the acknowledgement that I no longer had to share a world with my beast of a brother.

Cautiously, he sat down beside me, then he wrapped an arm around my shoulders and pulled me into a hug. "It's alright," he whispered. "He can't hurt you anymore."

My sobs began to shake my entire body, my tears soaking the shoulders of his shirt as I cried out years of grief and fury. I wanted so badly, to be strong and not cry, to just get up, dust of my hands, and walk away, leaving the memory of my brother and all he'd done behind me.

But I couldn't. So I cried, letting my twin console me in a way he hadn't been able to three thousand years ago.

When I was done, Atlas stood and held out a hand. Numbly, I let him pull me to my feet and lead me from the room where Nate and my brothers waited on the other side of the door. I avoided looking at Zeus, knowing he was probably furious that I'd just stepped out of line.

So I was surprised when he stopped in front of me and and exhaled a heavy breath.

Blinking, I looked up at him curiously, even more shocked when I saw that his eyes were full of understanding.

Jaw tense, he sighed. "It isn't much, only getting to destroy his body when he tried so hard to destroy your soul." Emotion flickered briefly in his eyes, and he sent an unreadable look at Hades before he continued. "Be content with the knowledge that he didn't, and never will, succeed."

Suddenly, I understood why he'd let me finish what Josh had started. Three thousand years ago, Zeus had been given the chance to destroy the Titan who'd imprisoned him and his siblings for centuries, but he'd chosen not to. Instead of delivering the permanent death Cronus deserved, he'd shown him mercy and let him live.

He'd never admit it was mercy. He'd say it was purposeful, but I saw the truth in his eyes. He hadn't been able to kill his father. Despite all Cronus had done, Zeus hadn't been able to end him permanently.

I cleared my throat and swallowed back the emotion that fact had brought out. "Thank you," I whispered.

He stepped back, then Nate took his place. Hades went with Persephone to take Menoetius to the Underworld, where his remains would be tossed in the Acheron, no longer anything more than a meal for the Hydra who dwelled there.

I turned and faced Nate, then took his hands and looked up into his midnight gaze. His eyes ran over my face, questioning.

I'm okay,' I said.

Taking me in his arms, he pressed his cheek to the top of my head. *'I know. I just need to hold you for a minute if that's alright.'*

Content, I tightened my arms around his waist and buried my face in his chest, inhaling his scent and doing my best to ignore the corpse that had just been removed from my brother's former cell.

'Tessa, a word?'

I flinched at the sound of Hades' voice in my head, then sighed. *'Where are you?'*

'Meet me on the steps out front.'

I wiped my eyes and looked at Zeus. "I'll meet you all back upstairs. There's something I have to do."

Zeus gave a sharp nod in return, still seeming a bit off-kilter.

Nate gave me a questioning look. *'Are you alright?'*

'Yeah. I'll be back soon.'

He kissed my forehead and gave my hand a squeeze.

I made my way through the palace and out the front doors to find Hades waiting for me on the steps. For the first time in as long as I'd known him, the emotion pulsing off of him wasn't anger but sadness.

When he heard my approach, he turned, and in seconds, had me wrapped in his arms.

I didn't try to pull away, knowing if he was showing this kind of emotion, his mind must've slipped into a bad place. "Hades, I'm alright," I whispered.

"I know," he murmured against my hair. "I'm not, though. You shouldn't have had to do that, Tessa."

I swallowed back the lump in my throat. "I needed to."

"I should've protected you better back then," he said, tightening his arms around me as emotion thickened his voice. "There was so much more I could've done."

"It's over now," I told him. I pulled back and put my hands on his face. "It's done, he's gone, and we don't have to worry about him ever again."

His eyes, more pained than I'd ever seen them, ran over my face. "I should've done more."

I shook my head. "You did all you could. You *saved* me back then, Hades. Don't ever question that."

He slid his hand over mine and kissed it, then took a deep breath. "Tessa, I will forever grieve what we lost, I want you to know that."

I tried to take a step back, but his hands tightened on my shoulders. "Hades—"

"Just listen," he said quietly. "That doesn't mean I can't be happy with where my path led me or where you've found yourself in your new life."

I closed my eyes as unshed tears began to slip down my cheeks.

Lips pressed against my forehead, and his arms went around me again.

"Nathaniel is a good man," he said hoarsely. "Make sure he always knows how strong your love is for him."

Unable to speak, I nodded, then wrapped my arms around his waist. Hades had never told me what he felt for me in my previous life, but I'd always wondered if what we'd had was more than what it seemed on the surface.

I would never know, though, and that was okay. We'd both found love—the kind people wait a lifetime for—and neither of us would change that for the world.

But it was also okay to be sad, to grieve what might have been, to be angry at the choices that had been taken from *us,* not just me.

Pulling back, he swiped away a few of my tears that had escaped. "I'm proud of you, Tessa. More than you know."

I smiled. "I'm kind of proud of me, too."

He laughed, then rested his hands on my shoulders. "I always knew you had it in you to do great things. It thrills me to see I was right."

I arched a brow. "As if you'd *ever* be wrong."

"That's an excellent point." He glanced back at the palace doors. "You should go on in. I imagine my dear brother's benevolence has hit its quote for the century."

As if on cue, Nate's voice sounded in my head. *'Hecate and Scylla are back. We need you.'*

"It would appear you're correct yet again," I told him. I took his hands in mine. "Thank you, Hades. Everything you did for me back then—it's what helped make me who I am today. I'll be forever grateful for that."

Cupping my cheek in his hand, smiled sadly. "You did more for me in return than you'll ever know." He gave me one last kiss on my forehead. "Goodbye, Tessa."

And then he was gone, leaving me, my tears, and my emotions standing on the palace steps.

Ever since getting my memories back, I'd known that was a conversation Hades and I needed to have. And despite how happy I was with Nate, feeling that absence as Hades left *really* fucking hurt.

Knowing I needed to have my wits about me for whatever Hecate and Scylla were going to report, I took a few minutes to collect myself and settle my nerves before going back inside.

When I arrived, Hecate was pacing, looking abnormally harried, while Scylla stood, arms folded and hip cocked, watching her mother in mute fascination.

"What's happened?" I asked, coming to a slow stop.

Hecate's pacing ceased when she heard me. "Oh, good, you're back," she murmured.

Frowning, I stepped forward. "Hecate, what is it?"

She gave me a pained look. "Tessa—gods, I don't know how I could've let this happen."

"We went to Renville," Scylla said, letting her arms fall to her sides as she faced us, "to look into the symbols Chiron and Persephone found and to examine the shields Mother placed over the home of Tessa's guardians. We also wanted to see if we could find what manner of protection or containment the other rings on the symbol signified." She sighed. "The symbols were still there, and I could feel the remains of Josh's magic in them. My guess is he stopped fueling them once you were came to Olympus and he left."

"Which makes sense," I said slowly, still looking at Hecate warily. "So why the pacing?"

"My magic was gone," she said, stepping toward me. "Every drop of magic I placed on your home was gone."

"Didn't you drop the cloaking spell when Tessa left Renville?" Nate asked.

"When the spell on Tessa's mind broke, all magical protections I had in place for her would've fallen, yes," she confirmed. "But magic leaves a residue. I should have been able to detect the remnant of my power when I went to the Averys' home, but there was nothing there. Not a wisp."

"There *was*, however, a good deal of Josh's magic present," Scylla told us. "Heaps of it, and as I suspected, it felt incredibly old." She held up the paper that held the symbol Chiron had found. "The innermost ring represents Leila, and we assumed the outermost ring represented him." She tapped her finger on the middle ring. "This ring seems to represent a protection spell he placed on your home, and the outermost ring protected your town, hence the markings Chiron and Persephone saw."

"That makes no sense," Epimetheus said. "There was already magical protection in place. Why erase it?"

"This is just conjecture," Hecate said. "But I believe instead of making her whereabouts invisible to those who might search for Tessa magically, he used a repellant form of magic that prevented others from wanting to search for her to begin with."

"Would that explain why he never came for me before my transformation?" A headache began to pulse in my temples. This was beginning to get far too complicated for me. I could understand a simple protection spell. But this discussion of rings of protection and containment, piled onto the events that had just unfolded in the basement, were starting to feel heavy on my mind.

"Yes, I would think so," Hecate replied.

"Okay, fine, then what does this mean?" I asked tiredly. "I'm already out of Renville. Josh is out of Renville. He's cut all ties with Leila. Why does it matter whether or not he screwed with your magic?" I looked at Hecate. "As the literal Creator of us all, is that really surprising?"

That drew her up short. Frowning, she shook her head. "No,

Tessa, it's not surprising. But your mother tasked me with keeping you safe, and well, it would appear I've done quite the opposite."

"Fine. Learn from your mistakes," I told her, nodding. "Next time you shove someone into the Void for their own protection, make sure you follow up on how your magic is holding up afterward. Until then, stop feeling sorry for yourself so we can move on."

Epimetheus rubbed a hand over his chin to hide his smile, and Scylla let out a throaty chuckle.

"Ah, Tessa. You are quite the wordsmith," Scylla said.

I kept my gaze locked on Hecate. "Now is really not the time to be stressing about the things you can't go back and fix. It's done. We need to focus on ending this."

She stared at me for a few seconds, her face unreadable. Then she let out a breath and nodded. "I know. It's very frustrating, that's all."

I gave her a smile that I hoped seemed reassuring. "I understand. For now, let's just move forward. Did you find anything useful while you were there?"

"No, unfortunately," Scylla said. "We have, it seems, reached the end of our rope." She looked at Hecate. "Which means we need to find more rope."

"What are you thinking?" Zeus asked.

"The Fates," Hecate said without hesitation. "Chiron is trying to find the location of any remaining first-generation deities, but we need to go about this the right way. The Fates are the ones who had instructed me to bring Tessa back, despite Menoetius' presence and the threat of rebellion. I believe they are also the only way we might gain an audience with one of the old gods."

"How do you expect to go about finding them?" Atlas asked dubiously. "The Fates are nearly as difficult to get to as the old gods."

"But it's not impossible," Hecate countered. "Tessa and I will be leaving immediately to seek them out."

"We will?" I shot a surprised look at Nate. "I thought I was going with you."

He looked at his father, exasperated. "As did I."

"You all have your orders," was Zeus' only reply.

None of us bothered arguing. It was no use, and at this late in the game, it didn't matter who went where or answered to who as long we succeeded. Things needed to be done, worlds needed to be protected, and we weren't always going to be together when we did those things.

And I, apparently, had to go convince the Fates to help us figure out how to destroy Josh before he destroyed us all.

I smiled brightly at Hecate. "When do we leave?"

40

MARY

When I woke the next morning, it took a solid minute for me to remember where I was. As my mind became more alert, the memories of the previous night came rushing back.

I'd never had a panic attack before, and I was hesitant to say it would be my last.

My mind felt a bit clearer today, most likely due to the heavy hits of magic I'd taken from Nate and his brothers the night before.

For a few minutes, I lay on my back and stared up at the skylight above the bed. Through the glass, I could see bright blue sky and thin, wispy clouds floating by.

Whenever I closed my eyes, I still saw that small square of sky in the ceiling of my cell casting a dim glow over the room. Once the sun went down, it had been so dark there that human eyes would've been completely blind. As it was, even with my immortal eyesight, each night, the cell had become a hundred times more claustrophobic.

But I wasn't there anymore. The square of sky I saw above me now wasn't a hole in a dingy cell. It was a something Nate had designed to help natural light flow through the house, just like the large picture window in the wall to my left.

I wasn't there anymore. I needed to move forward.

I swung my legs over the edge of the bed and stood, then glanced at the clock on the nightstand and groaned. It was nearly one in the afternoon. Not wanting to waste what was left of the day moping, I started digging through my dresser until I found a pair of gray leggings and a long-sleeved yellow shirt. Yellow was a happy, cheerful color, and I needed some happy cheerfulness in my life.

Once I'd brushed my teeth and dressed, I made my way out to the living room, not sure who I'd find. A good dozen people had come through Nate's house last night, but I had no clue who, if any, stayed.

The doors to the other two guest rooms—gods, Nate's house was bigger than I thought—were still closed, telling me Yana and Anette were still asleep. When I walked out into the living room, I was pleasantly surprised to find John and Analise sitting on the couch talking quietly.

"Morning," I said.

Both jumped to their feet, then Analise rushed toward me and wrapped me in her arms. "How are you feeling, honey?" She pulled me back and held me at arm's length, looking me up and down.

I gave her a wry smile. "Shitty."

She gave me a chastising look. "Well, it's good to see your attitude hasn't completely vanished."

I laughed, and something loosened inside me. It was slight, but that small twinge of security I felt as I was finger-wagged by Tessa's guardian gave me a sense of relief.

"Where is everyone?" I asked as I allowed Analise to lead me to the couch.

"Briefing," John said. He slid a paper cup of toward me that had to logo for the café in Olympia on the side. "Here. Coffee. You look like you need it."

Smiling gratefully, I took a sip, then closed my eyes and let myself bask in another small reminder that I was home and safe.

"I'm guessing my memories are a major subject?" I asked after taking a few more sips.

"More than likely," Analise replied. "I'm sure if they need you—"

"Nope." I held up a hand and shook my head. "Tessa, Nate, Apollo, Hades, Athena, and the gods know who else, have my memories now. They can be the messengers, because I have no intention of setting foot in that palace any time soon."

"Mary," John said cautiously. "If Zeus calls for you—"

"He can come down here and see me." My bravado was stupid, but I was so goddamn furious about what he'd done to me last night. I grew up thinking he was this amazing ruler, fair and just, then *bam*. He'd tossed me in a cell without so much as a warning to any of the people he trusted to protect this mountain.

"Ah, she is awake!" Yana walked into the room dressed in skinny jeans and a black tunic. "How are you feeling?"

I held up my cup of coffee. "I have coffee. All is good."

She smiled and sat down on the couch across from us. "That is all that matters, then. Chiron called. They just finished their meeting. He is going to get all of his research from the archives and come here." She glanced back down the hall toward the guest rooms. "Anette should be on her way out."

I gave her a curious look. "Wouldn't it make more sense to keep all his research there?"

She shrugged. "I would think so, but he said Nate said something about using this as a base, so…"

"This place has turned into a damn hotel, so I'd say that ship has sailed." I frowned. "Why were you guys sleeping in so late, anyway? It's after one."

"We were up 'til nearly dawn," Yana said. She inclined her head toward John and Analise. "Them, too."

"Why?" I looked at John and Analise. "You guys were here all night?"

Analise squeezed my hand. "We didn't want to leave until we knew you were going to be able to sleep. It took Dionysus several tries before he was able to finally settle you down. Once he did, we didn't want to leave right away, in case you woke back up."

"Well, thank you. I appreciate you staying. I'm sure Tessa appreciates it, too."

"Mary, I'm so sorry we can't bring Chris and Alan up here to see you," Analise said sadly.

My heart clenched at the sound of my guardians' names. I hadn't seen them in months, but I had known when I left Renville, there was a very good chance I'd never see them again. I'd prepared for it my whole life. But with Tessa's guardians right in front of me, I was beginning to miss them terribly.

"It's okay," I said, waving a hand and trying not to cry. "As soon as I can, I'm planning on going to Renville to see them. Screw that whole, 'leaving your mortal lives behind' bullshit," I added with a forced laugh.

"That's certainly something we can be on board with," John said, smiling. "Once this is all done, we'll go back, explain to them all that's happened."

Anette walked in wearing what I could only describe as Anette-wear. Leggings that were swirls of pink and purple, topped with a lilac tank top that fell to mid-thigh were complemented by the bright pink scrunchie that held back her bright blond hair.

As much as she drove me nuts when we lived together, she was without question, another piece of home.

Her steps faltered slightly when she saw me, then she grinned. "You're awake! How are—"

"*Fine,*" I said with a grumble. "Sorry. You're the third person in the last ten minutes to ask."

"It's alright," she said, sitting down beside Yana. "Will you three be joining the research team today?"

"We are, from what I'm told," Analise said.

"Ah." I nodded knowingly. "Well then, it looks like I am, too."

There was a knock at the door, and a moment later, Chiron and Dionysus walked in, each carrying a huge box. I was surprised to see Chiron in his human form, as he'd been coming in his equine form to training almost every day since week one.

He must've noticed me looking because he flashed me a smile. "Sometimes it's just easy to maneuver on two legs."

Setting down the giant box he carried, he held out his arms.

Without hesitating, I stood and launched myself at him, letting him wrap his giant arms around me in a bone-crushing hug. The tears that had threatened to fall just a few minutes before spilled over as I clung to the physical proof that he'd made it out of that arena.

Chiron had made it out. He'd survived.

"I was so worried about you," I whispered, not bothering to hide the emotion in my voice. "How—"

"I'm very old and very hard to kill." He stepped back and smiled warmly. "And Apollo is a phenomenal healer."

I laughed and wiped away the tears that had started to fall. "That he is." My shoulders slumped and I smiled at him. "I'm so happy you're alive, Chiron."

He chuckled and patted my shoulder. "Likewise, Mary. Now, let's get to work." Picking up the discarded box, he carried it over the dining room table and set it down.

Dionysus tapped me on the head, then shifted the box he held to his hip and held out his free arm. "Where's mine? I *did* get myself locked up for you, after all."

Rolling my eyes, I wrapped my arm around his waist and hugged him. "Thank you for getting yourself thrown in the dungeon with me," I mumbled against his shirt.

"Anytime, doll. Anytime."

I followed him over to the table, which was big enough to seat ten and wide enough to hold a feast for twice that many. Yana, Anette, John, and Analise walked over and watched as they began methodically began pulling out books, fragile documents, random objects, and scrolls of parchment. When they were done, nearly the entire table was covered.

"This is everything I've found that either explicitly or vaguely references Chaos as a living being and not just a Void or container for all life. There's also quite a bit on symbols used by the first generations of primordial deities, from what we can tell."

"Wait. Back up." I held up a hand. "*Chaos?*" I looked around the room, wide-eyed. "Does anyone want to fill me in on what I missed last night?"

Chiron looked at the others in surprise. "You haven't explained things to her yet?"

Anette shook her head. "We just woke up, and we thought Chiron might be the best option for telling her what is going on."

"Which is what, exactly?" I asked.

"Do we need wine for this?" Dionysus asked, brows raised. "Because if I have to hear this story *again*, I might need some wine."

"No wine," Chiron groaned. "Some of these items are ten thousand years old. So help me, Dionysus—"

"Will someone please tell me what's going on!" I put my hands on my hips and did my best impression of Zeus glaring. "Now!"

With a sigh, Chiron gestured toward the table. "Sit. I'll run through it all."

I obeyed, and the others followed suit. When we were all settled, I looked at him expectantly.

"In a nutshell, based on your memories and research we've done, I've concluded that the creature we're dealing with—Josh—is not a primordial witch, but actually the Creator himself."

My brow furrowed. "Huh?" I ran back over the memories that Nate had left me of my conversation with Josh. "Just because he said he knew Tessa before?"

Chiron shook his head. "No, we believe he was actually in the Void with her. That's what he was talking about when he spoke of her not remembering their time together."

"Okay..." I wasn't quite sure I bought it, but I'd hear him out before saying so. "So aside from my memories, what else is there?"

"When he mentioned wanting to destroy it all and his seeming obsession with wanting both sides to suffer equally in this war, I began to look further back than I had been. A few sources—poems, mainly—refer to Chaos as an actual being."

"It's not, though. It's a place."

"As is Tartarus, yet a being also existed who was the personification of Tartarus, the abyss at the bottom of the Underworld. That being existed within the walls of Tartarus, eventually giving over his energy and power to protect the entire realm, turning it into a place where evil could be locked away. Gaia did the same when she gave her power over to Earth, allowing the species that lived there to flourish."

"Right, but we've never—or at least, I've never—heard Chaos referred to as anything other than a place where the universe began."

He smiled pointedly down at the piles of research on the table. "Hence my recent stay in the basement archives."

I let out a breath. "Okay, I'll buy it for now. So what are we looking for? And we're not the only ones looking for information, right?" The thought that Zeus would leave the discovery of information on our biggest threat in the hands of two humans and three Ischyra was comical.

"No, but we are the only ones seeking information here," he said. "Zeus and I have sent out teams globally to search for things that may have never made it to Olympus."

"What about Tessa? Why does she get out of homework duty?"

Dionysus shook his head and laughed. "I think we should let her explain that when she gets home." He looked up at the clock. "Which should be soon. Or two days from now. You never know."

"I—you know what? Never mind. I don't want to know."

"So what are we looking for, exactly?" John asked. "It seems like our starting points are a bit vague."

"They are," Chiron agreed. "So we need to know where to go next. In particular, the locations and statuses of any first-generation primordial deities. There were a number who chose to release their energy and forsake their physical forms, but not all."

"*First* generation?" Anette asked.

"You're looking for the children of Chaos," Analise said quietly.

Chiron's expression turned grim. "I am. We know the location of a few, but there are others out there who might speak to us if we're unsuccessful with our current plan. They may be our only chance of finding out how to win this war."

"But no pressure," Dionysus murmured, barely managing the casual tone he tried to force.

Chiron shot him warning look. "I'll send you right back to the palace if you don't knock it off. I know you only offered to take research duty was so you could get out of going to Earth."

Dionysus grinned. "And wine. Nathaniel has a lovely collection of wine."

I exchanged an amused look with Yana.

"Okay, then," Analise said. "Where do we start?"

"Anywhere," Chiron said. "We're looking for any mention of Chaos, Nature, the Creator."

"As well as anything on weapons of unknown origin," Yana added. "Something that can destroy, that holds the ability to handle that much power."

John nodded. "Alright." He rubbed a hand over the stubble on his jaw as he eyed the piles and boxes that Chiron had just unloaded. "Let's get to it, then."

41

TESSA

In my previous life, the Fates lived on Mount Othrys, the original home of the Titans. Then after the war, they lived on Olympus, along with the rest of the deities. They'd kept to themselves, perfectly content to be left alone. They never ventured out or joined in celebrations; instead, they just existed autonomously with almost no interactions with the outside world. They would ignore anyone who arrived at their door unannounced, which, considering most people who sought them out wanted their lifelines altered in some way, was understandable.

In the twenty-first century, the Fates were, according to Hecate, the deific version of globetrotters. Whether or not one gained an audience with them wasn't thanks to their mercurial behavior, as it had been before. Now it was due to the fact that they were damn near impossible to find. And, apparently, if and when one *did* track them down, they'd have little luck convincing the Fates to even acknowledge their existence. They couldn't and wouldn't alter a being's fate once their lifeline was spun, so there was very little they could offer anyone who sought them out.

Hecate and I followed three false leads to New York City, London, then Tokyo, before finally traveling to Rome, the last place on the list.

It had been rumored they had been living there for some time, posing as college professors.

I didn't have it in me to be weirded out by news like that anymore.

I'd been to Rome once before with John and Analise when they'd taken me for my fifteenth birthday. The city had stunned me with its vibrancy and culture, and one of my favorite things to do was explore the tiny hidden streets and corners that would randomly reveal some structure or feature that was a thousand years old. Before coming to Olympus, I'd always hoped I might get stationed there one day. Living among those giant, historic structures, and going past the Colosseum and the Arch of Constantine every day was my idea of a dream placement.

Now, seeing it for the first time as an immortal in its modern state, it still sent a thrill of wonder through me, but something about it seemed... smaller. Even still, I wanted to stop and explore, peek in the stores, wander through the ruins of the Roman Forum, and take a stroll down the Appian Way.

Which, as it happened, was where we landed when we arrived.

Frowning, I looked up and down the ancient cobblestone road. "Where are they?"

Hecate gestured toward a path that led off the Way and onto a main road. "They've got a home just up there. Before we go, I wanted to talk to you."

I looked up at her curiously. "About what?"

"Come, sit." She gestured toward a small ruin that sat about ten feet away that looked like it had once been some kind of statue. It was wide and flat enough that it worked well as a bench.

Once we sat, she shifted, so she was facing me. "Tessa, I need to apologize for how horrifically wrong things have gone. When I used the spell to send you into Chaos, I *never* could've guessed that it could go so badly."

I bit back a sigh. Her apologies were becoming incredibly tiresome.

"Hecate, I appreciate the apology, and I know how regretful you feel about all of this, but it's done," I told her. "You didn't mean to send me into another dimension with a sadistic freak who wants to destroy the world, and there's no way you could've anticipated it." I shrugged. "We just have to do what we can to fix things."

She stared at me for a few seconds, her face unreadable, then closed her eyes and nodded. "Yes, I suppose you're right." She rubbed her hands on the thighs of her pants and stood. "Well, then I suppose we should be off."

I stood, then we began walking down the path toward the main road. "So how will this work?" I asked. "We just ring the bell? That seems awfully simple."

"Essentially. The difficult part is getting them to speak to you. If they choose not to, they'll just send us right back to Olympus and bar us from returning."

Lovely. "And if they do decide to speak with us?"

"Then we need to be very clear in how we ask our questions," she said. "They won't change a thing about where your life, or anyone else's, is set to go, nor will they tell you what's to come." She smiled wryly. "For that reason, their answers often come in the form of anecdotes, leaving you to interpret them as you will, so prepare yourself.'

"Which means asking them to tell us exactly how to kill Josh is a surefire way to get us kicked out?"

"Exactly." She winced. "And watch out for Lachesis. She tends to speak in riddles. Take note of *all* she says. She might seem a bit unstable compared to Clotho and Atropos, but every word she speaks has meaning."

I raked a hand through my hair and groaned as I followed her up the path to the street. "They should really make a damn decoder ring for this."

We came to a stop outside a two-story stucco house that was crammed on a small street between two other identical buildings. Compared to the ostentatious homes of the deities who lived on Olympus, this bordered on a hovel. By normal standards, however, the building was exactly the kind of place I could've lived. Wrought iron gates enclosed a small, manicured front yard bisected by a narrow stone walkway that led up to the first-floor porch. Beds of vibrant wildflowers bloomed on either side of the steps, and the porch was fitted with a wide porch swing, perfect for napping. The door was a deep terra-cotta with black iron hardware, the stucco siding, beige. Windows with shutters that matched the door were flung open on either side of it.

I looked to Hecate in question. "Now what?"

"Now we knock," she said grimly. She lifted the latch on the gate and held it open, allowing me to walk through first. When we reached the door, I waited for her to knock, but when I looked at her expectantly, she shook her head, then gestured for me to do it. "You're the one who is here for information, Tessa. You have to be the one to seek out their presence."

"Right." Steeling myself, I curled my fingers around the black, ring-shaped knocker and knocked three times.

There were a few seconds of silence, then after a moment, the door opened, and a short brunette with a heart-shaped face, a narrow, upturned nose, long, wavy hair, and Buddy Holly glasses opened the door.

"Ah, Tessa." She sighed and scratched the side of her head. "There you are." Holding out a hand, she forced a smile. "I'm Clotho."

Slowly, I took her outstretched hand and shook it. "I guess you knew I would be coming, then?" I joked.

"Of course, we did." She peered up at Hecate and frowned. "Your presence is unnecessary this time, Hecate. You've done what we asked. Now you can go."

Hecate opened her mouth, but before she could get her response out, she was gone.

I blinked slowly, staring at the space beside me where Hecate had just been.

Well. So much for backup.

Clotho took my hand and gave a hard tug to pull me through the door. I stumbled into the house as she shut the door. "Come. The four of us have much to discuss."

Righting myself when she let go of my hand, I looked at her curiously. "We do?"

She nodded curtly. "Follow me and mind your manners."

I pressed my lips together to hold back any response I might have. My manners had been the last thing on my mind in recent days, but now more than ever I needed to make sure I kept my annoyance and frustration in check. She'd let me in. The last thing I needed was to ruin my chances by saying the wrong thing before I even got to ask my questions.

She led me through the warmly-decorated Mediterranean-style home, through the living room and the kitchen until we'd reached the back door, which led out onto a backyard that was practically bursting with flora. Flowers of every color bordered the tall privacy fence that ran around the entire space, interspersed here and there with trellises of morning glory and bushes of honeysuckle. Every few feet, a tall bird feeder poked through the top of the blooms.

I smiled. It reminded me a lot of the garden Hestia had brought me to when we first met in a dream walk. It'd been just as beautiful, but in a different way. The main difference was, instead of meandering through the flowers, the cobblestone path led to a small sitting area that consisted of two wicker sofas and two matching chairs that sat around a propane fire pit.

Clotho's sisters, Lachesis on one sofa, Atropos on the other, sat facing each other.

"Sisters, she's arrived," Clotho announced when we came through the doors.

Lachesis, a willowy redhead with a smattering of freckles across her nose, gave a small nod in my direction. Atropos had a spiky, blonde pixie cut and a face that matched, with narrow features and a slight build. She watched impassively as Clotho led me toward them.

Clotho indicated toward one of the chairs with her hand. "Sit."

I obeyed, then wiped my clammy palms on my jeans as I tried to figure out what to say now that I'd made it in. I'd been hoping I'd have Hecate's guidance when we asked our non-questions, but clearly they had other ideas in mind.

"Thank you for seeing me," I told them. "I'm guessing you know why I'm here." I made sure there was no lilt at the end of my statement.

"Of course, we do," Lachesis said. Her voice fit her body perfectly; soft, slightly high-pitched but melodic. "Although you will leave disappointed."

Atropos sent her a warning look. "That is a matter of opinion, sister."

Lachesis shrugged. "Well, in my opinion, then, you are going to be disappointed when you leave."

"I understand I may not get the kind of help I would like from you three," I began. "I know there's only so much you can or are willing to give. There's too much at stake for me not to try, though."

"As anyone in your shoes would feel," Clotho said. "Although I cannot promise we'll be able to offer you much in the way of guidance."

"I'm not here to ask what to do," I said carefully. "I'm here because I need knowledge, not answers, necessarily." I bit my lip, hoping I was on the right track. "So I can make informed decisions and help those I'm working with do the same."

Lachesis' lips tilted up in a soft smile. "'The only true wisdom is knowing you know nothing.'"

"I—um, yes, I can see why that might be true. Is that a quote from something?"

"Mm hmm. Socrates. Died of hemlock poisoning, poor man. It's a shame you weren't around to meet him. He was quite smart." She sighed, a soft, musical sound. "They didn't like that about him, you know."

"Knowledge can both help and hinder, Tessa," Atropos said gently. "Sometimes in tandem."

"And yet," Lachesis held up a finger, "if one advances *confidently* in the direction of his dreams, he will meet with success unexpected."

Atropos rolled her eyes and gave me a knowing look. "Thoreau. Sort of. Lachesis has a love for poets as well as philosophers, but she doesn't always get them quite right."

"It's true, though," Lachesis said with a shrug. "Right or not."

"Yes." Clotho nodded. "There was a time not so long ago when I wanted to make a vegetarian meal—"

"She heard a vegan diet was healthier," Lachesis interjected. "Felt she knew all that she needed to make this—what was it? Tofu ravioli?"

Atropos made a sound of disgust.

"—but the local grocery was out of tofu, which was a main ingredient," Clotho continued. "There was quite a good deal of traffic, so I was forced to either drive thirty minutes to the next closest vegan grocery or make my own, which I've never done before, but I hear it's just *such* a hassle, isn't it, Atropos?"

Atropos *tsked* her agreement.

"Oh." I tried not to let them see my confusion as to why she didn't simply teleport to another store, or why she thought she needed a healthy meal to begin with. "I—um, yes, that kind of thing can be very frustrating," I agreed. I glanced at the other two and saw they were watching me, appraising my response.

Right. Hecate said their information often came in the form of anecdotes. Small stories that I would have to deduce meaning from. Easy.

"Did you cook often in your human life?" Lachesis asked curiously.

"Sometimes," I replied. "Not often, though."

"Well, you should take it up," Clotho said, wagging a finger. "It can be quite useful as a tool for stress management."

I smiled. "I think I know quite a few deities who could use some of that."

"I suppose we should get to it," Lachesis said with a sigh. "Tessa would like to get back to her mountain, so she can help save the world." She lifted a brow in my direction. "Ask what you want."

I paused a moment to gather my thoughts. This was it. I couldn't screw it up by asking my question in question form or some other way that might offend them.

"I know you can't give me answers about a specific lifeline," I began. "And I don't intend to ask you to change anything about mine or anyone else's. I'm not trying to change anything that's already been woven, but I would like to believe that ending up here, with you three, is part of the path you wove for me long ago." Hopefully that would pacify them enough that they'd be forthcoming.

"And if it isn't part of your path?" Lachesis asked smoothly.

"Then that would mean I or someone else has somehow managed to change my lifeline, and based on your reputations, you never would have allowed that to happen." *Score.*

She gave me a small nod. "Continue."

"I suppose the thing that might help me—all of us—the most, would be a history lesson. Simple knowledge. I'm sure there's some I already know, but I've never had the opportunity to learn from deities as ancient as yourselves."

The three of them exchanged a look, their expressions unreadable as they had some kind of silent discussion. Finally, Atropos turned and faced me.

"What is it you would like to learn about?"

I took a deep breath, hoping I wasn't about to get myself thrown out. "The creation of the universe... and also where you three came from."

They shared another look. Then, her expression blank, Clotho looked at me.

Without warning, I was teleported away.

42

MARY

I'd never liked research when I was a human. Any time I'd done a research project in school, it'd always been on something I had no interest in at all, so the work itself was almost always inherently boring. But I did it because to do otherwise would mean I'd suffer the wrath of my guardians for not working to my "full potential."

Blah.

Sorting through books, documents, and artifacts that came from the Olympian archives wasn't much better. The only thing that made sifting through the dusty old boxes remotely interesting was that I was potentially doing lifesaving work.

Also, it was distracting. It kept me from thinking about everything that had happened over the last two weeks.

It stopped me from wondering whether I'd be able to use my powers soon or if they'd return in full. I'd waited my entire human life to get my powers, to be put to work as an Ischyra, and now, I couldn't help worrying that I might not get that chance.

Quietly, I exhaled and opened the wood-bound book Dionysus had just handed me.

'You okay?' he asked.

'Yeah. Reading about—' I squinted at the small print on the cover *'"The History of the Olympian Metallurgists"' is totally my idea of a good time.'*

'Hephaestus had a hand in that one,' he said, amused. *'He's quite verbose, believe it or not, so I'm sure it's fascinating.'*

I slid him a look. *'Seriously? What are you reading?'* I reached over and shifted the book he was holding to see the cover, then gave him an incredulous look. *'You're reading the Olympic census records from four thousand BC? Sounds thrilling.'*

'Trade?'

'Not a chance.'

I set the history book down and rubbed my hands across my eyes, then looked up at the clock on the mantel. Eight PM. "It's been seven hours. Can someone go get coffee?"

"Wine?" Dionysus asked.

"No wine," Chiron deadpanned, not looking up from the scroll he'd been examining for the last half hour. "Go get coffee if you need a break."

Before anyone could offer to go, there was a *whoosh,* and suddenly I was on my feet in the middle of Main Street in Olympia, right outside the small coffee shop on the corner near the portal field.

I glared up at Dionysus. "A little warning next time, please. I don't do well with surprises these days."

He shrugged, then dropped his arm around my shoulder and started leading me toward the coffee shop. "You needed to get out of there."

"No, I didn't." *Liar.*

"I'm an empath, in case you've forgotten. My inclination is toward making sure people are happy. Joyful." He arched a brow at me and pulled the door open. I was immediately hit with the scent of coffee and sweet-smelling baked goods. "Which you, my dear, are not."

"Considering—"

"...the circumstances, no one would expect you to be, I know. I can't help it, though." He grinned. "It's my thing."

I scowled, torn between irritated and thankful. "Well, try to keep your *thing* to yourself unless asked to do otherwise," I muttered, then turned and faced the Ischyra who was standing behind the counter, a petite redhead who slightly resembled an elf. "Five large coffees, three with cream and sugar, one black, one extra cream, extra sugar."

She flashed me a smile and nodded. "No problem." She looked at Dionysus in question. "Anything, sir?"

"Triple shot of espresso, Nadia."

I wrinkled my nose.

He snorted. "Like your coffee-flavored sugar is *any* better."

The loud, hissing rumble of the espresso machine filled the little restaurant as Nadia began working on our order. I folded my arms and cocked my hip against the counter, eyeing the giant chocolate chip cookies in the glass case speculatively as I waited. Smirking, Dionysus reached behind the counter and grabbed a wax bag from beside the case, then nabbed two cookies, tucking them inside the bag. "There. Now you don't have to hem and haw."

With a sigh, I took the bag. It was very, very hard not to be frustrated with his constant need to help, but at the same time, it was also incredibly sweet. I knew he wasn't trying to be annoying, but I found myself trying to temper my reactions to his attempts to cheer me up more often than I liked. There were just times I wanted to be left alone to wallow, which I supposed was why he was always there. Wallowing is never good or helpful.

After Nadia gave us our order, we walked outside, then he gestured toward a bench that sat near the portal field. "I'm not sharing my cookie with any of those vultures back at the house," he said teasingly.

I couldn't help the smile—the very real smile—that formed on my lips.

He nudged me with his elbow. "Got one."

We sat there for the next few minutes in companionable silence. I almost outright laughed when I saw the look of disgust that filled his features when I dipped my cookie in my coffee.

"That's gross, even by my standards," he commented, grimacing.

"Don't knock it." Grinning, I shoved another bite in my mouth. "This is one of Tessa's favorites, too."

"Somehow, that doesn't surprise me," he mumbled.

I finished my cookie, then stared down at my coffee, trying not to let my mind wander back to where I'd been just yesterday. Being surrounded by so many people who loved and cared for me was helping immensely, not to mention the piles of research that were forcing my mind to focus on other things. And yes, if I was being honest, I was kind of glad Dionysus had pulled me away for a little while. I'd barely had a taste of fresh air since I'd been released, and I hadn't realized until now how much I'd taken it for granted. I'd been surrounded by nothing but the damp, musty smell of rot and sweat and blood for days, and my brain's adjustment to the lack of those things, the lack of emotions attached to them, was a bit jarring.

Slowly, I felt myself slip back into that dark place from the night before.

"Mary?" Dionysus asked quietly.

"Hmm?"

"Do you need another hug?"

Suddenly, I became aware of the tears that were sliding down my cheeks, dripping off my jaw and onto my lap, seeping through the fabric of my leggings. When I opened my mouth to speak, I couldn't get the words out, so I just nodded.

Setting his coffee down on the ground and doing the same with mine, he wrapped an arm around me and pulled me into his side, then rested his cheek on my head. A few seconds later, I felt the warmth of his magic wash over me as he held me, wrapping me in a cocoon of contentment.

"You're safe now," he told me. He nudged me back slightly, then put a finger on my chin and tilted my face toward his, forcing me to meet his eyes. "You're home, and you're safe, and that isn't something I intend to let change. Believe that. Know it. Look at what you're feeling and see that your fears aren't necessary anymore. Let your logic take over."

I took a few steadying breaths and tried to do what he asked, then let him pull me against his chest as I tried to envision what he was saying.

I wasn't trapped anymore. I was home with Tessa and her brothers, and Nate and his stupid brothers, and with Yana, Anette, Chiron, and John and Analise. I was safe, and I was helping them find a way to defeat the thing that had done this to me. I was going to come out a winner in all this.

And at least one of my tormentors was dead. It startled me, how easy it was for me to reflect on Iapetus' death and not feel fear. No, if anything, I felt relief. Happiness. Giddiness, even.

"There you go," Dionysus murmured, tightening his arms around me. "Hold onto that feeling."

I sniffed and nodded.

I felt his chest rumble with quiet laughter. "And stop calling me and my brothers stupid."

That got a watery laugh out of me. Sitting back, I wiped my eyes and tried to smile. "Well you guys *are* kind of dumb sometimes."

He used his thumbs to wipe away the rest of my tears. "Stubborn and foolish, maybe, but all of Nathaniel's brothers are the pinnacle of intelligence." He smiled warmly. "Better?"

"Some." I took a deep breath. "Much, actually. The objectivity that you give me when you use your magic... it helps a lot."

"And here you thought I just made people want to party," he said, shaking his head. Standing, he held out a hand. "Come on, let's head back before they think we ran off with the circus."

I rolled my eyes. "I'm pretty sure only one of us would cause them to think that."

He flicked my nose, then teleported us back to Nate's.

By the time we got back, the pile of "potentially helpful" information had grown slightly, but we were still no closer to finding a definitive conclusion about Josh' origins or weaknesses.

"Everyone, every *thing* has a weakness," Chiron said, drumming his fingers on the edge of the table.

"Weaknesses and vulnerabilities don't always equate to means with which to kill someone," Analise said. "Damage, certainly, but something as powerful as he seems to be... I just can't imagine anyone having the right kind of magic to destroy him."

"Pessimism serves no one," Dionysus said, wagging a finger at her.

"Do we truly believe he wants to destroy *everything*?" Yana asked. She looked at me. "Mary, the memory from your conversation with him is clear now, correct?"

I nodded. "It is. And no, I don't think that's really what he wants. Or not entirely, anyway."

"Why not?" Analise asked, her eyes curious.

I shoved back the heart-pounding fear that gnawed at my mind and forced myself to look at the memory, remember his words. "Because he talked about war as being a means of suppressing the oppressors, ridding the world of those who harmed what they viewed as beings that were beneath them. It's about killing the bad guys, which I guess in his eyes are us."

"So if that's the case, the only reason he would've started a war between the gods would be to destroy them, not the entire world," Dionysus finished.

I nodded. "But he doesn't seem to have any problem getting the humans involved," I said. "So that makes me wonder if he's gotten them thrown into the war for the same reason."

"Which leads us to cycle back to the original question," Analise said with a sigh. "Why won't he just do it himself?"

"He can't," Dionysus said. "And there has to be a specific reason why he can't."

"I agree," Anette said. "There is no other answer."

"But why?" I asked. "That's what doesn't make sense. Assuming he is who we think he is, if he wants to destroy the beings that are ruining the world he made, why not just wipe them out? He's got to have the power for it."

"It's in here," Chiron said absently, eying the books in from of us, a determined frown on his face. "There's got to be something here."

"Has anyone heard from Tessa?" Yana asked. "She has been gone for quite some time."

Chiron smiled wryly. "Hecate took her to hunt down the Fates," he said. "If she's been gone this long, it means they either haven't found them, or they've found them and were successful in gaining an audience, in which case, they could be gone for hours or days, depending."

"Are they normally hard to find?" Analise asked.

"Very," he confirmed. "So I'm hoping Tessa and Hecate's extended absence means they were successful and not flitting about the globe trying to hunt them down."

"Any idea what kind of info they might give her?" I asked.

Chiron pressed his lips together and shook his head. "None, unfortunately, and any information they do give may not be easily usable. They have a tendency to shy away from direct answers, especially when a question revolves around changing a person's lifeline.'

"So no hope of them just handing her some magical sword that'll slice him to bits?" I asked.

"I would say the chances of that are roughly nil," he said with a smile. "Although we shouldn't hold out hope that such a weapon actually exists or can be created."

Smirking, Dionysus handed me the book on Olympic metal workers I'd been avoiding picking back up. "Sounds like something you might find in a book on metallurgy."

"You know, you're totally right, Dionysus," I said with a bright smile. "And since you're the *older*, more experienced resident of Olympus here, maybe you should be the one to read it."

His mouth dropped open. "That is—that is *unfair!*"

I shrugged and plucked a scroll from the middle of the table. "You could go back to reading six thousand years' worth of census records."

"She's right, Dionysus," Chiron murmured, not looking up from the scroll he was examining. "You know a lot of the history that's in that book already, so you'll have context to go with it."

Preening at Dionysus, I waved the scroll at him and unrolled it, then began to read.

43

NATHANIEL

As a large portion of the Netherlands was now under water, Zeus sent us to the Ischyra headquarters in Berlin for a briefing on the attacks on the waterways just north of Amsterdam. When Eris, Epimetheus, and I arrived at the single-story concrete structure on the outskirts of Germany's capital, we were greeted in the lobby by a stern female who held the look of someone who couldn't be ruffled, no matter the circumstances.

"Thank you for coming," she said by way of greeting. "I'm Dona."

"What have you got?" I asked.

She gestured down a hallway behind her. "Come, I'll fill you all in. I've just sent a few teams in to get some more boots on the ground in Amsterdam, The Hague, and Utrecht, which have the highest populations of humans and supernaturals affected," she said over her shoulder, not slowing the brisk pace she'd picked up when we'd begun walking. She stopped outside an open door and gestured toward us to go ahead. The large meeting room was filled with about thirty Ischyra.

"Everyone!" Dona barked, then waited for the room to fall silent to begin speaking again. "Reinforcements from Olympus have just arrived. We're going to brief them as quickly as possible, then we need to get on the ground. Tomas, what's the latest?" she asked a wiry blond man who stood in front of a map, holding a sheath of papers.

He turned and gave us a brief nod in greeting. "We've just received updated reports that nearly two million homes and businesses are without power, and about half of those buildings are inaccessible due to the floodwaters. Ischyra in the affected areas have been working with the humans to rescue as many as possible, but even with our powers, the water is difficult to work against. Water and wind users have managed to hold it back in several areas, but it's slow-going."

I looked over the large map of the Netherlands and examined the red sections that indicated high levels of flooding. "Waterway control systems have all failed, then?"

"Some." Tomas tapped his finger to a large, U-shaped body of water. "There are several structures in the northern region that have burst, but this enclosure dam here—" he tapped a long, thin line that stretched across the top of the lake, separating it from the sea, "—formed the lake you see... here." He brought his finger down and touched another line further south on the lake that bisected the body of water. "When that dam burst, sea water began to pour through, the force of which led to the locks on the southern dam to fail."

Epimetheus made a U-motion with his finger. "So all of the cities along the banks have been flooded?"

Tomas nodded. "Quite heavily. Most of the outlying ones as well. A good portion of the country is below sea level, so the floodwaters have plenty of room to settle."

"Have you already called in other Elementals?" I asked. "Water, wind, earth?"

Dona nodded. "About a hundred are on their way from various parts of the world."

"Alright. Poseidon and his forces are spreading out, too, so they'll be able to help with the rescue missions." I looked at the map again. "Where do you suggest we head first?"

"That depends on what you're looking for," Dona said. "Are you attempting to locate those responsible?"

"And potentially prevent any secondary attacks," I replied.

"Then I would suggest starting at the lower dam. Despite the breach, it's still holding back a large portion of the seawater that flooded the lake when the closure dike up north burst. Flooding has been significant, but damage will be irreparable if the full force of the North Sea takes over that body of water."

"You've sent in units to search for potential survivors in the hardest hit areas?" I asked.

Dona gave a sharp nod. "Yes, and we've got several Remotes working from here, as well," she added, referring to the Ischyra who had the ability to look at any place on Earth without leaving their current position.

After radioing to the Ischyra who were on-site at the dam, she gave us coordinates for a rescue craft for us to teleport to.

When we arrived on the boat, the damage to the dam was immediately evident. Where a lock had once been was now a giant, gaping hole in the concrete, the gates ripped clean off, allowing water from the north to rush through the dam, unchecked. The local Liaison, Jerreth, stood on deck with a portly human who I assumed was one of the human contractors who had a hand in the dike's maintenance

The human held out a hand to shake mine. "Noah Van Alst, head of maintenance.

"Good to meet you. Can either of you tell me how this happened?" I asked.

"We don't know," Jerreth replied. "That water alone wouldn't have been strong enough to take the lock gates off."

"River gods would, though. Fucking Potamoi," Eris muttered. Frowning, she walked to the edge of the boat and looked down. "Question!" she called. "What is this water used for?"

"Recreation, fishing," Noah replied. "In times of lower than normal precipitation, the fresh water in the lake is used to keep the ground in the surrounding regions wet."

She dipped her finger in the water and touched it to her tongue, then made a foul face and spat. "Can you bring us closer to the breach? Right up against it if possible."

Noah motioned to the captain, who began steering the boat closer to the wall.

"Can one of you guys keep me from falling in?" she asked, peering up at the walls. She waited for Epimetheus to get hold of her belt, then leaned over until her fingers brushed up against the grimy wall.

"What is it?" I called.

"We've got a bigger problem on our hands," she said, turning to look at me. She held up her finger, which was coated in black. "Poison. The same stuff they've been using to poison the crops." She gestured toward the opposite side of the breach, at the walls that were visibly coated with the same black that was on her fingers. "It's all over the place."

My heart sank.

"This is a large body of water," Epimetheus said. "Even in high quantities, the poison would be incredibly diluted."

"Maybe. Just in case, get the shore waters tested," I told the Ischyra. "Your headquarters will have a sample of the poison that was used on crops in other areas of the world. Use that, compare it to samples of water from towns and cities around the lake. Once you've fully assessed the level of contamination, we'll know better how to proceed."

Jerreth nodded. "Right away." He pulled a radio from his waist and walked a few feet away to report to his commander.

I turned back to Noah. "The poison will need to be cleaned off the dam before the dam can be repaired. Once that's done, how long will it take to fix the damage?"

His face scrunched as he eyed the hole. "Temporarily? Days. Permanently? Months."

"Get going on that, then. We'll handle things on our end." I turned to Jerreth, waving him over. "What are your forces doing in the rest of the area?"

"Assisting with evacuations and scouring the region for any sign of perpetrators," he replied.

"Alright. Keep that up and report with any updates. We'll bring the information about the poison back to Zeus and see how we can go about starting a cleanup. In the meantime, we'll be sending back an antidote that you can have your Earth users replicate. If anyone falls ill, give it to them."

Jerreth gave a sharp nod. "Understood. We appreciate you coming in."

I glanced at the others. "Let's head back."

I LEFT Eris and Epimetheus with orders to head up the hunt for the creatures who'd damaged the waterways. Artemis was sending in a team of archers, and in addition to the one hundred Ischyra already being sent, Apollo sent an extra four hundred to help with the cleanup once the antidote for the poison arrived. By the time I returned to Olympus, Ares was the only one to have returned from his trip to assess damage. As with the Netherlands, water containment structures in a half-dozen spots in Russia had been tampered with. The reports coming back from Athena, Artemis, and several other team leaders Zeus had dispatched all had commonalities— dams, levees, and bridges had been destroyed in about two dozen places around the world, some causing minor damage, others, more major.

In all cases, the water had been poisoned.

"It's only freshwater that's been poisoned?" Zeus confirmed.

"It is," Ares confirmed. "We've sent word to have the water in each area tested and alert the humans in the surrounding areas to avoid water sports and drinking tap water for the time being."

"Evacuation might be better," I murmured, looking at the dark gray markers that indicated the sudden global appearance of the Potamoi, the freshwater gods that fell under Oceanus' rule.

"Well, that's something, I suppose," Zeus grumbled as he looked at the map, took note of the additional markers showing an increased presence of empousa and crocotta. "Let's just hope they used up the bulk of whatever stores of poison they had left on that water," he added.

"I think we need to get back to Earth," Ares said. "All of us. Things have escalated significantly in the last two days. Numbers on their side have increased more than we'd anticipated."

Zeus looked up at Ares. "What numbers are we looking at now?"

"Empousa have spread themselves out over the southern United States, crocotta have been sighted in three times as many places as Artemis initially reported, all three thousand Potamoi are out in full force, and the Naiads also seem to have joined the fray. Artemis has taken her archers, and Persephone has taken her trackers out to hunt in the areas where the water was tampered with. I told them to bring back a few prisoners for questioning. Nathaniel and I already instructed Eris and Enyo to begin field interrogations. The Centaurs and Satyrs have gone to assist in the more heavily wooded areas and mountainous regions."

"Has there been any success?" Zeus asked.

"Some. At last count, nearly seven hundred of the Potamoi have been put down. Enyo is currently questioning a few who were pulled aside, so I'm hoping we'll be able to get more from her. Ischyra have reported significant losses of empousa and crocotta in a handful of areas, but they seem to be popping up in just as many."

"They're back to having us chase our tails," I said. "How many human lives have been lost?"

"I've spoken to the continental human representatives briefly over the last few hours. Globally, human casualties resulting from attack by Cronus' forces are hovering around ten thousand."

Zeus grimaced. "Not horrible, considering, but still too many. And ours?"

"We've lost five hundred Ischyra thus far," Ares replied wearily. "About double that are currently recovering from godsbane wounds. One hundred fifty forest creatures, and half a dozen deities and demigods. In addition, five more witches have gone missing. We're assuming Cronus has taken them to replace the ones Josh returned."

Zeus braced his hands on the table, his fingers curling around the edge as rage twisted his features.

"Has Hephaestus gotten those weapons out yet?" I asked him.

He nodded. "He has."

"Currently, we've only enough to arm the deities," Ares said.

I frowned. "Wouldn't it make more sense to give the more vulnerable fighters the deadlier weapons?" I asked. "We can defend ourselves well enough without them."

"Agreed," Zeus said. "At the very least, let's split them up. Divvy up two-thirds of the blades to the Ischyra. The rest go to the deities whose powers don't lend well to combat." He looked at me expectantly. "Dionysus said he was helping Chiron and those Ischyra look into potential sources of information for Josh. Has there been any word?"

"None yet," I told him. "But now that Chiron's got more assistance, I'm sure they'll be able to come up with something."

Zeus grunted, his doubt about sharing the archival information of Olympus with non-residents quite apparent.

"Actually, there was something I wanted to discuss with you," I said, glancing at Ares, then back at Zeus. "What do you think about bringing on the guardians?"

Zeus stood up straight and frowned. "Humans?"

"Why not? We've developed their training regimen. They're strong fighters."

"None of whom have ever been tested in battle," Ares said dubiously.

Resigned, I looked at my father and awaited the inevitable refusal.

"Do it," Zeus ordered, surprising me and my brother both. "Contact the Liaisons and the lead guardians. I'm not going to pretend to like it, and I would far prefer to relegate them to only training Ischyra," he said when Ares shook his head. "We're at war. There is no such thing as too many allies."

"Infantry or humanitarian aid, only," Ares stated reluctantly. "If we go into full-on battle, the humans are the not to be on the front lines or the rear guard. They need to be off the battlefield entirely until absolutely necessary."

Zeus nodded. "For now. Send the guardians in to replace the Ischyra that have been called to help with cleanup operations for the contaminated water. Put the soldiers on combat duty. We don't need to throw the guardians into the fray unless absolutely necessary."

"I'll head out now, then," I paused, unsure I wanted to push my luck when he seemed to be in an amiable mood. "I'm going to bring John Avery if that's alright."

Zeus narrowed his eyes and stared at me, indecision clear on his face. Finally, he nodded his assent. "It may help to have one of their own vouching for us."

I was about to leave, when the door opened, and Hecate walked in. "I've got good news," she announced. "The Fates have allowed Tessa an audience."

I sighed with relief. I'd expected it to take far longer for them to track down the Fates, but if Tessa had managed to get an audience so quickly, hopefully she'd be able to get something useful from them.

I angled my head and narrowed my eyes. "I thought you were with her?"

Hecate's jaw tensed. "I was. Tessa got an audience with them. I did not."

"Why?" Zeus asked.

She sighed. "I would imagine it has something to do with how badly I've bungled the situation with Tessa."

"Well, regardless, Tessa is with them now, so let's just hope she brings back something we can use," Zeus said, then turned to me and gave me a brief nod. "Go get the guardians on board and report back as soon as you have their cooperation."

"You're bringing the guardians in to fight?" Hecate asked. "That's—"

"Unprecedented?" Ares said, turning back to Zeus. "You're aware this violates agreements we have with them, correct? When they're brought on, it's explicitly stated that they will not be asked to fight, only teach."

Zeus ran a hand roughly over his beard. "Yes, well, times change. and now we have need of them. I won't break the agreements we have with them by force, but Nathaniel, I hope you'll make it abundantly clear how bad this situation has gotten."

"Of course," I said. "I'll check in once we've spoken with them all."

After making the trek back through the palace, I teleported home, fully expecting to find half of my liquor cabinet emptied by Chiron and Dionysus. So I was surprised when I walked in and found all of them silently poring over old books and documents. The dining table that had just held a full family dinner days before was now covered in old, crumbling books and documents, scrolls, and a few physical artifacts.

"Find anything?" I asked, shutting the door behind me.

Nearly all of them jumped at the sound of my voice.

"Geez, warn a girl next time," Mary muttered, touching her hard to her chest.

I gave her an amused look. "Apologies." I glanced at Dionysus, who was sitting beside her. "I'm surprised you don't have a bottle in hand."

He glowered in Chiron's direction.

"No. Wine." Chiron didn't look up from the book he was thumbing through. "If I have to say it again, I'm going to toss something at that pretty head of yours."

Yana, Mary, and Anette all looked to be forcing back smiles.

'How's she doing?' I asked Dionysus, surprised and happy to see Mary's eyes a bit brighter than they were last night.

'Touch and go, really. I took her down to Olympia earlier, got some coffee and fresh air.' He flipped another page in the book he was holding and started running a finger down the edge. "Nathaniel, what do you know about woodworking?"

"Not enough to want to help," I replied with a grin. "I'm actually here for John."

John looked up, confused. "You are?"

I nodded. "I've spoken with Zeus about bringing the guardians on board. He's in agreement. I'm getting ready to make the rounds, visit the continental leads and Liaisons. I'd like you to come if you're up for it."

"Thank the gods," he muttered, slamming the book shut. He stood and stretched his arms. "I'm always one to help, but this..." he waved an arm over the mess on the table. "I've never been good at this part."

"Zeus really went for it?" Chiron asked me. "I never thought he would."

"Attacks have picked up significantly, and more witches have gone missing." I sighed and raked a hand through my hair. "We need more allies."

"But they're so..." Anette bit her lip and looked sheepishly at the Averys.

"Breakable?" Analise gave her a knowing smile. "But it's still our world. We teach you all how to defend it. We should get the chance to do the same even if we don't make it through the other side."

John leaned down and gave her a soft kiss, then brushed a thumb over her cheek and smiled. "I'll be back soon."

She held his hand against her cheek for a moment, and I thought I saw her eyes shine with unshed tears. "Be safe." Shooting a pointed look at me. "You'd better keep him safe."

"I will. We'll check in as soon as we get back."

Mary stood to face John, concern clouding her features. "Are you sure?" she asked quietly.

He opened his arms and pulled her in for a hug. "Absolutely."

44

TESSA

I landed on my rear on a hard, rocky cliff side moments after the Fates sent me to... wherever it was they sent me. Groaning at my stinging tailbone, I rolled onto my side and opened my eyes, trying to figure out where I was.

A wide stretch of grass led up a soft incline from the cliff ledge where I sat, stopping a few feet away at the start of a forest. The chilly wind and scenery told me I was back on Olympus, although I had no idea *where*.

Sitting up, I turned to face the cliffside. I scanned the scenery in front of me, beneath me, and above, looking for any kind of feature in the landscape that might be familiar. What I saw made my heart both leap and plummet.

The view from where I sat was the Olympic range, but from the cliff I sat on, I could very clearly see a jagged, rocky, and very familiar outcropping directly below me. It was large, about the size of a football field and slightly different from the last time I'd seen it. The edges had crumbled, making it quite a bit smaller than it had been, and the bushes that had once clung to the side of the cliff were long dead. But I knew it as sure as I knew myself. It was one of the few places Atlas had trained me as a girl.

I was home.

Home.

My heart leapt in the same moment disappointment struck. This had been home to me for seven hundred years. Now it was just another part of the mountain that had been overtaken by nature.

Heart pounding, I spun around and faced the forest behind me. It was new, unfamiliar, the complete opposite of the wide, sweeping lawn that had separated our house from the edge of the cliff way back then.

Without hesitating, I ran into the dense trees, struggling to orient myself as I went. I'd only been in the forest for about thirty seconds before I skidded to a halt in front of the three Fates, who were sitting on the ground around a small heap of stone.

The only remnants of the house I'd been raised in.

"Why—you brought me home," I said.

"We did," Lachesis replied. "It's where the heart is, after all."

"I always loved coming home after a long stretch away," Atropos said wistfully. "Traveling the globe is so fun, but there's just no place like home."

But this wasn't really home. There was nothing left here. The house had been destroyed so long ago that a forest had completely overtaken the swath of grass that had surrounded it. Nothing about this place was familiar, but I also had a strong urge to ask what had been done with everything that had once been inside.

At the same time, it didn't matter. The gifts my father, brothers, and Hades bought me were just trinkets, most of which were attached to feelings of remorse, regret, or deceit. I'd enjoyed the baubles and pretty dresses and beautifully illuminated books at the time, but now I knew they were all little more than means of appeasement or, in my father's case, a way to ensure I remained loyal.

"The universe began, not with a bang, but with a whimper," Lachesis said.

Atropos gave her a chastising look. "That's not how the expression goes, sister."

"But it's just as accurate," Clotho countered. "And besides, saying the world will end with a whimper is quite melancholy, don't you think?" She huffed. "Wouldn't we all want to go out with a bang?"

"The world—" I had barely had time to be shocked that she was talking about the world ending when reason kicked in and told me she wouldn't state something like that so explicitly. "That was in a poem, right?"

"It was. Long ago, in human years. Just yesterday to us." Lachesis frowned, considering. "Not you, though."

"No, not me," I said with a sigh.

"Now for your lesson." Lachesis shifted so she was sitting cross legged and smiled. "I've always loved teaching."

Gingerly, I sat down beside them, putting the meager remains of my childhood home at my back. Maybe I would come back here someday and further grieve what I'd lost, or maybe I'd just toss the last remains over the edge and be done with it all. Maybe even both. Not today, though.

"What we're going to give you is information that has already been disseminated," Clotho said. "Some more easily found than others, as your fellow Olympians are currently discovering. It's just history. This changes *nothing,* and you're better off just listening."

There was no mistaking the warning her words carried, so I just nodded. "Understood."

"She'd like to hear of our past, too," Lachesis said primly. "We're quite interesting."

Atropos made a "hmm" of agreement. "True, but not in full today, sister."

Clotho cleared her throat and looked at each of us, waiting until she had our attention. Atropos, Lachesis, and I all sat around her, watching like three children at storytime, obediently waiting for her to start her story.

"When our universe was in its infancy, opposites fought against one another, canceling each other out. Pure disharmony. For Chaos to create worlds, there had to be limits to what he could do. He had the ability to balance between light and dark, hot and cold, life and death, but after creating that balance, he was forbidden from destroying it. He was given one chance to create what he saw as the perfect world, a world of harmony, of all parts working together as one, instead of a meaningless pile of bits and pieces."

"Forbidden by—?" Immediately, I clamped a hand over my mouth.

Clotho arched a brow, but it was Atropos who answered. "Beings far older than you or I spoke to him, girl. Far older than my dear mother, older than Chaos, himself. He may be the Creator of *our* universe, but he is not the Creator of all things. The faces of those who are will never be seen by our eyes, at least not in our lifetime."

"So what Chiron said was accurate, then? That Chaos was given permission to bring order to the universe?"

Clotho nodded. "When Chaos began to create life, Nature required a give-and-take, which was how Nyx came to bear us. When we were created, we were given knowledge of the rules of Nature. There exists a system of checks and balances, so to speak. Each time Chaos created something, he had to give a bit of himself over to his creation to fill it with life, so prior to bringing something into being, it had to be perfect. Energy that once existed within him is what fuels every aspect of life in this universe, from the saplings to the gods. That energy cycles from one thing to another, tree to animal, land to sea, earth to sky. If a species goes extinct, the energy used to fuel that species gets returned to the Creator, who could then choose how and when to divert that energy. In the case of Chaos, seeing that his machine was humming along nicely, he funneled that energy back into the Earth to fuel the evolution of species on Earth. He left it unchecked."

My brow shot up in surprise, but the look on her face kept me from voicing my shock that he'd essentially kicked his baby universe out of the nest to see if it could fly, not considering what might happen if it crashed.

"At the behest of *his* maker, we were created not long after he began, as keepers of order and energy. And, of course, destiny. Our main purpose was to ensure Chaos would never be tempted to destroy what he created. If Chaos chooses to eliminate one of his species with his own two hands, whatever energy of his that had been in that being would come to us and be lost to him forever. We created the witches as the holders of that power, the primordial power that so many of them have. The more primordial witches that exist, the less power he has. It's why there are so few."

"I thought that power came from the other primordial deities?"

"Some," Clotho allowed. "But not all. In most cases, the most powerful witches have the power he forfeited in his early attempts to destroy what he made."

"But when one door closes, another opens," Lachesis said quietly.

"He found a loophole," Atropos said. "Which I'm certain you've worked out by now."

"The war," I murmured.

Clotho nodded slowly. "Since he'd only be tangentially responsible for any large-scale deaths, not much more than an instigator, really, there would be very little blood on his hands at the end of this war."

Anger surged in me. I wanted to snap at them, lash out for not warning us, not giving us the chance to nip the stupid rebellion in the bud. Fates or not, they were talking about their existence just as much as mine. If Josh wanted all the deities to be dead, they would certainly fall on that list, considering they essentially controlled how he used his power.

Instead, I aimed my energy at steadying my breathing and cooling my temper.

"Was there a reason you couldn't tell us? This seems like it would be outside the bounds of what you normally keep under wraps."

"We are the holders of destiny, but we do not control it," Lachesis said patiently. "That which created us gives us knowledge of what a creature's lifeline will look like, but they gave us the inability to speak of it. Just as Chaos cannot disrupt the flow of energy in the universe, we cannot disrupt the flow of destiny. Our own lifelines were woven for us just as yours was for you."

"We've tried," Clotho said calmly. "Many times. When I saw your lifeline, where it would lead you, I tried to re-spin the story I'd already spun, prevent Hecate from making the choice to send you into the Void."

"It's nice to know you cared, I suppose," I muttered.

"I didn't," she said simply. "Not about your personal outcome, but that of the rest of the world. Believe me, Tessa, if I could have unmade you, I would have. Instead, we had to ensure your return."

"Oh. Wow. Okay." Even though she'd been clear that unmaking me wasn't an option, the fact that she'd had no compunctions about trying was more than a bit unsettling. "Does that mean my soul wasn't actually decaying in the Void?"

"More or less."

"Please don't take what my sister says personally," Atropos said. "But you must know that your presence in the Void, your time there, feeding Chaos details of what had been done to you in your past life, only served to fuel his desire to find a way to unmake his creations. Your anger and feelings of betrayal strengthened his conviction to start over, even if it was unintentional. Please don't blame yourself!" she said quickly, holding up a hand when she saw the look on my face. "He'd already planned to try. You simply gave his ideas agency."

"Hecate never would have been able to recall your soul if Chaos did not want you to return," Clotho said. "When we told her it was time for you to be remade... we knew he would ensure your safe passage to our dimension."

"Yes, he said he sent me back," I replied, recalling his words from before. "But couldn't you—"

"—have instructed Hecate not to retrieve you?" Clotho shook her head. "We are slaves to destiny, just like you. And... Hecate was our loophole."

"She put you on the track on which you've found yourself," Lachesis said, gesturing toward the ground in front of me. "Placed your feet *just* where they needed to be."

Standing, I turned and paced away, processing all they'd just told me. The thought of a power even higher than Josh was far too big to wrap my head around at the moment, so I focused on the smaller things. He couldn't facilitate the extinction of a species, which seemed to be what he wanted from the gods, for whatever reason. Humans, too, based on the amount of attacks that had been launched on regions that held no deities at all.

Based on all they said, a true death for Josh wasn't in the cards. But at his core, he was built of energy. Far more than any other being known to exist, but energy just the same. So the answer had to lie there.

"There was one other thing I wanted to speak with you about," I said carefully, knowing my time was almost up. "I was hoping I might be able to speak with one of the primordial deities who are still alive."

Clotho narrowed her eyes. "You mean, you want to speak with our mother."

"She's one of the first generation of deities he created and one of the few who hasn't chosen to pass into the afterlife. I'm hoping she might be able to provide information that could give us further insight into Josh—Chaos'—history. I need to find his weaknesses, and I know you can't tell me what those are."

Atropos gave me a speculative look. "What makes you believe she would agree, even if we tried?"

I shrugged. "Nothing. I know absolutely nothing about her aside from the fact that she's one of the oldest beings in existence." I sighed. "So, I guess hope is what makes me think she'll see me."

Clotho gave me a single nod. "We will speak with her. I cannot make any promises as to what her choice will be. Nyx enjoys her privacy. Even we haven't seen her in several thousand years."

"I appreciate the attempt," I told her with a smile. "More than you know."

"There isn't any more we can tell you," Lachesis said. "Your friends are on the right track, though. Go back to them, tell them to stay the course. There may be miles to go before they sleep, but they should have all you need soon enough."

"We'll send word once we have a response from Nyx," Atropos said.

I took a deep breath and closed my eyes, trying very hard not to show them how disappointed I was that they couldn't, or wouldn't, give me more. I could only pray that Nyx, Night incarnate, would be willing to help. "Thank you."

Clotho gave me a small nod. "We wish you the best of luck."

45

NATHANIEL

The first place John and I went was Philadelphia, the home of Jerome Atwood, the lead guardian for the Northeastern United States. With the exception of crop poisonings in New Jersey, the region had seen little in the way of supernatural activity in recent weeks, so it seemed the best place to start.

Also, Jerome was an old friend of John's, and John seemed to think it would take little to no convincing to get Jerome on board.

"Jerome, thank you for seeing us," I said, reaching out and shaking his hand when he answered the door.

"Of course." The lanky Ischyra turned to John and gave his hand a quick shake in welcome. "John Avery, as I live and breathe! Good to see you!"

"Likewise," John said, grinning. "I wish it were under better circumstances."

Jerome waved us in, then led us toward a large sitting room. "Come sit down. If you're here visiting me, things must've gotten bad, but let's talk over a cup of coffee, shall we?" He grinned. "I haven't gotten my third cup in yet."

I smiled. "I'll take water if you've got it. I've never had a taste for coffee."

He *tsked* and shook his head but disappeared into the kitchen and returned a moment later with two mugs of coffee in his hands and a bottle of water tucked under his arm.

"So, what can I do for you gentlemen?" he asked once we'd gotten settled.

I glanced at John and gave him a small nod.

He took a deep breath, then leaned forward and rested his elbows on his knees. "Things with this rebellion have taken a turn, Jerome, and I think it's time to consider that thing we talked about a few years back."

Arching a brow, I slid him an incredulous look and noticed he was studiously avoiding my gaze.

Clever man.

Jerome glanced at me nervously, then let out a short sigh. "That bad, then?"

John gave him a grim nod. "That bad."

"Have you spoken to the others?" Jerome asked. "Callie, Julius, Meg?"

"You're our first stop," I told him. I gave them both an amused look. "I'm guessing this topic has come up before now?"

"It has," John confirmed, not looking the least bit abashed. "It wasn't ever something we planned to bring up unless it became apparent you could use the aid."

"I suppose that will make the job of convincing the others fairly easy, then?" I asked.

Jerome bobbed his head back and forth, then grimaced. "Some will be easier to convince than others. Most of the guardians currently raising Ischyra are unlikely to want to leave their posts."

"They may not have a choice," John countered.

I held up a hand when Jerome's face shifted toward indignant. "There's always a choice. The Elders have sworn agreements not to force the guardians into war." I let my hand fall into my lap. "That said, if the lead guardian in a region orders them to enter a fight, they would have to."

Jerome nodded slowly. "What exactly would you expect us to do?

Understand, you have my full support, and I will help you bring on as many as I can. But I need to bring my people information, not just orders."

"A number of waterways around the world have recently been attacked, the water poisoned, the surrounding communities put in danger. They need protection, help with water cleanup, oversight of recovery efforts," I explained. "Currently, your assignments would center on cleanup, recovery, rebuilding, that type of thing. Fighting will be a last resort."

Jerome drummed his fingers on the arm of his sofa and sipped his coffee. "So humanitarian aid, then?"

"Essentially," I replied.

"And healers?"

"A number of healers will be left at each site to help the wounded and to be on hand if things go sideways," I assured him. "In addition, a handful of Ischyra with battle magic will also remain behind. We have no intention of leaving any region defenseless, but we would like to put the bulk of our soldiers in the field, if possible. This fight will eventually come to a head, and we'd prefer the mortals be left out as much as possible."

"Alright. I can work with that. My region will be on board, and I can nearly guarantee the Northwest, southeastern Canada, and the Southeastern US will be willing as well. If you need me to get on the phone, we can touch base with the rest of the North American leads, get them on board."

"That would be incredibly helpful, Jerome."

He set his coffee down on the end table and stood. "Not to rush you out, but if I'm going to get things moving for you, I'll need to get going on it now."

John and I stood. "We'll check in a bit later," John told him. "Do what you can, get the others to do the same. Emphasize that we're not asking them to fight, just help."

Jerome pulled John in for a one-armed hug and patted him on the back. "I never thought I'd see the day our drunken banter came to fruition."

John chuckled and stepped back. "The surprises keep coming these days, it seems. We'll talk soon."

Once we stepped outside, I turned and faced John, stopping him mid-step. "The others?"

He let out a resigned sigh. "One night a few years back, after the last generation of Ischyra was sent to Olympus, a group of us got together. One thing led to another, and we ended up talking about how Olympus might be missing out on using a valuable tool when it came to the guardians once their charges had left the nest."

My eyebrows shot up. "Does Tessa know?"

He shook his head. "It was a somewhat radical idea, and we didn't want to bias her in any way. Our job was to train her, raise her as our own, and make her a strong fighter who made her own choices. And at the time, there was no need for us to even be considered in that capacity."

I wondered what Tessa would think, knowing how strongly her guardians felt about being put into battle.

"So, where to next?" John asked. "Jerome and the others will have the US in hand soon enough."

"South America, then we'll move west. Hopefully we can get this done in the next few hours."

After sending a brief update to Zeus about our discussion with Jerome, I teleported us to Santiago, Chile, home of the lead guardian for the western South American region.

The Chileans took a bit more convincing but were finally swayed when John pointed out that their country was precariously located on an active fault line that could easily become the target of any enemies who could wield any form of elemental magic. He also reminded them that a very large portion of attacks by the crocotta had occurred in South America, so it was to their benefit to help the Ischyra get back to fighting instead of working on cleanup.

All told, sixty of the seventy-five lead guardians had no qualms with assisting us, and most of those were convinced by John with very little help from me. Those who pushed back didn't outright refuse but promised to get back to us with their answer once they convened with representatives from various districts within their regions.

"I'd like to check in with Eris and Epimetheus in the Netherlands," I told John as we left the home of the lead guardian in Wales.

"If it's alright with you, I'd like to head back to the States, reconvene with Jerome and the others," he said.

I agreed, and after returning John to Jerome's house in Philadelphia, I checked in with Epimetheus.

'There have been a few smaller attacks on nearby towns,' he said, 'but we've managed to thwart most of them. Head to the Amsterdam headquarters and I'll fully brief you.'

When I arrived on the steps of the Ischyra headquarters in Amsterdam, I was happy to see that the water had receded a good deal, thanks to the water and wind users that had been sent to assist. Making my way inside, I was greeted by Eris and Epimetheus in the lobby.

The three of us started to walk through the building toward the main conference room.

"Any casualties?" I asked.

"So far, about five hundred human casualties throughout the country, most due to the flooding," Epimetheus told me. I cursed under my breath. "Normally they're well-prepared for widespread flooding, but something like this..." He shook his head. "Fire users, Naiads, and the Potamoi have been destroying smaller towns, and empousa and crocotta have been coming in to take out the stragglers."

"Any response on our side?"

"We've taken out a few hundred Potamoi, several dozen crocotta, and about as many empousa," Eris said. "But the Naiads are being slippery. I've pulled in a few captives for questioning, as well, so we're hoping to get something from them."

"Any news on the status of the water?"

"Water in about thirty towns around the lake has been tested and has come back positive for high concentrations of both hemlock and castor seed," Epimetheus said with a sigh as we reached the conference room. "It's the same poison they were using on the crops."

"What's been done for the locals?" I asked, pausing before going in.

"I had the antidote dispensed to all towns and cities surrounding the lake," he replied. "With orders for the locals to refrain from using tap water until we can be certain the groundwater isn't contaminated, too."

"Alright, good." I jerked my chin toward the door. "Let's head in. I've got some news."

We went into the conference room, a large, sterile-looking space with a single long table stretching almost the entire length of the space that held about thirty chairs, about half of which were filled. A dozen or so Ischyra were scattered around, poring over maps, speaking into radios, and talking amongst themselves.

When Jerreth, the Liaison from earlier, noticed me, he yelled for everyone to be quiet. Once they were all settled, I dove right into the plan to have the guardians join us at each site that was attacked to assist with the cleanup and recovery efforts. At first, I was met with dubious and even annoyed looks.

"Clearly, this is unprecedented," I told them, trying to mask my own annoyance at their reluctance. "The work that's being done here is incredibly important, but we need you all in the field, hunting, tracking, and taking down our enemy. Not all of the guardians have agreed to come on board, but I believe the last few who are holding out will join us. Once I have final numbers, I'll be sending a few dozen here to replace any Ischyra who have magic that is best-suited for combat. Fire, wind, Mentalists, and light, in particular, will be sent out in larger numbers, although we'll be keeping a few of each here for protection, along with most of the water and earth users and any with healing abilities." Raising my brows, I looked around the room, meeting everyone's eyes. "Questions?"

Before anyone could respond, several of the radios in the room began to squawk, quickly followed by calls for help.

"The lake has been attacked!" Jerreth announced.

"Where?" I demanded.

"Shipyard just outside Lelystad," he replied. "It's where the largest cleanup is happening."

"Coordinates?"

He rattled off a few numbers.

"Hands, everyone!" I called above the din. Eris, Epimetheus, and I waited until everyone had connected hands, then teleported them all to the lake.

When we landed, we were met with the sounds of fighting, flashes of fire and electricity, and water that churned with the power of the water gods that had attacked.

"Crocotta," Epimetheus bit out when he saw the pale-skinned creatures who were overrunning the shipyard we'd just landed in. "Bastards."

"Get out there," I ordered. "I'm calling for backup." I glanced at Eris. "Get back to headquarters and keep working on your prisoners. We'll handle this."

She cast a furtive glance at the melee, then nodded and disappeared. Epimetheus shot forward, launching himself into the fray alongside a dozen Ischyra.

On instinct, I called out to Apollo. *'Attack at a boatyard in Lelystad. Get here and help me out.'*

Seconds later, my brother appeared at my side, a ball of blinding light in each hand. He smiled grimly. "We truly need to find a better way to bond," he muttered.

I huffed out a laugh, then sent out my Coercion, slamming it into half a dozen crocotta who were on the docks attempting to incapacitate a group of Ischyra that had been siphoning the poison from the water. The moment the creatures were stunned, Apollo threw his light, disintegrating them on the spot. The Ischyra bolted up the docks onto dry land.

I heard a hissing screech behind me and ducked just before an empousa latched onto my back. Pulling a dagger from my waist, I swung out, sliced through her throat, and tossed her to the ground just before Apollo burned her body to ash. Several more followed, each one ending in the same fashion.

One after another, we and the Ischyra took down the creatures that continued to throw themselves at us, until eventually, the ship-yard was nearly silent.

Suddenly, screams sounded from the docks, followed by the splash of bodies hitting the water. I ran toward the sound and found a half dozen humans thrashing in the water, desperately trying to avoid being pulled under by three Potamoi.

Shit.

'Freeze them,' Apollo ordered. *'Nathaniel, are you up for this?'*

No, I certainly wasn't looking forward to slaughtering deities, no matter what their allegiances might be. But this was war, and they were my enemy.

'Do I have a choice?'

Without waiting for his response, I froze the group of roaring gods, then forced myself into the minds of the humans, momentarily taking away their fear and pain enough that they could swim back to shore where healers waited with antitoxins.

'Are you sure, Nathaniel? It's been quite some time.' He ducked as another crocotta launched itself at us, then tossed back a ball of light and incinerating it.

'It needs to be done, and it'll be faster if I help.'

Aiming all my power toward the still-frozen Potamoi, I reached deep into their minds until I touched their magic, their life force. Seconds later, I felt Apollo's power join my own. I felt their power shrink back, their minds quiver under the pain of our combined power.

'One... two... three!'

With a vicious pull, we yanked the gods' energy from their bodies. Apollo hurled a ball of searing light at the bodies. Seconds later, nothing remained of the three gods but an ugly black smear on the water.

I TRIED VERY hard to shake off the feelings that clung to me after killing three deities. It had to be done. I knew that. But taking lives had never been a thing I relished, not the way some of my relatives did.

Once we got the shipyard cleared of all enemies, Apollo began going around to the injured, healing as needed, while Epimetheus and I scanned the area in search of any stragglers. When we were done, we teleported back to the headquarters in Amsterdam to check in with Eris.

Her prisoner, an empousa who looked like she'd been run over several times with a bulldozer, sat chained to a chair in a small interrogation room. Her stringy hair fell in a dirty curtain around her face, obscuring what might be left of her facial features. Blood dripped down her face, arms, and legs, forming a puddle on the floor around her. Several small lumps were scattered in the blood. Fangs, I realized upon closer inspection.

Disgust at what was in front of me was quickly suppressed by a feeling of relief that I hadn't been the one doing the interrogation this time.

Apollo arched a brow at Eris, who sat on the table in front of the empousa, cleaning her fingernails with her dagger.

"What?" she asked, giving him a wide-eyed look. "You three were taking forever."

I rubbed the bridge of my nose. "Did you at least get anything useful from her?" I frowned and tilted my head to get a better look at the empousa's face. "Is she still alive?"

A quiet, angry hiss rose from the creature, telling me she was still aware.

"I figured I'd wait until you got here to finish her," Eris said, setting her knife down. She stuck her foot out and nudged the empousa. The creature groaned in response, then hissed.

"What have you gotten from her?" I asked, averting my eyes from the mess my sister had made.

"The orders they got from Cronus yesterday were to spread their forces out into as many of the flooded areas as they could and take out anything they came across—human, Ischyra, chipmunk. She doesn't know much about what the other factions are doing, but she *does* know that the Potamoi are out in full-force. All three thousand troops, along with the Naiads."

"Does she have any knowledge of their movements?" Apollo asked.

"Coastal areas only. Once they get the coasts in hand, the empousa were ordered to move inland and start plucking out small cities and towns."

"We can assume the crocotta and any other non-water creatures have gotten the same orders," I said.

Apollo nodded his agreement. "Even still, three thousand Potamoi might be a lot, but not spread across the globe."

"Not by a long shot," Eris agreed. "But if what she says is true and the Naiads have joined up with them, that's another few thousand right there. I'm guessing they're going to focus on the more highly populated regions."

"We're done with her, then?" I asked my sister.

She nodded, then hopped off the table, knife in hand. Before she could go in for the kill, I ripped into the empousa's mind and shred it into nothing but scraps, killing her almost instantly.

"Dammit, Nathaniel!" Eris cried. "Come on!"

I shrugged. "You've had her all day, and we don't have time for you to waste dragging out her death."

"Which you would have," Apollo added.

"I fucking hate you both," she muttered, sheathing her knife angrily. "Palace?"

Apollo nodded, then the three of us teleported back to Olympus to fill Zeus in on all that had happened.

46

TESSA

When I walked into Nate's house, my head spinning from my meeting with the Fates, I was surprised to find everyone still poring over the research Chiron had said he was bringing over nearly ten hours earlier. Chiron and Analise were sitting at the dining room table, but Yana and Anette had spread themselves out on the floor, each sitting cross-legged in the middle of the living room with papers and books spread all around them. Mary had stretched herself out on the sofa holding a book up, a small frown on her face as she read. Her legs were crossed at the ankles and propped against Dionysus' thigh, who sat at the other end of the sofa. His feet were up on the coffee table, his head resting against the back of the couch, and his eyes closed as he tapped rhythmically on her shin with his thumb. A stack of papers sat near Mary's feet, abandoned.

"Productive day?" I asked, causing everyone in the room to jump and Mary to drop the book she'd been holding on her chest.

"Dammit, Tess!" Sitting up, she rubbed at her sternum where the corner of the book had hit. "Knock next time."

I gave her an amused look. "You guys have immortal hearing, and

I wasn't quiet when I came in. It's not my fault you weren't paying attention."

"Tessa, how did it go with the Fates?" Chiron asked, jumping to his feet.

"Good, I think—" I frowned, taking in the occupants one more time. "Where's John?"

"He went with Nate to meet with the lead guardians on Earth," Analise said. She sighed and set down the papers she'd been studying and leaned back in her seat. "Zeus has agreed to let the guardians get involved in the war."

I gave her an incredulous look as my heart plummeted. "And that's what you both want? To fight?"

"Wouldn't you?" was her only answer.

I rubbed my fingers over my eyes and huffed. It was done. My guardians were going to get themselves involved in this war whether I wanted them to or not, knowing full well that they might not come out alive. A fight between humans and supernaturals nearly always led to the death of mortals. It was just the way it worked—the one with the better weapons, the more cunning, usually came out on top.

"So?" Yana peered up at me from her spot in front of the fireplace. "Did you get an audience with the Fates?"

"I did." I sighed, then walked over to the liquor cabinet and poured myself a giant glass of wine. "They were... odd."

"Hey!" Dionysus exclaimed. "Why does Tessa get to drink?" He let out an *oof* sound when Mary kicked his leg.

"Tessa gets to drink because she just spent an hour at the site of her former home getting a history lesson from the Fates," I said dryly. I eyed all the archival materials Chiron had brought over. "And she's not currently handling ancient artifacts."

I took a seat at the opposite end of the sofa and toed off my shoes, then sent out a call to Nate.

'I'm back with info. When will you be home?'

It took a few moments before he answered.

'Leaving the palace now.'

"What happened?" Mary asked.

"I'd rather tell it once," I told her. "Nate's on his way back. Then we'll compile what we have and take it to Zeus."

A few moments later, Nate walked in. I expected to see John at his side, but he was nowhere to be seen. Before I could ask, Analise was on her feet.

"Where's John? Is he alright?"

Nate nodded. "He's fine. He stayed behind to help get the other guardians on board."

"Of course, he did," I murmured.

Nate dropped down on the sofa next to me, his face drawn. Tension radiated off him.

'What's wrong?' I asked.

He slipped his hand into mine and squeezed. *'Later.'*

With a sigh, I set my glass down on the table and rested my forearms on my knees, then I addressed everyone. "So the Fates were potentially helpful, but I think I'll need you guys to help figure out what, if anything, they said might be useful."

Once everyone was paying attention, Dionysus and Mary on the couch, Yana and Anette on the floor, and Chiron and Analise standing behind the couch watching with furrowed brows, I started to recount my experience with the three Fates—from Hecate's explanation of how to handle them, down to their agreement to try and get me an audience with Nyx. When I was done, I looked around the room, hoping at least one person would be on the verge of an *Aha!* moment.

No such luck.

"Okay, so to be clear, I was right?" Dionysus said, holding a hand in the air. "Because I absolutely said he hasn't destroyed the world himself because he doesn't have the ability."

Mary snorted, then shook her head when he shot her a scowl and swatted her foot.

That was still resting in his lap.

I arched a brow at Yana. *'What's that about?'*

'He helps her,' was her only absent response.

Later. I would deal with it later.

I sucked in a slow breath through my nose, then looked at Chiron. "So, thoughts? Ideas? Suggestions for anti-apocalyptic weapons?"

He shook his head. "If anything, I think that's even less likely now. All this talk of energy and the sheer amount he must possess to be able to hold the power of creation... there's no weapon that can contain that much energy."

"We should talk to Hephaestus," Nate suggested. "He might have some insight."

While we waited for Chiron to contact the forger, I looked at Mary. "So did you guys find anything new?"

She smiled wryly. "Well, I'm quite well-versed in the Olympic history of metallurgy."

Chiron gave her an exasperated look. "Weapons and other magical objects are very often made from metal, Mary."

She smiled sweetly. "That doesn't make the subject matter any less dull."

"I'll be sure to tell Hephaestus when he arrives that you don't care for his manner of writing," he replied.

She wrinkled her nose and stuck out her tongue.

Chiron and I shared a quick glance, and I knew he saw what I was seeing. Even though there was still a haunted look in Mary's eyes, and her sadness still hung over her like a cloak, Mary, *my* Mary, my snarky, bitchy best friend, was starting to peek through.

A few minutes later, Hephaestus arrived, still wearing the same forging clothes I'd seen him in previously, now smudged with soot. His red-black hair was shoved back from his face and his eyes were weary as he leaned heavily on his cane.

"Chiron," he said with a nod. "I came as soon as I could, but I don't have much time." Frowning, he looked around the room, as if suddenly realizing we were all there. "There are quite a lot of people here."

"Yes, we've been trying to dig up whatever information we can on Josh," Chiron explained. "It's been a long day, but Tessa's just returned from a visit with the Fates and we were hoping you might have some insight as to what she was told."

Hephaestus gave me a curious look, his eyes kind despite the coarse features of his face. "The Fates spoke to you?"

"They did." I stood and gestured toward the couch. "Come sit down. This won't take long."

He made his way over to the sofa and sat, setting his cane against the seat next to him. "What can I do for you?"

"When I met with the Fates, they talked a lot about energy, about how much Josh has, where it goes when he creates new beings, that kind of thing. The problem is, we have no idea how to go about killing someone with that much power inside them. Even with a living, breathing universe still in existence, thriving off his power, he's still got enough available to him to create entire species, new worlds."

"There is no type of weapon that exists that can extinguish that much energy," Hephaestus said with a shake of his head. "Certainly not with any material or magic I've ever forged with."

"Do you have any thoughts on what type of weapon might need to be used?" Nate asked. "If one did exist?"

Hephaestus pursed his lips and tapped calloused fingers on his thighs. "Not that I can think of at the moment, but can you give me 'til morning? I can mull it over a bit more, go over some resources I have at my home. We're meeting at the palace first thing to discuss what the others may have found, so I might have something for you by then." Standing, he looked around the room at the various unfamiliar faces. "I'm sorry I can't offer more than that just now, but I will do my best."

"Thank you, Hephaestus," Chiron said. "That's all we can ask for."

Once Hephaestus left, Chiron rubbed a hand over his face and sighed, suddenly looking more exhausted than I'd ever seen him. 'I think we've done all we can for today. It's late. Let's get some rest and regroup in the morning." He waved a hand at the research material that was scattered all over the living room and dining room. "Put aside anything that's got information we may want to bring up tomorrow when we meet at the palace and leave the rest."

As everyone stood and stretched out their limbs, Analise walked over to me and wordlessly gave me a hug. Closing my eyes, I wrapped my arms tight around her waist.

"I am so proud of you," she whispered. "So goddamn proud."

My smile wobbled a bit as the emotion in her voice pricked at my heart. "I couldn't have done it without you," I whispered back.

With a watery laugh, she pulled back and met my eyes. "I've seen you these past few days, Tessa. The connections you've formed with your brothers, your new friends, this whole place... that's all you, sweetheart."

"Analise?" Chiron asked as he came to a stop beside me. "Thank you again for your help today. I'm sure this wasn't what you expected to be doing once you came here."

She laughed softly. "To be honest, I didn't know quite what to expect. If I'm helping, though, that's all I care about."

He grinned and gave her a small nod. "I can take you back to the village if you'd like."

After giving me a quick kiss on the cheek, Chiron and Analise teleported down to the village, where I hoped John would be checking in soon. Yana, Mary, and Anette all said their goodnights and headed off to bed, and Dionysus stretched out on the couch with an arm draped over his eyes.

"You staying?" Nate asked him, stretching his arms above his head and yawning.

"She's had a rough day," Dionysus replied, not bothering to open his eyes. "It'll be better if I'm nearby."

Nate and I exchanged a look, then he gave me a questioning frown when I quirked a brow.

'I'll be there in a few,' I told him. *'I want to talk to him first.'*

Once Nate had disappeared into our room, I sat down on the couch next to Dionysus, then nudged his foot with mine. He let his arm drop from his eyes and looked at me curiously.

"What's up?" he asked.

"Dionysus, you know I adore you, right?" I lifted my eyebrows in question.

He gave me a crooked, sleepy grin. "Who wouldn't?"

"That's... kind of my point."

He sat up slowly, his eyes a bit more alert now. "What do you mean?"

"I—look, normally I wouldn't say anything because it's not my business, but Mary's my best friend." I took a deep breath. "I need to know that you're not clinging to her like this—" I gestured toward the couch "—because she's giving you a power fix." I groaned when I saw his confused expression. "You're drawn to people who are miserable, Dionysus, and she's the epitome of unhappy, and now here you are, spending the night in case she needs you."

He cast a glance down the hall toward her room, then looked back at me, his expression looking almost insulted. "No, I am *not* here because of my incessant—and biological, might I add—need to improve the spirits of others, Tessa." I was surprised to hear a bit of annoyance in his tone. "This past week has been horrific for her, and I have the ability to help her get through that without making her forget. Why in all the realms wouldn't I do what I could to help?"

I closed my eyes and scrubbed my hands over my face, recalling I'd done something very similar with Leila. Dionysus was one of the nicest gods I knew and it was incredibly unfair of me to basically accuse him of using Mary. "You're right. I'm sorry. It's just—"

"Ah." He gave me an understanding nod. "You're concerned she's going to develop feelings for me." He shook his head and laughed quietly. "Tessa, if that happens, I can tell you without hesitation that it won't be because of my magic. I'd never allow it."

"I know you would never do that intentionally. Just promise me... if it looks like that's where this new... friendship is going, if it's not what *you* want, don't give her false hope. She's had her heart broken in the past, and with everything that's happened..."

His smile this time was warm. "You know, she's lucky to have you as a friend. I know you'd absolutely kick my ass if that happened." His smile shifted into a dazzling grin. "Which it won't. Now go to bed because I'm beat."

I was still shaking my head when I walked into our bedroom, barely having enough energy to brush my teeth and put my pajamas on. Nate had already gotten in bed by the time I came in. The lights were out, but there was just enough moonlight to see that his eyes were open. Quietly, I climbed in next to him and slid under the covers, then wrapped my arm around his waist and rested my head over his heart.

"Hi," I whispered as he started stroking my hair. I closed my eyes, immediately soothed by the motion.

He shifted his body so he was facing me, and for a moment, we just looked at each other. It was clear we were both beyond worn out after the day we'd had, but there was something keeping me—and possibly him—from wanting to sleep.

"What happened today, Nate?" I asked softly. The tense look he'd worn when he got home still weighed on my mind, because I knew it meant the day had gone badly for him.

"A lot," he said with a sigh. He was quiet for a few seconds, then he closed his eyes. "I killed three gods today."

Empathy rose in me at the sadness on his face. "Potamoi?" I asked.

He nodded. "And don't get me wrong—they deserved it. It's just... back when I would help my father and Hades with traitors, I was never the one who performed the executions, and even then, I only witnessed the execution of one god. The rest were demigods, Ischyra, some other beings. It's something that takes a lot of power and, for someone with a power like mine, is much more... personal, I guess, because you're so closely tied to their power and mind when you pull their energy. It's all there, exposed, with nothing to filter out their thoughts or feelings."

"You felt their pain," I whispered after a moment, trying not to let my horror at that fact show. His eyes went tight, so instead of waiting for him to respond, I put a hand to his cheek and kissed him. "I'm so sorry," I murmured.

He put his hand over mine, holding my palm to his cheek. "I knew this would happen," he said. "When I have to break into a being's mind to destroy them instead of just using a weapon to do it, it's almost impossible not to feel what they're feeling." He sighed. "I'm just... very happy you're here."

I smoothed his hair off his forehead and smiled. "I just want you to be okay."

He gave me another kiss. "I'll be fine, Tessa. I just need to get my mind on something else."

"Like?"

He gave me a crooked smile that didn't quite reach his eyes. "What did you have to talk to my brother about?"

I rolled my eyes. "Like you don't already know."

"I make it a habit not to eavesdrop on private conversations."

I sighed. "Fine. I told him that if he hurt Mary, I'd kick his ass. Well, I guess he deduced the ass-kicking part himself. I may not have been explicit."

Nate looked on the verge of laughter. "Tessa, Dionysus is the last person you need to worry about hurting anyone."

"I know. I guess my mama-bear came out a bit."

He brushed a hand across my cheek. "Do you think it's headed that way?"

I shrugged. "I knew they were friendly before Mary was taken. After last night, getting locked up with her like he did, I don't know... It's certainly not something I'm going to bring up with Mary now, not when he's clearly helping her more than any of us can, but I'm worried she'll end up getting hurt."

"It wouldn't be the worst thing, you know," he said softly, sliding closer. "We could double date," he teased.

I brushed my lips over his. "I suppose you're right, but..."

He slid his hand up the back of my shirt and pulled me against him. "Can I suggest something without you getting angry?"

I narrowed my eyes, suddenly very distracted by how close he was. "Maybe."

"I think..." He brushed a strand of hair off my forehead and touched his lips to mine, "you should let it be."

Before I could tell him I absolutely would *not* do that, his mouth was on mine, his lips molding to my own and pulsing enough emotion through me to send all thoughts of anyone who wasn't me or him skittering away.

He rolled onto his back, pulling me with him to straddle his hips. Our conversation forgotten, I kissed him furiously, my fingers gripping his hair as though this were the last time we'd ever have this chance.

I pulled back long enough to slip my shirt over my head and drop it to the floor, then I gave a startled yelp and giggled as he flipped me onto my back.

'*I want you to do something for me,*' he whispered as he settled on top of me, drawing my legs around his waist. The weight and warmth of him was nearly consuming.

I sucked in a breath as he began kissing my neck, then my collar bone. '*What's that?*'

'*Open yourself to me.*'

A thrill ran through me at what his words implied.

He wanted to feel me, all of me, while we made love.

I ran my eyes over his face, taking in every feature. Sharing my mind with his like that, opening fully, giving him access to everything that was there, was a true test of trust and the ultimate expression of our feelings for each other.

Yes, that was something I could and would give him.

'*Have you ever—*'

He shook his head. '*Never.*'

'*Only if you do the same. I want to feel what you feel.*'

Smiling softly, he dipped his head down and kissed me gently. There was a quiet touch of lips, the soft brush of tongues, and then he let his shields fall. I felt everything inside him that made him who he was—his love, compassion, and goodness—brush my mind, seeking permission to enter.

I dropped my own walls, allowing him to settle his consciousness with mine. It was different than the other times he'd entered my mind. This time it was soft as a kiss and filled with pleasure.

Mine. His. Ours, all wrapped together as one. I felt the weight of his feelings for me, heard it clear as a bell as we moved together in the darkness. It flowed through my mind like water, touching every corner, filling me with his love and devotion.

In all the years I'd lived, not a moment existed that was more perfect than this.

And that right there, that perfection, that deep, searing love that humans and gods were capable of giving one another, was *exactly* what I was going to fight for.

SEVERAL HOURS LATER, I was wide awake, unable to sleep. My mind wouldn't stop turning over everything the Fates had told me.

In particular, Lachesis' slightly erratic way of speaking.

If one advances confidently... he will meet with a success unexpected.

It *had* to mean something. All of the random things Lachesis said... Hecate told me to pay attention.

The only true wisdom is knowing you know nothing.

Irritated, I sat up and swung my legs over the side of the bed, annoyed that her fortune-cookie clues were so incredibly unhelpful.

Home is where the heart is.

Miles to go before we sleep.

The bed shifted behind me, and a moment later, Nate's hands slid around my waist. "What's wrong?" he whispered.

I leaned into him and sighed. "A lot of what the Fates said was crystal clear, but almost *all* of what Lachesis said was just... odd."

"How so?" he asked.

"She spoke almost entirely in inspirational quotes. It was... bizarre."

"Hmm. What did she say?"

"Um... something by Thoreau, about advancing confidently. Another about the world ending with a whimper, and 'miles to go' and something by Socrates—'the only true wisdom is knowing you know nothing.'"

He chuckled and rested his chin on my shoulder. "Well, I don't know about the first few, but I can tell you that the Socrates one has a few flaws."

"Which are?"

"There's no real proof he actually said it, for one. Anything you see that's attributed to him was written by one of his contemporaries."

"But it seemed like she knew him," I said, frowning. "And she's a Fate, so I kind of took her word for it."

"She could be right, but if she's as mercurial as you say, it's more likely she was leading you toward something else, don't you think?"

I bit my lip, turning over all they'd said, then looked back at him. "Did you know him?"

He shook his head. "No, not personally. He was a wonderful teacher, from what I've been told."

"What was so great about him?"

"He was very... open-minded about things, like social status, gender, class."

"That's why they killed him?"

"No, they said he denied the gods of the state and corrupted the young," Nate replied.

I frowned. "Is that true?"

"I don't believe so. If he corrupted anything, it was the status quo, which isn't always a bad thing."

I tapped my fingers against his thoughtfully.

Perhaps Lachesis was just giving me some words of wisdom, but it was more likely she was directing me toward something specific. It didn't make sense, as least to me, that she would attribute words to a man who may not have actually said them, but at the same time, it was quite possible she actually heard those words spoken.

The only true wisdom is knowing you know nothing.

Socrates, a man convicted of crimes he may not have committed, who went against the status quo and what was considered socially acceptable.

Slowly, I started to piece things together, until an idea began to form in my mind. One that went against the norm. One that I would've considered sooner if I hadn't let what I thought I knew get in the way of my better judgment, had I not let my prior knowledge hinder me.

Nate kissed the side of my head. "What's going on up here?" he asked quietly.

"Potentially bad ideas," I said ruefully.

"Such as?"

I turned and faced him, then took a deep breath. "I think I need to go talk to Scylla."

He arched a brow. "About?"

"Going against the status quo."

47

MARY

First thing the next morning, I was informed that my presence was expected—*not* requested—at the meeting at the palace.

"You hold valuable knowledge, Mary," Apollo said somewhat impatiently. "I believe my father has moved past questioning whether you might pose a threat, but you still need to be present if anyone decides to question our accounts of what your mind contains." He shot look at Nate, who huffed out a sigh. "Athena will be here shortly to look through your memories so she can provide additional insight into what you experienced."

"Is that really necessary?" Dionysus asked. "Everyone on this damn mountain has heard what she saw, most of us several times," he added with a grumble.

"No, it's fine," I told him. I'd resigned myself to this happening since Zeus' wild overreaction the night I'd returned. As much as I despised the thought of anyone else being in my head, if it had to be anyone, I didn't mind it being Athena. Aside from being a general for Zeus' army, she was my friend. She was no Tessa, but I trusted her not to do anything that might hurt me.

There was a brief knock, then the goddess in question walked in. She gave me a sympathetic smile.

"Don't worry, Mary. This will be quick, and if you'd like, Nathaniel can block you from seeing what I pull forward."

That offer was more than a little tempting. I'd been replaying the memories over and over since I'd gotten them back. Watching them play out in full technicolor wasn't something I was super keen on doing.

But I also wasn't a wimp, so I shook my head. "I'm not going to shy away from those memories. If anything, replaying them might help me be more helpful."

Tessa stepped forward and stood beside Athena. "Mare, are you sure?"

I pulled in a long breath, then sat down on the couch. "Yup. Let's get this over with."

Athena sat down beside me, with Tessa on the other side holding my hand. Gently, Athena turned my face toward hers. "Close your eyes. This'll be over before you know it."

And thank the gods, she was right. When she was done, it felt like only minutes had passed, not the hours or days I would've expected.

Unfortunately, though, I got nothing new from what I saw.

Letting her hand drop from my face, she smiled. "Thank you, Mary. I think that will satisfy our fearless leader." She looked around the room at the faces of the people who'd basically been living here for the last few days. Yana, Anette, Chiron, Dionysus, along with me, Tessa, Nate, and Analise had all gathered in the living room for one last discussion before we left.

"Have you found anything new?" she asked. "Anything we need to discuss before heading up?"

"No, unfortunately," Chiron told her. "There were some allusions to a *thing* that could hold the amount of energy he has, but nothing definitive on what that might be. Based on what I know and what I've learned about how magic and the power that fuels us work, any weapon we attempt to use on him would fail almost immediately."

"Hmm." She tapped her finger on her chin. "Alright. Well, hopefully, once we convene with the others and pool what we have, we'll have something more concrete."

Anette, who hadn't pulled her nose from a book yet, held up a finger. "Wait." Setting aside the book she'd been reading on the floor by the fireplace, she leaned forward and shuffled through a stack of old documents Chiron had brought back. Tossing them aside, she picked up an old book with a crumbling red cover. As she flipped through the pages, the rest of us exchanged a look.

"What is it, Anette?" Tessa asked. "Do you have something?"

"Nothing concrete, but I may have an idea." Frowning, she set the book down and picked up another, then another, until she found what she was looking for. Anette held up the book, but I didn't catch the title before she began flipping through. "I thought I saw... Ah! Yes! Oh." Her face fell. "Maybe..."

"Oh for the love of us all!" Apollo groaned. "What is it, girl?"

She gave him a sheepish look. "Sorry. I was thinking... this book —it seems to be a diary of some sort—it doesn't mention containment of energy, specifically, but it does discuss transformation or..." she squinted at the page. "Transference? I think that would be the correct translation."

Dionysus peered over her shoulder. "Here, let me see that," he said, holding his hand out for the book. He read for a few seconds. "Tessa, all that talk of energy the Fates gave you... it was about how energy cycles throughout the universe but is never actually destroyed, right?"

"Transferred from one thing to another," Tessa murmured. "Yes, that's what they said."

Nate sat down and took the book from Dionysus. "You think we might be able to transfer his energy into something else? Instead of killing him? That's a lot of power to funnel into one spot."

"It's still worth consideration," Apollo said. He gave Anette a brief nod. "We'll discuss it at the meeting." He glanced at the clock. "Which we need to get to."

Reluctantly, I stood. "Are you sure we all need to go?" I asked Athena. I looked at Yana and Anette, who both wore expressions of hesitance that I was positive matched mine.

Athena nodded. "This is, as they say, the eleventh hour. The activity on Earth has picked up far too quickly in the last few days to indicate anything other than our enemy attempting to finish us off. We need everyone who holds any information in one place to figure this thing out."

I scrubbed my hands roughly over my face, then nodded. "Yeah, I guess you're right."

"Before we go," Analise said, stepping forward. She gave Athena a steady look. "I'd like permission to go with the other guardians," she said. "There's nothing more for me to do here, at least not right now. I'd be of more use on Earth with them."

Tessa opened her mouth to protest but was shut down immediately by the mother of all mom-glares from Analise.

"We talked about this, Tessa. I'm not going to stay up here and do nothing any more than you will, and that's final." She looked back to Athena, then Apollo. "Do I have your permission?"

Athena and Apollo exchanged a look, then Apollo nodded. "Yes. John is in Tokyo helping with cleanup there, if that's where you'd like to go. I'll take you myself, so I can brief you more fully once you're there."

Her shoulders loosened a little with relief. "Thank you. It—I appreciate the opportunity to help." She gave us all a sad smile. "I never, not in a million years, would've expected to be here."

"Analise, are you sure?" Tessa asked, her voice wobbling a bit. "You're so much safer here."

"But I don't belong here, Tessa." She stepped forward and laid a hand on Tessa's cheek. "You know it as well as I. Just come find us when it's all over, okay?" She grinned. "We'll do a barbecue back in Renville and invite Grandma Avery so she can see how amazing you are."

My heart stuttered a bit as I listened to their exchange and watched as Analise tried to hide exactly how scared she was. We all knew that the humans who'd gotten involved were the least likely to come out alive. Knowing Josh's true intentions, it wasn't a stretch to say that barbecue was as likely to happen as Josh walking through the door with a Chaos-killing weapon in his hand.

Tears streaming down her face, Tessa wrapped her arms around Analise's shoulders and whispered her goodbyes.

"Come," Apollo said, putting a hand on Analise's shoulder when Tessa stepped back.

A moment later, they were gone.

I turned away, unable to watch as Tessa collapsed into Nate's arms and cried at what she knew could have been the last time she saw Analise.alive. She didn't need to see me crying. If she did, I'd think of my guardians, and they were the last thing I wanted to focus on right now. If I did, I'd probably be breaking down worse than she was.

Dionysus reached out and took my hand. "Come on, you can come up to the palace with me," he whispered, nodding toward the others. "In case my father gets any ideas about throwing you back in the dungeons," he added with a smirk.

Even though his tone was light and I kind of wanted to hit him for joking about such a serious situation, I was reminded of how incredibly lucky I was to have friends like him who'd be willing to sit locked in the dungeon to keep me safe. I exhaled nervously and squeezed his hand. "Thanks. I appreciate it."

When we got to the palace and made our way into the war room, he didn't leave my side. The room was filled to the brim with deities and other beings, making it more than a little claustrophobic. At five-three, I pretty much felt like I was going to get trampled at any moment by the giant gods and Titans who milled around me. As I scanned the faces in the room, my heart leapt when I saw the seven Pleiades standing at the side of Atlas and Demeter. Taygete, Alcyone, and Celaeno looked radiant, their power seemingly restored now that they were back with their sisters.

My own magic stirred a little in my head, reminding me of its presence.

I know, I know. We're going to war. You'll get your time.

A moment later, Tessa appeared beside us. "Take her to the back," she told Dionysus. "Chiron can handle reporting anything you've found, and it'll give you a quick way out if you need it."

"I'm okay," I told her. "I'm the one that was locked away with Josh, so I shouldn't be hiding in the back."

She pursed her lips and gave me an assessing look, then nodded. "Alright, if you think you're up for it. But Zeus isn't the only one who's likely to ask questions," she warned. Her eyes shifted to Dionysus, then back to me. "I know you can handle it, Mare, but just know that you don't *have* to."

"I want to," I said. "I won't get better if I'm constantly shying away from this stuff, so just let me figure it out on my own, okay?"

She gave me an understanding smile. "I get it. If that's what you want, I'll back off."

I let out a quiet breath and nodded. "Thanks."

As she turned to walk toward the front, I arched a brow at Dionysus. *'What did you say to her?'*

He didn't look at me as he responded. *'I told her she was doing to you exactly what her brothers did to her when she came back.'*

'Which was?'

'Coddling. Hovering.'

'You hover,' I pointed out.

He gave me a crooked smile. *'But I don't coddle. Come on, they're starting.'*

I followed him toward the front of the crowd where the leaders and most high-ranking of our allies stood around the map of Earth. When I saw the amount of markers that covered it, indicating where our enemies were currently killing us off, a level of pissed off I'd never experienced before hit me.

I felt a tap of calming magic on my mind.

'Thanks,' I murmured.

'Just save it for the battlefield.'

For the next half hour, the leaders of each group went over the remaining numbers of fighters on our side. Athena, Ares, and Tessa's brothers all reported casualties on Cronus' side, and I was thrilled when the numbers came out to far more than ours.

Ever the pessimist, Apollo shattered that glee almost instantly.

"We can assume, if what Josh said is accurate, that he'll want to balance the scales, take away our advantage."

"The Potamoi appear to be handling that for him," Poseidon said. "The information Eris got from the empousa she questioned in Amsterdam appears to be accurate. The Ischyra on coastal regions throughout the world are reporting heavy losses of both soldiers and humans at the hands of the Potamoi. Their presence has opened the inlands up to be taken by the empousa, crocotta, and other allies."

Zeus held out his hands expectantly. "I'm open to suggestions." His expression was flat, angry.

"Spread troops out further," Athena suggested. "Have teams centered in the highly affected regions."

"No." Atlas shook his head and tapped his fingers to his lips. "That's no more than a band aid at this point. Quell one attack, two others appear. That's been the pattern in recent days."

"Then what do you suggest?" Athena asked.

"Draw them here." A Titan—he had to be, based on how damn tall he was—stepped forward.

"Pallas—" Hecate said, but Zeus held up a hand.

"Why?" he asked. "Why bring them here?"

"If we concentrate them in one place, on our own turf, we'd have a better chance of defeating them," Pallas explained. "Leave a portion of our allies in the field to combat attacks by any who don't take our bait but bring the bulk here."

"That's incredibly risky," Ares said, shaking his head. "We'd be opening ourselves to a siege, not to mention the safety of Earth."

"Leave the Ischyra on Earth." This time, it was Cornelius who spoke. "This is what we were designed for, isn't it? Despite our losses, we're still thousands behind those of our enemy."

"Cronus will see right through it," Oceanus said.

"He might, but if Josh is really the one pulling his strings, it won't matter," Tessa said, frowning. "If Josh—Chaos—whatever you want to call him truly wants to keep the scales balanced and ensure equal loss of life on both sides, he'll make sure it happens."

"And if Cronus refuses to move his forces there?" Ares asked.

"He won't," Taygete said quietly, casting a quick glance in my direction. "Even if he sees it as a trap, he won't have a choice."

"What makes you so certain?" Zeus asked.

"He's scared of him," I said, not moving my eyes from the map to see who might be looking at me. "Cronus is scared of Josh. He knows what he is."

"Are you certain?" Ares asked.

I lifted my eyes to his and nodded. "When I was there—he referred to Josh's 'kind.' He thought... he thought Josh was trying to use me for—he said, 'I wasn't aware your kind had the type of needs she might fulfill.' And when Josh killed Iapetus—" I sighed. "Cronus was scared."

"Josh has been well-hidden," Celaeno said. "Even we did not realize he was in charge until just before he returned us."

"Did he seem as though Cronus knew Josh's intentions?" Apollo asked. "We've seen the memories, but what of your opinions?"

Alcyone shook her head. "No, he was far too cocksure," she said. "He may have known his identity but it's unlikely Cronus knew his true plans."

"Whenever he tried to assert himself, Josh just smacked him back down," I added.

Ares and Zeus exchanged a look, then Zeus nodded. "It could work." He glanced at Pallas, tight-lipped. "Although I agree with Ares. If it's a siege they want and we falter even a little, they'll get it."

"Then we don't falter," Poseidon said with a shrug. "We've done it before, brother. We can do it again."

"Or we don't bring them here at all," Nate said, stepping forward. He pointed at a mountain toward the south of Olympus. "Take them to Mount Othrys."

A silence fell over the room, followed by a few scattered murmurs.

Zeus, Hades, and Poseidon all exchanged a heavy look.

"You want to lure him home," Atlas said quietly. "To his birthplace."

"I do," Nate replied. There wasn't an ounce of hesitation in his voice. "Cronus wants to take Olympus, but there's no way he'll let us overtake his original home, too."

Hades nodded slowly. "He's too proud. He'd never allow it."

Zeus cleared his throat. "Yes, that could work," he said. "That could certainly work."

"But how do you expect to get them there?" Oceanus asked.

"Let it get out that we're evacuating all deities from Earth, calling them home," Ares said. "Keep the Ischyra on Earth, as Cornelius suggested, but bring all deities, including our own forces, to the mountains. We'll leave a portion here, but the bulk with go to Othrys. That will draw them there."

Prometheus frowned. "And if they don't take the bait?"

Poseidon shook his head in resignation. "Then Olympus will likely not be our home much longer."

48

TESSA

I had to hand it to Nate. Playing on Cronus' pride, his unwillingness to forsake anything that had once been his, even if it was a place he hadn't touched in millennia, was smart. But as I looked around the room at the other Titans who were present—Pallas, Hyperion, Theia, Phorcys, Mnemosyne, and Perses—I couldn't help but notice the pained expressions a few of them wore as their old home was put forward as a battleground.

Mount Othrys had never been my home. My mother and father lived there long before I was born, then made their home on Olympus with the rest of the Titans when Cronus overthrew Ouranos, not knowing that Cronus had left his children imprisoned on the mountain when he left. I didn't feel the same connections to the mountain that the others did, but I could certainly understand why they might be reluctant to risk destroying the place they grew up.

"It's the best option," Perses finally said, his voice tight. "It's unpopulated, and any structures that remain from before the war are nothing but ruin. The only things there to destroy are tree and rock."

"That's where we'll go, then," Oceanus said with a nod. "We'll draw them there, make them think we're creating temporary settlements for deities who've lived on Earth." He nodded. "Yes, that's where we'll make our stand."

Zeus looked at Hecate. "You'll need to ensure the wards around both mountains are rock solid. Can you handle that?"

"Yes, of course," she said quietly.

"When?" Hades asked. Grim satisfaction was written all over his face.

"Give the rumors a day or two to spread," Ares said. "We'll begin planning the best way to go about trapping them."

"Take care of it," Zeus told him. He looked at Athena. "You and Ares get to Earth with Poseidon and Oceanus. Give your orders to the Ischyra and start corralling any deities who live down there."

He turned and faced the rest of the room. "Now, let's shift to what we've found to combat the inarguably larger threat we're facing." He looked around the room expectantly. "What have we got on how to defeat Josh?"

Hestia stepped forward. "There was very little to be found on Earth, even in the oldest archives. The most common thread we found was talk of harnessing great power within a vessel. It's vague but usable, potentially." Her mouth tightened. "There was nothing anyone could find regarding any type of weapon that can destroy a creature with the amount of power he holds."

"A vessel?" Zeus asked. "As in, a container for his energy?" He dubiously eyed the other deities who'd visited Earth in search of answers. "I have a feeling this will be far more complicated than your typical disassemblage of a deity."

"One of my researchers found something similar," Chiron said. "Anette found a good deal of information on transference, particularly of large amounts of energy. She's digging a bit deeper into it now, but if we can't kill him or destroy his power, that may be the only option."

"Tessa has just returned from a meeting with the Fates," Hecate said. "Perhaps she can shed some light?"

Taking a deep breath, I nodded, ignoring the looks of surprise that were sent my way. "The Fates were very clear that his energy can't be destroyed. It's what fuels all life in the universe, shifting from one thing to the next but never truly disappearing. So, yes, I think transference technically would be an option. It's just a matter of finding something that won't break under the weight of all that power."

"Have we determined why he hasn't simply destroyed it all on his own?" Phorcys asked.

I nodded. "The Fates told me that his hands are tied when it comes to his creations. He can only create; he can't unmake, which is what it seems he wants to do with the gods and humans."

"What happens if he attempts to destroy his own creations?" Athena asked.

"The power that he'd funneled into them would become inaccessible to him, unavailable for future means of creation. It would get sent to the Fates, who funnel it into supernatural beings." I inclined my head toward Scylla. "Witches. It's what powers many of your primordials. It's why some of you are so much more powerful than others."

"We've always been told our power derives from primordial deities," Celaeno said. "Are you saying that power may very well come directly from the Creator, undiluted?"

I nodded.

"Hang on." Nate held up a hand. "Scylla, didn't you say several witches just went missing?"

Frowning, she nodded. "Five. All primordial."

He looked at Zeus grimly. "How much do you want to wager their power was once his?"

"Do you think he's going to try and siphon their power?" Hecate asked.

"The Fates said he found a loophole to destroying his creations," I said slowly. "It could be he found a loophole to getting his power back as well. At least some of it."

"What would be the point, though?" Alcyone asked. "He still wouldn't be able to destroy his creations."

"A failsafe," Athena said quietly. "A witch's power regenerates just like anything else. If he decides it's taking too long for this war to have the desired consequences, he may take matters into his own hands. Destroy his creations but have a power bank on hand to ensure he has power at the ready to create more."

"Why not do that anyway?" Epimetheus asked.

"It would take too long," Alcyone said softly, her eyes pained. "When Cronus siphoned our power," she began, nodding toward her sisters and Mary, "it took hours just to get enough to fuel him for a few days."

"The amount of power a being like Josh would need to be at all effective would be far greater than that of Cronus," Celaeno added.

"And even if we assume Josh's methods would be more efficient, he would still only have a finite amount at a time," Taygete said. "The power he took would burn up, and he would have to replenish often."

Atlas held up a hand. "Let's not forget that Cronus could just as easily be the one to benefit. He lost his power source when the sisters were returned home. I don't think we should assume this is a contingency plan just yet."

"Alright, we'll circle back to that," Zeus said. "For now, that's just conjecture. We need to focus on what's in front of us. If multiple sources, vague or otherwise, suggest energy of this magnitude can be contained, let's figure out how."

"I'm currently working on a few leads regarding materials that would be required to manage such a feat," Hephaestus said. "They're a bit meager, however. If I could examine any sources that have been unearthed thus far, it would be greatly appreciated."

Zeus gave a short nod. "Hestia and Chiron will get you all they have."

"There's one aspect of this that we've yet to discuss," Perses said. "Say we find a means of containment for his power. Then what?" He lifted his eyebrows and looked around the room. "What do we do with it once it's done? That type of object would be far too dangerous in the hands of any being, mortal or immortal, but we need to ensure it doesn't fall into the hands of someone who would attempt to wield it."

The room fell silent as we realized that the hardest part of this might not be containing Josh, but actually keeping him from being released. Something told me there was nothing in the universe that could hold him indefinitely.

Hecate cleared her throat, then glanced at me, then my brothers, before addressing the room. "We'd need to send him back."

"Hecate is well-versed in that type of magic," Atlas said with a humorless smile. "So I suppose it's a good thing you're on our side.'

An uncomfortable silence followed as my twin glowered at her. He'd yet to have it out with Hecate regarding the spell she'd used to send me away, something I knew he'd been wanting since he returned. Emotion poured off him. Anger, disgust, sadness, and everything in between swirled around him.

Now wasn't the time to be holding grudges.

Apparently on the same wavelength as me, Zeus rapped his knuckles on the table. "As it happens, I agree. The rest of you have your orders. Get moving."

I frowned up at Nate, confused about Zeus' abrupt dismissal.

'Things between Hecate and Atlas may get ugly, but we need to know everything she can tell us about that spell,' he explained.

Slowly, the room emptied out until, finally, only Nate, Zeus, Hecate, my brothers, and I remained.

"Tell us everything there is to know about this spell, Hecate," Zeus ordered.

"It's more or less the transference Chiron mentioned," she began. "It requires the use of two beings—one who is the subject of the spell and another to fuel the shift of a soul from here to another dimension." She gestured toward me. "In Tessa's case, I transferred all of Clymene's energy, her life-force, from her body into Tessa. The mechanics of the spell itself allowed Tessa's soul to remain intact, protected by the magic Clymene sacrificed as it was sent into the Void."

Atlas looked so furious at her words that I nearly Coerced him to leave. Instead, I just sent him a silencing look, hoping I could pull off Analise-level scorn.

"What about when you brought her back?" Zeus asked.

"When the Fates told me it was time for Tessa to return, I used the reversal spell I'd created when I drafted the original. It allowed me to recall her soul from the Void, return it to her body."

"Hecate, my guardians said I wasn't born, that you made a body for me when I came back," I said. "How?"

She smiled sadly. "A lock of your hair. When you died, I cut a small piece off and spelled it so it would hold the energy that bound your body to your soul. I used that to fashion you a body, magically. When I activated the spell, your soul responded to the pull of that residual energy. The moment it hit the vessel I'd made for you, the two combined, and you were reborn."

Under any other circumstances, that would've fascinated me. As it was, I had every intention of going back to Hecate once this was all over, and, assuming we survived, asking her to give me the details of my return to Earth. It had been something I hadn't questioned much since I'd come back, unsure whether or not I'd actually wanted to know. Now I was kind of curious.

"If you give me a bit of time, I may be able to tweak that spell so that it's suited for what we need to do," Hecate told Zeus.

"We've got one day, two at most," he told her. "It won't take them long to mobilize against us if they take our bait. That's all the time I can give you."

"I'll do all I can," she replied.

"In the meantime, keep searching," Zeus said to the rest of us. "Hecate may be on the right track, but we need more than just possibilities."

"We'll head back and dive in with Chiron and the others," Nate said. "Unless you need us elsewhere."

"No," Zeus said gruffly. "Ares and the others are working on directing Cronus' forces toward Othrys, and the guardians and Ischyra have their duties covered. Rest now, because you may not get to again soon."

Silently, the six of us looked at each other, absorbing the fact that this could be our last night outside the Underworld. I'd never been involved in the last war, so I was surprised at the level of ease I felt being so involved in this one. I knew that was very likely to change the moment I stepped onto a battlefield, but for now, I was content to know that I wasn't shying away from this fight. I was running into it head-on with the people I loved, to protect a world that I treasured despite its imperfections.

"I'll go gather the witches," Hecate said quietly. "We'll work on a barrier spell for the mountain to keep the battle contained within." She inclined her head toward Zeus. "You and your brothers will need to get Cronus isolated so I can perform the spell to take his energy. It makes no difference to me which of you kills him, but I need to be there to catch his power."

"Will one Titan be enough for this?" Prometheus asked.

Hecate looked hesitant to give a definitive answer. "I'm honestly not positive of that, Prometheus. As it stands, he's the most powerful being we'll be facing and is therefore our best chance."

Zeus nodded slowly, then turned and paced toward the window.

Understanding we were being dismissed, the rest of us left the room and went outside to teleport home.

"What do you think will happen afterward?" I asked as we walked through the palace.

"Unrest, in the early days," Atlas said. "From those who remain on the opposing side and any on our own who feel slighted by the way we handled things."

"We have the advantage of Cronus being locked away for most of the time the rebellion was building," Nate said. "With Menoetius gone, I'm hoping that period won't last too long."

"What if it does?"

Epimetheus draped an arm around my shoulder. "If it does, baby sister, then we'll face it and move forward."

I patted his hand and smiled up at him, hoping it would be that easy.

The sun was sinking beneath the horizon when we stepped outside, the wind, for once, not beating down relentlessly like it often did up here.

I'd just set foot on the bottom step when chills slid over my body. Before I could speak, something tugged in my chest, a hard pull that had me pausing midstep.

"Tessa?" Nate stopped, looking at me curiously.

"I—" Another tug, and the light around me began to dim. I heard the shouts of Nate and my brothers, then I was being sucked away, drawn toward something that pulled at the core of me like a magnet.

When I slammed to a halt in a gray cement room, my heart stuttered in my chest.

A tall, ethereal woman with skin the color of alabaster stood before me, her hands clasped in front of her. Her hair was the color of midnight and hung in a straight curtain to her waist, falling over her shoulders and brushing against the red fabric of her dress. Piercing black eyes studied me from a face that was as beautiful as it was ancient.

Her form wobbled a bit, as though she were underwater.

"Who are you?" I mentally patted myself on the back for not sounding as petrified as I felt.

A small smile tilted her red lips. "My daughters said you had need of my counsel. I'm Nyx."

49

TESSA

Nyx.

Night incarnate, one of the oldest beings in existence, standing in front of me.

I tried to slow my thundering heart as my brain caught up to my circumstances. I absolutely could *not* blow this.

"It seems things have gotten a bit out of hand," she said with a curve of her lips. "Would you agree?"

"I—yes, I would."

What do I say, what do I say, what do I say.

"I think," she said slowly, "you should begin by asking a question." She smiled in understanding and gestured toward two chairs that suddenly appeared in front of us. "I am not quite so reticent as my offspring, so I will help you as best I can."

We sat, and I took a few seconds to consider what we needed to know. I didn't know how long she would keep me in whatever place this was, but we were down to the wire. I needed to make the best of what time I *did* have.

"How do we defeat him?" I asked. Direct and to the point.

"Ah. That's an answer I can't give you, because I don't know, myself." When she saw my disappointment, she held up a long, slender finger. "Wait. First, tell me what you have so far."

As succinctly as possible. I ran through everything we'd learned, from when Mary was returned until the conversation I'd just had with the others in the war room. As I spoke, I became a bit disheartened when I realized just how much of what we were basing our plans on was conjecture, opinion, and circumstantial evidence.

"So," I finished. "Our plan as of now is to find a way to transfer his power into an object, then send that object back into the Void, using the same spell Hecate used on me."

She nodded slowly and stared absently at the floor. "Yes, that is a good plan," she said after a few moments. "But it has flaws."

Unsurprising.

"What would we need to do differently?"

"The transference of energy from Chaos' vessel to an inanimate object is the correct path, but the difficulty will lie in the spell you plan to use to send him back. Where do you intend to get the energy to fuel the spell?"

"Cronus," I told her. "He's the most powerful deity out there, in terms of energy."

"He will not be enough," she said simply. "The way Hecate sent you to the Void does not truly open a door between dimensions; it merely thins the veil that separates them."

"So my soul was pushed through the veil?"

She nodded. "In the case of Chaos, you'll need far more energy to weaken the walls enough to send him home and even more to keep him from returning."

"How much?"

"I can't say," she said.

"Can't or won't?"

"Can't," she said patiently. "Because I don't know. You will not be able to match the amount of power he holds inside him, no matter how many creatures you sacrifice, but you will need to get as close as you can. Once you have it, you must ensure every drop is funneled into your spell otherwise the chances of him being able to return will increase."

"How do we contain him first? I know we won't be able to draw his energy like a normal deity."

"Hephaestus is on the correct path, if I'm not mistaken," she said quietly. "The material he seeks is a stone, ancient and unchanged since the days of creation. A blade made of *that* is what will bind Chaos long enough for you to perform your spell."

Relief and elation roared through me as I received what might've been the first straight answers I'd gotten since we found out who Josh was. Quietly, hope began to bloom inside me.

"What type of stone?" I asked carefully, hoping her knowledge didn't end there.

"We used to call it by another name, long forgotten. It holds the power to transform, but it can only contain something like him for a few minutes. Tell Hephaestus. He'll know where to look. The blade will disable Chaos long enough to perform the spell, but it must be done *immediately*," she stressed. "It will only hold him for a few minutes before his power breaks through."

"And if it does?"

"You will have a very angry Creator on your hands."

I leaned back in the chair, my mind racing over what she'd just told me.

Clear, specific answers. That's what she'd given me, at least for the most part. I could only pray she knew what she was talking about.

"I appreciate your help," I told her with a smile. "I'm sorry to have disturbed you."

She waved off my apology. "I existed in this universe with four other beings for thousands of years before it became such a highly populated place. Chaos' original children—Earth, the Abyss, Darkness, and Night—helped him build the foundations of the world you live in. We wanted it to be as perfect as he did."

"What changed?" I asked quietly.

"He thought he'd achieved perfection," she said with a sad smile.

"So he sat back and let his machine hum along, self-sufficient. No matter how hard we tried to convince him to do otherwise, he wanted to let the universe continue to evolve on its own."

The sadness of that statement struck me hard. At his core, Chaos had been hopeful that he'd created a world that balanced the imbalance, made order from disorder. He'd wanted to succeed, but in his eyes, he had failed.

Who hasn't felt that way a time or two in their life?

"That's all I can tell you, Tessa," Nyx said. "Take what I've given you and disseminate it as you will." She stood and smiled down at me. "I do hope you manage to succeed. The world he created may be imperfect, but that doesn't mean it's wrong. He thought he knew all he needed to know about the creation of a world, thought he'd been given it all by *his* Creator, but that turned out to be his downfall."

I nodded and let out a quiet breath. "Thank you, Nyx. I can't tell you how much I appreciate it."

She smiled warmly. "Oh, and Tessa?"

"Yes?"

"The transference that your friend spoke of—it doesn't *only* have to apply to the transfer of a being's energy or life-force. It can apply to magic, too."

"Mag—"

Of *course.*

How could I have been so stupid?

Relief mixed with annoyance as I realized what I'd been missing in recent days.

I tucked away my newest revelation, eager to put what I'd just discovered to the test when I returned.

"Thank you again," I told her. "For everything."

She gave a small nod, then I felt myself being pushed back to where I'd come from.

THE FRONT LAWN of the palace was silent when I arrived, completely empty of the others who'd been there just a short while ago. Assuming I was correct, I'd been gone for a good half hour...

Sure enough, I found them all back in the war room, and *panicked* was too mild a word for what I found.

In addition to Nate, Hecate, my brothers, and Zeus, Persephone had arrived, along with Apollo.

Nate was the first to see me when I opened the door. In seconds, he was on me and lifting me clean off my feet.

"Where *were* you?" Emotion thickened his voice, his fear nearly palpable as he buried his face in my neck.

Atlas was beside him in an instant, and Nate set me down long enough for Atlas to pull me into his arms in a suffocating hug. I expected a barrage of questions, but whatever he was feeling prevented him from speaking.

"What happened?" Zeus demanded.

"I was just about to try to track you," Persephone said, confused. "They all said you vanished."

"*What happened?*" Zeus roared.

"Nyx took me," I told them.

A collective silence hung over the room as they absorbed my words.

"Nyx—she agreed to see you?" Hecate asked incredulously. "I'll be damned."

"I can get into specifics later if you want, but right now we need to get Hephaestus up here," I told Persephone. She nodded, her eyes going blank as she called out to him.

"She told you what kind of weapon we need?" Prometheus asked.

"Sort of. According to her, she and his other children tried to convince him to maintain his creation instead of letting it evolve on its own. He didn't listen, which he's now regretting. I don't know if she told me because she actually wants to save the world, or because she wants to deliver a big, fat I-told-you-so to Dad, but it doesn't matter."

Just then, Hephaestus walked in, looking harried. "You've found something?" was his only greeting.

"A stone," I told him. "Nyx said you need to create a blade using a stone that's ancient and unchanged since the days of creation and has the power to transform. Sound familiar?"

"Ancient and unchanged, you say?"

I nodded.

"This is good news, Hephaestus. It's our first true lead," Epimetheus said, frowning when a resigned look formed on the forger's face.

"Yes, yes, of course, but..." Hephaestus sighed and looked around the room. "If I'm correct, the stone Tessa is referring to is called *staria*. It's a mineral that can bear an astronomical amount of stress. It will shatter, but it will never shift form or combine with other rocks. The problem lies in its size. The largest crystals are only a few centimeters in length, if that. I can fuse them to create the blade, but I'd need a day, at least, to gather the necessary stone and forge. Did she say anything about a handle?" he asked me.

"No," I said, trying to hide my disappointment. Anything else, Hephaestus would be able to forge in hours, minutes, even, depending. My heart sank as I realized the only weapon that could help us might not be attainable at all.

"Get going on it, then," Zeus ordered. "The armies will have to make do with whatever weapons you've given them, but this is your priority. Get the Earth users out gathering up what you need *now*."

Hephaestus gave him a quick nod. "Of course, Father. I'll let you know the moment it's ready."

When he was gone, I turned to Hecate. "She also said the life-force of one deity won't be enough to send him back to the Void." Quickly, I explained the part about weakening the veil between dimensions enough for his energy to be returned to its home.

"Alright, then," she said with a resigned sigh. "Did she say how much more?"

"She didn't. She just said a lot."

"What about an entire army's worth?" Nate asked.

We all looked up at him, then I glanced at Hecate. "Could that work?"

"Siphoning the energy from all of Cronus' soldiers?" Hecate lifted a delicate brow. "Potentially, but you'll need something to hold all that energy until you can use it."

"Hephaestus may be able to help with that as well," Zeus said. "Check in with him when you leave."

"I'll begin gathering the witches after that," Hecate said. "I'm going to need help casting a spell this large."

Zeus nodded, then turned and looked directly at me. "It would seem your powers of persuasion when it came to the Fates may have just won us this war."

WHEN WE ARRIVED BACK at Nate's, I pulled him to a stop at the bottom of the porch steps.

"Before we go in, there's one last thing I need to talk to you about."

As I laid out my plan, the smile that blossomed on his face told me I was doing the right thing.

As if in confirmation, he laid a kiss to my forehead, then just held me.

"I love you. For everything you do."

I smiled. "I love you, too."

Mary leapt to her feet the second we walked through the door. "What happened?" she demanded.

Dionysus picked up a bottle of wine he'd opened that sat on the coffee table and gestured for me to take it. "Here. You look like you need it."

I gave him an amused look. "I think clear-headed is best right now. We've got a lot to plan for." I cast a glance at Yana. "And there's something I need to do before we get started that I think requires full sobriety."

She frowned at me curiously. "What is it?"

I looked at Nate who gave me a reassuring nod. I stood, then crossed the room and sat beside Yana on her normal spot on the floor in front of the fireplace. Shifting into a cross-legged position, I held out my hands. Hesitantly, she laid hers in mine.

"Close your eyes," I told her. "And try not to fight me."

Doubt filled her features, but with one last dubious look, she shut her eyes.

Doing the same, I reached deep inside myself, far back into my memories of my time as an Ischyra when my powers were first developing. I thought back to the morning of my first date with Nate, the day he'd taken me to the springs, and we'd shared our first kiss.

Mary had come to my room to help me get ready and had decided Yana needed to do my hair. I'd been about to get dressed when Mary had fallen to the floor, scowling in pain because Yana, annoyed at Mary's attempts to wake her, had just shocked her with a heavy dose of her electricity.

Carefully, I watched the memory, and when I saw the tiny spark of magic float away from Yana toward me, I reached out with my power and touched it, felt the way it worked, assessing its makeup. Then I turned further inward toward my well of power and searched for that same spark. When I found it, I carefully pulled it forward, feeling a strange *yank* as I did, and guided it out of my mind and into Yana's.

Her shocked gasp was all the confirmation I needed that it had worked.

I pulled myself from her mind and opened my eyes to find her staring in wonder down at her hands, her blue eyes bright with tears.

"You gave it back," she whispered, unable to pull her gaze from her hands and the vibrant green electricity that now sparked from her fingers. "You gave... it back."

"I'm so sorry I didn't think of it sooner," I told her, my own voice thick with unshed tears. "It should've been the first thing I thought of." I felt the absence of the tiny pearl of magic that had been mine for the last few months. A small hole that I knew would never be refilled. Not with Yana's power, anyway.

Pulling her power back inside her, she wiped her eyes with the back of her hands. "Tessa, I never would have asked this of you. It was your power."

"No." I took her hands in mine. "It was *yours*. Unequivocally."

Wordlessly, she nodded, the tears that had been hovering on her lashes finally breaking free and sliding down her cheeks. Silently, she began to sob.

Sliding closer, I wrapped my arms around her and pulled her into a hug, then let her cry.

50

MARY

I shouldn't have been surprised that I couldn't sleep that night. The moon was full, so the light that filtered in through all the damn windows Nate had put in his house lit up my room too brightly to fall asleep easily. That and my mind refused to shut up.

So after two hours of tossing and turning, I slid out of bed and wrapped my blanket around myself, then tiptoed out to the front porch, sliding quietly by Dionysus snoring lightly on the couch. Hopefully a change of scenery and some fresh air would clear my head enough to let me fall asleep.

I jumped, startled when I found Yana and Anette already outside and talking quietly on the porch.

"Ah." Yana gave me a knowing smile. "We are not the only ones, then."

I smiled ruefully and took a seat next to Yana, angling my chair a little so I could see them both. "What are you guys talking about?"

Anette shrugged. "We are going to Earth tomorrow to help the guardians." She bit her lip and looked at me with wide eyes. "I don't think I am ready."

Yana reached over and squeezed her hand. "None of us are, Anette. That is why they are not sending us in to fight."

"She's right," I told Anette Apollo had informed us we would be sent to help the guardians at the sites of the waterway attacks, assisting with cleanup and any recovery efforts. It wasn't exactly how I pictured my first foray into a war going, but considering the circumstances and my current state of mind, it was for the best. "I'm freaking petrified right now, but we're going in, whether we want to or not."

"How is your power feeling?" Yana asked me, cocking a brow knowingly.

"It's there," I muttered. "I haven't tried to use it yet, though."

"How come?" Anette asked, frowning. "It was the first thing I did when I was free."

Yana smiled wryly. "There were frogs hopping around the bathroom."

A smile spread across my face. "You got your Illusionist powers back and decided to make frogs?"

Anette gave me a sheepish grin. "They were small, only tree frogs, but I needed to see if I could still do it." She stared down at her lap where she'd started wringing her hands together. "I could feel it the whole time I was in the dungeon. My power—it felt so—"

"Lonely?" I asked quietly. "Yeah."

She gave me a sad smile. "You shouldn't neglect it, Mary. It needs to be let out."

"She is right." Yana held up her hands and wiggled her fingers, which were coated in sparkling green electricity, then started pouring the sparks back and forth between her hands. "I have hardly stopped."

I couldn't help but smile at the childlike way she was letting her electricity flow from hand to hand, fidgeting with it like a small toy. I knew if I pissed her off, though, she wouldn't hesitate to toss a few of those sparks my way.

I pulled my legs up onto the chair and wrapped my arms around my knees, then rested my chin on top. "I know I need to use it," I said after a moment. "And I will."

"You do not think you have it all back," Yana said.

Perceptive brat.

I stared straight ahead, willing myself not to cry for the umpteenth time since I'd been brought home. "I don't know."

"So try." She mimed flicking a whip and sent a handful of sparks toward me, all fizzling out just before they hit. "You will not know until you do."

"I know. And I will," I assured her when I saw her disparaging look. "I just... I don't know. Not now. I need to be clear-headed, and I'm not even close to that."

The door opened, and Dionysus stepped out, bleary-eyed, his brown hair sticking up in all directions. "What are you girls doing?"

"Sorry if we woke you," Anette said sheepishly. "We couldn't sleep."

He rubbed the sleep out of his eyes, then leaned against the railing in front of us. "Which I'm guessing is why I can't either. You guys are miserable. It woke me up."

I arched a brow. "Did you try counting sheep?"

Yana bit her cheek to try and hide her smile, then stood. "I think I am going to try to get some rest." She smiled down at me. "Think about what I said."

Before I could respond, she'd grabbed Anette's arm. "Come, Anette. You look tired, too."

"I—" Anette cast a confused look at me, then Dionysus, before smiling. "Yes, goodnight. I'll see you both tomorrow."

"Night," I murmured as Yana tugged her through the door. Sighing, I looked up at Dionysus. "Sorry," I told him. "None of us could sleep, and I guess talk got a little depressing."

He sat down in the seat Yana had just vacated and propped his feet up on the railing. "It's fine," he said with a smile. "Par for the course these days."

"Being woken up?"

"There's a lot of misery on this mountain, in case you haven't noticed." He smiled wryly. "Far more than what I'm used to, which means far more for me to either block out or fix."

"Huh. I'm sorry to hear that."

He shrugged and rested his head against the back of the chair, then closed his eyes. "*C'est la vie.*"

"*C'est vraiment con,*" I grumbled.

He opened one eye and looked at me. "You speak French?"

I smiled sweetly. "No, but I'm quite fluent in profanity."

He snorted. "Of course you are."

I looked out over the lawn and up toward the summit of the mountain. The moon was reflecting off the clouds, making everything seem brighter. Lights from the houses of the other gods and demigods dotted the mountain in a few places, but other than that, all I could see was the moonlight bouncing off the trees.

I hadn't really taken the whole place in yet, having only been to Nate's house a couple of times before everything happened. It really was an amazing spot to live, though. It was so peaceful and serene. On a normal day, it would've been impossible to feel as tightly wound as I did.

"So you haven't used your power yet?"

I jerked my gaze back to Dionysus. "You were eavesdropping?"

"'Overhearing' would be the more appropriate term, considering I was all of ten feet from where you three were talking." He raised his eyebrows expectantly.

I rolled my eyes. "No, I haven't tried to use my power yet."

"Because you're scared?"

"Yes." I averted my eyes again, surprised that I'd actually answered honestly. I didn't mind talking with Yana and Anette about how I was feeling because they could empathize. They understood exactly what I was feeling and why. Tessa, too. All four of us had our powers taken from us by force at some point, so we'd all felt that helplessness, the *emptiness* that existed when we couldn't reach that part that had become so ingrained inside us. No one else could ever understand, and I'd certainly never want them to.

Dionysus stood, then lifted me out of my seat. Before I could squawk out my protest, he'd sat back down and settled me on his lap, draping the blanket over both of us.

"Relax," he ordered, wrapping his arms around my waist.

I snuggled against him and waited for the push of his magic to settle my nerves, but I didn't feel it. All I felt was the steady rise-and-fall of his chest and the warmth of his body.

"Try to do it without my magic," he whispered.

Knowing it was for the best, I exhaled a quiet breath then rested my head against his shoulder and closed my eyes. I tried to remember the way his magic worked, how it calmed me, eased me back from whatever hysterical cliff I was about to topple over.

It was hard. I didn't realize how hard until I tried to talk myself out of the hole my conversation with Yana and Anette had started to send me down. I wanted to use my power so badly, but the thought of trying, then finding out Cronus had possibly taken a part of it from me permanently, was beating back that desire like a freaking billy club.

"Talk to me," I whispered. "That'll help."

"Okay." His arms tightened around me. "What are your plans for when this is all over?"

I sat up and looked at him incredulously. "Seriously? Right now, I'm in the 'we're all going to die tomorrow' type of headspace. Asking about my plans for after—"

"Gives you something to hope for," he said simply. "Which, believe it or not, can be a great motivator."

"Since when are you so wise?" I muttered, laying my head back down on his shoulder.

"You should know by now that I'm *much* more than just a pretty face," he joked.

Wasn't that the truth?

I sighed. "I don't know. I've only done a couple of months out of my full training year, so I guess I'll need to finish that up. Then I'll just have to wait for my placement." I had no idea what they were going to do about Yana, Anette, and me now that we were the last three recruits who weren't dead or locked up. New mentors would have to be brought on, training would have to be scaled down for three recruits instead of fifty.

Regardless of what they did, training with two other recruits instead of several dozen was going to be really freaking depressing.

"Where do you want to be assigned?" he asked.

"I don't know. Someplace that doesn't suck?" I smiled. "And that isn't cold."

He chuckled quietly. "There's never been a place in the world you've always dreamed of living?"

"Maybe. Tessa and I always talked about Rome. I've never been, but she has. Or maybe France somewhere."

"Because their profanity manages to sound both insulting and perfectly refined?" he teased.

I laughed. "What better reason?" I shifted so my legs were dangling over the arm of the chair. "What about you? Where will you go?"

"Not sure. It's been a good decade since I spent a decent amount of time on Earth, so I'm about due to enroll somewhere. Probably somewhere in Europe. I've done schools in the US the last three times."

"What do you do when you go to college?" I asked. I'd been curious about that since I first found out he enrolled in college every decade or so. I knew he got a big power fix, between the parties and drunken misery that tended to abound on college campuses, but there had to be something aside from power use that kept him going.

"Pick a major, go to class, join a fraternity," he replied. "The last time I worked in the student health center as a counselor."

I looked at him, surprised. "Seriously?"

"Sometimes people just need to talk," he said, tapping me on the nose. "I'm a very good listener, in case you haven't noticed."

"Huh." I settled back against him, feeling a little guilty that I'd just assumed he always used revelry and partying to feed on. If these past few days had shown me anything, it was that many of the gods I'd thought I'd known were a lot different than I'd first assumed. Layered, not shallow like I'd always imagined.

"Have you ever thought about going to college?" he asked.

"Not really," I replied. "No, that's not true. I did when my human friends were applying and getting their acceptance letters, but never so much that I wanted to go."

"What would you major in if you went?"

"Some kind of science. Maybe chemistry. Or physics."

Now it was his turn to be surprised. "That's... not what I expected. I would've pegged you for liberal arts."

I shook my head. "Nope." I hadn't cared all that much about grades back in Renville, but I always liked my science classes the best. After being called as an Elemental, I was glad I'd taken more of an interest in chemistry and physics, because both came in really handy when I was trying to make my ice weapons.

I missed my ice arrows. I'd never gotten to really perfect the daggers I'd wanted to make, and I really wanted to try and make an ice-version of Athena's spear. And possibly sweet talk her or Artemis into gifting me a bow. I'd thought water was such a boring element at first, but then, once Chiron had explained a few ways to weaponize it, I was hooked on trying to create the best weapons I could.

"You're calmer now," Dionysus remarked. "Give me your hand."

Frowning, I held it up. He took it in his, turned it so it was facing palm-up, then looked at me expectantly. "Go on."

I scowled, knowing he wasn't going to let me leave until I tried. No. He would let me leave. He would just make me feel shitty about it if I did, which to be fair, I'd deserve. I wasn't a wimp. I never had been.

I was letting my damn fear control whether or not I used something that was *mine*.

I closed my eyes and focused on the air around me, on the tiny specks of water vapor that floated in it.

You can do this, Mary.

It took a moment, but then I felt it. My magic, thrilled to be acknowledged, surged forward, seeking out all the water in a fifty-foot radius and drawing it toward me. I opened my eyes and watched as the tiny specks slowly turned into drops, drifting across the porch and up from the lawn until finally, there was a golf ball-sized ball of water undulating over my hand.

I grinned, then couldn't help the giddy laugh that bubbled out of me as I watched its shape tighten up, its surface smooth and still as glass. Narrowing my eyes, I set it spinning on its axis, then, smirking, I raised it in the air over Dionysus' head.

He grabbed my wrist and gave me a chastising look. "Don't. Even. Think about it."

I widened my eyes in mock-innocence. "What*ever* do you mean?"

He ducked his head when I sent the ball of water careening toward his face. "Mary!"

I laughed, a full, outright laugh that surprised even me.

"See? It's not so hard." he said with a smile. It faltered a little, then his eyes ran over my face, lingering on my lips for a moment before meeting my gaze.

Something inside me tripped.

The smile on his face shifted, and I felt my eyes widen, just a little.

Without warning, he closed his fist over the ball of water, then ran his soaking wet hand down my cheek, shaking off the excess on my shirt.

Bastard.

51

NATHANIEL

We were up late into the night, ignoring my father's instruction to get some rest.

None of us had been around to fight in the last war. Yana, Mary, and Anette had only just put a dent in their formal Ischyra training, and Tessa was just now coming into her true powers as a fighter.

The power that Tessa returned to Yana the night before had given everyone a much-needed morale boost. No one was going into this empty-handed. We each had our weapons, some physical, some mental, but we *all* had the ability to defend ourselves and others.

If Tessa heard Mary and Dionysus' talk on the front porch in the middle of the night, she didn't say anything about it the next morning, and I chose not to ask. I was a little bothered that she'd seemed so hesitant about the two of them becoming closer, but I tried not to let it show. He was my brother. I wanted the best for him, and it had been a very long time since he'd formed a relationship with a female who tempered him the way Mary seemed to. I didn't know if their relationship was heading toward romantic, or if it was strictly platonic, but whatever it was seemed to make them both happy.

So, as I had told Tessa to do, I let it be, even at dawn when we found them asleep on a porch chair, a blanket draped over them both.

"Still no word from Hephaestus?" Tessa asked as we prepared to head out to the attack sites on the second day.

I shook my head. "He'll come through, Tessa. He may not seem it, but my brother is like a dog with a bone when it comes to things like this. If he's told he can't create something, he'll work ten times harder to see it's done."

"Has he ever failed?" she asked.

"Never."

She slid her arms around my neck and kissed me. "That's good," she murmured. "Let's just hope he figures it out in time."

As Ares, Athena, and Tessa's brothers planned out battle strategy with Zeus, Poseidon, and Oceanus, the rest of us spent the next day-and-a-half teleporting around the globe to monitor evacuation efforts and assess the status of our enemy's forces.

Potamoi had been seen teleporting into Greece just outside the wards that surrounded Mount Othrys, scouts that Cronus had sent to investigate the sudden movement on the mountain. Thanks to a team of Illusionists, all they saw was temporary housing and hundreds of deities with powers that leant poorly to combat seeking safety.

I had just reached Prince Edward Island in the afternoon of day two when I got the call from Ares that Cronus was withdrawing a large portion of his troops from Earth, meaning whatever the Potamoi had reported was significant enough for Cronus to send backup.

I sent word to Tessa, then teleported to a plateau high on Othrys that overlooked the valley below.

All the gods and other creatures who'd pledged their allegiance to Olympus were there or on their way. Ares, Athena, and Pallas were busy doling out orders, organizing troops, and divvying up the last batch of godsbane-infused weapons Hephaestus had made.

"Alright, everyone, listen up!" Zeus roared over the din of voices around us. "Approximately five thousand of Cronus' troops are in that valley, and another three are on the way. We're at a twenty-five percent disadvantage. Do *not* let that cause you to falter. Half of the creatures he has fighting for him hold no true power, no magical weapon they can wield. Empousa, crocotta, any remaining Telchines, in particular. You'll be inclined to go after those first because they're easier to kill in large numbers. Take out what you can but remember that the deities and creatures who wield magic are the larger threat, despite the numbers." He gave me a nod. "Nathaniel, Tessa, Apollo, Rosalind, Christophe, and Callum," he motioned to three Ischyra with Coercer powers, "will work the flanks to keep the enemy contained."

I squeezed Tessa's hand, thankful that we would be near each other.

A shout rang out from below. My father looked down at the valley, and his face turned grim. When I followed his gaze, I saw that a solitary creature stood in the center of the valley, tall and imposing.

Cronus had arrived.

'He seriously bought it,' Tessa commented.

'Or he didn't have a choice,' I replied. Cronus might be evil, cruel, and a hundred other things, but he wasn't stupid. *'My money is still on Josh ordering him to be here.'*

"It's time!" Zeus turned back to face us. "But leave my father to me and my brothers," he said with deadly calm.

'Do you think he'll do it this time?' Tessa asked as she eyed my father. *'A true death?'*

'I don't think he'll have a choice.'

"Are you ready, brother?" Apollo asked as he came to a stop beside me.

"As I'll ever be."

'When this is done, I would like to talk if that's alright with you.'

I hesitated. The estrangement between Apollo and me had been lessening a good deal lately, which I wasn't entirely opposed to. Talking out our problems had never been our strong suit. But I had to try. *'I'd like that, as well.'*

"Think we can just Coerce them all into going home?" Rosalind joked.

I huffed out a laugh. "Wouldn't that be nice?"

"No, nice would be if they all had those damn poisoned teeth," Tessa said with a sigh. "That would *certainly* make it nice and easy."

Apollo, Tessa, and I took the hands of the three Ischyra and teleported down to the valley. Tessa, Rosalind, and I took the left while Apollo and the others took the right.

Cronus stood facing his sons halfway between the front lines of our opposing armies. Unlike the Potamoi, who wore spelled armor that would deflect the sharpest of blades and poisons that would devour normal metals, Cronus wore simple brown pants and a gray shirt, his sickle dangling from one hand, a scythe at his back.

"My sons," he sneered. "Do you truly think I would allow you to take my home?"

"We needed the space," Hades deadpanned.

"Sadly, I won't be handing it to you that easily," Cronus growled.

Then with a shot from Artemis' bow, it began. The poison-laced head flew toward the front line of Cronus' army and found its mark under the arm of a Potamoi, dropping him where he stood.

Both sides surged forward, powers flying, weapons swinging.

The Oceanids and Nereids faced off against the Naiads and Potamoi, water against water, freezing, shattering, and disabling long enough for others to tear their life forces out. Artemis' archers fired rapidly from above, the sky quickly filling with barrage after barrage of poisoned arrows.

Noticeably absent was the use of poisoned *anything* from Cronus' side, telling me we'd done our job well in Iceland.

All the while, Hecate and her witches silently cast their spell from above.

Rosalind and I each threw our power along the flanks of Cronus' army, while Tessa used her fire and Apollo's light to burn the creatures we Coerced into immobility to ash.

Bodies fell around me as I ran. Some burst into ash, coating me in a fine dust as I passed them; others fell heavily, downed by one of Artemis' archers, a poisoned dagger, or a swift beheading.

It was hard not to check in with Tessa, but I shoved that desire to the back of my mine. I had faith in her abilities and the last thing she needed was to get distracted.

When we reached the center of Cronus' forces, both armies mixing into a single mass, my Coercion suddenly stopped working.

A Potamoi rushed me, barreling right through the power I was flinging at him. Just as he was about to hit me, I flung out my dagger, hitting him square in the throat, deep enough to sever his spine. I continued to run forward, snagging my knife and shredding his life force as I did.

'I think he siphoned Menoetius' disabling power,' I told the others. *'My Coercion isn't working.'* A swing, a slice, and a hissing empousa fell to the ground in front of me. *'Anyone else?'*

'I'm good, but I'm still in the rear,' Rosalind said.

'Same,' Callum replied.

'I'm alright, too,' Tessa answered.

'Their range must not be far, then,' Apollo said. *'Warn everyone in your immediate area.'*

I sent out a general warning to any mind I could touch within a hundred-foot radius for deities to check their powers. Seconds later, a dozen balls of searing light came arcing over us, deftly taking out ten of the water gods who'd begun to converge on me.

'Thanks,' I said. I readjusted the grip on my dagger and called out to Artemis. *'Let your archers know there are some Potamoi disabling powers down here. Have a few aim for any that are coming at me or the other Coercers, especially Tessa. I'll draw them forward, but we need to keep them from taking out the stronger Mentalists.'*

'On it.'

Hermes and Athena appeared beside me, armed to the teeth. Wordlessly, we continued to mow down our enemy. I tried not to worry about Tessa, but as I sliced my way through one empousa or crocotta after another, as I ripped the life-forces out of the Potamoi who came at me, I could only pray that she still had fully functioning powers.

We fought for what felt like days. When I was finally able to pause and send out a call to Artemis to assess numbers from above, she told me Cronus' numbers had dwindled to about one-third. Ours, half.

We were finally ahead, but barely.

'To me, Nathaniel!' My father roared.

I teleported to where Zeus, Hades, and Poseidon still faced off against Cronus. Poseidon had thrown up a wall of water around them, but some of the Potamoi were hitting it with a barrage of their own water power, trying to break through and get to their leader.

'Handle them!' Zeus ordered, not breaking stride as he ducked under Cronus' sickle and shot out a bolt of furious blue lightning.

I threw out my Coercion and watched as the three Potamoi who'd been trying to tear down Poseidon's wall stopped in their tracks.

"Finally," I muttered. Hopefully that meant whichever creature had been disabling powers had been killed and wasn't just out of range.

I was about to end the Potamoi in front of me when Apollo appeared at my side.

"Get the rest," he said as he hit them each with a ball of light.

As our father and his brothers fought inside the watery cage they were held in, Apollo and I worked tirelessly to keep Cronus' forces out.

Suddenly, Cronus roared with laughter. Casting a glance over my shoulder, I saw that Hades had managed to get Cronus to his knees.

"Ah, Zeus," he said, glaring balefully up at his son.

I shoved my dagger into the chest of a Potamoi who'd launched himself at me, pulling his life force from him and shoving him to the ground in a single motion.

"It's nice to see we don't all have sons who choose to rebel against their fathers," Cronus said, then broke off at a hiss of pain from a bolt of Zeus' lightning.

'Just kill him already,' Apollo muttered as he shifted to the other side of their circle to take on a group of empousa who'd just appeared there.

"Although that one... I could see him following in your footsteps one day." Another hiss of pain. "He's your youngest whelp, isn't he? Just like you? Just like me?"

That made me falter.

'Focus, Nathaniel!' Apollo snapped. *'They're just words.'*

To his credit, my father didn't waver when Cronus tried to shift suspicions.

But I did.

Something latched onto my back, pulling me to the ground with it as it sunk its teeth into my shoulder. Hissing in pain, I sent out a burst of Coercion, immobilizing the thing on my back. Flipping around, I grabbed the empousa by the hair and sliced her from chest to navel. She shrieked in pain as the poison on my blade flowed through her. With a final stab through her skull, I rolled off of her, trying to steady the dizziness her venom had brought on.

Apollo was on me in seconds, dragging me to my feet.

"Shake it off!" he ordered, slapping me on the back and throwing two balls of light at oncoming Potamoi.

There was a hard thump, and I spun to see Hades gripping Cronus' head, forcing what I could only imagine were horrific things into his mind. Poseidon drew all the water around them back to himself, forming a single, long stream that he shoved down Cronus' throat, pinning him to the ground. Then with a roar, he ran his golden trident straight through his father's chest. Blood gurgled through Cronus' lips, spilling onto the rocky ground beneath him as everything around us seemed to freeze.

"Now, Zeus!" Hades roared.

'Hecate!' I called, my eyes wide as I watched Zeus and his brothers converge on their father one last time.

'Say your goodbyes now, Nathaniel,' she said quietly. *'You may not get another chance.'*

Slowly, the white light of Cronus' life force began to rise from his body.

Heart pounding, I reached out to Tessa. *'You'd better get going, love.'* Three empousa ran at me, slamming full-force into a wall of Coercion that tore their minds apart.

'Are you sure?"

Hecate appeared on a cliff high above the battle. The incantation the witches had been murmuring this entire time rose in volume, causing many of those who were left on the field to pause. As one, the witches all raised their hands, and a great, white light began to lift from the valley floor.

'Do you have everything you need?' I asked Tessa.

'I guess we'll find out.'

'Then it's time.'

'When this is done—'

'Antarctica?' I joked as I watched the light climb higher.

'Disney World.'

I sent a touch of laughter and love into her mind. 'Wherever you want. Now go!'

'I'm going.' She paused, and I saw a flash of light fly up from where I'd last seen her. 'Be safe, okay?'

'I'll find you soon. I love you.'

'I love you, too.'

With that, she was gone.

52

TESSA

As soon as Hecate gave me her signal, I set my thoughts to Josh's location. I didn't know where he'd be, but I knew without question that he wouldn't do anything to prevent me from finding him.

When I located him, I teleported away, coming to a stop on a narrow strip of sandy beach. The water rolled slowly against the shore, not an ocean, but some other large body of water.

The moment we locked eyes, a wide, wicked smile spread across Josh's face.

"Finally!" he called over the loud, whipping wind. "Now we can accomplish something!"

The Sirens that hovered in the air just behind him looked on, their tails swaying and expressions stony as I slowly made my way across the hard sand to where he stood.

The small beach wasn't particularly well-designed for air assault, but with their newfound legs, I knew they could be just as deadly as they were in the air. As one, the Sirens plunged toward the ground, their tails transforming into legs just before they landed gingerly around Josh.

I'd taken a gamble coming here alone. I could only hope it would pay off.

Josh smiled and snapped his fingers. Suddenly, the beach was littered with bodies.

With a cry, I stumbled back, nearly tripping over the body of an Ischyra behind me.

Ischyra, gods, Titans, and humans.

Guardians who'd chosen to fight instead of help with recovery efforts, only to find death, cruel and permanent, waiting for them, all stared up at me, lifeless.

I dragged my eyes from their faces, snapping my gaze to Josh's and reminding myself of my purpose here.

He needed to pay, and I was going to make damn sure that happened.

"I thought you didn't make it a habit of killing your own creations?" I called. I gestured around us. "This seems counterproductive."

He smiled the warm, easy smile that I'd once thought was so genuine. "While it may seem a bit counterintuitive, the power I've lost by killing them is really only a drop in the bucket for me." He waved a hand out behind him, gesturing toward the body of water and the world beyond it. "If I took out the rest of your kind," he nodded toward the dead body of a guardian, "and theirs on my own, well, we're talking billions upon billions of lives." He shook his head. "I can't have that."

"For good reason," I pointed out as I continued to walk closer.

"I suppose. I'm glad you finally made it," he said when I came to a slow stop ten feet from him. "I was beginning to think you wouldn't show."

"I was actually surprised you and Cronus came," I admitted. "I didn't think you would. Or, I didn't think he would, anyway."

Josh laughed quietly. "He didn't have much choice in the matter, and his pride wouldn't let his former home be retaken, no matter how small the sentiment might be."

"I suppose that shouldn't be terribly surprising, then." I gave him a wry smile. "Well, I think it's time we try to hash things out, don't you?"

The corner of his mouth tugged upward in an amused, crooked smile. "Hash things out? And here I thought you were here to surrender." He cocked his head to the side and eyed me curiously.

I slid my hands in my pockets and looked around the beach. "What is this place?" I asked. "Why here and not Olympus or Othrys?"

He jerked a thumb over his shoulder. I followed the motion and saw a lighthouse in the distance.

Frowning, I cast a quick glance over my shoulder and saw a giant stone monstrosity of a home looming over us. It looked like a small castle, with turrets at each corner, and wide, arched windows just visible over the rampart that appeared to encircle the entire structure.

"This is where you held Mary and the Pleiades."

"It certainly is."

Frowning, I looked back at him. "Where are we?"

"Louisiana," he said. "On the gulf, near the border of Texas."

"I—why?" Of all the places in the world to find a random castle, Louisiana would not be anywhere close to the top of the list.

"I was hoping you would get the hint I left in my school records and come searching down here," he said, shaking his head as though disappointed. "You would've found her that very day if you'd tried tracking her here."

Idiot. I'd been a goddamn idiot not to even consider he might be holding her in the place he listed in his records. Telling myself to save the chastising for later, I frowned. "But we tracked Mary to Greece."

"Haven't you figured out that I'm quite good as misdirection?"

"Alright, I'm done with the banter," I snapped, still pissed off that I'd missed what now seemed like such an obvious clue. "Actually, no. I do have one question. Why can't we find a middle ground? I can't fathom that you hate what you made so thoroughly that you want it to be gone forever."

"Middle ground?" He let out a loud, bawdy laugh. "I'm going to remake the *world!* There is no middle ground there, Tessa!" He paused, then gave me a considering look. "I've been meaning to ask .. you haven't had anyone retrieve your memories of our time together in the Void. Why is that?"

I swallowed hard. "Because I'm not what you say I am. I don't want to destroy the world. The only people I wanted dead after I was killed were the ones responsible, the ones who made Hecate and my mother send me away. If you had a lick of common sense, you would know that no sane person would want to destroy the entire *world* just because of a handful of selfish gods."

"Hmm. It's a shame, really. I thought you were different." He let out a suffering sigh. "Oh, well. I suppose we'll have to agree to disagree, then."

I let my hands fall to my sides and took a deep breath. "Disagree all you want, but I'm still here to end you."

"How?" He frowned. "With that silly little dagger in your pocket? Come on, Tessa!" He spread out his arms and took a step back. "I'm the Creator! Do you *really* think that trinket can contain me?"

"Maybe." I slid the knife I'd gotten from Hephaestus from its sheath and touched the point to my finger. He'd delivered it to me on the battlefield not an hour ago, finding me in the midst of the melee and shoving it into my hands, rattling off hurried instructions before teleporting away. Its smooth, brown blade glittered in the sunlight. "Maybe not. It's worth a try, though, right?"

His eyes dipped to the blade, then back up to me. "I see Hephaestus found my *staria*." He snapped his fingers, and the blade was ripped from my hand and deposited into his. "It's a beautiful thing, isn't it?

"Hey!" I lunged forward, hands outstretched to grab it, but he snatched my wrist in a vise grip and spun me so I was pinned against his chest.

Holding up the knife so the vivid gold fibers glinted brilliantly in the sun, he sighed. His breath was cold against the shell of my ear. "It's so... small. Puny." He tapped the blade. "And wrong." With a hard shove, he sent me tumbling to the ground. Then, leering down at me, he slid the knife in his pocket.

I glared at him. "You shouldn't have done that."

He raised his eyebrows. "Why? Because you hoped to banish me back to the Void? Good luck with that, Tessie Bear, but you're missing a key ingredient." Frowning, he scanned the area behind me. "You know, I'm surprised you didn't bring your sidekicks with you. Have they made you the sacrificial lamb? Or is it the other way around? They're off fighting while you're here with me?"

Even as he spoke the words, Josh's cocky smile faltered just a little, and I knew without looking that my brothers and Nate had all just appeared beside me.

"Ah, Nathaniel." Josh smiled indulgently when he'd recovered himself. "Have you come to save your damsel? I would've thought you'd be nursing your wounded, mourning over the bodies of your fallen comrades."

Nate stepped forward, coming to a stop beside me. "People die in war. I can't waste time mourning them now."

"Well, that's not very honorable, now is it?" Josh clicked his tongue, and gave Nate a disapproving look.

"Honor has no place here," Atlas growled. "If others have to die to ensure your banishment is permanent, that's a sacrifice we're willing to make."

I hated how much I agreed with that sentiment.

Suddenly, Josh's entire body jerked as two ice arrows shot into his back, piercing straight through his body.

Stunned, he stared down at the razor-sharp points that now protruded through his chest. Gripping one of the arrows in his hand, Josh slowly pulled it out, then held it up as he turned to face Mary, who'd just appeared behind him with Dionysus at her side.

The small gold threads of *staria* that Mary had worked into the ice glittered in the sun.

'*Told you she could do it,*' Dionysus said with a wink as he stepped back and let Mary do her thing.

'*One of your better ideas, definitely,*' I replied.

Josh tossed the arrow to the ground and began to advance on her. "Nice. Try."

Stone-faced, Mary drew back her bow and fired again, then again.

The Sirens remained still. Josh's steps began to slow just a little as the *staria* powder began to weaken him.

The expression of fury he wore when he realized what she'd done was enough to bring a grim smile to her face.

She fired again.

'*Now, Tessa!*' Nate shouted.

Taking aim, I flung the knife I'd had sheathed at my hip right at Josh's back, where it embedded square between his shoulder blades.

It had its intended effect.

Josh stopped mid-step, then turned to face me, his face turning ashen. Mary held her bow still at the ready.

He reached behind him and yanked the knife free, then held it up to examine it. He gave me a confused look. "This is no more than a steak—"

There was a flash of green beside him. The next moment, Saia had Josh by his hair and had kicked out his knees. Whether he went down because of his weakened state or shock, I didn't know, but I didn't waste time wondering.

"Do it, Mimic!" Saia growled.

Another arrow found its mark in Josh's left flank.

I took a deep breath.

Please don't let this be a mistake. Please don't let this be a mistake.

Quietly, I spoke the words Scylla had reluctantly given me the night before.

"Be free now. Your curse has ended."

Saia faltered slightly as the magic Scylla had forced on her so many centuries ago lifted. Then victory flashed in her eyes as the bodies of her and all of her sisters began the process of transformation.

Josh roared and shoved back against her, trying to take advantage of her momentary distraction. Before he could gain his footing, Mary fired into his torso again, then again until Saia—now standing solidly on two very strong, deep brown legs—regained her composure. She tightened her grip on his hair, bringing her other hand around to grip his throat. He struggled against her hold, but the *staria* had weakened him too severely for his efforts to have any effect.

Mary fired another arrow into Josh's side for good measure, giving me precious seconds to call on my telekinesis and pull the blade from the pocket he'd slipped it in. I grabbed it in midair as I ran forward, then slid to a stop in front of him, plunging the blade deep into his chest.

Saia pulled a second, smaller blade from her own sheath and stabbed it through his back.

I gave him my brightest smile. "Made you look."

With an inhuman growl, he tried to get to his feet, but the knives we'd maneuvered into his heart had already begun the process of containment.

Of transformation.

Power surged through the handles, shooting out and knocking Saia and me both on our asses. I scrambled back, letting Epimetheus drag me to my feet as Josh struggled to lift his arm. We all backed up further when he got a hand around the handle and pulled.

When nothing happened, his arms fell to his sides, limp.

Mary stared wide-eyed at the scene in front of her, the bow Artemis had gifted her hanging at her side. Dionysus stepped closer, then gently laid a hand on her back. She leaned against him, letting him support her as she stared numbly down at Josh.

I approached him again, then glanced down at his chest, heaving with the exertion of trying to fight the magic that was pulsing through him. Curiously, I bent down and touched my finger to the black stone that was slowly spreading out from the wound.

"How—" He struggled against the pressure and magic of the stone that was overtaking his body.

"It turns out," I said, "that I can *also* mimic the power of witches, as long as I have their permission." I ruffled his hair and smiled. "Isn't that something?"

He scowled.

"I knew if I came right at you, there was no way I'd win," I told him, standing back up. "I'm not naive enough to think otherwise." I inclined my head toward the Sirens. "So I got help."

"Tessa can be very persuasive when she wants to be," Saia hissed in his ear. "Scylla gave us our freedom with no conditions of allegiance after today."

"Sometimes it just pays to be nice," I said with a shrug.

"Demeter—" he rasped.

"Is none too pleased with me *or* Scylla right now." I shrugged. "She'll get over it soon, though, I'm sure."

He opened his mouth to speak again.

"Shh." I patted his cheek. "You don't want to get stuck with your mouth open." I wrinkled my nose. "A bird might find it to be a good place to nest."

The stone that had been spreading across the rest of his body began to creep up his neck. A hint of panic flashed in his eyes.

"I *will* be back for you," he ground out. "These blades won't hold me forever."

Standing, I folded my arms and took a step back. "True." I let my eyes drift to his neck, which was quickly becoming encased. "But, Josh?" I smiled down at him, then held out the tall, slim bottle Atlas had slipped into my hand that swirled with bright white energy. "That missing ingredient you mentioned? It's right here."

His eyes widened, but just as he opened his mouth to say... whatever it was he was going to say, the stone that had been slowly containing him overtook his mouth, then his nose, then his eyes.

Then he was nothing more than a statue of a man on the sand.

Saia shook her head and stepped back. "I suppose he should've taken your advice, Mimic. He looks like a gaping fish."

I tried to laugh, but it came out as a hysterical huff.

"Tessa? It's time," Nate said, looking down at the bottle of energy that had once belonged to Cronus and all of the other dead soldiers —both allies and enemies—in the valley.

I looked at Josh and saw that cracks were already beginning to form as his own power began to break down that of the *staria*.

Nate took my hand, and Epimetheus squeezed my shoulder.

"Are you sure you're up for it?" Epimetheus asked.

"You've done enough, Tessa," Prometheus added. "You really don't—"

"No, I need to do this." Stepping away from them, I held out a hand for my twin. "Atlas?"

Quietly, almost hesitantly, he stepped toward me, then took my outstretched hand. "Together?"

I nodded, then uncorked the bottle. "Together."

He wrapped his other hand around mine, and we slowly tilted the glass container onto the statue that was once my old friend. As soon as the energy touched the stone, it began to swirl, twisting around the mass of him like steel cables. It began to pulse brighter, until the light was nearly blinding, but I continued to watch as it consumed him.

I closed my eyes, recalling that day in the woods when I'd been in his place, when Clymene's energy enveloped me, killed me, and shoved my soul through the veil between dimensions to live in the Void with a creature that wanted to destroy the very world she was protecting me from.

The blinding light condensed into a small pinprick, then it and all that remained of my former friend, was gone.

EPILOGUE

TESSA

In the days and weeks following the war, the world, of course, continued to spin. The remainder of Cronus' army had been destroyed, the wounded were healed, and the dead were burned and mourned. Altogether, nearly six thousand allies—Ischyra, deities, demigods, and other creatures—had died. The energy of those allies who'd died on the battlefield had gone to help send Josh back to the Void. Hades had ensured all would have safe passage to Elysium once they crossed into the Underworld, regardless of any dark spots they may have had while they lived.

We'd won, but we'd also lost.

Cronus' body had been burned on the battlefield by Zeus, Poseidon, and Hades after Hecate and her witches sucked every last drop of power out of him. As his corpse turned to cinders along with the rest, all three of the brothers had looked on peacefully. For once, there wasn't a look of anger or discord between them. Only... relief. Their tormentor was finally gone, his death permanent, and the threat of his return erased.

About a week after the dust settled, Andrei was executed. I'd considered asking Zeus to just give him an eternal sentence in the dungeon, but I didn't have it in me to carry that much anger. So, on a sunny Tuesday afternoon, I watched from the front steps of the palace as Zeus swung his sword and sent Andrei from this world for good.

Hades made no promises as to how Andrei's soul would fare as he made passage into the Underworld, although I wouldn't have been surprised to hear Cerberus found himself a new chew toy.

Before any other decisions were made that involved our own little group, Mary and I traveled to Renville for what would probably be the last time to visit Leila and attend a small memorial service for Eric.

When we arrived in town, we told Leila everything except for Josh's role in the war and what he'd used her for. She was in a good place, and whether it was due to the Coercion I'd used or her own ability to heal, I wasn't sure. She'd ended up applying to a handful of colleges and was planning on doing a semester at community college before transferring over to one of the local schools.

With the exception of me and Mary, no one from Olympus attended Eric's memorial.

It was an overcast September day when we said our final good-byes to him. Evan and Joanne spread his ashes along the shore of the lake where we'd grown up, and afterward, we'd gone back to John and Analise's, who'd offered to hold the wake so the Andersons wouldn't have to.

I'd been back in my old home for over an hour before I finally worked up the nerve to go up to my old bedroom. Everything about the house seemed so much smaller than it had before I left. Simpler. Better.

Mary and Leila found me sitting on my bed, still made up with my purple paisley comforter and lavender sheets. Quietly, they came in and sat down next to me.

"I'm surprised they haven't gotten rid of everything," I commented, staring at the black trash bags that John and Analise had yet to take to the donation center.

"You can bring it back with you," Mary suggested. "Now that you've got a big old house to put it all in."

I smiled. "Yeah, maybe I will."

Slowly, I slid to the floor and pulled one of the bags toward me and opened it. When I looked inside, I almost closed it back up. It was a bag of stuff my guardians had insisted on keeping. Mementos, mainly. Souvenirs from vacations, a few books, some clothes, and, right on top, a stack of pictures.

"Don't," Leila said when I moved to retie the bag. She held out her hand. "We had good memories, the five of us. Even if Josh and Eric are gone, those still exist, right?"

Mary and I exchanged a look, and I reminded myself that this was why we'd agreed not to tell Leila about Josh. She was able to look back on their time, our time, fondly now. It should stay that way for as long as possible.

So, I split up the pile, and we began to go through them all, laughing at some, while more than a few brought on some tears. I tried very hard to not see Josh's face in each picture, but it was impossible not to remember the fun we'd had together.

Part of me wondered if there was ever a time that he'd enjoyed living with humans, if we'd ever given him pause to question whether destroying us all was what he really wanted. It was hard to look at his smile, one that seemed so warm and genuine, and see the same thing that had wanted to kill us all.

The other part of me didn't want to know. If I knew that any part of our life together had been genuine, I might tip over the ledge that I'd been very precariously balancing on since I'd watched him vanish that day on the beach.

Instead, I remembered the smiles we brought to each other's faces, the stupid pranks we'd pulled, and all the other memories we shared growing up in this small town, knowing the feelings attached to those experiences could never be taken away.

SIX MONTHS *Later*

. . .

NOT LONG AFTER Mary and I said our last goodbyes to Renville, she, Yana, and Anette decided to move back to Olympia and get an apartment together while Zeus figured out what to do with the remainder of this generation's recruit class. There'd been talk of sending them right into the field, treating them the same way humans would treat interns, and that seemed to be the way the Elders were leaning. There were skilled Ischyra all over the world that they could mentor with, so their options for educators would be pretty extensive.

"Are we still going to take that vacation?" Anette asked one day not long after they had moved into their three-bedroom bungalow. The four of us had met up for pizza at Nico's and had been promptly joined by Athena, Nate, Apollo, and Dionysus, who, it seemed would *not* be returning to Earth any time soon.

Instead, he sat down next to Mary and draped an arm around her shoulders. Absently, she slid closer to him, tucking herself under his arm.

I'd been worried about my best friend starting a relationship with a god who had a reputation like his. But I knew Dionysus, and I knew his reputation didn't truly represent who he was. What I *also* knew was that, when I saw the way he looked at her as she fired those arrows into Josh, and when I watched the way they unconsciously sought one another out, she didn't need me to worry about her or protect her.

Maybe it would turn into love, or maybe it wouldn't, but for now, the contentment I saw on their faces was enough to tell me I'd been wrong to ever question his intentions.

Mary gave Anette a questioning look. "We're going on vacation?"

"I think a vacation would be well-earned," Athena said. "Where to?"

"Disney World, if I recall correctly?"

I grinned when I heard Chiron's voice as he approached from the street.

"We're going," I told him. "You in?"

"Only if we can convince Apollo to come," he said, smiling wickedly. "I want to see him in mouse ears."

"I will do no such thing!" Apollo snapped, his eyes wide with incredulity, glaring at Nate when he laughed at him.

"Didn't I tell you that you need to loosen your girth a bit, brother?" Dionysus said, shoving a slice of pizza in his mouth.

Nate snorted. "He's right, Apollo. A trip to the happiest place on Earth would certainly help with that."

Apollo scowled at his little brother, but the tension that had been there previously had begun to give way to humor. Or as much humor as Apollo was capable of.

The two of them had a long way to go before their relationship was anywhere close to what Nate had with his other brothers, but day by day, they seemed a bit closer to getting there.

"Every last one of you are a disgrace to your professions," Apollo muttered.

Athena grinned. "So that's a hard *maybe,* then."

WE WERE able to convince Apollo to go to Disney World with us, but he'd drawn the line at mouse ears. A group of immortals traveling to a theme park was, according to him, borderline shameful, so he was going to make sure none of us did anything to mar our reputations.

Hermes said it was because he liked funnel cake.

So, we took a week's vacation to Orlando. Nate, Dionysus, Hermes, Mary, Yana, Anette, Apollo, Athena, and even my brothers and Eris, who insisted on getting pictures with every villain we came across.

On our third day there, Nate and I stole a few private moments on a bench near Cinderella's castle while the others grabbed something to eat.

"You know," he murmured, "Hera's been asking questions."

I couldn't help the smile that curved my lips. "Of course she has." Turning to face him, I grinned slyly. "How mad do you think she'd be if we came home from Disney World already married?"

He let out a laugh, possibly the happiest I'd ever heard from him.

"I *think*," he said after catching his breath, "we would spend an eternity suffering her wrath."

"You mean I'd suffer," I muttered. "You're her baby boy, after all." I glanced over at our friends and eyed Eris as she and Epimetheus laughed over a funnel cake. "Tell her to bother them."

Grinning, he touched a finger to my chin and kissed me. "You'll marry me one of these days, right?"

I smirked. "I suppose I *might* consider it."

He leaned in and put his lips to my ear. "I'll get you that house with a porch swing you wanted," he whispered.

"Oh, well in *that* case," I teased. I leaned up and kissed him. "Then yes. One of these days, we can discuss the possibility of maybe getting married."

Laughing, he wrapped his arm around my shoulders and kissed the top of my head. "I love you, Tessa."

"I love you, too."

FOR THE NEXT FOUR DAYS, we rode the rides and took photos with the characters and did all the things a bunch of human tourists would do, because why not? Four of us had lived as humans for the last nineteen years, and regardless of who we might be now, that was always going to be a part of who we were. Those years had given me a family and friends who were irreplaceable. I would never turn my back on what my human life had given me simply because of who I used to be.

After all, that was what I'd fought for.

IF YOU ENJOYED *Entropy* and want to see a bit more into the world of Olympus, signup for my newsletter here to get some exciting bonus scenes!

Continue reading for a preview of The Valkyrie's Bond, book one in the Half-Blood Rising series...

1

Freya swooped over the docked ships in the Bay of Brystone, deftly slipping between towering masts and furled sails as she approached the darkened bulkhead before her. A shadow moved, a thing slithering up the slick wood toward the dimly lit street that ran along the harbor. As the stench of decay stung her nostrils, she let out a muttered curse and closed in.

It had been a slow night so far. Her aerial patrols had yielded little more than a few angry tavern-goers who needed only to sleep off their inebriation at the marshal station before finding their way home in the morning.

When the scent of a Jotnar draug hit her, she couldn't say she was disappointed that her night seemed to be picking up a bit. They always seemed to think coming into Lindorothian lands through the waterways was a surefire way to avoid being seen, yet the one and only reason Freya patrolled the bay was because of the incessant stupidity of the creatures who thought they could pull one over on her.

She slipped on a glamour to conceal her presence, circling wide before setting her feet down in an alleyway facing the bay, then darted toward the bulkhead. As the creature neared street-level, the cloying scent of death became stronger, mixing unpleasantly with the briny odor of low tide and causing Freya's nose to wrinkle.

Moments later, a set of clawed, bile-brown hands covered in pustules reached over the splintered wooden ledge, and a tall, black-haired draug appeared—a creature who'd managed to sneak from the northern lands of Jotunheim to hunt the citizens of Lindoroth.

If he was lucky enough to get past Freya, that was.

Cocking her hip against the stone building, Freya folded her arms across her chest, waiting until the creature found his footing on solid ground before announcing her presence. She forced back the desire to tug on the black vambraces protecting her forearms that itched thanks to the thin film of sweat that had formed underneath.

"Hello, there!" she said brightly, letting her glamour fall as she stepped forward, revealing broad, gray wings and sturdy armor made of thick, spelled leather.

The creature stopped, momentarily startled, then growled, low and guttural, when he took her in.

"You're a Valkyrie," he hissed, his gnarled hands clenching into fists at his sides.

"And you've got eyes," Freya replied dryly. She gestured toward the bay. "You know these waters are infested with kraken, don't you? They aren't so particular about what they eat, so you really should take more care when sneaking about."

"Kraken," he scoffed, the sound a mix between a growl and a hacking cough. His nostrils flared and the thick tendons in his neck trembled with the anticipation of a fight. "I thought your kind kept to the north these days. I'd be rewarded well if I brought you and those fancy feathers of yours back to Jotunheim."

Wrinkling her nose at the offensive odor that wafted toward her, she tightened the cord that fastened her long hair off her face and wordlessly curled her fingers in challenge.

The draug roared and lunged, his claws reaching for her neck. Just as he would've gotten his hands around her throat, Freya struck out, bringing the heel of her hand to his nose in a wet, satisfying *crunch* while the other fist found purchase in his gut. She spun, and the ridge of her wing sliced through the air and to his temple. Blood, black as pitch, spurted from his nostrils and ear as he roared in pain. Before he could regain his balance, she twisted his arm behind his back and pulled him hard against her chest. Plucking a single feather from her wing, she dragged the metallic, venomous tip across his neck, tearing his throat open from ear to ear, sending out a long arc of arterial spray. His gnarled hand flew up to grab her wrist, but he'd hardly gained purchase when he went slack against her. His entire body stiffened, and seconds later, he began foaming at the mouth as her venom made quick work of his insides.

Freya dropped the gurgling body to the ground, wincing as her feather regrew, the burn of venom filling the shaft. It was a sting she didn't think she'd ever get used to. Shaking it off, she wiped her hands, now reeking with blood, on her leather pants, scowling at the scrubbing she—or more preferably, her aunt—would have to do when she got home.

"Gloves, Freya," she muttered to herself. "Get yourself a damn pair of gloves."

With a huff, she hefted the draug's body over her shoulder and took to the skies once again, aiming this time for the wide, deep ravine that ran along the outskirts of Watoria, separating the small capital of Allanor from the dark expanse of evergreen forest that stretched for miles all around. The dark crevice worked well as a means of defense but was also the perfect dumping ground for pesky bodies that stunk to the heavens if burned.

Not wanting to waste time landing, Freya dropped the body into the black abyss, hovering above only long enough to hear the satisfying *thunk* when it landed on the rocky floor before changing her direction back toward the city.

A moment later, her feet came down quietly on the roof of the local town hall, a three-story building that sat in a large public square in the center of town.

The square was a bustling area for shopping during the day, the small shops around it and down the sprawling side streets offering all manner of goods, from foods and freshly dyed fabrics, to talismans and potions imported from the other four realms of Lindoroth as well as the neighboring lands of Jotunheim and Dystone. Now, in the dead of night, it was silent, lit only by the few sparkling pixie lights that dotted the air along the stone sidewalks.

Crouching behind the building's wide brick chimney, Freya watched the street below, the building giving her the advantage of height without revealing her position. A few marshals, oblivious to her presence above them, ambled through the streets, no doubt keeping an eye out for mischief makers. The marshals were in charge of roaming the city streets, but it was Freya's job to climb and fly where no one else in Watoria would or could go.

Satisfied there were no immediate threats in the area, Freya scanned the city, assessing where she'd be most useful. The town-hall's rooftop was slick with rain, making any movement a bit cumbersome, so she waited, choosing her next location carefully. Settling on a brighter area toward the north, she took off toward the busy North Ward, a place rife with dancing, drinking, and debauchery. If she was going to find anything more to occupy her time tonight, it would be there.

For the next few hours, she flew low over the roofs, stopping here and there to avoid being seen by any ruffians or other such trouble-makers in the darkened streets and alleyways. Despite the usefulness of a Valkyrie's wings, they were, in fact, wings, which were pretty damn hard to miss in the sky, often making the element of surprise difficult to maintain unless she wanted to drain her power by wearing an invisibility glamour for every patrol.

After depositing two more brawling drunkards at the marshal station, she landed on the clock tower of Watoria's secondary school —the school that had been her second home up until a few short months ago—and sat down on the edge, letting her legs dangle over the side. Leaning back on her hands, she looked around the city, watching as the last lights winked off in Watoria's late-night establishments.

She closed her eyes in contentment and tilted her face toward the night sky. *This* was her favorite time of night—when she was on patrol but also able to take just a few moments to enjoy the silence that cloaked this part of the city. Even her home in her own neighbor-hood in the South Ward, posh as it was, didn't hold the same level of tranquility she found sitting forty-feet above the rest of the world.

Casting her eyes toward the northern sky, she found the large grouping of stars that represented her namesake—Freyja, the goddess and progenitor of all Linds. The triangular shape was low to the horizon, telling her dawn would arrive in just a few hours. She pulled herself to a standing position and yawned, stretching her arms above her head as she took one last look around.

She saw nothing of import in the street, so she spread her wings, smiling to herself as the damp night wind rushed through her feath-ers. She shot forward, staying as low over the rooftops as was wise, for one final sweep over the city before returning to her quiet neigh-borhood.

Ana, her aunt and fellow Valkyrie, was waiting in the warm kitchen when she arrived wearing a green silk robe knotted tightly at the waist, a steaming cup of tea in front of her, her chin-length blond hair mussed from sleep. A flame, small and vibrant, floated inside a lantern in front of her, casting a soft glow over the room.

Freya paused at the sight when she stepped through the door.

Ana leaned back in her seat and arched a single, blonde brow as she walked in. "Busy night?"

With a sigh, Freya fully retracted her wings.

"Not so bad," she hedged as she kicked off her shoes and began to divest herself of her leathers, dropping her pants, shin guards, jacket, and vambraces until she was left in her underthings and a thigh-length beige tunic. She dropped down into one of the chairs with a huff, gladly accepting the cup of peppermint tea her aunt offered.

Ana gave her an expectant look. "Well?"

Freya took the tea and sipped before answering. "There was a draug," she said, setting the cup down. "I killed it. Aside from that, a few drunks got a bit rough with one another. They're sleeping it off at the marshal station." She jerked her chin toward her pile of leather. "One ripped a fastener off my jacket, the bastard."

"Then I suppose it's a good thing we've still got your mother's sewing kit. Go get changed," Ana said wearily, running a hand through her knotted hair. "Those clothes will start stinking if you've gotten any blood on them. I'll start them soaking. Once they're done, you can do the fastener repair." She held up a long finger. "And don't even think about asking me to do it, young lady. I told you ages ago you needed a new jacket."

Freya made a face, knowing there was no point in arguing. "Can I at least finish my tea first?" she complained.

"No. Now, go. Your tea will be here when you get back."

Grumbling, Freya made her way to the bathroom, stopping in her spacious bedroom to get a change of clothes on the way. She made a face in the mirror when she saw the messy state of her thick reddish-brown hair and the smudge of draug blood on the tip of one of her ears. Picking up a washrag, she scrubbed at it, wincing when she had to rub extra hard to get the blood off. After changing into a pair of soft silk pajamas, she pulled the tie out of her hair and ran her fingers through, then brushed out the tangles before wrapping it up into a high bun.

She cracked her neck, still a bit sore from carrying the weight of the draug across the city, and sighed.

Then, picking up her dirty shirt and underwear, she went back out to the kitchen to finish her tea.

Ana had just entered the kitchen when Freya returned. As Ana poured herself another cup of tea, Freya saw she wore a pursed expression.

"What is it?" Freya asked, sitting down and sliding her lukewarm tea toward her.

"I spoke with Nadya down the street, who heard from one of the marshals who heard from the commander. Aldridge is expected to send scouts out to gather up any remaining students who haven't yet arrived on campus." Turning, she took a slow sip of tea, her eyes narrowed at Freya over the rim. "Oddly enough, there seems to be just one who hasn't made her way there." When Freya merely stared back, Ana huffed out a sigh. "You were supposed to be on a ship four days ago! Now, Freya, I've been lenient with you, considering, but do you know how it looks—"

Freya rolled her eyes. "The first school term doesn't begin for five days, and I've already booked passage for tomorrow afternoon. Most of my things are packed. The only thing I'm missing out on is—"

"*Four* days, and you're missing out on getting to *know* people, reconnecting with people," her aunt lamented. "Gods above, Freya! Training at Aldridge is a gift most can only dream of and it's important you show your appreciation for it! I thought you'd be happy!"

Freya snorted and turned to gaze out the window. "I'm fairly certain my happiness is the last thing I need to worry about." She smirked at her aunt and circled her finger in the air. "You, on the other hand..."

"*I* will be returning to Iston, where I plan to live out my last few centuries happily with the rest of our kind. As honored as I was when your father chose me to raise you in his absence..." She sighed and smiled at her niece. "I'm eager to return home, just as you should be eager to dive into this new phase of your life."

"I'm going, aren't I? I have no intention of shirking my duties, Aunt Ana." And, as hard as it was for her to admit, she was excited to go back to Iladel, Lindoroth's capital, so she could finally learn and train under experienced professors. The physical training she'd received from the marshals and her aunt, her father's sister and a battle-tested Valkyrie, had been of the highest quality, but the education she would receive at Aldridge Academy, a small, elite university, would set her on another level.

"They won't change you as much as you fear," Ana said quietly. "If that's what's worrying you."

Freya was silent for a few moments, letting her mind wander over her future—one that had been laid out for her when she was just a child. Traveling several hundred miles to Iladel was something that had always loomed on her horizon, getting closer as each day, each *year* slipped past. It wasn't something she feared, but lack of fear did little to quell her anxiety of returning to a place and people she hadn't seen in years.

At the age of thirteen, her nineteenth year had seemed a million years away. Her mother, a general in the Allanorian army that helped protect the western lands of Lindoroth, had just been killed. Freya's father had decided she'd no longer be summering with the royal family, who were long-time family friends. After that, she was sent on her way. She'd trained and fought in Watoria, the capital of the realm of Allanor, earning herself a reputation with the local marshals at the age of sixteen as an ally worth having, while also ensuring she excelled in academics.

Her graduation from secondary school had come and gone three months' past, and since then, a clock had been ticking relentlessly in her mind, counting down the hours until she left her home for good. The obligations she'd made for herself here in Watoria would soon be replaced by those that had been set on her shoulders by others, that would recreate the female she'd grown into.

With a sigh, she drank down the dregs of her tea, wincing at the bitter taste of the leaves that had found their way through the infuser.

"It will be alright, Freya." Ana stared down at her own cup. "When you go… it will be alright."

"I know it will," Freya muttered.

2

Freya was woken several hours later by rough shaking and her aunt hissing in my ear.

"Freya, wake up! There's been an attack!"

Freya bolted out of bed, her mind instantly alert as she lunged toward her armoire.

"Where?" She flung the wardrobe's doors open and pulled out a fresh pair of leathers and began tugging them on. "Was it draugs?"

"Yes, at Keranal's," Ana replied breathlessly.

Freya paused in the middle of fastening her jacket. "Draugs attacked a tavern? What in heavens for?"

Ana shook her head. "Not a clue, but the marshals are there now and there are at least a dozen patrons injured. Ashton just called for you. Do you need me to come?"

"No, stay here. If I need any backup, I'll send for you."

"Alright. Be safe, Freya."

Once her protective gear was secure, Freya stepped onto the front porch and let out her wings, leaping into flight and shooting toward the tavern she'd been dragging raucous drunks toward the marshals' wagon not three hours prior. She did a quick loop around the area to check the side streets for any movement before landing silently in front of the small building.

A marshal stood a few feet from the door, a male called Gideon, who she'd been friends with since she began working with them four years ago.

"What do you have?" she asked him.

He jumped at her sudden and silent appearance. "Freya! You startled me."

She flashed him a quick grin. "Apologies. My aunt said you called for me?"

He nodded gravely, then jerked his chin toward the door. "Ashton is just inside. I think he's waiting for you."

Nodding her thanks, Freya stepped through the doorway and cast her eyes around the darkened establishment. The smell of old ale mixed with death assaulted her nostrils as she stepped further inside, causing her face to scrunch. The stench was forgotten as she took in the scene before her, though. Ana's report had been accurate—there were about a dozen patrons bearing injuries of an attack. A few clutched their heads, no doubt thanks to hard blows, while others were pressing rags against seeping wounds.

"Ah, Freya." The warm voice of Ashton Carinald, one of Watoria's five senior marshals, reached her. She and Ashton had become friends not long after she moved to Watoria when she was thirteen. Three years her senior, he'd been the first to suggest she train with the marshals. Their friendship teetered on the edge of romantic at times, but considering her imminent departure from Watoria, she tried very hard to keep from giving him any type of false hope.

She frowned as he approached. "How long ago was this?"

He dragged a hand through his blond curls and blew out a breath as he gazed around them. "Maybe three hours ago, so far as we can tell."

"Three hours? How—" She huffed out a breath though her nose. "They were entranced?"

Ashton shook his head. "Poisoned. We found a vial of widow

venom on the ground outside and the doors were locked. They're only just waking up."

Frowning, she began to make her way around the room, examining the patrons as she went. She crouched down beside a witch with skin pale as chalk who was clutching her heart.

"May I see?" she asked gently.

The female nodded and pulled her hand away, revealing four vicious claw marks across her chest, the edges hard and blue.

"I didn't see much." Her lips trembled as she struggled to meet Freya's gaze. "I felt the hit, then it all went black."

"These are draug claw marks," Freya said, glancing up at Ashton briefly before continuing. "It may take a bit longer to heal, but give it a few hours and you should be good as new," she told the female with a smile.

The female returned her smile, and Freya gave her hand a squeeze before shifting position so she could get a better look at the male bear shifter slumped on the floor beside her.

She assessed the large gash across his neck and gave him a questioning look. He grimaced, then nodded and tilted his chin up.

Touching a finger to the male's jaw, she nodded. "These are draug marks as well. Slightly different, though. A bit more jagged than hers," she said, indicating toward the female. She winced and lightly touched the edge of the wound. "Have you tried shifting to heal yourself?"

The male nodded. "It was the first thing I did, but my strength still hasn't returned."

Freya gave him an encouraging smile. "Give it time. I know how painful draug venom is."

"A pack was seen roaming the outlands a few days ago," Ashton informed her. "They emptied the till and relieved all patrons of their valuables before leaving."

Freya gave a hum of annoyance and stood, wiping her hands on her pants as she turned to face him. "I killed one earlier. It was climbing over the bulkhead across from the fishery. He was alone, though."

"What did you do with the body?" Ashton asked sharply.

"I dumped him in the ravine." She cocked her head to the side, her lips quirking. "He made a nice *crunch* when he landed."

Ashton ran a hand over his face and shook his head. "Considering how strictly Caelora guards the Jotunheim border, don't you think it would have been wise to report that when it happened?"

Freya's eyes narrowed. "This isn't the first time Jotnar draugs have gotten into our lands. Caeloiran knights are strong, but until they agree to send more support to the coast, draugs and their ilk will continue to come in by sea. And as I said, I dealt with it."

"And you're certain he was alone?"

"Yes."

Ashton's brow lifted in question.

"Yes, Ash, I am certain he was alone," she said with a smirk. "They're defensive creatures. If he had others with him, they would've come after me. That and he was talking about dragging me back to Jotunheim in exchange for a handsome reward. It's unlikely he would've been willing to share such wealth."

Ashton chuckled darkly. "I would've paid to see that fight." He scanned the patrons around them. "Is there a chance this could be payback, then?"

Freya's eyes widened at his insinuation. "You think this is *my* fault?"

He shifted his stern gaze back to her, and a small muscle in his jaw twitched. "I think retaliatory attacks are something draugs are known for, *considering* their defensive nature."

Freya blew out a small breath to keep herself from delivering Senior Marshal Ashton Carinald a backhand worthy of his title.

"If that were the case," she said slowly, "they would've come after me and Aunt Ana, not a bunch of people I don't know."

"Maybe. Maybe not. Are you certain you killed it?"

"I stunned it and sliced its neck with my own feather. It's dead as a goddamn doornail."

Ashton's warm brown eyes ran over her face, then cast a glance toward the door where another officer had just entered and gestured for her to follow him outside.

When they stepped into the cool night air, his expression softened, and he brushed a thumb across her cheek. "You're right. I'm sorry. I didn't intend for it to seem as though I don't trust your judgement."

"Apology accepted." She grinned, then backed away when he tried to reach for her and pull her closer. "I'll do a few more sweeps around the city and let you know if I find our assailants. And, if it will ease that pretty mind of yours, I'll also confirm that the body I dropped earlier remained where I left it."

A smile tugged at the corner of his mouth, one that melted the bit of annoyance she'd allowed to creep in.

Once outside, she stormed away from the building, frustrated at the turn the night had taken. With a leap, she was airborne, banking hard to arc over the nearby buildings. She flew down dark alleys and streets, her wings pinned to her body, cutting through the air soundlessly. Keeping her eyes and ears peeled for any sort of disturbance, she did a thorough air patrol of the North Ward, moving next into the East Ward's marketplace, and, finally, the residential neighborhoods that dotted the Southern and Western Wards.

As she continued her sweep, her concerns seemed to be valid. A few drunks stumbling home, a couple fornicating behind the town hall, and a few vagabonds settling in for the night under a bridge were the only activity she saw. When she glided over the outermost neighborhoods, her worry grew. If the draugs had already fled the city, there was little chance they'd be caught.

When she'd covered the rest of the city, she turned eastward, aiming for the spot where the sun was beginning to lighten the sky. In the soft glow of dawn, the deep ravine appeared like a thick black line drawn in the ground around the city. Banking low, she eyed the surrounding area carefully. It was unlikely any draugs in the area would attempt to recover their fallen comrade, but it wasn't in Freya's nature to assume anything of those creatures, wretched as they were. The Jotnar were, on the whole, quite intelligent and not unlike the

Linds, although the lower strata of their society—draugs, huldra, and their ilk—couldn't make that same claim. They ran on instinct and greed, which was often more than enough to get them killed.

Rubbing her fingers together, she blew on them, forming a soft ball of glowing light that illuminated the air around her as she descended into the darkness. Coming to a silent stop, she held the light at shoulder-height and looked around.

The draug was just as she'd left him—dead, his body broken, the boulders he'd fallen on coated with blood and whatever muck had spilled when his flesh tore on contact with the sharp granite.

Annoyed that Ashton's words had caused her to question her own methods, Freya pulled a vial of accelerant from the pouch at her waist and cracked it open, pouring the contents over the thing's ruined body. She flicked the small light that still glowed in her hand downward, setting the corpse ablaze. After watching for a few moments as the green flames slowly turned the draug to ash, she took to the air for what she hoped would be the last time for the night. She'd check in with Ashton later in the morning, but for now, she wanted—needed—rest.

Freya landed quietly on the cobblestone street in front of her house, keeping her steps silent as she ascended the stairs toward the front door. She knew it would be of little use—if she knew her aunt, Ana had refused to go back to sleep until she knew Freya was home and safe in her own bed. At times, it annoyed Freya that her aunt had fallen so effortlessly into the role of mother after her own had died. But despite Ana's softer nature, she was nearly as good a fighter as Freya, having been subject to the same training regimen in her youth, centuries ago. Unlike Freya's father, though, Ana hadn't followed the same path most of their kind did, by entering the military or law enforcement field. Instead, she'd chosen medicine, acting first as a physician in the field for Lindoroth's royal army, then as a traveling physician in Watoria, a job that kept her aunt busy most days.

Freya turned the knob as quietly as she could, hoping in vain she could avoid the annoying screech that almost always sounded halfway through a full turn. Much to her dismay, the old mechanism squealed, sharply announcing her entry.

When she stepped through the foyer and into the kitchen, she came to a halt, her eyes widening, then narrowing to slits as she took in the scene before her.

Her aunt sat at the table, a look of resignation on her face, her hair rumpled as if she'd actually attempted to get back into bed. A fresh cup of steaming tea sat in front of her. Four males, slender and resplendent in their gold-adorned navy blue uniforms, stood at attention in the four corners of the room, the white epaulets and bronze shields pinned to their lapels identifying them as Iladel's palace knights. The crest of House Harridan, Lindoroth's ruling family, was carved into the metal—two large, golden lynx reared on their hind legs in mid-battle. Each guard wore a longsword at one hip and an onyx-handled dagger at the other.

Freya's nose twitched as she took in their scents, the sharp, earthy smell identifying them as wolf shifters, the type most commonly employed by the monarchy.

A fifth male, tall and foreboding, with dark brown hair shot through with streaks the color of cinnabar, stood beside Ana. His uniform was pitch black with mother-of-pearl buttons. The gold epaulets identified *him* as the commander of King Salazar's Royal Army. The corner of his mouth quirked up when Freya appeared, amusement at her surprise lighting his aged gray eyes.

Freya allowed herself three seconds to recover, then tilted her chin up and folded her arms across her chest. "Commander."

He inclined his head in greeting. "Freya."

"Are you here to drag me off?"

The commander set down the glass of water he'd been drinking and folded his arms, mimicking Freya's pose. "You should have been on a ship days ago."

She walked toward the stove and poured herself a cup of tea from the kettle that still sat there steaming. Ignoring the guard to her left, she busied her hands doctoring her tea with cream and a bit of honey before turning to face the commander again. Leaning against the stove, she crossed her legs at the ankle and took a slow sip of the steaming liquid. She held back a smug smile as the tension in the room thickened, refusing to acknowledge the dirty looks she was sure her aunt was sending her way.

"Is there a reason you couldn't wait until daylight to make this visit?" Freya asked. "It's been a busy night, as I'm sure you know."

"Ah, yes." The commander nodded knowingly, and she winced at the impending barb. "You killed a single draug that was sneaking onto a deserted street, if I'm not mistaken, while twelve of Watoria's citizens were being beaten and robbed less than a mile away." He strode forward, stopping a foot away from her, hands now clasped behind his back. The authority behind the gesture, the kind one had achieved after spending several centuries as a warrior, oozed from him, slapping Freya's own sense of confidence down in a single hit.

"Odd coincidence, isn't it?" he mused. "One draug keeping one of the city's strongest fighters occupied while his comrades attack elsewhere."

Freya ground her teeth together. Commander Balthana delighted in irritating others when they misstepped, and the pleasure he took in goading her, trying to get a rise out of her, was clear in his eyes.

"Yes, I suppose that would be an odd coincidence," Freya said slowly, cursing herself for not considering the possibility when she'd spoken with Ashton. "Although, organized crime has never been their strong suit."

"Quite true." He held up a finger. "But a good warrior knows that her biggest enemies are ignorance and assumption. You allow your assumptions of a creature's behavior to be dictated by what you think you know."

With a sigh, Freya straightened her shoulders. "If you're going to cart me off to Iladel, I'd like to at least get a few hours' sleep before I go. May I have that, at least?"

The commander clicked his tongue and shook his head. "Unfortunately, no. Your disdain for your obligations has caught the eye of those above me. I'm under orders to bring you—kicking and screaming, if necessary—to the capital *now*."

"But—"

He held up a hand at her protest. "No, you may not rest. The belongings you've already packed have been taken to the carriage and will be loaded onto the ship for Iladel shortly. What you *may* do is change out of those filthy clothes and be in the carriage out front in ten minutes. I have an army to lead, and chasing the king's wayward students is preventing me from doing my job." He ran his eyes over her hair and sighed. "And do something about that hair. It looks as though you've been rolling in mud."

She held his stare for several moments before giving him a small smile. "I'll be ready shortly. Feel free to let Ana go back to sleep," she added, glancing down at her aunt, who already appeared halfway there. "She's had a rough night as well."

Not waiting for permission, Ana stood.

"Safe travels, Officers," she said quietly. "Commander."

He nodded a farewell, then turned back to Freya once Ana left the room. "Ten minutes."

Pushing herself away from the stove, she brushed past him. "Make yourselves comfortable."

When she reached her room, she found her aunt perched on the edge of her bed, Freya's repaired jacket draped over the back of a chair.

"Thank you," Freya said softly, picking it up.

"I couldn't very well trust you to do it right, could I?" she mumbled. "Half-witch or not, using your magic to sew has never been your strong suit."

"Are you sure you don't want to come with me?" Freya asked, sitting down gently on the end of the bed. This was a conversation they'd had countless times, and though Freya knew the answer, she needed to ask one last time before she left. "I'm sure there are plenty of opportunities for healers in Iladel."

Ana smiled sleepily and shook her head. "No, my job here is done. I'll come visit when I can, though."

"I know," Freya said with a sigh. She flopped back on the bed and closed her eyes. "Gods above, why does he have to be so... tyrannical?"

"Centuries of experience being such? Best not to goad him, dear," Ana warned. "It's a long way to the capital from here, and the king and queen don't take kindly to their commander being harassed."

"Harassed," Freya scoffed. "If anyone's being harassed, it's the two of us." She gave Ana a small frown. "Shouldn't you be in bed?"

"I'll go to sleep once you're gone," Ana said, sitting up. "I don't think either of us intend for you to leave here without packing the rest of your things, so let me help."

Freya grinned. "You couldn't be more correct."

NEARLY AN HOUR LATER, after multiple rounds of Commander Balthana banging on Freya's locked and spelled bedroom door, she emerged with a knapsack slung over one shoulder packed with the few articles of clothing she hadn't had time to stuff in her trunks.

Ignoring Ana's exasperated look and the expression of pure annoyance Balthana wore, Freya strode down the front walk toward the first of two large, black carriages that waited at the street's edge. Each was pulled by a single black stallion and bore the royal crest on the door. She held her head high as she climbed inside, taking great care to kick her feet on the sill before sitting on the red-cushioned bench. Once settled, Ana stepped up to the door and reached inside, taking Freya's hands.

"Be good, Freya," she said, the warning clear in her tone. "It's been a long time since you've been in the capital and at court. Things change over the years."

Freya smiled. "Have you known me to be incapable of adapting?"

Ana gave her a pointed look, her eyes sliding to the left toward where the commander stood before responding. "Incapable and unwilling are two different things."

"I am fully willing to adapt to my imminent change in circum- stances. I promise." She squeezed her aunt's hands for extra emphasis. "I'll get all my brattiness out before we've reached midway, don't worry," she teased.

"Please see that you do," Ana said wearily. "Salazar and Ordona are lovely monarchs, but even they have their limits."

Leaning out, Freya planted a kiss on Ana's cheek. "It will all be fine. Try not to worry. I'll send word when I get there. And, Aunt Ana? Travel safe."

"I will, dear. You do the same."

"Time to go," the commander said.

Smiling reluctantly, Ana stepped away from her. "You be good, Freya," she said in one last warning. "I'll see you at Winter Solstice."

Balthana pulled himself up inside the carriage and took a seat across from Freya.

With one last farewell, Ana waved and stepped back from the road.

Freya took one final look at the house she'd lived in for the last six years, surprised when she found herself struggling against a lump in her throat. Slowly, the carriage pulled away, the tall wheels rattling so loudly on the cobblestone Freya knew better than attempt to sleep on the short trip to the port.

"You'll be happy to know I received word from Officer Carinald," Balthana said. "They located a cadre of draugs in the forest less than an hour ago. The draugs have been destroyed, and the stolen goods are on their way back to their owners."

Freya let out a quiet breath, relieved to know she wasn't leaving the city behind with a mess for the marshals to clean up. "Thank you for the update. I appreciate it."

He gave her a curt nod.

Not wanting to dive into a full conversation just yet, she contented herself with resting her forehead against the cool glass, watching as the rows of familiar houses slipped past, drinking it all in one last time before she left Watoria behind for good.

3

A short while later, Freya found herself settling into a first-class cabin on the ship leaving Watoria for the capital.

A small bed covered in lush velvet the color of new spring leaves caught her eye, contrasting with the carpeted floor in deep colors of autumn. With the white-paneled walls, gauzy curtains in shades of sunrise, and touches of gold in the fluffy bedding, the cabin seemed to encompass all five of Lindoroth's regions in one small space. The beauty of it made Freya feel a bit remorseful about her filthy shoes, so as soon as she sat down on the small bed, she tugged them off and changed them out for her spare boots, ignoring the commander's smug look as she wrapped her dirty boots in a tunic and shoved them into her bag.

Satisfied, she slid her bag under the bed and met his stare, jolting slightly when the ship let out a loud *creak* as it pulled away from the dock and into the Southern Canal, which would take them south through Saith and Edhil, the two southernmost realms of Lindoroth, then east to the capital realm of Iladel.

"Will I go straight to the academy when we arrive, or do you have any stops planned?" she asked.

"You'll be taken straight there," he told her. "Classes start in four days and you'll need to get settled in before then."

"And what about supplies? Clothes?" She gestured toward the simple nature of her outfit. "As much as I'm loathe to admit it, my current wardrobe isn't well-suited for the capital, considering. I'd planned to take one last trip to the markets before leaving this afternoon."

"All of those things will be provided to you. We'll arrive in Iladel in two days' time, so take the third to acquire your supplies and make a trip into Iladel this week to purchase some new clothes. Everything will be billed directly to the capital."

Her brows shot up in surprise. "That's a dangerously long leash to give a girl," she said, smiling. "What if I find a sudden taste for Errestian jewels? I hear Edhil's mines have been quite fruitful this year."

He gave her a dry look. "Your 'leash' consists of clothing, texts, and whatever other supplies the professors at Aldridge require of you. Your roommate will show you the best places to purchase what you need."

Freya wrinkled her nose in distaste. "So I'll have a roommate, then? Have you met her?"

He nodded. "Grevillea Calliwell. A cousin to Prince Aerilius and daughter of Orin Calliwell, the Governor of Edhil. Her mother is the queen's sister."

Freya gawked. "Grevil—good heavens, is that the name she goes by? Please tell me it's not!"

He gave her a warning look. "She goes by Lea. She's quite lovely.'

Freya gave a noncommittal *hmm*, unsure if she was ready to trust the commander's version of 'lovely' just yet. It had been her experience that females who lived in the capital could be *lovely* in their own way, but that way typically involved a long look down pointed noses at anyone who wasn't a lifelong Iladelian.

"A schedule of upcoming events you'll be required to attend will also be made available, although some final adjustments are still being made."

Freya rubbed her fingers across her forehead as a small headache began to form behind her eyes. "What kind of events?"

"A few dinners, the annual commencement ball, and the Winter Solstice celebration, among others. I would recommend bringing Lea with you when you're choosing attire for those."

She narrowed her eyes. "Lea..." Freya couldn't bring herself to use the poor girl's proper name. "Should I expect her to act as my shadow, or will she simply be my roommate?"

"That is entirely dependent on you, although the hope is that you'll become friends."

"And is she aware of who I am?"

"She is."

"Lovely," Freya murmured.

He flicked a glance out the small porthole window, then tugged the heavy velvet curtains closed to block out the light. "We'll be on the water for some time. You might as well get some sleep. My cabin is just down the hall if you need anything."

THERE WAS a favorable wind behind them as they sailed, so the trip to the capital took just under three days, much of which Freya spent abovedeck talking with the crew, sunning her wings, and generally lazing about. The commander made appearances now and then, but for the most part he was off doing whatever it was he did. He was a curmudgeonly fellow on a good day, so Freya wasn't overly eager to bask in his company.

When she awoke on the third day to the steady sound of the sloshing water and the call of gulls, the sun appeared high in the sky, and the flowering fields of the southern realm of Edhil were drifting past outside the porthole beside her bed.

There was a knock at her door. Groggily, she rolled out of bed and opened it, then greeted the commander with a tired wave.

"It's nearly noon," he said by way of greeting. "You shouldn't have stayed out so late."

"The crew wanted to wish me well before the start of term," she muttered, ignoring his chastising tone as she flopped back down on the bed. "How much longer until we arrive?"

"About an hour and a half." He stepped aside as a servant set a pot of coffee and a paper-wrapped sandwich on the bedside table. "We passed through Saith and into Edhil about three hours ago. We're just outside Errest now, so pack up your things."

Once the commander and the servant left the room, she began to eat the sandwich, wincing a bit as the crusty bread scraped against her still-dry throat. The roasted chicken was juicy and flavorful, though, and by the time she was done, she felt more alert and less like she'd been up half the night with the crew members.

After packing up her belongs and tugging on a pair of soft linen pants and pale blue tunic, she went abovedeck and spent the rest of the time watching the lush scenery of Edhil slide past.

Her home realm of Allanor consisted largely of grasslands and evergreen-covered mountains dotted through with a few towns, with the largest city being Watoria, the realm's capital. But where Allanor was full of vivid golds, greens, and reds, the region of Edhil that drifted past now was filled with all color imaginable. Far to the south sat the Edhilian desert, a dry, hot expanse of land that spanned most of the southernmost portion of the continent. The waving grasses appeared greener, the trees taller, and even the sun's golden glow seemed to glitter a bit brighter.

The sun was well past its midpoint by the time the captain rang the bell signaling their arrival. As the crew began to prepare to dock, Freya got her first view of the capital, a sight she hadn't seen in nearly six years.

The bustling city spread out before her, rising to the foothills that led up to the craggy peaks of the Aldridge Mountains. Five hundred years earlier, the region had been a shared capital between humans and the Linds, a race of shifters and magic-wielders. When a chain of earthquakes shattered their lands and weakened the humans, the Jotnar, a race of witches and warlocks who lived to the north of Lindoroth, had attempted to take the human territories for their own, taking any opportunity to kill, capture, or enslave every human they could find. After nearly a decade at war, the Linds assisted in negotiating a treaty that allowed the humans safe passage to settle on the eastern continent of Dystone, while the Linds and Jotnar divided the western continent.

Freya cast her eyes upward as the ship slid into the port. From her vantage point, she could just make out the high, sharp turrets of the palace peeking over the lower part of the mountain far in the distance. When the crew dropped anchor and began throwing out ropes to tie down, her attention was drawn down to the busy port, where she saw gray-uniformed guards bearing the official seal of the capital swarming the area.

"Why are there so many guards?" she asked the commander beside her, lowering her voice to a whisper once they disembarked and stepped onto the aged wooden dock.

"Guard presence increased last week when students began arriving at Aldridge. Prince Aerilius will be attending Aldridge this year." Balthana gave her a curious frown. "How do you not know this?"

Freya's heart stuttered a bit and her words carried a sharp edge when she responded. "How would I?"

"Hmm. You received all of your correspondence from Aldridge, correct?"

"Yes, of course," Freya replied, hefting her duffel over her shoulder as he began to lead her up the dock toward the roadway.

The prince had been a good friend of Freya's in their youth—one of her closest—but time and distance had caused that friendship to wane, and now nearly six years had gone by since they'd last spoken. While she knew she'd see him soon enough, she was surprised to hear she'd see him every day.

"Well, had you taken the time to read it," he admonished, "you would've received news of the increased guard presence in the capital and on campus due to the attendance of the crown prince." He didn't bother looking back at her as they quickly navigated the busy port, his purposeful stride and black uniform parting the crowds like water. A long line had formed at the tall gates that led into the city all passengers who'd just disembarked, each going through the process of stating their business before being allowed through.

Freya quickened her pace to keep up with him, ignoring the glares and grumbles of those queued up beside them. The commander stepped through a narrow door cut into the gate, giving a terse nod to the guards as he passed, then held it open for Freya to step through and onto the paved walkway.

"Why is he attending? That wasn't—surely he can acquire training of equal measure privately and without all the fuss?" Freya adjusted her bag on her shoulder. "It seems a bit unfair to the rest of the students, wouldn't you say? Having a prince on campus, attending classes?"

"Perhaps, although the same could be said for you, considering your background. The assumption, of course, is that he'll find a mate and choose his queen while he's there."

Freya snorted quietly. "A farce, if I ever heard one. Everyone knows the king and queen will choose his betrothed. Will he be living on campus?"

The commander gestured toward a black carriage trimmed in gold and bearing the royal crest waiting at the curb. "No, he'll continue to live at the palace. Come, let's get you settled in."

As was her habit, Freya took in her surroundings as she walked, letting her eyes drift about as she stepped toward the carriage. The city's tree-lined cobblestone thoroughfare stretched away from the station, the foot and carriage traffic neatly separated by a long, narrow flowerbed that bisected the road that stretched off into the distance. Looking skyward, Freya imagined the pale color of the stone would appear as a long, white ribbon from above, stretching from the port clear across the city before splintering off into the rolling hills beyond.

"You know," she commented, turning to face him as he sat down on the bench across from her, "it's quite unprecedented for the royal commander to be escorting one wayward student to school. Might I ask your reasoning?"

He gave her a stern look. "The king and queen don't take kindly to 'wayward students,' especially when an invitation to Aldridge has been handed to her *personally*. As the king, queen, and royal commander are aware of said student's propensity for flying off, they thought it best she have an escort."

"If said parties are so aware of my propensities, they should also know that I wouldn't shirk my duties simply to spite them."

"Certainly, but one can't blame them for being a bit overcautious."

Freya made a face but didn't argue. Her invitation to Aldridge had been written just after her fifth by the king himself when her status as a true halfblood—a Lind who inherited equal parts witch and shifter blood—became clear around her sixth birthday. In unions like those of Freya's parents, where one was a shifter and the other a witch or warlock, witch blood always won out. It was incredibly rare for a person to be both shifter and witch, but on the rare occasion a half-blood was born, they were prized, often coveted.

One morning when her father had taken her down to the training yard to learn with the children who were training to become squires, the king came down to check on the progress of the students. After watching Freya hit archery targets thirty yards away and fling knives made of magic alongside the prince and some of the best squires of the king's Guard, Salazar had insisted she attend once she came of age. Her parents and aunt had been proud, as had she, but her pride had faded years later, when her mother, a highly-respected witch who worked for the crown, was killed on a routine patrol of the northern border between Caelora and Jotunheim.

Ever since, her father had become distant, immersing himself in his work and checking in only once or twice a month to ensure both she, the marshals, and her teachers in Watoria were keeping up with her training, continuing to prepare her for life in the Capital. Her aunt Ana had ensured the sums of money left behind when Cina passed were used for housing, food, schooling, and anything else she might have needed.

"You know, I was under the impression you were eager to attend Aldridge," Balthana commented, breaking her from her reverie.

She looked at him. "I was just dragged from my home after patrolling and fighting all night, put on a boat for three days, and now I'm being taken to meet this new best friend that's being forced on me. It's not lack of eagerness that has me down, it's exhaustion and a strong desire to bathe."

"Fair enough." He nodded. "But I trust you'll keep your thoughts to yourself once you arrive. Get it out of your system now because Headmistress Dyren won't tolerate it."

"Your lack of faith in my ability to simper is appalling."

"No one expects you to *simper*, just to behave."

"So long as I get a few hours of sleep before I'm expected to present myself to anyone, I will be the picture of propriety," she said primly.

Exasperated, Balthana shook his head. "A lie, if I've ever heard one."

4

They rode the rest of the way in silence, Freya occupying herself with watching the citizens of Iladel bustle about the city as their carriage rolled along the cobblestone streets. Iladel really was a beautiful place, and despite having been absent for six years, Freya felt a sense of home as they rolled past the people stepping in and out of shops and restaurants. It was nearly three times the size of Watoria and seemed to run at double the pace, but Freya had always enjoyed sinking into the capital's exuberance as a child. She and her mother had taken many trips into the city, wandering the busy streets and strolling past restaurants and taverns, dressmakers and tailors, florists, jewelers, and art galleries that burst with goods and wares from across the realms. As she and the commander traveled now, apartment buildings and homes rose above the din, and when she turned to look through the rear window, Freya could make out the tops of tall masts of ships docked in Iladel's port slipping off in the distance.

When they finally pulled down the shady road that led to Aldridge, Freya shifted in her seat to get a better glimpse of the tall, wooden gates that loomed ahead. Towering oak trees bordered the sprawling grounds of the university, and as unseen magic opened the gates to usher them inside, neatly-trimmed lawns rose away from the main road. A stone path that bisected the vibrant lawn led from the gates to the behemoth stone structure that housed the classrooms of the academy. Some students lounged about on the front lawn, while others walked along the paths in small groups chatting with one another.

She thought it would be rushed, more fitting to the capital, but instead it seemed... serene.

As Freya hopped down from the carriage, taking the footman's hand when he reached out to help, she inhaled deeply, taking in the scent of the woods, the pines and oaks that towered above, and the flower beds overflowing with blooms that waved gently in the breeze along the fence. The unfettered scent of nature was a far cry from the brine-and-soot smell of Watoria, and while she felt a bit homesick being so far from what she'd become accustomed to, she had to admit this wasn't the worst place to call home. Everything about it carried an air of serenity, something she was suddenly eager to explore in depth.

"I take it by your expression you aren't entirely disappointed to be here?" Balthana asked.

Keeping her eyes trained forward, she huffed. "I suppose circum-stances could be worse," she admitted. "Although I've never once said I wouldn't like it here."

"Come, I'll take you to your dormitory."

Freya desperately wanted to get a lay of the land from above, but instead chose to follow the commander as he led her away from the carriage.

Despite her skills, her rarity and parentage often caused others to either avoid her entirely or attempt to slip into her good graces. She knew it was only a matter of time before her true identity was revealed, but for the time being, she just wanted to bask in her anonymity. A student eager to succeed, just like everyone else, as opposed to the daughter of one of the fiercest warriors and most gifted witches Lindoroth had ever seen.

Tightening the strap of her bag on her shoulder, she followed the commander through the wide gates and up the path toward the main building. Matching her stride to his, she eyed the busy campus warily.

"Shouldn't I check in somewhere?" she asked when he began to veer off the main path toward a cluster of four stone buildings nestled along the woods away from the academic building that had rose with grandiosity in front of them. Small turrets rose at all four corners of each, the windows tall and arched. If the buildings hadn't been so lovely, the silence and ivy snaking up the walls would've made them seem abandoned, Freya thought.

"That's already been taken care of," he replied. "You're to meet with Headmistress Dyren tomorrow morning to go over your coursework, schedule, and whatever else she feels needs discussing."

"What am I to do with myself for the rest of today, then?" she asked, annoyed. "You were in such a rush to get me here, after all."

"Meet your new roommate, get to know the campus, hopefully make some friends," he said, ascending the three marble steps that led to the glass dormitory entrance. "I'm quite sure those skills aren't beyond you."

Clenching her teeth, she sent him a stormy glare as she passed him and entered the building, where a wide, curved staircase greeted them. On the left, an archway opened into a quaint common area with overstuffed couches and a fireplace, and to the right, a second archway revealed a small study area, the walls lined with shelves of books from floor to ceiling. A fireplace was set in the far wall, and three long wooden tables sat in the center of the room, giving Freya a clear image of students hunched over texts and whispering softly. Both rooms were brightly sun-lit through the curtained windows that faced the busy grounds of campus, with gas-fueled lamps installed on the walls to chase away the gloom come nightfall.

As the door shut with a *thud* behind them, Freya noticed it was conspicuously quiet inside.

Freya peered into the other rooms. "Where is everyone?"

He started up the stairs, not looking back as he answered. "On their way to a gathering with the headmistress. I thought it best it not be made obvious I was the one settling you in."

Knowing better than to ask why he hadn't brought her there, Freya followed him up two flights of stairs to the top floor, pausing to look out the large window on the landing of the staircase. The building was laid out in a square with a large central courtyard that appeared to offer outdoor living space that could be enjoyed in Iladel's warmest months.

When they reached the hallway that contained her living quarters, he pulled a large brass key from his pocket and opened the door, then gestured for Freya to go in.

A short entryway led away from the door into a large room. Two wood-framed sleigh beds were pushed against the walls on either side, one already made up with a soft pink quilt and airy-looking pillows. A small stack of books sat on the nightstand beside it. Matching armoires were built into the walls on either side of the window seat that overlooked the campus grounds. The walls were a similar color to the exterior stone—a pale, unassuming gray—and the floors were made of deep brown hardwood that had been smoothed with age. A pale blue rug embroidered with a complex floral pattern covered most of the floor, which Freya hoped would keep some of the chill at bay once night fell. Despite the summer heat that still permeated the capital, nights in the mountains, even as low as the foothills, often turned chilly in the summer.

"Lea should be arriving a bit later," the commander said, hovering at the mouth of the entryway. "So go on and get yourself settled. And Freya?"

Turning to face him, she gave him a questioning look. "Hmm?"

"Be nice."

She feigned offense, pressing a hand to her heart and letting her mouth drop open in an O of shock. "What little you think of me!"

He gave her a chastising look, then left the room.

There was a slightly musty smell lingering in the air, no doubt a result of the building having been sealed up for several months while the academy was closed for the summer holiday. Moving to the window, she pushed the white sheers aside and slid up the sash, letting in a soft, warm breeze.

She dropped her bag onto the unclaimed bed, then groaned when she realized all of her belongings were still on their way from the port and likely wouldn't arrive for several hours. Cursing Balthana for his haste when they disembarked, she threw open the wardrobe on her side of the room and opened the drawers, breathing a sigh of relief when she found a small pile of white sheets and a blue quilt. They would do for the time being, although she was desperately wishing for the down quilt from her bed in Watoria.

After making her bed, Freya eyed her bag of belongings before looking back at the soft mattress. Seeing no choice between unpacking or sleeping, she kicked off her boots and flopped down on the bed, burying her face in the pillow.

"Do you think we should wake her?"

"I don't know!"

"Well, I wouldn't!"

"I don't think Valkyrie take kindly to being woken by strangers."

"They don't," Freya mumbled into her pillow. "And you've already done it so you might as well stop hissing over there." Rolling onto her back, she rubbed her eyes, then sat up, frowning as her mind tried to adjust to the dim light coming through the windows. It seemed she'd slept longer than she intended.

Running a hand through her hair and frowning when her fingers snagged in the tangled brown locks, she looked at the three people standing across the room. A dark-skinned, waifish female with wide, bright blue eyes—Grevillea, she assumed—stood between two males, biting her lip. She had curly, black-brown hair tied up in a chignon and wore a flowing blouse and pants set in pale blue and beige. The male to the girl's right had similar coloring and striking green eyes, with short black hair cut close to his scalp.

The second male, the one who stood to her left, had hair that was a vibrant shade of red, with pale skin and a smattering of freckles across a perfectly straight nose.

Freya inhaled a bit, taking in their scents. The female carried the sweet scent of a witch, but the two males smelled heavily of wolf.

"A witch and two wolves." She stood and gave them all an appraising look. "I'll assume you're Gr—"

"For the love of all that's holy, please do *not* finish that sentence," the girl said, holding up a hand and closing her eyes. "Call me Lea. My proper name was a cruel, drunken trick on my parents' part that I have yet to forgive them for. And yes, I'm a witch."

Freya's lips quirked up in a smile. "Lea it is, then." Angling her head, she addressed the two males. "I don't know who you are, though."

The one on Lea's right lifted a hand in greeting, his green eyes brightening as he smiled. "I'm Lazarus Cailen, Lea's cousin. You can call me Laz."

"Cailen, as in Governor Cailen of Caelora?" Freya asked.

"The very same." Laz confirmed. "Rischa Cailen is my father."

"And King Salazar's cousin, making you one of Aerelius' cousins, too." She arched a brow at the other male. "And you? Are you a governor's son and cousin to the prince, as well?"

"Nephew, actually, and no, there's no relation. I'm Collin Maddix. My uncle is Gunnar Maddix of Allanor," the auburn-haired male said.

"Ah!" Freya smiled. "Yes, I believe my grandfather named your uncle as his successor. I've only met him once, but Governor Maddix seems to be a good man. He's done well by Allanor since he was appointed." As was tradition in Lindoroth, each governor chose their own successor prior to retirement. Freya's grandfather, Governor Jora Enrieth, had retired fifteen years past, naming in his place Lord Gunnar Maddix to succeed him.

"Yes, he always spoke highly of Governor Enrieth and was quite saddened by his passing," Collin told her, tilting his head to the side and running those stunning blue eyes over her. "Don't mind me saying this, but you look different than I expected. More... plain."

Lea smacked his chest. "She doesn't look *plain*, you buffoon."

Collin's eyes widened. "No, I only meant—"

She gave Freya a smile, then stepped forward and held out her hand. "Ignore him, please. He doesn't get out much. They live in the dorm just next door," she said, gesturing toward the window where their building could be seen about twenty yards off.

Freya shook the outstretched hand as she eyed them all suspiciously. "Are you all to be my watchdogs, then?"

Lazarus and Collin exchanged a confused look.

Lea's eyes widened in surprise. "Heavens, no!" She clicked her tongue then made a sound of disgust. "Is that what Balthana told you? Oh, I'm going to wring his—" Cutting herself off, she took a deep breath. "No, Freya, none of us are going to be your 'watchdogs.' Commander Balthana simply wanted to ensure you roomed with someone well-suited to helping you reacclimate to life in the capital. As Aer's cousin, I am just that. These two just like to follow me around," she added, jerking her thumb over her shoulder. "They're easy enough to ignore, though."

Freya bit back a smirk. "Alright, then. I'll hold you to that." At that, her stomach rumbled, reminding her that all she'd had to eat was the sandwich the commander had given her hours earlier. "Well, now that we're such good friends and all, care to tell me where I can get something to eat?"

"The dining hall is open for a few more hours, and we were just about to head over for dinner," Lea said. "We were hoping you'd join us."

"That sounds great," Freya said, surprised at how easy her answering smile came.

"Alright, then!" Lea beamed at her. "Let's go!"

"So, Freya, the most important thing to remember here is that Aldridge is full of cliques," Lea said quietly as the four traversed the grassy expanse of Aldridge's grounds toward the brightly lit stone building that housed dining hall. "Some are better than others, but it'd be in your best interest to cement your status as quickly as possible to avoid the wrong types trying to sink their claws in."

"The wrong types?" Freya eyed her dubiously, hoping her initial opinion of females in the capital wasn't about to be confirmed. "What does that mean?"

"Oh!" Lea covered her mouth with her hand when she realized how her words had been construed. "I don't mean—no, it's just that opportunism is rampant here. There are certain groups who are, to put it simply, cruel. Females, mainly, hoping to detract attention from others in the hopes of finding a mate." She rolled her eyes. "It will be especially awful this year, what with my cousin attending and all."

Freya sighed. "Well, I'm not here to find a mate, so they're in luck."

"They don't know that, though," Collin replied from beside her. "You're quite pretty, and considering your background and the fact that you're a halfblood..."

Lazarus snorted. "What my darling Collin is trying to say is, you will be, without question, competition. Or perceived competition. You won't be given time to prove otherwise before some of the more rabid females here make that determination."

Once again, Freya became suspicious. "How do I know you three aren't simply saying this to keep me close-by?"

Lea looped her arm through Freya's as they approached the outside stone patio of the dining hall, where the scent of deliciously cooking food from inside was wafting toward them. A dozen or so tables were scattered about, some crammed with students, others sitting empty.

"Again, you don't," Lea told her. "And nothing any of us say will convince you otherwise."

Freya looked at her, surprised. "So why should I trust your intentions?"

"Do you trust Commander Balthana?" Lea asked, arching a brow. "Do you trust his judgement?"

"Now and then."

"Then that's all you need for now." Lea paused as Lazarus opened the door for them. "The rest will come in time, Freya, but I do hope we can be friends."

Smiling, Freya followed the three of them into the dining hall, quietly and surprisingly finding herself hoping for the same thing.

Echoing voices buzzed throughout the large hall, far more than Freya had expected, despite the busy nature of campus earlier. Students sat at round tables, some perched on top, others in the benches around them, talking, laughing, and eating. There was a carefree air about the room, the sincerity of which Freya immediately questioned.

Lea tugged on Freya's arm and waved off the males. "Come, let's take a table while Laz and Collin get us some dinner."

Collin looked at Freya in question. "They've got most everything here, so is there anything you don't like?"

"Not in the least," Freya told him. "Feel free to surprise me."

As Lea led her toward the back of the room, Freya noticed two black-uniformed guards standing sentry along the wall. Her eyes were immediately drawn toward the table they were watching over, already knowing what, or who, she'd find there. There, holding court with a number of male and females, was Freya's old friend, the dark-haired Prince Aerelius of House Harridan. A striking female, blond with all the signs of a would-be royal, sat at his side, laughing with the small group that surrounded him. She looked the type to set her goal for a mate high.

There was no question who the female had set her sights on.

Despite not having seen Aerelius for six years, she immediately noticed the muted look of vexation on his face, one he wore when he was annoyed and trying not to show it.

Before Freya could glance away, Aerelius' dark eyes lifted and he sent a look of pure exasperation at Lea before his gaze slid to meet Freya's. His face took on a confused expression, then his lips tilted in a smirk, the same infuriating one she remembered from their youth. The one that somehow made his handsome face even more so.

"He's only here for dinner because the meeting with the head-mistress ran so long," Lea whispered, ignoring him and dragging

Freya's attention away from the prince's table. "I told the boys we wouldn't be sitting with him if the social leeches had descended before we got here, if that's what's got that look on your face. Unless you want to..."

"No, it's fine." Freya forced herself to focus on her roommate "I'd rather get to know you three, if that's alright."

"Oh, I completely understand, trust me. And to be fair to my cousin, he can't stand the lot of them. He's just got to be polite, you know." They came to a stop at an empty table in front of a picture window that looked out over a large pond. "Maybe now that we have a Valkyrie witch to scare them all off, he won't have to worry about being bothered anymore."

Freya replied with a noncommittal hum as she took a seat across from Lea.

"Well, what can you tell me about this place I'll now call home?" she asked.

Lea puffed out a breath of air, blowing a few stray curls from her forehead. "Goodness, where to begin? Let's see... have you gotten your schedule yet?"

"No, I'm to meet with the headmistress tomorrow."

Lea nodded, narrowing her eyes as she bit her lip. "Well, there's only so much I can say without knowing who your professors will be, although those I've met already seem to be quite fair. As for the student body... I would keep to yourself for the most part, observe more than you interact for the first few days or even the week, otherwise you won't get a proper feel for the place."

"But above all, make sure you mark your place here," Lazarus said, setting two trays down and taking a seat beside her.

"Ideally in Combat," Collin said, putting a tray with a small bowl of soup, a piece of seeded bread, and a plate of fruit in front of Lea while setting another tray loaded with food down at his own place. "Otherwise, females like Myria—the shameless blonde fawning over the prince—will challenge you at the first opportunity they see."

"Yes, make it clear that you are *not* to be fucked with," Lea added sagely.

Freya nearly laughed at the way the curse sounded coming from the pretty girl's lips.

"But you just told me to observe more than interact," she pointed out, picking up her silverware and cutting into the roasted chicken Laz had just given her.

"Socially and in classes," Lea clarified. "I don't quite know what your social skills are like—"

"Lea!" Lazarus hissed.

"Well I don't!" Rolling her eyes, Lea looked at Freya. "You lived in the capital each summer, correct?"

Freya nodded. "Until I was thirteen, yes. Winter Solstice, too."

"Considering your parentage and the length of time you lived in the capital as a child," Lea continued, "I would assume you have some fairly-honed social graces and are highly intelligent. Therefore, you'll have a fair number of males attempting to court you."

All true, Freya thought, but her "fairly-honed social graces" told her not to confirm that.

"Well, I suppose we'll see how things go," Freya said. "I'm certainly not here to be courted."

Collin nodded slowly. "I'd suggest getting that information out there as soon as possible."

"Somehow I don't think that will be an issue," she muttered.

ACKNOWLEDGMENTS

To my husband for putting up with my addiction to white boards and pens, to my oldest daughter for becoming the best writing partner a girl could have, and my youngest for just being her.

To the best critique partner on the planet, Eric, for your brutal honesty. You helped me become a better writer, for which I'll always be grateful. Hopefully I've finally done Mary justice.

To Katy, Wendy, and Kelly—I couldn't have done this without you three.

To my ARC readers who took the time to read, review, and offer feedback on my writing.

To my profanity translators (Waves at Ulli)

To Ovid, Homer, Hesiod, Socrates, Plato, and of course, Keats.

To my middle school English teacher for introducing me to the amazing world of Greek mythology and my college professors who introduced me to the rest.

To the entire indie community—words can't express how thankful I am to be a part of such a wonderful group of people.

Finally, to my readers. *You* are what's made writing so exciting for me and you are the reason I'll keep on going.

ABOUT THE AUTHOR

Lucy grew up "down the shore" in New Jersey, where her love of the mythological was born when her middle school English teacher introduced her to the Odyssey. After high school, she received Bachelor's degrees in Psychology and English Literature before continuing on to her Master's degree in Library and Information Science. In her spare time, Lucy loves to read, cook, and go hiking with her husband and two daughters. Chaos is her debut novel.

Stay up to date! Hop over to www.lucyroyauthor.com to sign up for Lucy's newsletter, follow her on social media, and read up on news and other bookish things!

ALSO BY LUCY ROY